STUDIES OF GREAT COMPOSERS

This edition published 2024
by Living Book Press
Copyright © Living Book Press, 2024

ISBN: 978-1-76153-841-4 (hardcover)
         978-1-76153-802-5 (softcover)

First published in 1887

A catalogue record for this book is available from the National Library of Australia

STUDIES OF GREAT COMPOSERS

by

CHARLES H. H. PARRY

PALESTRINA.

CONTENTS

PREFACE

THE following short studies were originally written for a periodical for young people. They, therefore, do not attempt to deal with the profounder and more abstruse questions which are of interest to advanced musicians and students, and professed masters of artistic philosophy.

Though the conditions of their first publication necessitated their being cast in a form which admitted of each article's being separately intelligible, they were not from the first intended to be absolutely distinct or independently complete but a connected and continuous series.

The object of the work as a whole was to help people of average general intelligence to get some idea of the positions which the most important composers occupy in the historical development of the art; by showing their relations to one another, and the social, personal, and historical conditions which made them individually the representatives of various branches and phases of musical art.

The biographical portions were intended mainly to show the circumstances which made them severally what they were, and the immediate external influences and traits of character which had so much to do with the style of their works and the lines of art which they pursued.

As the authorities which must obviously be used to get and check sufficient trustworthy details of the lives of the most famous composers are to be numbered by hundreds, it has not been thought necessary to cumber so slight a work with references; but the writer is glad to acknowledge his special indebtedness for biographical matter to the admirable and exhaustive articles in Sir George Grove's *Dictionary of Music and Musicians*; on Haydn, by C. F. Pohl; on Wagner, by Edward Dannreuther; and on Beethoven, Schubert, and Mendelssohn by the Editor.

I

PALESTRINA

P EOPLE often talk of music as the modern art, but it is not probable that they always realize clearly how very modern it is in the shape in which we know it. The sister arts, which comprise painting, sculpture, architecture, and decorative work of various kinds, can show masterpieces which still impress us as perfect and complete objects of beauty, though they were made or carried out more than two thousand years ago. But if we go back as much as two hundred years in music, we feel as if we were among things in a crude and incomplete condition, like barbarous examples of the sister arts of races and nations even before history began. It seems, indeed, as if all other arts began with the beginnings of civilized life, but music came only with its well-advanced development.

The ancients had some sort of music, but it certainly was of a very slight and unimpressive kind, not calculated to please us much or to move us at all. Such as it was, however, its system and some of its actual melodies lasted on through the dark ages between the collapse of the great states of ancient times, like those of Greece and Rome, and the days when modern states like Germany, France, and England were rising towards the condition they are in now. Something in the way of art of various kinds was just kept going in churches and in the monasteries where monks lived secluded and kept their intellects alive with study and work and interchange of ideas. But music was in such a low state that as little as eight hundred years ago, people had not even the means of putting down a tune in which the notes were of unequal length; and they did not dream of such things as bars till quite four hundred years nearer to our time. About the time of our William the Conqueror, they were beginning to puzzle out elementary details and were trying to come to some sort of understanding as to how music might be put down on paper or parchment, and how sundry scales could be settled which would be fit to make music in. But they worked very slowly, and for a long time, they did not even get so far as to find out how to make two voices go together in parts, nor even how to sing the simplest second to a tune; and some modern speculators on these subjects think that when they did discover how to do it, it was quite by accident — as if somebody was singing one tune, and somebody else, for fun, sang another, and as they found the effect amusing, they tried a little more of it, till by slow steps they really found out how to make a couple of voices or so sing different parts in a tolerably agreeable manner. But when they began to consider part-singing or counterpoint — as they called it — seriously and to make rules to control composers, they became very particular and would only allow very simple chords indeed. In fact, they were puzzled to know what to do with discords and probably thought they were just ugly and nothing more, so, of course, they had not much to make effective music with. A composer nowadays uses more discords in one page than musicians in those days did in a week; and if he was not allowed to use them as freely as he pleased, he would certainly give up composition as hopeless. But though their music was so limited, the mediaevals contrived to make some fine effects with it, and the plain-song, which was the traditional music they sang in churches, had a dignified character about it which still impresses moderns as well worthy of the occasions and purposes for which it was reserved.

In that part of the world's history which we know as the middle ages, from about the days of the Norman Conquest onwards, Italy was the artistic center of the world. This was partly because it was in the best position for commerce and partly because the land itself was so very rich and productive; and the great cities like Rome and Milan and Florence, which had been established in the days of the ancient empire and had lasted on in tolerable prosperity through troublous times, served as seats of learning and centers of activity. Here painting and poetry began to thrive very early, and here, too, music began, after a time, to be appreciated. But curiously enough, it had to be fetched from other countries; for it was not among the Italians but among the Netherlanders that it first made the most successful strides, and the most distinguished members of choirs and church establishments in Rome and Venice and elsewhere for a long time were Dutchmen or Belgians. The most successful of all of these was a composer called Josquin de Prez, who lived from about 1450 till 1521. He was, in his time, the great and favorite composer of Europe; and though his works, which are all for voices, seem to most people nowadays singularly unexciting and severe, there is no doubt that they were as much in request amongst musical people of the time as successful operas and oratorios are in the present day. He was even personally courted and made much of by princes, grandees, and dignitaries of the Church. For instance, there were Louis XII of France, the Emperor Maximilian, and great Italian dukes like Hercules of Ferrara, in communication with him at different times; and it is especially interesting to us to know that Henry VIII was acquainted with his music, and that unfortunate Anne Boleyn is somewhere recorded to have learnt to play arrangements of some of his works on the little keyed instruments which served in those times in the place of the pianoforte.

Josquin was really a great and remarkable genius and produced works which have real beauty in them; but all his compatriots had not the sagacity to aim so surely as he did at genuine artistic beauty. In fact, they got upon a wrong tack and began to mistake learning and ingenuity for art. They invented queer musical puzzles which had nothing to recommend them but their difficulty and spent all their lives working them out; and the consequence was that the pre-eminence in composition passed by degrees away from them; and then it was that it took root and flourished among the Italians, and with them, it arrived before long at a very high pitch in the peculiar style of the time — so much so, indeed, that some people still speak of the age just after Josquin as the golden age of music.

This was, indeed, a very noteworthy time in many ways. Things had got into a very lax condition among the very people who ought to have set the best example to the rest of the world. There were, no doubt, good priests and monks to be found, but the influence of the bad ones preponderated. And not only those in the lower ranks of the clergy, but even the highest dignitaries, such as cardinals and popes, lived the most worldly and disreputable lives. When Luther came and the Reformation, that frightened them into a better frame of mind; but it did not mend matters all at once, for the corruption in the old Church was too general and deep-seated. But their evil ways came to a climax in the end, for after such a pope as Alexander VI, it was almost impossible that they could get worse; and then the reaction began, and for some time it certainly was the object of most men of authority and power to get a better tone into the papal court and to elect men as popes, not for worldly motives, but because they were most likely to adorn the high position they occupied and to purge out the accumulation of abuses which had crept into the Church.

It was about this period that the greatest composer of the age came into the world. The name he is generally known by is Palestrina, but this is in reality only the name of the town in which he was born, which is in the Campagna near Rome. His full name given in Italian is Giovanni Pierluigi Sante da Palestrina, and we find it Latinised into Joannes Petraloysius Preenestinus, or J. P. Aloysius. His parents were poor people, and that appears to be all that is known about them; and even the date of his birth is not known for certain. It probably was somewhere about 1524; so it must have fallen just at the beginning of the reign of the most unfortunate of all popes, Clement VII, and would be making him come to years of discretion just at the time when a better spirit was coming over the papal court, which was no small matter for him, and influenced his career in a healthy way.

As usual, there are stories about the early years of Palestrina, as there have been about most celebrated musicians and artists; and they are probably not less mythical in his case than in most others. At the same time, these myths, even if not true in details, often have a germ of value in them, in so far as they put under the vivid form of anecdote something which at bottom is characteristic of the man or his circumstances. It is, of course, in reference to his poor origin that the story is told of his having been taken out of the street and put in his choir by the principal musician of the church of Santa Maria

Maggiore, who happened to hear him singing; and the anecdote has a peculiar appropriateness through his close connection with that Church later in life. And indeed it is extremely probable that his career began in such a way, as did those of so many other great composers, who were thereby subjected to solid and dignified influences from their earliest years. People might have been able to find out something about his early history with more certainty but for the fact that the registers of his town were destroyed a few years later by the soldiers of that same terrible Alva, with whose name we associate such a host of horrors and massacres in the wars between Spain and the Netherlands. The first thing we really do know for certain is that Palestrina settled in Rome and became the pupil of a certain Flemish or French composer called Claude Goudimel. This fact does not on the face of it seem particularly interesting, but it is really rather curious, and worth taking note of. What is known of Goudimel is that he was born near Avignon, and having great musical abilities, naturally moved to Rome, where he set up as a teacher of music. He first wrote quantities of music after the manner of the Roman Church, such as masses and motets; but later he is said to have become a Protestant Huguenot and was one of the earliest composers who set a metrical version of the Psalms to music. It had been one of Luther's great ideas that if the people had the Psalms in a metrical form with metrical tunes to sing them to, it would be a great help to their religion; he himself carried it out with great success; and we still sing some of the splendid tunes written for the purpose by himself and his followers, and very much finer and nobler they are than anything that is produced for the purpose in modern times. Luther's tunes were, of course, written to German words, Goudimel's to the French version by Marot and Beza. Goudimel is said to have become rather prominent as a Protestant in consequence of this work, and the fruit of it all was that when that terrible night of St. Bartholomew came in 1572, and the French Catholics treacherously set upon the Huguenots in Paris and other great towns of France, Goudimel was one of those who were massacred in Lyons. And this certainly gives additional interest to the curious fact that Palestrina, the greatest representative of Roman Catholic music before 1600, was the pupil of one of the earliest representatives of Protestant music — but of course Palestrina's music is not like the music which Protestant composers wrote for their metrical Psalms, but like the earlier music of his master, which was in the ecclesiastical style of the old Church.

Palestrina probably came to Rome about 1540, and for eleven years we hear nothing much about him. He must have been working hard, and learning to master all the science of music as it was then understood; and it is clear that he was also learning some of the quaint puzzles and ingenuities which the Dutchmen thought the highest aim of art; for in the earliest work which he made public there are traces of this unsatisfactory influence. The first actual post that he was appointed to was that of chapel-master in the Capella Giulia in the Vatican in 1551, and it was soon after this appointment that he published his first musical work above mentioned, which was a set of masses. This book he dedicated to the pope of that time, Julius III.,[1] and it is said to have been the first musical work that was ever published and dedicated to a pope by a native-born Italian. In return for this, Pope Julius made him one of the singers in his private chapel. But this was not a very fortunate or wise thing to do, for it is said that Palestrina had a very poor voice as a man, whatever he may have had as a boy; and, besides this, he was a married man, which ought properly to have excluded him from such an appointment. But popes were able to do pretty much as they pleased in those days, for people had not begun to be so very particular about such details as they became shortly afterwards; so it may have appeared a pretty fair and promising advance for Palestrina at the time. But in the end, it stood him in very poor stead, for he had to resign his first appointment when he was promoted to the new office, and therefore had nothing to fall back upon if the latter fell through.

When Pope Julius died, a most excellent and earnest man was elected, who took the name of Marcellus II, and his election marks a sort of turning point in the history of the Church. But Marcellus himself, after making people hope much from him, only survived twenty-three days. Paul IV, who succeeded him, though not a man of quite so high a stamp, still had his mind set on doing well and honestly, and began at once to reform in all directions, small as well as great. Poor Palestrina was one of the first sufferers. The pope rightly turned his attention to

1 The portrait subjoined is taken from the title-page of the second edition of this collection, in which Palestrina is seen presenting his work to the pope.

the affairs of his own household, and finding that some of the singers in his own private chapel had no right ever to have been appointed if the regulations about laymen and married men had been properly observed, promptly turned them out. So poor Palestrina, after being fourteen years in Rome, with a wife and a family of several growing boys, was turned adrift upon the world without any post or definite occupation that could bring him any money — for composition did not put him in funds any better than it did Schubert or Mozart, or hosts of other composers who have starved for their noble devotion to their art.

For the time, Palestrina was completely beaten down. He despaired utterly of his prospects and became seriously ill. All the pope could do for him was to allow him a very small pension, which can have been hardly enough to keep his head above water. But, fortunately, Palestrina was not destined to be forgotten or neglected. He was, after all, only without a regular post for about a couple of months; for towards the end of the same year he was made chapel-master at the Lateran, and the pope allowed him to keep his pension as well; so he was not so very badly off considering, though his whole pay seems to have been ridiculously small. He next stepped on to a still better position, namely, that of chapel-master at Santa Maria Maggiore, in the choir of which church he is said to have sung as a boy; and there he remained for fully ten years, during which time he definitely formed his style, achieved some of his greatest masterpieces, and gained a very high position among composers.

This was no doubt a happy and contented time for him. He had enough to keep himself and his family, and his care must chiefly have been to make his music as good as he possibly could, and to further the musical part of the services at the church with which he was connected. He also took his children's musical education in hand, and three of them promised to do exceedingly well in his own line, which must have afforded him no little contentment.

It was moreover while he was connected with this church that a very important event in his life and in musical history took place, which made him stand out as the champion of the Church music of his day. In order to understand how this came to pass it is necessary to go back to some of the abuses which had got into the services of the Church in the lax and evil times before referred to.

The Dutch composers who invented the perplexing puzzles and ingenuities which became the fashion just before Palestrina's time applied them very unsuitably to the services of the Church. This soon had very bad results; as the music appeared to have next to nothing to do with the sentiment of the words either in character or expression, and only proclaimed itself as so much dry science and barren cleverness. But this was not the only evil nor the worst. Composers in those days, as now, were obliged to have some sort of principle or basis to work upon, and one of their favourite methods of making a piece of music was to take some old bit of plain-song and give it to the tenor voices to sing, and then to add other parts for the other voices to sing with it. If they wanted a long movement, they put the tune into very long notes and made the music last just as long as the tune lasted; in this form, the other voices sang the words over and over again to different kinds of melodies — counterpoints, as they were called — and ending when the tune ended. They used to vary the process in different ways — as, for instance, by writing the principal tune for the voices to sing backwards; and though this seems rather absurd to us, still, as the effect depended more on the way in which the other voices were managed than on the style of the tune, the composer was often able to ensure very good general results all the same. But then they did not always choose tunes which had been originally connected with sacred words. Sometimes they chose common secular tunes and set the sacred words to them; and there were certain secular tunes which were particularly in favour for such a purpose, as, for instance, one called L'homme armé, which was used by many different composers. This practice seems to have answered very well at first, but by degrees, composers got lax in their choice of tunes and used some which were associated with frivolous and absurd words; and tunes, too, which the people who went to church were quite familiar with. And the consequence is said to have been that when the music was performed, the choir used to sing the sacred words as arranged in the books, but a great part of the congregation used to take up the secular tune with gusto, and even sing the secular words to it. Of course, this produced a very discreditable medley of sacred and profane, and the wiser and more earnest men among the ecclesiastics were very much scandalised; and finally, it was decided that the subject should be taken seriously into consideration at one of the great ecclesiastical councils which were held at Trent. The difficulties in the way of reform were so great that they almost despaired of curing the evil anyhow but by making a clean sweep of all the more elaborate Church music and returning to the picturesque but rather crude simplicity of the early plain-song. Fortunately for art, there was among the cardinals a great and notable man called Borromeo who believed firmly in Palestrina; and he persuaded the rest of the ecclesiastics to give him a trial as a last resource; and it was understood that if he failed, the most uncompromising measures were to be taken, and Church music of any artistic value was practically to be reformed away altogether. Palestrina turned his hand bravely to this crucial task, and so as not to rely upon one experiment only, he wrote three masses at once.

They were all three sung privately first, and as they were generally thought promising, the pope allowed them to be performed in the Vatican. The trial took place in 1565, and the result was an extraordinary outburst of enthusiasm. The pope and the cardinals and everybody concerned were quite carried away with delight at the effect they produced, and all sorts of curious sayings are recorded as having been made by distinguished persons on the occasion, from apt quotations from the poets to comparisons to the music thought likely to be sung by angels. And the fruit of it all was that artistic Church music was held to be saved by the genius of the composer, and the cardinals were spared the necessity of framing rules for the regulation of style, which would certainly in the end have proved either impossible or ruinous to the art. The most successful of these masses is Palestrina's most famous work, and is known as the *Missa Papa Marcelli*, after the good pope of that name. In recognition of his achievement, the pope made Palestrina composer to the pontifical choir, which was probably in those days the highest musical position in the world, and a few years later, he was reappointed to the office of chapel-master in the Capella Giulia.

His financial position was not, however, much improved by these appointments; in fact, Palestrina must have been very poor throughout the whole of his lifetime. The posts which he occupied were worth absurdly small sums; as his salary as chapel-master at Santa Maria Maggiore was only sixteen scudi a month, and for the work in the pope's chapel, he had nine more, amounting in all to a little over five pounds of our money. To this, he could have added very little from other sources. He had scarcely any pupils except his own sons, and his compositions can have brought him in next to nothing. It is possible that he may have had presents from great people for whom he wrote works, but that could have only been an occasional windfall, not much to be trusted to help him with the daily wants of his family. However, we cannot tell that he suffered from his poverty, for there is not much information to be got about his private life. In those days, people were ready enough to record events, and even the sententious remarks, of people of high birth and position, but they had not developed the taste, which has become so conspicuous in later times, for keeping and handing down characteristic deeds and words of really great and able men. It seems likely enough, too, that Palestrina's life and character is all told in his musical work. His education in lines apart from music must have been very slight, and his opportunities of social distinction scanty, for the relations of musicians with great people, even up to the time of Mozart, were singularly subservient. The grand people hired composers or performers just as they would butlers or valets, and treated them much in the same way. They often made much of them, and petted and praised them, and were really proud if they had a musician of mark in their service; but their praise and pride alike were much of the same quality as if they had been concerned with clever cooks or coachmen. The musician waited on his employer with his work and received his criticisms without having the option of explaining or defending himself; and when the verdict was unfavourable, if he was worldly wise, he went home and tried to make something which would go more in accordance with his master's views. A curious story has been told in connection with a mass called *Assumpta est Maria*, which Palestrina wrote in 1585 for Pope Sixtus V., and it gives a very good picture of the sort of way in which popes and grandees were considered to have taste and judgment on all subjects, and how their remarks were received in a meek spirit by people who generally knew much more about the subject than their critics. The story is that Palestrina wrote a mass for the pope when he was elected, early in 1585, and the pope did not find it to his taste; and instead of praising the composer as he came out of church, he said, "Pierluigi has forgotten the *Missa Papa Marcelli* and the *Motets on the Canticles*," by which enigmatical remark he evidently meant that the new mass did not please him, and he thought it showed a falling off from such great works as those he quoted. What Palestrina said is not recorded, but he certainly was not happy at the rebuff. However, he took the most sensible course on the whole, which was to set to work upon another mass at once, to try and please the pope better. This new work was performed first on the Feast of the Assumption, and was received by the pope in a very different manner. For when he came out of church this time, he said, "The mass of this morning is of an entirely new character, and could only have been written by Pierluigi. On Trinity Sunday, we found fault with his music, but to-day he has fully satisfied us, and we hope that he will often revive our devotion as sweetly." This is perhaps quoted after a historian's manner and may be a little more grandiloquent and sententious than the actual words of the pope were, but it still gives a good idea of the feelings which men had about the relation between musician and employer in those days. The great people of the day had, however, the taste and sense to realize what a genius Palestrina was, and he had many friends in high places. Cardinal Borromeo has already been mentioned, as it was chiefly owing to him and another cardinal, called Vitellozzi, that Palestrina had the opportunity of producing the famous masses which decided the difficult question about the reform of Church music. Another great helper and admirer was Cardinal Ippolito d'Este, to whom he dedicated an important volume of motets. A more interesting friend and patron was Filippo Neri, who after his death was canonised. He was founder of a religious body called the 'Congregation of the Oratorians' and had a great idea of extending and strengthening the influence of religion generally by giving a more popular character to some kinds of Church music, something after the manner that Luther had done for his people. Among these ideas was that of performing music in connection with sacred or biblical subjects, such as the history of Job or the Prodigal Son.

These performances were begun in 1540 and took place in the oratory of his convent, and from these circumstances we get the name of "oratorio," which we use in modern times for a class of work of much more elaborate and dramatic character but of the same main principle. Actual oratorios they were not, but rather a kind of play interspersed with hymns and such music; but it is a curious coincidence that the first work which can be fairly called an oratorio was performed in 1600 in the oratory of Filippo Neri's church, and it is likely enough that the composer, whose name was Cavalieri, took his idea from Neri's earlier attempts. And this Neri was one of Palestrina's best friends and was probably the one whom in the end he most valued.

This connects Palestrina remotely with one of the most important kinds of modern music, but he himself had nothing to do with oratorio of any kind. His art was all of one description, namely, the highest and purest kind of choral music. In his time, instrumental music had scarcely begun, and there were hardly any instruments sufficiently well constructed to be fit to play anything worthy of the name of music upon. Such things as sonatas and symphonies and overtures had never been attempted, and there was not anything as yet in existence like our familiar kind of vocal music with accompaniments, such as songs and recitatives, and accompanied choruses and cantatas. All such things had even yet to be begun. What Palestrina and his fellows had to make music for was sets of more or less numerous voices; and this he did in the most beautiful and refined way possible. It was the most ideally perfect religious music that could be conceived — pure and serene, free from agitation or excitement, though rising at times to a high pitch of exaltation and vigor in the expression of praise and thanksgiving. There was no sentimentality in it, and when he was at his best no affectation. The means he used were the very simplest; for he used very few discords, and those which he did he used so carefully as to take away a great deal of their harshness. Men who live in the exciting mental atmosphere of the nineteenth century can hardly get into the condition of mind to understand and feel the beauty of his work. After going through all the turmoil of operatic music and the powerful effects used by composers of instrumental music, it is difficult for them to enter into anything which is not made exciting with discord or captivating with pretty and effective tunes, and their musical senses have got so far blunted with great volumes of sound and brilliancy of effect that they can hardly realize for themselves the excessively delicate beauty of such music as Palestrina's. Almost the only chance they have of enjoying it is to hear it in its own home — in some great church, where it can echo down the aisles and float in the great spaces of choir and nave, and where all the old associations are still strong enough to give it a poetry and a tone which in a concert-room must always be wanting. It seems to belong almost to a different world from ours, and people who have not wide sympathies and a feeling for what is loftiest and noblest in religion have hardly any chance of entering into it in the fullest sense. And so it comes to pass that the name of Palestrina has a sort of mysterious halo round it, and men know and feel the sanctity that belongs to his work without being able to come within the circle of its influence themselves.

But though the number of people who can enjoy such music thoroughly is limited, it never can become old-fashioned in the conventional sense. When people use the word old-fashioned, they generally mean that the thing they refer to is not thoroughly and completely good and mature but depended for such success as it had upon some fancy or affectation of the time when it was produced. Second-rate art and second-rate music become old-fashioned very soon. People often win success by hitting some trivial fancy which has taken hold of the public, and as long as that fancy lasts, their works please the world; but when the light humor comes to an end, if the work has not something solid and thorough behind its tricks and manners, it is only fit for the dust-bin or the fire-grate. It often happens that people in their younger days read books and see pictures and hear songs that strike them as delightful; and when, after a few years, they come back to them, they are utterly astonished to find them dull, stupid, and without any character except affectation. They themselves may not have improved in judgment, but they have passed out of the mood that was tickled by the special kind of affectation, and they find nothing else left to care for. But if, on the other hand, they have had the good luck to come across some really good and sound work and to have been pleased with it when they were young, they may come back to it twenty, thirty, or even more years afterward, and their children and grandchildren too, and yet it will never become old-fashioned. Palestrina's music is of this kind. It is like Greek statuary or the painting of the greatest Italian masters or the architecture of the finest English cathedrals; its beauty is so genuine and real that the passage of time makes no difference to it. As long as religion and religious emotions last, Palestrina's music will be the purest and loftiest form in which it has been expressed.

Palestrina wrote very little secular music, and what he did write strikes people who are not familiar with refinements of style as being very like his sacred music. The only difference they can see is that the words are not sacred. In truth, people in those times liked a much more solid kind of art than they do now. They could be carried along by music as music without the help of tunes or dance rhythms; and even in their secular music, they appreciated beauty of a more refined and delicate kind than is popular in our time. Palestrina had not the chance of being led astray by opportunities of writing either for money or display; everything tended to keep his work up to the highest level, and it is wonderfully to the credit of the taste of his day that the works which made his fame even in his own lifetime were those which have been felt by the most intelligent of his admirers in later times to be really his loftiest and most perfect achievements. His principal encouragement must of course have come from the people of high rank in Church and State, but one popular demonstration in his honor is recorded. This was in the year 1575, which was called the year of jubilee, according to some arrangements made by popes in the Middle Ages for the purpose of getting money. In this year, people flocked to Rome for ecclesiastical or religious reasons; and one of the bodies of devout worshippers who came were fifteen hundred men and women from the town of Palestrina in the Campagna, who marched into Rome in procession singing all together the music of their great fellow townsman. It must have been a very extraordinary scene, and to us in these days almost inconceivable. But no doubt the organization of the Church was then more able than it would be now to drill her flocks to such a remarkable feat as marching into a town in a body of fifteen hundred singing such difficult and austere music as Palestrina's. If such a thing could be done in these days, it would be worth going some hundreds of miles to see.

Palestrina at this time was passing middle age, but his steadfastness to work was not flagging and never did flag to the last. He lived for his work, and the great turmoil of the world and the exciting scenes of warfare and intrigue which went on in Italy, and indeed all over Europe, in his lifetime do not seem to have affected him. In his own home, trouble and sorrow came upon him in his declining years. His wife Lucrezia, to whom he appears to have been constantly devoted, died in 1580; and the three sons who showed most promise all died before coming to years sufficient to make any mark in the world, leaving him only one extremely worthless son Igino, who not only did his father no credit in his lifetime, but disgraced his name as soon as he was dead by a fraudulent use of it as a means to get some money. Beyond these family matters, the story of the latter part of Palestrina's life is little more than the record of the production and publication of successive works, such as motets, masses, litanies, offertories, and madrigals. The popes tried to do what they could for him in the way of bettering his circumstances; but it appears that his fellow musicians stood in the way, for what reason we cannot say — possibly from jealousy; and they tried to prevent the popes conferring on him the title of Maestro as late as 1586. At any rate, he could never have been at all well off, and we can only fancy him spending a simple life, unenlivened by gaieties or luxuries, in the constant production of music. It went on so to the last, and without apparent falling off of his powers. Of course, his works were not all at the same level of beauty and perfection. People generally hold that he never surpassed the famous mass called *Missa Papa Marcelli*, which was written in 1565, but he kept on producing works of the very highest beauty till the end of his time. At the beginning of 1594 he was busy looking after the publication of a collection of his masses when he was taken ill with pleurisy. He was soon too ill for any hope of saving his life, and his son Igino and Filippo Neri attended his bedside. To Igino, he gave directions about the publication of some of his works which were still in manuscript, "to the glory of the most high God and the worship of His holy temple," and then bade him farewell, and spent the rest of his few hours of life in the company of his friend, in whose arms he died on February 2nd.

It had been a curiously quiet and uneventful life, devoted as far as we can discover almost entirely to work. Of the character of Palestrina it is almost impossible to guess anything. That he was devout in the highest sense we can be certain of from his music, and that he was patient and steadfast we can guess from the enormous amount which he produced. But as to his manner of living, and his affections and so forth, record is blank. His music itself was, of course, from the moment of its triumph in 1565, recognized as the model for composers of Church music to imitate; but, curiously enough, the perfection of his art was so great and wonderful that it took the heart out of composers who would have followed in his steps. It seemed impossible to compete with him, or to produce anything of the same kind which was worth hearing by the side of his work. Some few did try, but the effort did not continue long, and within a few years after his death composers had started on an entirely new line, which was almost as far removed from Palestrina's style as could be. They began to try and make music for solo voices with accompaniment, like recitatives and airs, and as they understood next to nothing about it they had to begin at the beginning. Instead of being elaborately and completely beautiful like Palestrina's music, theirs was for a while childishly simple and elementary; but it led to great things in the end, no less indeed than all the great triumphs of modern music. Palestrina's art of his own kind was complete with him and in order to do anything more in art it was necessary to begin on another road. It is much as if men had been climbing a big mountain for a long while. When Palestrina finished his work they were at the top, and could not go any higher that way; and in order to get to the top of another high point they had to go back almost to the bottom again.

II.

HANDEL.

AFTER Palestrina the world had to wait nearly a hundred years for another great composer of the highest rank. In reality, the time that passed before works of anything like as great calibre as his were produced again was considerably over a whole century, but to count from the year of his death to the year when Handel and Bach were born is actually ninety-one years. That certainly is a very long interval, and it seems the more remarkable if it is compared with the ninety-one years immediately before the present day. In that time some of Haydn's best symphonies have been written, and his *Creation* and his *Seasons*, all Beethoven's symphonies and masses, and his opera *Fidelio*, and Weber's *Freischütz*, and Schubert's songs, Mendelssohn's oratorios, and Chopin's pianoforte music, and Schumann's many beautiful productions, and all Wagner's immense music dramas; and if the time is expanded just to a century it will take in all the greatest of Mozart's symphonies and his *Requiem* as well; so it seems to hold almost all that is most interesting in thoroughly modern music. And in the same amount of time, from Palestrina's death onwards, the world was, musically speaking, almost dumb. But it is not really so strange as it looks on the surface; for in that hundred years there was an enormous amount of work to be done before men could climb to the top of the next mountain — fully enough to have taken more than a hundred years, if composers and musicians had not worked very hard and wisely.

It was quite clear enough to men's minds that Palestrina had made the best music possible in his particular style. There were just a few composers who went on trying the same line, but most musicians turned their energies into new directions, where they had chances of new effects by using instruments and combining voices and instruments in ways that were quite different from the old style of Palestrina and Josquin. In fact, within six years after Palestrina's death they had almost abandoned the grand old style and were trying their hands at little operas, and oratorios, and cantatas, which were not much like what people understand by such names now, except in principle, and were even more utterly unlike in appearance as well as principle to anything Palestrina had ever done.

In reality, these works were only unlike modern works of the same names because they were first attempts, and because everything that makes modern music what it is had to be found out. Composers knew next to nothing about chords and keys, and such effects as men can produce by them now, and they only began to use chords by themselves in the ways modern composers do, as a sort of experiment; and keys and modulations they had to find out, more or less, by accident. Besides these drawbacks, they had scarcely any serviceable instruments, and those few they had they did not know how to play upon; and even if they had known how to play on them tolerably they did not know how to combine them with effect. Then, again, though they had done an enormous quantity of singing in combination, and some of it very difficult and elaborate work, they had scarcely tried at all to write anything artistic for single voices with accompaniment, and consequently the development of solo singing had still to be gone through.

So, in reality, it is not such a wonderful thing that it took a hundred years to come to another great composer; the wonder ought to be that they could get through all the work they did in the time. To anyone who understands the music of the early part of the seventeenth century it seems as if composers made the most wonderful strides. In comparison with the infantile experiments of that time the works of Carissimi and Cesti and Salvator Rosa, who wrote about fifty years later, are quite rich and definite; while Lulli and Alessandro Scarlatti seem already like full-grown men in many respects compared with their predecessors. For Lulli and Scarlatti could both write very effective airs of some size, and, with good luck, even effective movements for instruments alone; and their operas as wholes have some sort of mature completeness about them, which is an amazing advance to have made from such beginnings, and in the face of such difficulties, in so short a time. While in other lines men had not only found out how to make some of the most beautiful instruments the world has ever seen, in the shape of the famous old Italian violins — which the world cannot even match in these days — but they were finding out how to make real musical effects with them, and how to write agreeable and thoroughly artistic music such as Corelli's for them. And, in the same way, they cultivated their voices so successfully that they were within a short distance of having some of the most beautiful singers that have ever been heard, if report is to be believed.

This is not bad work to spend a hundred years over; and while so many elementary difficulties had to be contended against, it is not to be expected that any composers of the highest rank would make their appearance. But, at length, when men had by manifold and most invaluable labours arrived at a mastery of these new artistic resources, the climax came, and in the same year (1685) two of the greatest composers in the history of the world made their appearance together—and not only in the same year but within a month of one another. Handel was born on the 23rd of February and John Sebastian Bach on the 21st of March. Handel was therefore a little the older of the two giants, and as he looked back and linked himself more closely with what had been done before him than Bach did, it will be as well to consider his life first.

How Handel came to be so great a musician is one of the strangest things to unravel for people who believe in the special directions of hereditary genius. No doubt it would be easier to understand if we knew more about his mother; from his father he ought apparently to have got next to nothing to help him in his art, unless it was that obstinacy which may be much the same thing in the end as dogged perseverance. His father was a surgeon in Halle, in Saxony, who is said to have had a very decided aversion to music, and a strong determination that no child of his should devote himself to it. If accounts may be believed he was horrified at the appearance of musical gifts in his son George Frederick, and did all he could to stamp on them and turn his energies in another direction. He thought it would be a good thing to make a lawyer of him, but it would certainly have been a difficult thing to get him properly taught even the rudiments of legal science; for his horror and dread of musical infection was so great that he would not send him to school for fear of his finding any opportunities of hearing music or getting any encouragement or help while he was away from the strict watchfulness of the parental eye. But, as the story goes, the parental eye was not sufficiently active and penetrating to prevent the dreaded evil coming to pass, even within the walls of the house to which the boy was in this manner confined; for somehow or other, a small and very soft instrument, probably one which is known as a clavichord, was smuggled into the house, and away into some corner where the father rarely troubled himself to go, and there the boy began to puzzle out his own education. Luckily, keyed instruments were not in those days of the sonorous and rattling description moderns are familiar with. If, as is extremely probable, it was a clavichord that the young musician got conveyed into the higher regions of his father's house, no ingenious trickery of damping the strings for moderating the sound would be wanted, for the father might go even into the next room and hear nothing; for though it is a very expressive and sweet-toned instrument, it is so soft that it is difficult to hear it even in the same room at any distance from it. At any rate, the boy appears not to have been interrupted, and no doubt he managed to learn some-thing of the way to use his fingers before he was seven years old. At this age, the crisis of his early years arrived. His father went off to a place called Weissenfels to visit a relation who was in the service of a duke of Saxe-Weissenfels, and the little boy managed to persuade his father into taking him with him. While there, he was naturally drawn to make friends with the musicians whom the duke, like most great German magnates in those days, kept in his household; and he some-how gave them such an idea of his abilities that the duke was told of it, and after hearing him play, set to work to persuade the reluctant father to allow his son to study the art thoroughly with the view of devoting his life to it. Of course, the father was difficult enough to persuade, but the duke was too great a person not to have his way, and so it was arranged that the obvious inclination of the boy should not be any longer thwarted.

It is a pity there is no account of the state of mind the boy must have been in at this all-important decision. No doubt he was stubborn and tough enough to have stood a great deal of bullying and opposition on the score of his beloved art, and he would most likely have had his way in the end, however much his father had driven him towards the law. But it must have been a triumphant moment when the obstacles were removed, and he found himself in the way of being thoroughly helped by competent musicians, instead of having laboriously to grope his way in the dark and find out everything for himself. The master to whom the task of developing and guiding him was first confided was the organist of the Liebfrauen Kirche at Halle, where they lived, whose name was Zachau. This very excellent man accepted the responsibility with enthusiasm and exercised his pupil severely. He helped him to learn four different instruments and made him study and copy out the compositions of the most famous musicians then known and put him through long courses of counterpoint and such forms of composition as were then understood; and expected him to produce such things as motets as weekly exercises. So it went on for three years, at the end of which time Zachau's wits were exhausted, and he thought his pupil so proficient that he had better go elsewhere to develop himself further, if it were possible. So the young musician went to Berlin for a while, where he made a great impression on everyone who heard him play, whether courtly amateurs or able musicians, like the Italians Buononcini and Ariosti, who were there at the time; but he does not seem to have arrived at any definite conclusion on how to pursue his education further. He wanted to go to Italy but could not find the means, and, as nothing else could be contrived, in the end, he went back to Halle and began to work again nominally under Zachau. But very soon he had to turn his powers to practical account and develop them in a different way. His father died, and he was left to provide for himself and also for his mother; so he had to look about for such musical employment as would bring him funds at once.

The first place he went to was Hamburg, where there was a famous German opera house in the hands of Reinhard Keiser, who was one of the very first men who ever attempted musical settings of German plays after the manner of an opera. Handel got a place in this establishment among the inferior violin players, and in this slender way began his public career. But he was not destined to remain in such a subordinate position for long. The bands that were used in operas in those days were very different from what they are now. Among a moderate number of violins, and a considerable number of hautboys and horns, the harpsichord — the old counterpart of our modern pianoforte — was a very prominent instrument. In fact, there commonly were two harpsichords in an old opera band: one for the man who answered to a modern conductor and kept the band in order as he sat at the instrument; and another for a man who did great part of the accompanying of the recitatives and even airs. Both were important positions and required able musicians; and through the lucky accident of Keiser being one day absent, Handel had the opportunity of showing his abilities on this instrument and his efficiency as a musician, and he was thenceforward no longer called upon to play a subordinate violin part, but to take the prominent duties of harpsichordist. This very shortly brought him into collision with the man in Hamburg who was, in the course of time, his best friend and admirer — a collision which was not far from bringing his career to an abrupt termination and depriving the world of some of the greatest of musical masterpieces.

There was in Hamburg at this time an eccentric and very clever young man called Mattheson, who had studied law and was an able *litterateur*, and at the same time a composer and a singer. In 1704, an opera of his called *Cleopatra* was performed, and in it the composer himself took the part of Antony. It was not uncommon in those days for the composer of an opera to preside at the harpsichord, and Mattheson evidently considered that playing a part on the stage did not annul his right to play a prominent part also on that instrument; so when he had done acting the part of Antony, he came down into the orchestra to take his place there. Handel, however, had no inclination for giving up his seat and refused to move. Mattheson must have looked rather foolish and was certainly in a great rage, but he could not give vent to his feelings on the spot and had to wait until the performance was over. Then, as they were going out of the theatre, he appears to have warned Handel to be on his guard by trying to box his ears, whereupon they both drew their swords and fought. It is most likely that Mattheson was the better fencer — at all events, he got through Handel's guard, and if the story is true, as he himself told it in later years, Handel's life was only saved by a big brass button on his coat, which broke Mattheson's weapon. After that, friends stepped in and prevented further fighting, and the two combatants were very soon good friends again; and it is to this same Mattheson that the world owes a great part of the information it has about Handel's earlier years.

The very next year the first of Handel's numerous operas was produced at the Hamburg theatre. This was called *Almira*, and he did not wait long before bringing out another called *Nero*. They both appear to have been pretty successful; but his style can hardly have been mature by this time, nor completely characteristic of the composer as the world knows him in his later works, for much of his familiar style was gained through later experiences in his life, when he was in Italy. He appears to have stayed on in Hamburg for only a year or so more, and this is the part of his life about which least is satisfactorily and clearly known. He produced two more operas at Hamburg, and it must have been finally about the year 1706 that his most important journey to Italy took place. He had long been wanting to go there, to study on the spot what were then considered the classical models of composition and to meet the representative Italian composers; but funds had been wanting, and when some Italian grandee offered to take him, Handel could not bring his independent spirit to submit to the appearance of charity. But, however it was, it is clear from dates which are found on the manuscripts of his compositions of this time that he did manage to get to Italy and to visit Venice and Rome and Naples.

This Italian journey was a very important point in his history and certainly coloured his style for the rest of his life. He may have gained something of an Italian manner even before that time, through his acquaintance with Italian operas, which were almost the only models of that branch of composition; but in all the compositions of his maturer years, the influence of Italian style is so strong as almost to counterbalance the native German element; and there is nothing which distinguishes him so strongly from his countrymen, especially Bach, as the softness and suavity which he got from more intimate acquaintance with the Italian musicians. Some of the most characteristic turns and figures in his music come from Corelli; and his types of melody and even the style of his counterpoint are much more like those of the Italian than the German school.

The details of his life in Italy are unfortunately the reverse of full, and it is quite impossible to piece together a continuous account of it. There is no doubt that he impressed musicians and amateurs alike with his wonderful powers. One of the stories which illustrates this most strongly is that of his first meeting with Domenico Scarlatti. This famous musician was the son of Alessandro Scarlatti, who was one of the most powerful and versatile composers of the time between Palestrina's death and Handel's birth. Domenico, following his father's steps, tried his hand in opera and church music at first, but ultimately settled down exclusively to playing on the harpsichord, and writing for it, and in this province he had no rival in Italy. The first time he heard Handel play seems to have been by accident, as he must have come upon him unexpectedly and without knowing who he was, and his exclamation of astonishment is recorded to have been, "It must either be the devil or the Saxon," for the fame of *il Sassone*, as they called Handel, had gone before him. But these great minds seemed to have been above jealousy, and they were easily brought to a point of friendly rivalry, in which each readily acknowledged the superior merits of the other, wherever they were perceptible. Scarlatti had, no doubt, the greatest agility and the greatest brilliancy of style; but Handel had the greatest solidity and breadth. It is recorded of Scarlatti in his later years, much to his credit, that his admiration of Handel's harpsichord playing remained unimpaired, and when his name was mentioned he would cross himself in token of his respect; while, if anybody praised his own playing, he would turn it off gracefully by reference to his early rival.

About the time that Handel was in Italy, the Italians had no very great love for the harpsichord, as they were beginning to understand and feel the superior qualities of the violin; and the great school of Italian violin players was just beginning to flourish in the person of its first master, Corelli; but, all the same, they had enough interest in the keyed instrument to be amazed at Handel's performances, and were inclined to think that there was magic at the bottom of them. Handel seems to have come into contact with all the greatest of representative Italian musicians in the course of his stay. At Rome he met Alessandro Scarlatti, Domenico's father, then in the very zenith of his powers and reputation; but there is no information to be had about the circumstances of their acquaintance. With the famous violinist and composer Arcangelo Corelli he must have come into frequent contact, and Corelli — then getting on in years — found considerable difficulty in coping with the passages Handel wrote for him to play. On one occasion, Handel is said to have seized hold of the violin Corelli was playing, in a fit of impatience, in order to show how he wanted a passage to be played. Whereat the gentle Corelli remonstrated a little, saying, "But, my dear Saxon, the music is in the French style, which I don't pretend to understand." The place where this happened was the house of a certain Cardinal Ottoboni, who was a great patron of the arts, and altogether one of the most magnificent grandees of the time, drawing enormous revenues from the Church, which he spent in a most princely and effective way; while at the same time he held numerous ecclesiastical offices, among which was that of secretary of the Inquisition; which did not prevent him from being very good friends with the staunch Lutheran Handel. The Cardinal used to have meetings of musical amateurs at his palace, for whom he provided the best performers and the best music to be had; and here Handel won some of his most important triumphs while he was in Italy, one of these being his first Italian oratorio, called *La Resurrezione*, which was probably written at Cardinal Ottoboni's suggestion. But, indeed, he seems to have been received with enthusiasm wherever he went, whether it was to Rome or Naples or Florence or Venice. His first *bona fide* Italian opera, called *Rodrigo*, was produced at Florence in 1707, and was such a success that the Grand Duke gave him a grand service of plate and a great present in money; while the principal singer, Vittoria Tesi, was so infatuated with the music that she got leave to follow Handel to Venice to sing in his second Italian opera *Agrippina*, which was performed there in 1708, with, if possible, even a greater success; for the people went on shouting "*Viva il caro Sassone!*" all through the opera, whenever a pause in the music gave them a chance. It had what was considered in those days a wonderful run, and was played later in Hamburg as well.

In the midst of his successes, he was learning all he could from the Italians. It was a characteristic trait in him, as it was later in Mozart, that he was always ready to absorb the best qualities of the styles of the people with whom he was brought into contact. Even when he was working under Zachau, it is curious what various schools he took his models from, and how many composers' works he copied out by way of learning their methods of art. Under that worthy master he had learned all the most solid things to be known; with Mattheson at Hamburg he had learned a good deal of dramatic art, and had no doubt improved his ideas of melody; but he appears to have been deficient in the art of writing with full effect for the voice. When he came amongst the Italians he was in the midst of the most admirable school of vocal writing in existence, and by the time his Italian journey came to an end he was as great a master in that respect as he was in every other; and no trait is from that time more characteristic of his music than its peculiar smoothness and singableness. The Germans, as a rule, as was the case with the great John Sebastian Bach, were always inclined to express their music better for instruments than for the voice; and when they wrote for voices, they often gave them rugged passages which were much more fit for instruments to do; but with Handel after this time it was quite the reverse, and his instincts seemed to be more towards what was vocal than what was instrumental. The origin of this spontaneous instinct of Italians for vocal music is easy enough to understand when it is remembered that their language is the easiest and most natural to sing in the world; while German and all northern or Teutonic languages are by nature difficult to sing, and incline to produce harsh sounds unless managed with considerable art. Italian words produce beautiful sounds when pronounced just as in ordinary speech, but in most other European languages an artificial way of pronouncing has to be learned before it is possible to produce really good musical tone in singing; and there has consequently been a strong influence among the northern races against the development of a natural instinct for a pure vocal music of a high order.

Handel in these respects ceased very early to be like the rest of his compatriots, and he really represents a compound of different schools, combining the solid and intellectual qualities of the Germans with the softness and smoothness of the Italians. The circumstances of his life were all against his making any return in the direction of pure German style, for he was never again in the whole course of his life subjected to German influences for any space of time together, but always met with warmest encouragement and found his most cordial sympathizers among people of other nations.

This most important visit to Italy came to an end in 1710, the last place he visited being Venice, from whence he went to see his mother once more in his native town of Halle. He could not have stayed there long, for he was very soon in Hanover, where the Elector made him his *Kapellmeister*, without being very exacting as to his attendance to his duties. Here again he certainly stayed but a very short time, for before the end of the same year, 1710, he made his first appearance in England. What led him to this step is not known. He certainly met several distinguished Englishmen in the course of his stay in Italy, and he was as certainly highly appreciated by them; and it is very probable that they may have suggested to him the visit which had such important consequences.

At that time, music in England was in rather an unsatisfactory condition. National opera had made one short start with Purcell, but with his early death, fifteen years before Handel came, it had collapsed. But people were evidently inclined for entertainments of the kind, and as there was no one to supply them with a satisfactory native product, they were beginning to content themselves with Italian works; and as the managers could not bring together entire Italian companies, the operas had to be performed partly in Italian and partly in English. Buononcini, whom Handel had met as a boy in Berlin, was one of the first Italian composers whose works were represented in London in this way. His *Camilla* was performed at Drury Lane in 1707, with a mixed company, who sang it in different languages at once. In 1708, *Pirro e Demetrio*, by the great composer Alessandro Scarlatti, was played, and several other operas followed in succession up till the year 1710; so that English audiences were, by this time, beginning to get quite into the habit of going to operas, and looked upon it as a matter of course that there should be a regular supply. Handel came just at the right moment; for his fame had gone before him, and there were, in those days, what there are not now, enough people of spirit and taste among the richer classes to support really good work when they could get it. No time was lost in inviting him to write a work for the same company that had been playing the other operas, which contained some of the finest singers to be found. A subject, under the name of *Rinaldo*, was chosen, and an Italian poetaster, called Rossi, was set to work to throw it into verse. Handel began to write the music at once; and he wrote so fast that the unfortunate poetaster had terrible work to keep up with him and, in the end, was reduced to beseech the leniency of the public for his deficiencies in the following terms - "I implore you, discreet readers, to consider the speed I have had to work, and if my performance does not deserve your praises, at all events do not refuse it your compassion, or rather your justice; for Signor Handel, the Orpheus of our age, has scarcely given me time to write it; and I have been stupefied to see a whole opera harmonised to the highest degree of perfection in no more than a fortnight." Fortunately for composers in those days, operas were not what they are now, or the fortnight would have been an absolute impossibility. But even as they were, Handel must have worked furiously hard and written as fast as his pen could travel to get it finished; and notwithstanding the speed, the fruit was the finest work of the kind in every way which had been produced in England up to that time, and the musical public seemed to have been worthy of it. The first performance was on February 24, 1711, and it was then played for fifteen nights in succession, which, in those days, was considered a wonderful run. The famous male soprano, Cavaliere Nicolini Grimaldi, better known for short as Nicolini, took the principal part of Rinaldo, and the other parts were well filled. The opera was put on the stage with unusual magnificence; one of the features of the entertainment being that hundreds of little birds were let loose on the stage in a scene which represented an enchanted garden. But even without all this unnecessary show, the music would have made it the most successful work of the kind ever presented in London up to that time. Selections from it were played and sung by every person with any pretensions to taste in the kingdom. The march in it was adopted by the band of the Life Guards, who played it for forty years. A song, called *Il tricerbero umiliato*, was turned into a popular drinking song, and when that singular concoction, the notorious *Beggars' Opera*, was put together, the robbers' chorus, "Let us take the road," was borrowed from the same source; while the beautiful air, *Lascia ch'io pianga*, which was adapted from a Sarabande in an earlier opera, can scarcely be said to have lost its popularity even at the present day. The fortune which the publisher Walsh made out of it was so great, and what the composer got was, of course, so proportionately small, that Handel suggested to him that next time, Walsh should write the music and he should publish it.

When the opera season came to an end, it was high time for him to attend to his duties as *Kapellmeister* to the Elector of Hanover, and he appears to have remained in Germany for a year, during which time he managed to go and see his mother again at Halle; but very little of importance to his musical career happened. Finally, in November 1712, he got back to London, and in a short space of time produced two new operas, *Il Pastor Fido* and *Teseo*, and by January 1713, he had completed a work in a new line of great importance. All his operas had hitherto been after the Italian manner, and all those that had been performed in England had been set to Italian words. When the peace of Utrecht was finally concluded, it was determined to hold a great festival of rejoicing, and Handel was desired to set the *Te Deum* and *Jubilate* for the occasion. This was his first English work, and therefore the first in that line which led to his greatest masterpieces, *The Messiah, Israel in Egypt, Judas Maccabaus*, and so forth. The first performance took place in St. Paul's Cathedral in July 1713 and was received with enthusiasm. Queen Anne was ill at the time and could not go, but she had a performance for her own benefit at the Chapel Royal, and gave Handel a pension of £200 a year for the rest of his life, as a recognition of his success.

It must have been about this time that Handel was on friendly terms with a curious character called Thomas Britton, who is known to history as the Musical Small Coal Man. This man lived close to Clerkenwell Green, in a house which had been a stable and was now divided into two stories. The bottom part of it held the coals which he retailed in the daytime, and the upper — a long, low room, in which a tall man could barely stand up — served as his concert room. He seems to have had an enthusiasm for instrumental music and attracted the most famous players of his time to his meetings and a most distinguished audience; the ladies among whom, such as the Duchess of Queensberry, who was a famous beauty of those days, must have found it by no means easy of access up the rough flight of stairs, which is described as little better than a ladder. But, whatever the place, and however difficult and out of the way it was to get to, Thomas Britton's house is famous in history as the first place in England where concerts of instrumental music were attended by an appreciative audience. And here, at one time, Handel was frequently to be heard playing upon the harpsichord or upon a very small organ which Britton had managed to squeeze into his singular concert-loft. Britton's career began some time before Handel's appearance in England, and it only lasted till 1714, when he died, in consequence of an unfortunate practical joke.

Handel had promised, when he left Hanover in 1712, that he would not long desert his duties there. But there was too much to be done in England; and by one thing or another, he was kept from going back till things turned in a direction which was rather awkward for him. Queen Anne died in 1714, and on the same day, Handel's master, the Elector of Hanover, was proclaimed king of England. The new king arrived very soon and was crowned in October. Handel was consequently in disgrace with the whole court of the country where he had now cast his lot, and for a long time, he was ignored. Members of the royal family were present at a performance of one of his new operas, called *Amadigi*; but no notice was taken of him personally till far on in the year 1715. Several of his friends were at work to bring about a reconciliation, but no opportunity occurred, till an occasion when the royal family went for a water party in the royal barge from Whitehall to Limehouse and back. It was then suggested that Handel should write music for a band to play in another boat, as a sort of water serenade to the royal party on the way home. The performance came off successfully under Handel's own direction, and the king was very pleased and only waited a short while for a fit occasion to receive Handel again into favour. The opportunity arrived in the person of a violinist, Geminiani, Corelli's famous pupil, who was to play certain violin concertos at the palace. He said it was necessary for him to have Handel accompany him, and the suggestion was favourably received. Handel came, and after making his excuses, was not only readily forgiven but allowed an extra pension from the king of £200 a year over and above that which he had already received from Queen Anne. The music which was the cause of this very successful reconciliation is well known under the name of "the Water Music," and it was again performed on a grand scale later for the benefit of the king and royal family, on an occasion when they went to a grand party given in Chelsea in 1717.

The next time the king went to Hanover, he took the precaution to take Handel with him to make him attend to his duties there. Fortunately, they did not stay very long, for it was not the place to stir Handel to any important musical work. The only thing he appears to have done in this journey to Germany was to write a second Passion Oratorio in German, for performance in Hamburg. The first he had attempted in this line was in 1704, and this was on a much larger scale, to which he was probably moved by the rivalry of several other composers who had lately been engaged on the same subject. Very little is known of its reception beyond the fact that Mattheson records that his own setting was preferred. This was the last time that Handel attempted to set a work of any size in his own native language, which is not much to be regretted as he was always more successful in setting a foreign tongue than in dealing with his own.

He most probably came back to England early in 1717, to look after fresh performances of his operas Rinaldo and *Amadigi*; and when the opera season ended in June of that year, his occupations in connection with opera ceased for some years, as there were no performances of the kind till 1720.

In the mean while, he found a magnificent patron in a certain Duke of Chandos, who appears to have amassed a colossal fortune in the same way as Charles Fox's grandfather did earlier; namely, through the singular opportunities the office of paymaster of the forces afforded for waylaying public property. The duke built himself a palace called Cannons near Edgeware, in which everything was devised on the most expensive and luxurious scale. He kept a regular guard, which was no doubt necessary to protect him from highwaymen, with whom he had several collisions on his way home from London; and he also had a private chapel in the palace, which must have been a large and sumptuous place in its time, but like the rest of the enormous and extravagant establishment has now entirely disappeared. At this chapel, the services were conducted on a splendid scale, with instrumental band and choir, after the manner customary with German grandees and princes. Dr. Pepusch was his first *Kapellmeister*, but in 1718 it was somehow arranged that Handel should take his place. This was in many ways an advantage for Handel as things then were, as it brought him into contact with many of the distinguished men whom the duke invited to Cannons, and also led to the composition of some important works. Among these were several compositions for performance at the services of the chapel, which are known as the *Chandos Anthems*, and two settings of the Te Deum. But far more important than these was the first version of the work now known as *Esther*, which was written for the duke and performed on August 20, 1720. This work, though not on a level with the great oratorios which he wrote later, has many fine movements in it and is specially interesting as the first of the series of works upon which the greatness of Handel's name really depends. It was followed by another choral work of lighter quality, which has surpassed it in prolonged popularity; namely, the Serenata, *Acis and Galatea*, which was also written for performance at Cannons. It is not quite certain when the first performance took place, but it was probably either in 1720 or 1721. And yet another work, which is among his most popular and enduring productions, made its appearance about the same time. This was the first set of *Suites de Pièces*, or Lessons for the harpsichord. The work was advertised in the *Daily Courant* of the 2nd of November, 1720, to appear on the 14th. In a few days, the publication had to be pushed on, and when the first edition came out, there was an amusing note on the title page from Handel himself, saying that he had been obliged to push on the publication because surreptitious and incorrect copies had got abroad, and he concluded, "I have added several new lessons to make the work more useful, which, if it meets with a favourable reception, I will still proceed to publish more, reckoning it my duty, with my small talent, to serve a nation from whom I have received so generous a protection."

These *Suites*, or lessons, as they were called in England, were probably the most popular high-class pieces ever written for the harpsichord. They were reprinted in every civilised country and have maintained their position so well that the greatest pianists of the present day, such as Rubinstein and Bülow, have played them at their pianoforte recitals. The *Suite de Pièces* was the best and completest form of instrumental music in those days, answering for players on harpsichords to what sonatas do for players on the pianoforte in our time. Most of the *suites* written by all sorts of composers consisted of strings of dance tunes all in one key, and there was a regular order in which they followed one another; Handel followed the order in some cases, but he as often varied it according to his humour with fugues and airs with variations. Among these latter is the celebrated set on the air popularly known as *The Harmonious Blacksmith*. The amount of discussion which has gone on about this piece and the strong diversity of opinion which exists among men of judgment are bewildering. The most familiar, and most mythical, account of it is that Handel was caught in a shower of rain while walking near Cannons and took refuge in a blacksmith's shop, where he found the blacksmith whistling or singing the famous tune to the accompaniment of the ringing sound of his anvil. Another account is that the air was republished by a certain Lintott in Bath, and he called it *The Harmonious Blacksmith* in honour of his father, who had been a blacksmith and was fond of the tune. In the early editions of the *Lessons*, it is merely called *Air et Doubles*, which was the common way of describing any theme with variations in the days when *suites* were popular. How it received its familiar name, and why, is now most likely beyond the possibility of discovery; but a great many people believe in the blacksmith and the shower of rain — and the very anvil which is said to have accompanied the tune on the momentous occasion, which probably never occurred, is still preserved.

Handel's connection with the Duke of Chandos did not last very long. No doubt the quiet ways of life at Cannons were not altogether satisfying after the excitement of his operatic experiences; and when a very important venture, called the Royal Academy of Music, was started with a view of giving fresh performances of operas, Handel did not want much persuasion to throw himself into the work. This "Royal Academy" was supported by a grand array of peers and distinguished men, headed by the king himself, who subscribed £1,000 towards the venture. Handel was invited to take the management of the musical part of the business and to find the singers, and with him were associated Buononcini and Ariosti. He had to go abroad to find his company of performers and travelled to Düsseldorf and Dresden, and also to Halle once again to see his mother. While he was there, John Sebastian Bach, who was at Cöthen, heard of it and thought to seize the chance of seeing his great brother composer, and went over to Halle with that object, but unfortunately, Handel had started on his return journey to England the day before; and so it came to pass that the two giants in the course of their long lives never once met.

Handel was back in London and ready to begin operations by April 1720, and the new undertaking was begun with an opera called *Numitor*, by a certain Porta. This, however, soon gave place to another opera of Handel's, called *Radamisto*. Anticipation about this work was wrought up to the very highest pitch, and the excitement over the first performance was of the most extraordinary description. All the royal family came, and the demand for tickets was such that many had to be refused even at extravagant prices, while others who had the apparent luck to procure tickets had the bad luck not to be able to get in, and the struggling and scrambling of the *elite* of London society was such that dresses were torn to pieces and unfortunate ladies had to be carried out fainting. The enthusiasm with which Handel was received was unbounded, and the opera was the mainstay of this first successful season of the Royal Academy of Music till its close in June.

Its second season began before the year was out and with even greater promise than the first, for on the first night, one of the most celebrated male singers in the world made his first appearance in London in an opera of Buononcini's called *Astarte*. This was Francesco Bernardi, who is known to after ages by the name of Senesino, from the place of his birth. Handel had come to terms with him at Dresden the year before, but Senesino had not been able to present himself during the first season. His appearance at this time must have seemed the harbinger of complete success to Handel's career as a manager, but he was destined in the end to be one of the main causes of its failure. Another element of danger very shortly made its appearance. This was the fruit of a curious idea of the directors that it would be a good stroke to get the three composers, Ariosti, Buononcini, and Handel, to write an opera together. The subject chosen was *Muzio Scevola*. The play was divided into three acts, of which the first was to be written by Ariosti, the second by Buononcini, and the third by Handel. It is not certain whether the first act was carried out as intended, but the other two were, with the natural result that Buononcini was eclipsed, and a dangerous jealousy was roused in his not too friendly breast, which more than counterbalanced the temporary excitement of the public over such a curious experiment. However, for the present the matter was tided over, and the Royal Academy went on. In the next season, a new star was introduced in Cuzzoni, who was, according to Horace Walpole's account, "short and squat, with a cross face but a fine complexion," but nevertheless took the public by storm with her splendid singing, and even arrived at the point of setting the fashions for ladies' dresses. Handel and she fell out over *Ottone*, the first of his works she was to appear in, and she refused to sing a certain aria which he had written for her; whereupon Handel gave her a terrific rating, and seizing her by the arms threatened to hurl her there and then out of the window. At which form of conciliation she was so far taken aback as to agree to attempt the air in question; and, no doubt much to her surprise, made a great success with it.

Handel went on producing opera after opera, and every new work had something which arrived at a high pitch of popularity. In *Ottone*, there was a gavotte which, according to Burney the historian, was played on every instrument in the land from the organ to a salt-box. In *Rodelinda*, the next but one, was a song called "Dove sei, amato bene," which still holds its place in churches and cathedrals as "Holy, holy!" And then came *Scipio*, the march from which is played by the band of the Grenadier Guards still, as it was more than a hundred years ago, and probably has not worn out a tithe of its popularity.

Just before the appearance of *Scipio*, Handel went through the ceremony of becoming, as far as the law could make him, an Englishman and a British subject. An Act was passed for his naturalisation; and he took the oaths of allegiance on February 20th, 1726.

Very soon after this, the Directors of the Royal Academy prepared for themselves a new danger. They had got one star of the first magnitude in Cuzzoni, and were paying her 2,000l. a year; and they thought to make their prosperity even greater and more secure by engaging Faustina Bordoni, who was almost the only remaining star in Europe who was likely to rival her. To Handel was intrusted the herculean task of getting them to work together. It is a perfect marvel that for a time he succeeded. In a new opera called *Alessandro*, he provided them parts with such wonderful ingenuity that it was impossible to tell which had the preference. He even managed so that they should sing a duet together. But it was a combination which could not possibly last. They soon carried their jealousy of one another wherever they went; and the scenes they caused at parties to which they were invited caused amusement to the public and trouble to their entertainers in about equal proportions. The great ladies in society, after finding it amusing for a certain time, ended by entering into the quarrel, and formed themselves into parties on the sides of the rival singers; and they carried it so far that they used to applaud and to hiss alternately according as the singer they supported or her rival was on the stage, without the least consideration of the merits of either. The signs of the Royal Academy's approaching collapse were thus already becoming apparent on the one hand in the behaviour of its audiences; and matters were getting quite as bad on the other with its financial condition. The salaries paid to the rival singers were so enormous that the directors were incessantly losing money, although the tickets were run up by competition to a price of five guineas or so a night. They got through the season, however, and began a new one on January 7th, 1727. For this, Handel produced an opera called *Ammeto*, which was very successful indeed. It was followed, after a good run, by Buononcini's *Astyanax*, which was the signal for a wild outbreak of partisan excitement; and the voices of both Faustina and Cuzzoni were drowned in the hisses and shouts of their respective supporters.

This was the last work Buononcini wrote for the Royal Academy, and before Handel was called upon for further services in the same direction, he had to turn his hand again to the writing of sacred music. George I died, and was succeeded by George II, who was crowned on October 11th, 1727. Handel had to write the music for the coronation, which consisted of the fine work known as the "Coronation Anthem."

Then the Royal Academy of Music resumed its career; but it was already tottering. Handel did all he could to save it, and produced opera after opera. But people were beginning to be tired of the wild behaviour of the partisans of the rival singers, and began to drop off. More of their audience too was drawn away by the extraordinary success of the *Beggars' Opera*, which had been started at a theatre in Lincoln's Inn Fields; and when the season ended in June, the directors found they had lost 50,000l. over the affair, and had no chance of getting it back again, and so it was decided to put an end to the undertaking and let the rival *prime donne* and the rest of the admirable company go where they would.

For this institution, Handel had written no less than fourteen operas, all of which contained solid as well as attractive music, and attained unbounded popularity in their time.

His faith in the future of operas in England was not extinguished by the failure, the causes of which he could clearly see were not in his music nor even Buononcini's, and he soon made up his mind to try a new venture at his own risk. He entered into partnership with a man called Heidegger, who was chiefly famous as the ugliest being in London, and they took the King's Theatre to begin another course of operas as soon as possible; and Handel went off to the Continent at once to secure singers. While on this journey, he heard that his mother, who was by this time getting old, was very ill after a stroke of paralysis. He hurried off to Halle as soon as he could and found her better than he could have expected, but blind. He stayed there as long as his duties would allow him, and then bid her farewell for the last time, as he was not destined to see her again. She died at the end of 1730, nearly eighty years of age, and was buried beside her husband.

Before this sad event took place, Handel had got his new company together and had started his venture at the King's Theatre with a new opera called *Lotario*. His undertaking prospered fairly well for a time, and passed on through several seasons with the production of several new operas, and the reproduction of such old favourites as *Rinaldo* and *Rodelinda*, while in Lent, 1733, he brought forward his second English oratorio, *Deborah*. He re-engaged Senesino for a considerable salary, and had a company worthy of him to carry on the work, and things must have looked smooth and promising enough. But meanwhile Buononcini had plenty of time for working underground. His plan of operations was to make a strong party among the aristocracy by paying court to great ladies. His tactics were successful, and were aided by the treachery of Senesino, who, for no comprehensible reason, suddenly left Handel's company and took with him several of the most important performers. A sort of reaction seemed to set in against Handel in all quarters, and scurrilous articles and letters against him appeared in the papers, and to make the danger more pressing, a rival opera-house was started at the end of 1733 with the support of Buononcini's aristocratic patrons, with Senesino and others of Handel's own company as singers, and Porpora (a new rising composer, destined later to be the friend and master of Haydn) as conductor and composer to the establishment. Buononcini had been obliged by this time to leave the country. He just lasted long enough to give rise to the well-known epigram of Byrom –

> Some say, compared with Buononcini
> That Mynheer Handel's but a ninny;
> Others vow that he to Handel
> Is scarcely fit to hold a candle.
> Strange all this difference should be
> 'Twixt Tweedledum and Tweedledee.

However, his departure and the death of his most prominent patron, the Duchess of Marlborough, did not put an end to the contest. The rival opera-house was practically started, and it was inevitably come to a case of war *à l'outrance*. But Handel was not a man to be easily beaten. He filled up the ranks of his company, and had the good luck to secure a splendid singer called Carestini, who quite made up for the defection of Senesino. The campaign was carried on with extraordinary vigour, and must have been very amusing to the aristocrats who were trying to ruin Handel at this crisis. As soon as Handel's lease of the King's Theatre came to an end, they secured it, and drove him to the little theatre in Lincoln's Inn Fields, made famous a little while before by the success of the *Beggars' Opera*. They engaged the most famous male soprano in Europe, Farinelli, and the old favourite of the London public, Cuzzoni, as well. Handel a little later moved to Covent Garden Theatre and carried on the campaign by producing yet more fresh operas, one after another, and supplementing them in Lent when operas were forbidden by bringing forward new works of the oratorio order, such as *Athalia* and the ode called *Alexander's Feast*, and by all other devices he could think of. In the rival house, the operas played were chiefly by Porpora and Hasse, both rising composers, the latter destined before long to be the most popular opera writer in Europe and the husband of the famous Faustina Bordoni as well. The contest was kept up till 1737, when the opera supported by the aristocracy collapsed. Handel had at least the satisfaction of holding on for another fortnight, but when finally he too was forced to bring his undertaking to a conclusion, he found that he had lost over 10,000l. in the struggle; and the fruit of the cruel strain of work and anxiety was a breakdown in health of a serious paralytic kind, which necessitated complete rest for some time, and a visit to Aix-la-Chapelle in the hope that the sulphur waters there might revive him.

Handel must certainly have been a man of immense strength of constitution, for by November in the same year he was back in England again and at work. Apparently, the first task undertaken by him was the sad one of writing the funeral anthem for Queen Caroline, who had been a good friend to him, as she had been to all men of intellectual ability in her time. The work is known as *The Ways of Zion Do Mourn*, and is a most noble production, worthy both of the composer and the subject, and showing no traces of such failing as might have been expected after such a serious illness.

But though he got the better of his illness so soon, the disastrous failure of his experiments as an opera manager marks an important period in the story of his life, for he almost entirely gave up writing operas after this time. Heidegger made one more attempt to draw the public to performances at the King's Theatre in the Haymarket in 1737, and the last few operas Handel wrote were performed under his auspices. The last of all was *Deidamia*, which he finished in 1740; but by that time his attention was already being drawn away to a different class of composition; and though he was considerably over fifty years old, the greater portion of those works for which the world holds him in highest honour had yet to be written.

Mention has been made of the performance in the opera house of *Deborah* and *Alexander's Feast*. These works were to all appearance of somewhat similar construction to operas, but were performed without dramatic action, and depended for their effect more upon choruses than solos. In operas, long and elaborate choruses are impossible because of the difficulty of learning them by heart. But in the class of works which are known as oratorios, there are all the advantages of the story and the dramatic outline, with the additional impressiveness of the great effects which can be produced by a large choir; and it is this admirable balance of chorus and solo which has given the oratorios the lasting popularity which the constant alternation of recitative and aria in the opera failed to maintain. The English public had already showed signs of a liking for this kind of work. *Esther* had been received with every sign of delight when Handel revived it in a revised form some years after it was written for the Duke of Chandos, and the same had happened with *Acis and Galatea*; and he had thereupon gone on to the production of *Deborah*, *Athalia*, and *Alexander's Feast*. The latter drew an immense crowd and produced such evident satisfaction that Handel — though for some time afterwards continuing to devote much of his strength to operas — must certainly have felt that there was a great opportunity still open in this new direction. Moreover, now that he was getting on in years, it seems as if he thought a more serious style of art than opera would be more fitting; and even before he had put his hand to writing the score of the last opera, he had finished the most complete and effective oratorio which had appeared in the world up to that time. This was *Saul*, which he finished in a little over two months, in the year 1738. In this oratorio, Handel gave the public the benefit of a story full of human interest, much as they were accustomed to in operas, and together with splendid and characteristic choruses, such as "Envy, Eldest-Born of Hell," an attractive quantity of solo music.

In his next venture in the same line, he tried what could be done by putting all the weight upon his choruses, taking out most of the human interest of the story and reducing the prominence of the solo portion of the work. This was *Israel in Egypt*, which he finished very soon after *Saul*, in the same year, 1738. This time he appears to have tried his public too much. Though they liked choruses and solos in tolerably equal proportions, they were not quite ready for a work in which the choruses were all-important. And though the work impresses people of later ages as among the greatest and sublimest of his productions, he was obliged in the end to help the audience of his day by putting opera airs for his favourite singers in between the choruses. In modern times, anyone with any pretence to musical feeling understands the great descriptive choruses which deal with the plagues and storms and other terrible operations of the forces of nature; but in those days, people were unaccustomed to anything of the kind, and they did not know how to take it, and so it fell comparatively flat. *Israel in Egypt* has been the subject of a good deal of discussion on the score of Handel's curious ways of reproducing parts of his own early works in the works of the later part of his life and also, sometimes, of reproducing parts of other people's works too. He used to write at the most extraordinary speed and always had an immense quantity of work to do besides composition; and whether it was for the sake of saving time or for bringing forward afresh music which was more or less lost in some earlier work, he exercised remarkable ingenuity in adapting old materials to new situations. In *Israel in Egypt*, there is more of this sort of thing than usual. Some of it is borrowed, without doubt, from another composer's work, whose name was Kerl. More, again, seems to be borrowed from another composer called Stradella; while a very large quantity was taken from a Magnificat, which some people think to have been written by a certain Erba, because his name is written on the manuscript, and other people think to have been an early work of Handel's own. The music forms the duller part of the oratorio as it stands, but whether it was originally Erba's or Handel's is a question which it seems impossible to settle decisively one way or another. At any rate, whichever way it was, such borrowing was not regarded in the sort of light it would be now; and, on the other hand, if all that was reintroduced into *Israel in Egypt* from other sources was taken out again, there would still be left all the finest part of the work, and all which no one but Handel could have written.

After *Israel* was done with, and the series of his operas had ended with *Deidamia*, Handel turned his hand at last to the noble work upon which his great fame mainly rests. Fortunately, he was very careful in dating all his works, if not always at the beginning, almost invariably at the end. In the case of The *Messiah*, every part is successively dated. The beginning is dated 22nd of August, 1741, and the conclusion, including some extra touches and filling in, the 14th of September. So that the entire writing of one of the most important musical works in existence took him only twenty-four days. No doubt he had been thinking about parts of it before he actually began to put any of it down, and sketches exist of some of the more elaborate parts of the choruses. But, notwithstanding such qualification, it certainly is a most extraordinary feat to have accomplished in such a short time.

Curiously enough, London was not destined to have the honour of being the first place where it was performed. In the same year that he wrote The *Messiah*, he had several invitations to pay a visit to Dublin, which was in those days blessed with lively and cultivated society of its own, which was very appreciative of music. From the accounts he received, he gathered that it might be a very favourable opportunity, and so in the latter part of the year he started for Ireland. He was delayed a good while on the road, to the advantage of the famous musical historian, Burney, who saw him at Chester and gave a most amusing account of the attempt of a Chester musician to sing at sight some of this new work, The *Messiah*, which Handel was taking with him to Dublin, and the wrath of Handel at his incapacity. Handel arrived safely in Dublin and was welcomed cordially. He began his campaign with *L'Allegro*, and *Acis and Galatea*, and The *Ode for St. Cecilia's Day*, playing organ concertos between the parts, as was his custom. And at last, on the 13th of April, 1742, the new oratorio, The *Messiah*, was performed for the first time in the music hall in Fishamble Street. The people of Dublin seem to have been worthy of the honour, for they considered it the finest music that had ever been written. It certainly was the finest they had ever heard, and it is most creditable to their discernment that they found it out so quickly. They asked to have it performed again later, so it was given, with organ concertos between the parts as usual, as the last of the series of oratorios before Handel went back to England. In fact, the people of Dublin appreciated him as well as ever he was appreciated anywhere in his life, and he no doubt was sorry to leave the many friends he had made there; but London, even in those days, was a still more important centre, and supplied the real field for a composer of his powers, and to London he had to return, and arrived there towards autumn in 1742.

The *Messiah* does not, however, seem to have been performed at once in London, and it seems strange to most people now to think how slow the public was to appreciate it fully in this country. Even that able but singular character, Jennens, who was the author of the book of the words, seems to have been disappointed with the music, though he was an enthusiastic admirer of Handel's. He thought there had been gross faults in the composition at first which he had with difficulty persuaded Handel to correct; and that there were "some passages far unworthy of Handel, but more unworthy of The *Messiah*." The musical public in these latter days think that it would be difficult for anything to be more worthy either of the composer or the subject, but in those days, people were in no hurry to come to a better mind, and when Handel came back to London the first new work brought forward was not The *Messiah* but *Samson*. This work Handel had begun very soon after he had finished The *Messiah*, and before he started for Ireland; but it had been interrupted for an unusual length of time, and the whole was not finished and dated till a year later, when he was back again in England. Then he determined to start a series of performances of oratorio with the best singers he could get; and *Samson* was the first oratorio given, on February 18th, 1743. The first performance of The *Messiah* soon followed, on March 23rd of the same year, when it was described merely as "a sacred oratorio." It certainly made an impression upon the more sensible portion of the audience, and it is said that the regular established custom of standing up during the "Hallelujah Chorus" first began from the spontaneous impulse of the king and the audience, which caused them to do so on this first occasion. The oratorios, as a rule, do not seem to have been appreciated with such spontaneous outbursts of enthusiasm as had been the case with the operas. It took longer for them to take complete hold of people's minds, but when they once had done so, the hold never relaxed again; and no works in the history of music have had such wide and lasting popularity.

For the rest of his life, Handel reserved most of his energies for this class of composition. The most important of the later works were the *Judas Maccabaus*, which he wrote in July and August, 1746; *Joshua*, which appeared in the next year; and *Solomon* in 1748. *Theodora*, which Handel himself thought very well of, was produced in 1749; and the last, and certainly not the least in beauty and interest, was *Jephtha*, which he wrote in 1751. One other very important work he wrote in this late period which does not come under the head of oratorio. This was the *Te Deum*, which was written for the occasion of the national thanksgiving for the victory of Dettingen, in June, 1743, when George II had himself been in command of the army. This noble work was fully appreciated by the public of that time, who thought it worthy both of him and of the occasion.

It was about this same year, 1743, that symptoms of failing health began to make their appearance. It appears that some troubles similar to those which attacked him in 1737, after the struggle between the rival opera companies, again presented themselves, for which Handel tried the once fashionable cure of the Cheltenham waters for a short time. Besides these troubles, there were also symptoms that his eyes were going wrong. Things continued to get worse with him for successive years, and about the time that he was composing *Jephtha*, his spirits began to fail as well. The troubles of his eyesight show themselves in the peculiarities of his writing; while the condition of his mind seems to be shown in the fact that his system of writing straight on with a sort of certainty of inspiration began to give way to alterations and changes more frequently than of old. Besides which, according to the dates which Handel put in at various points, the work was often interrupted, and for at least one long period at a stretch. He began it in January, but he did not get it done till the end of August, which was a very long time for him.

Soon after *Jephtha* was finished, it became necessary that Handel should undergo an operation to his eyes; and as the malady he suffered from, namely *gutta serena*, or cataract, has frequently been cured, it was hoped that his eyesight might be restored. But the operation ended in failure, and the announcement of a contemporary journal of the sad event ran in the following terms: "Mr. Handel has at length, unhappily, quite lost his sight. Upon his being couched some time since, he saw so well that his friends flattered themselves his sight was restored for a continuance, but a few days have entirely put an end to their hopes." Yet he struggled against this misfortune with all the strength and courage of his disposition and made his appearance at performances of the *Messiah* and other works, and played concertos and accompaniments as usual.

The hostility of the aristocracy, which had lasted on even after the rivalry of the two opera houses, gave way in his later years, and the apparent reaction against him about the time he produced the *Messiah* turned again; and towards the end of his life, he attained to all the reverence and admiration possible, while his blindness roused such feelings of tender sympathy as are akin to love. People began to understand the greatness of the *Messiah*, and from 1751, Handel gave regular annual performances of it for the benefit of the Foundling Hospital, which was one of the many charities in which he took an interest. In 1757, he began to be convinced that his strength was definitely giving way, but he did not give up work or make any apparent alteration in his ways of life. In 1759, the usual season of oratorios was undertaken. Handel directed nine of the performances, and for the tenth, on April 6th, the *Messiah* was advertised. Handel duly made his appearance and directed the work as usual, but after the performance was over, an ominous faintness came on, and he foresaw that the end was coming. It was indeed the final seizure. The immense strength which had again and again reasserted itself after previous collapses was at last worn out, and the long life, devoted to strenuous and almost incessant labour, ended peacefully and nobly in the early morning hours of Saturday, April 14, 1759.

He had certainly filled well the measure of his days, and it has been the lot of very few men to do so much so thoroughly. Though he seems always to have written at a most astonishing speed, the rapidity did not affect the completeness or thoroughness of his work. The scale on which he worked was always large and free; but the details were not carelessly dealt with but were generally worthy of the ideas upon which the work is based. His mastery of his art was supreme in almost every branch, but most especially when he was dealing with voices, whether as solos or in choruses. This he had gained by his intercourse with Italians, as he had gained a peculiar kind of sentiment and smoothness of style, while from his German blood, he gained force and depth of feeling. And this is a thing which gives him rather a peculiar position in the history of music, for he is, as has been before said, as much Italian as he is German. In him, too, some of the most valuable qualities of the school of Palestrina, which had been neglected by the early composers of the seventeenth century, make their reappearance; combined with the fruits of the work which the new school had done during the intervening century.

In character and person, he was, as he was in his music, large and powerful. Even his appetite seems to have been like a giant's, while his temper was perfectly volcanic. Many characteristic and amusing stories are told of its explosions, for when he was roused, he was entirely without respect of persons, and was quite as likely to rage and swear at a prince as at a drummer or a parish clerk; and the people who understood him bore his outbreaks without ill-will. He had humour of a robust kind, and a vein of poetry too, and a considerable amount of dramatic feeling, which comes out in his oratorios as well as in his operas. But one of the strongest elements in his composition appears to have been a deep religious sense of a healthy and generous cast, which found its finest expression in the *Messiah*.

His style has suited the English better than any other nation, owing probably to its directness and vigour and robustness; and also, no doubt, because the nation has always had a great love for choral music, of which he is one of the greatest masters that ever lived. His influence has been extremely strong upon the English composers who succeeded him, but he so thoroughly worked out the possibilities of his style that very little more could be done in the same direction without failing in freshness and character, while it was scarcely likely that the force and power which are such a conspicuous element in his work would be likely to appear again very soon in another composer after such a pair of giants as Handel and J.S. Bach.

III.

JOHN SEBASTIAN BACH[2].

Everything about John Sebastian Bach is in strong contrast to the history and circumstances of Handel, except his greatness and the noble breadth of his style of composition. To begin with, next to nothing is known about the family of Handel, and his musical gifts seem to have sprung from nowhere, for it is never recorded that musical tastes ran in his family. Bach's family, on the other hand, traced back their pedigree for many generations, which spread over more than a hundred years. And they not only knew their pedigree, but they knew a good deal about each individual member of it; and what his character was, and what were his occupations. Moreover, the quality which connects them all together most remarkably is their constant devotion to music. This was so great as to force itself upon the attention of the public; and in Erfurt, one of the towns where they filled prominent musical positions, it even came to pass that the town musicians were generally called "Bachs" from habit, whether there was a member of the family among them or not. They made Thuringia their home, and their affection for their native country was almost as great as their invariable devotion to their art. As generation succeeded generation, their fame as musicians increased and spread abroad, till the time of the great John Sebastian, when it arrived at its culmination; and it still survived to a considerable extent in his sons, and then abruptly came to an end.

The earliest member of the family of whom much is known that is

___

2.		The original text refers to the composer as "John Sebastian Bach." The correct name is "Johann Sebastian Bach."

worth knowing was Veit Bach, who was born somewhere about 1550. He was not by profession a musician, but a miller and baker. He had decided tastes for music and is said to have spent the spare time he could find from attending to his mill in playing on some instrument like the zither. He had a son called Hans, who was a carpet weaver by profession and a merry man by nature, and played upon a fiddle of some sort. Hans travelled much from town to town, amused people with his fun, and pleased them with his playing; and he became a well-known and popular character throughout all Thuringia. He had several sons, all of whom had musical tastes, but the most important of them was Heinrich, who had the same cheerful bright disposition as his father and better developed musical abilities. He became organist at Arnstadt and lived on even after John Sebastian was born, till 1692, by which time he had officiated in that capacity for more than fifty years. He was not only important for his own abilities, but as the father of the two most distinguished members of the family before John Sebastian, both of whom he educated himself. These were John Christoph and John Michael. The former was court organist at Eisenach, famous as one of the greatest performers of his day, and as a masterly and noble composer. The latter, who was the younger brother, was organist at Gehren, a place near Arnstadt, and was also distinguished as a composer; and he is also memorable as the father of John Sebastian's first wife, Maria Barbara. Besides these, there were a great many more who were notable musicians, and sterling, healthy, true-hearted men; so that all things tended naturally to the culmination in John Sebastian.

He too was directly descended from Veit and Hans Bach, but not in the same line as John Christoph and John Michael. His father, John Ambrosius, was their cousin, and in the earlier part of his life had lived at Erfurt, where he gained distinction as a musician, and married the daughter of a furrier named Lämmerhirt. In 1671 he moved and settled in Eisenach, where John Sebastian was born in 1685, probably on March 21, as is guessed from the day of his baptismal register, for there is no actual register of the day of his birth. He thus came into life surrounded by family traditions, which besides their musical aspect always had a very strong German character about them. He had too all the strongest and deepest influences of German Protestantism around him; and these things had so much effect upon his development that they can be traced as the causes of all that is most characteristic in his works. There is nothing indeed which sums up the nature of his style as a whole so strongly as German earnestness and sincerity, and the characteristic vein of religious sentiment, which seems to belong to his race.

He did not long enjoy the protection of his parents but was left an orphan when he was only ten years old. His father can, therefore, have had but little influence upon his musical education; but it is said that the first musical impressions the boy received were from hearing him play upon the violin: and he began to learn that instrument very early under his father's direction. When his father died, his elder brother, John Christoph, took care of him for some years. He lived at Ohrdruff, a place not far off from Eisenach, on the other side of the Thuringian forest. Here John Sebastian began to settle to his musical education; though not to the exclusion of general culture, as he went in for the regular course of study at the "Lyceum" of the town, and learnt his Latin thoroughly enough to be able to make use of his knowledge serviceably later in life.

The violin which his father had begun with fell to a certain extent into the background, and his attention was given more constantly to keyed instruments. The pianoforte was not invented, but its predecessors, the harpsichord and clavichord, were the most useful and popular instruments of their kind, and upon one or both of these, the young musician soon made rapid progress. In fact, his progress was rather too fast for his elder brother Christoph, and jealousy seems to have caused him to put some obstacles in his way. John Sebastian devoured all the music that he could lay hands on and learnt all the best of it by heart. There was one particular book that he was anxious to have the contents of, which was a valuable collection of the very best and finest organ music by German composers, which Christoph had got together. Christoph did not want his young brother to be level with him in everything, so he carefully kept this book locked up. But John Sebastian's eagerness for it was so great that he finally managed to get it out, possibly by rolling it up and slipping it through the lattice work of the bookcase, and then at night time and by moonlight, whenever the moon was bright enough, he managed slowly to copy it all out. It took him six months to do it, and then at last the elder brother found out what he had been about, and ruthlessly took his own book and the precious copy away.

From such circumstances as these, it is obvious he had soon learnt all he could from his elder brother; and from this time forward the greater part of his education was worked out by himself with extraordinary energy and perseverance. He got some experience of choral music at the school of the Lyceum, for there was a boy's chorus at Ohrdruff, as in many other German towns at that time, and it was an important part of the school course. This chorus used to have to sing motetts and other choral works at all sorts of celebrations, such as marriages and funerals; and the boys also did a great deal of singing before people's houses in the streets, as Luther had done long before in Bach's own native town of Eisenach. John Sebastian had a remarkably beautiful voice as a boy, and he rose to quite an important position among his fellows. But his education here was not destined to continue for long; for when he arrived at the age of fifteen, his brother began to find his house and income rather too small to keep more than his own increasing family; and the young musician had to start on his own resources. His beautiful voice seems to have stood him in good stead at this crisis, and he was received into the choir of the church of St. Michael, at Luneburg; and when his voice broke, he was found so serviceable as an accompanist on the harpsichord, and as a player on the violin in the band, that he was still kept on in employment.

He was at this time beginning to show signs of the powers which in later years made him most famous next to his compositions. In Northern Germany, there were at that time a good many distinguished organists. At Luneburg, Bach had chances of hearing some of them, and no doubt learnt a good deal from them. But at no great distance off, at Hamburg, was a greater than any of these, named Reinken, and Bach soon made up his mind he must somehow get there to hear him. So when a holiday came, he started off on foot, and trudged away with a cousin called John Ernst, and got safely to Hamburg and heard the famous organist. But one hearing did not suffice for him, and many journeys were made to and fro to learn what he could from such a master. It had all to be very economically done, and a story was told by Bach himself in later years, which shows how close they had to keep. One time when he had been to Hamburg, and was on his way home, but still far from his destination, he found nearly all his money gone, and sat down on a seat outside an inn, taking what tantalising pleasure he could from the savoury smell of edibles that came from within. Suddenly, up above, a window was opened, and a couple of heads of herrings were thrown out near him. Curiosity, or the hopes of lingering fragments of eatable fish, prompted him to pick them up, and to his surprise, in each there was a very serviceable piece of money. He never succeeded in discovering who was his benefactor; but he made a characteristic use of the unexpected addition to his funds, for he turned about at once and went back to Hamburg to hear Reinken once more, and then had enough left to take him all the way home.

At Luneburg, he had but very poor organs to practise on; but, such as they were, they stood him in good stead; and though there is no account left of the impression his playing made upon anyone there, it is obvious from what happened soon after this time that he was arriving at very considerable mastery of his favourite instrument. At the end of three years, he moved to Weimar for a short time, and while he was there, it so happened that the municipality of Arnstadt — a town not far off — had rebuilt one of their churches, which had been burnt down, and had put a fine organ into it, and were much in want of an organist who could do it justice. Bach happened to go over there to see some of his relations and played upon the organ. The authorities no sooner heard him than they were convinced he was the man for the place. Before long, he was installed and began from that moment the definite line of that career which made him, in the end, one of the few greatest among the world's musicians. The music of the place was not in a very inspiriting condition, but he had a good organ to play upon, and a choir to compose for, and opportunities of hearing instrumental music occasionally; and these spurs were enough for the time. He began writing some of the earliest of the long series of church cantatas and also wrote one of the first and the most curious of his works for the "clavier," the name commonly given to the old counterpart of the modern pianoforte. This work was the "*Capriccio on the Departure of a Beloved Brother*," which he wrote when his brother, John Jacob, went off to join the Swedish guard of Charles XII. This is the solitary example among his works of what is called programme music, each separate movement having a title prefixed which explains

its meaning and purpose: such as "A General Lamentation by Friends,"
"Friends Coming to Take Leave," an "Aria di Postiglione," and a fugue
on a post-horn tune.

Bach lived a quiet life of steady work at Arnstadt for two years and
was always improving and strengthening his powers. But he still felt
the need of some guidance. He wanted the opportunity to hear yet
more of the performances of the old German organists; for he knew
instinctively that no man can arrive at the highest pitch of art without
learning all that has been mastered by the best intellects of previous
times. At Arnstadt, there was little opportunity of improving himself
by observing other artists; and he began to be restless and longed for
another expedition like his former ones to Hamburg to hear Reinken.
He appears to have become rather negligent of the duties of his office
as organist, and it is inferred that he did not keep the choir up to the
mark by sufficient drilling and practising. His mind was too strongly
occupied by eagerness to develop his own powers to be able to give
sufficient attention to choir practices. At last, the opportunity came.
He had managed to save sufficient money to keep him going for a
while; and he asked leave for a holiday for four weeks and started off
again on a long journey on foot to Lübeck in the North. His object was
to hear the famous Danish organist and composer, Buxtehude, who
had been the most interesting and powerful performer of his time;
but by 1705, when Bach was seeking him out, was getting an old man.
Nothing is told of their meetings or relations with one another; but
it is quite obvious that Bach was not disappointed in the old master,
and it can hardly be imagined that Buxtehude, in his turn, can have
failed to appreciate and sympathise with a nature which had so much
in common with his own. Not very much remains of his compositions,
but from what there is, it is easy to see how much he influenced the
younger artist. There is a richness of counterpoint, and fullness and
vigour of harmony, and a glow of noble imagination about some of his
works which make them extraordinarily like Bach's, and in some cases,
the latter evidently copied the plan and style of the older composer.

The short four weeks passed, and he was due back at Arnstadt,
but he could not tear himself away. He felt, perhaps, that the risk of
losing his place there was more than worth running for the sake of
such an opportunity to learn, as he felt himself to be learning, day by

day, at Lübeck. Possibly he was too infatuated to care. Art was all in all to him, and he was yet too young to be hampered with a sense of personal responsibility when such a passion possessed him. He stayed on and on till the end of the year, and it was not till he had been away for four times as long as he had asked for leave of absence that he managed to tear himself away; and having said his last farewell to old Buxtehude, journeyed back to Arnstadt about February 1706. The consistory were naturally not pleased by his behaviour and took it seriously into account. They not only objected to his extension of his holiday without asking, but they found many other things in his conduct reprehensible. He had not kept his scholars in order, and he had not had enough rehearsals; his preludes to the hymns were too long; and he used to play such extraordinary harmonies in accompanying the chorales that the congregation got confused. There was a formal examination held, the amusing report of which is still in existence in the form of question and answer between the consistory and Bach. One of the points runs as follows: "We charge him with having hitherto been in the habit of making surprising variations in the chorales, and intermixing divers strange sounds, so that thereby the congregation were confounded. If in future he wishes to introduce some 'tonus peregrinus,' he must keep to it, and not go off directly to something else." Bach's answers were short and not very submissive. He may have felt ashamed of the liberty he had taken in extending his leave, but with regard to his playing, he knew quite well what he was about, and that if the consistory did not understand his harmonies, that was their stupidity and not his license. But the consistory were really very patient with him, and though they said they must have an answer in eight days, they allowed things to drift on without severer measures, though his answer never came for eight months. They occasionally sent him a reminder of his duty; and latterly they found fresh ground of complaint, for in one of the reports there stand the words, "We furthermore remonstrate with him on his having allowed the stranger maiden to show herself, and to make music in the choir." This sounds as if things were getting seriously strained between the consistory and the organist, and it is evident that they could not go on in such a manner for much longer.

But the mysterious stranger maiden points to the approach of another important event in Bach's life. The daughter of old John Michael Bach had come to Arnstadt after her father's death, and John Sebastian had fallen in love with her, and before long they came to the conclusion they must marry. But Arnstadt was not the place to settle in, and Bach began to look about for a more congenial home. At length, a favourable opening was found at the church of St. Blasius at Mühlhausen. The organist there had just died, and the council who had the duty of electing his successor did not hesitate long when Bach offered himself, and he was safely installed in June 1707. A little time had to be spent in getting ready for setting up house, and then in three months he went back to Arnstadt to fetch his bride. Mühlhausen was a much better place for music than Arnstadt, but nevertheless, it was not destined to keep Bach for long, as a still better opportunity for the development and use of his powers at Weimar offered itself; and in June of the year after he arrived, he sent in his resignation to the authorities, who had treated him well and accepted his resignation with evident regret.

At Weimar was the court of a most excellent and earnest man, Duke Wilhelm Ernst of Saxe Weimar. His interests were chiefly centred in the religion of the German Protestant Church, and he did all he could to strengthen and enliven its influence; and Bach, as a great representative of the best form of music of that Church, was sure of the ready sympathy which is so necessary to draw out an artist's full powers. He had by this time mastered enough of the art of the great organists, such as Reinken and Buxtehude, to go on with his own development alone in safety, and in the quiet nine years he lived at Weimar, he at length brought his own art to that marvellous pitch of power and perfection which has left him absolutely unrivalled and even unapproached as a composer of organ music in all the history of the world.

People are often surprised at the limited amount of really first-rate organ music there is in existence; but a little patient consideration soon shows how inevitable its scantiness is. The organ is too grand an instrument to be tractable. There is a good deal of romance about it, and long associations with religion and religious art of all sorts have cast a sort of glamour over its sounds, which enable people, up to a certain point, to make great effects with very simple means. It seems easy to produce very attractive results by extemporising; and in a theatre, an organ has almost always a very telling effect in a church scene of any kind. But when music comes to be written down, or taken away from the illusive conditions of a theatre, it is judged by everybody, consciously or unconsciously, in a very different way; and then, nothing but that which is worthy of the instrument will stand. To be that, it must rise to the highest pitch of grandeur, dignity, and power. Prettinesses and tunes in such circumstances may take people in for a while, but they cannot stand the test of time; while the average showpieces, such as modern marches, offertories, and fantasies, made to display the misdirected abilities of organists at the expense of their noble instrument, are nothing less than ignoble and repulsive. It is but rarely that things act so as to bring that energy, clearness, and healthy nobility of character together which is necessary for the production of music worthy of the organ; but they had so converged before the time of Bach. The organ seems to be essentially the instrument for the accompaniment or performance of religious music of a pure kind. Not that kind of religion that is fostered by trumpery kickshaws, and tinsel and dressed-up dolls, and every kind of theatrical trickery, which is only an external tickling of the senses, and has its part in the outer man — but that religion that lives in the innermost soul of man, and holds its place and exercises its influence in his deepest emotions. Such, no doubt, was the form of religion which took possession of the northern races of Europe, especially the Germans, after the time of Luther. The simplest form of musical expression, and the backbone of their religious art, were the famous hymn tunes known by the name of chorales, which began with Luther, and were produced in considerable numbers by his most ardent and earnest followers. These tunes had all the power of national songs and were as familiar to all Protestants in Germany as their daily bread; and it so happened that their dignified and noble simplicity made them especially fitted for treatment on the organ. The organists learnt to use them in much the same sort of way as the early Italian composers had used hymns or secular tunes in the vocal masses and motets. They made them, as it were, the inner thread of the piece they were developing, and wound round their simple melodies many dexterous lines of counterpoint of rich and expressive effect. This was the kernel and centre of their scheme of organ playing; and generation after generation developed it to greater perfection. Buxtehude had been a great master of the art; but Bach surpassed everyone before or after him by his richness, freshness of invention, and nobility of thought in works of this kind.

Another most important form of organ music was an adaptation of a choral form called the fugue. This, too, had been elaborated by various composers in the course of preceding generations, and was brought to a very high degree of perfection, only leaving, as it were, the top-stone of the edifice to be put on by John Sebastian. The most suitable style of expression for the organ had been developed under these various influences; and soon after his arrival at Weimar, the tree which had been so long growing began to come to its fruit; and before the nine years which he spent there were over, many of the works which are familiar to every organist of any taste and ability, and the delight of everyone who appreciates great music, were completed. Bach was, of all things, first and foremost, an organist. He developed marvellous powers as a writer for stringed instruments and for the clavichord, and his choruses, arias, and recitatives are as fine as anything of the kind which exists in the world; but behind all these other forms, the organ seems to serve as the foundation. Even in writing for voices, or for the violin, or the clavichord, he uses forms of expression which are borrowed from the organ style. The effect of the works as wholes is sublime; but in details they are sometimes less perfectly adapted to the means of expression than works by later composers. This amounts to no more really than saying that, as perfect art, his organ works stand at the top of all his compositions; though in many other works the spirit which expresses itself is as great and beautiful, and even more so at times, in defiance of mechanical drawbacks.

As an organist, he certainly had no rival in his lifetime, and he probably has had none since. Many things which he did were totally new to the people of his generation. He could do infinitely more with his fingers than any other man; and the way in which he used to fly about with his feet on the pedals seemed to them almost incredible. But it must be believed that it was not only his agility which astonished them, but also the impressive grandeur of his style. The time when he was at Weimar is also interesting for the production of some of the most attractive of his church cantatas. These were works which occupied something of the position in German Protestant services that anthems do in the Anglican Church; but they were rather more developed both in style and length, and commonly had a band as well as the organ to accompany them. Bach had, up to the time when he was at Weimar, a difficulty in finding any man who could write a cantata text fit to inspire him. At Weimar he had the good fortune to fall in with a man of really poetical temperament, of the name of Salomo Franck, who wrote many religious poems for him to set in the cantata form; which commonly consisted of a mixed series of choruses, recitatives, and arias, and ended with a chorale. The one which has been most popular in this country, called *Ich hatte viel Bekummerniss*, or *My spirit was in heaviness*, was written by Franck, and was one of the earliest of those composed at Weimar; and many more noble works of the kind followed in rapid succession. But in these times, Bach was more famous as a performer than as a composer. He began to have pupils both for organ and clavier, and to be called to visit various towns to play upon the church organs for the enjoyment of the local public. In this way, he visited Halle, Handel's native town, and even had overtures made to him to take the organist-ship there. At another time, he went to Leipzig, where he played the organ in one of the principal churches, and conducted the performance of the cantata *Nun komm, der Heiden Heiland*. The most famous of these journeys from Weimar was one to Dresden in the autumn of 1717. In those days, there was a great deal of music of all sorts going on in Dresden. There was a lively court, and a theatre, and it was a centre which attracted many musical celebrities. When Bach was there, it so happened that one of the most famous of French harpsichord players was there also, by the name of Marchand. He had been organist to the King of France, and was a great favourite with the musical public of Paris; and he really deserved his fame, for he was gifted with considerable execution and taste; and his reception at Dresden, where he had played to the king, had been as favourable as in his native country. When Bach came, people began to talk about their respective merits and were inclined to pit them against one another as the representatives of German and French art. In the end, Bach was driven by his supporters to offer Marchand a sort of challenge. He was willing that Marchand should prescribe the terms of the contest, and he would play or read or attempt any other feat of skill proposed, on the conditions that Marchand would do the same. The contest was to take place in public, and on the day appointed, a considerable company assembled to witness the curious trial of skill. Bach arrived and waited long for his antagonist. People became impatient, and a messenger was sent in search of him. But he could nowhere be found, for he had left Dresden that morning by fast coach. It was supposed that he had come to the conclusion that Bach was too great an antagonist for his mettle and had retired with precipitation. But Marchand was, in fact, a worthy antagonist, and Bach himself was well acquainted with his compositions for harpsichord before this time and, as is natural, the whole story was considered to be greatly to Bach's honour, and to the honour of German art.

Very soon after this, Bach's connection with Weimar came to an end. He was probably disappointed at a man of far slenderer abilities being preferred before him as capellmeister there; and when the Prince of Anhalt-Cöthen invited him to come to him as his capellmeister, Bach readily closed with the offer. This was a comparatively untried field for him, but it was one which he was quite ready to cultivate. Up till this time, his energies had been chiefly directed to organ and clavier playing, and composing works for the organ and church cantatas. His reputation in all these departments had reached a very high point, but the greater part of his achievements in the line of secular instrumental music was yet to be begun.

Secular instrumental music is the most modern part of the modern art of music. In the early times, when the art was beginning to grow, scarcely any attention was paid to it at all, and when people who looked upon music more or less seriously began to try and make music with such instruments as they had, they only imitated or made arrangements of vocal pieces, such as madrigals and motets. Their instruments were also very poor in comparison with what are in use in more modern times. Instead of violins and violoncellos, they had cumbrous, coarse-sounding instruments called viols; and instead of the pianoforte, they had the twanging harpsichord, which was almost incapable of expression, or degrees of loudness and softness, or the little clavichord, which was very capable of expression, but so soft that it could hardly be heard a few yards off. Before Bach's time, things had got better in the matter of the instruments which were played with the bow, like the violin, but for keyed instruments, they still depended on the harpsichord and clavichord. The different forms of instrumental works of art were still few and limited and different from those which are familiar in the nineteenth century. Sonatas and symphonies and overtures of the familiar kind written by Mozart and Beethoven were not so much as thought of; and the whole process of discovering what could be done in that style had to be gone through. And even what there was of secular instrumental music before Bach's time was very crude and poor in comparison to choral music, or even organ music. Besides the imitations they had made of choral works, composers had begun to imitate some of the things they played on the organ, such as preludes, fugues, and toccatas; but the most important of all the works of any size was known as the Suite. This was the work which corresponded in those days to the sonata of modern times; it was their most important form of instrumental composition, and, like the sonata, it was divided into several movements. But the movements were not worked up with anything like the style and freedom of modern sonata movements, but were in principle just complete dance tunes and no more. Men had begun to see, as early as Henry VIII's and Elizabeth's time, that it was effective to play two dance tunes of different kinds one after another for the sake of the contrast to be got out of them; and when they had got so far, it did not take them long to see that there was even more interest and variety to be got by playing three or four after one another. They had very good opportunities of hearing all sorts of different kinds of dances, for men used to travel about from one country to another, playing their national dances at inns, and fairs, and such gathering places. And besides that, the greater part of the nations of Europe were always fighting and quarrelling in those days, and different sets of nations and peoples were, by that means, brought into close contact in fighting against other sets of nations, and when they were not busy fighting, they amused themselves a good deal, in camps and towns alike, with dancing and merry-making. And as national dances were more distinct then than they are now, composers had a very fair choice of variety when they came to try and see what effect they could make by artistically balancing different dance tunes together. They had pavans and galliards and correntes or corantos from Italy, and bourrées and passepieds and gavottes and minuets from France, and sarabandes from Spain, and jigs and hornpipes from England, and allemandes from Germany, and polonaises from Poland, and many more besides, and many were the experiments they made in arranging them. But by degrees, they got more and more systematic, as they found the best artistic effect was to be got by having a kind of solid quick dance or two to begin with, and a slow dance in the middle, and a light and merry dance to end with. Several old masters had written very fair suites of this kind before Bach's time, both for harpsichord and for violins, but it remained yet for him to bring this form of art to perfection.

There is another point, too, about instrumental music which is worth considering, which was the slowness with which people developed what is called execution, or *technique*. Corelli, noble player as he was on the violin, could not face certain kinds of difficulties, which mere children in the present day would think nothing of; and in harpsichord playing, it would have been much the same. The reason for such a state of things in connection with keyed instruments was, chiefly, that they were so slow in learning the art of fingering. Many men thought it really did not matter how the fingers were used so long as the notes were sounded, and up to Bach's time, they hardly ever used their thumbs at all. Even on the organ, great organists like Buxtehude and Reinken seem only to have used their thumbs in stretches which were too wide for the fingers alone. In relation to the harpsichord, this seems quite natural, as it was no use striking the keys as players do the keys of the pianoforte; for however hard they were struck, no difference was made in the loudness of the tone. Consequently, instead of playing with the hand bent or crumpled up, as is done in pianoforte playing, harpsichord players kept their hands quite flat and their fingers straight out, and wagged them up and down like sticks fastened with a hinge to the knuckles of the hand; and in that position both the little finger and the thumb were too far back to reach the keys without inconvenience. People used to play their scales by turning the middle finger and the third finger over one another as best they could, and they used their little fingers to help them out of occasional difficulties. Just before Bach's time, people were waking up to the possibility of using the thumb now and then. Couperin, the famous writer of harpsichord music in the time of Louis XIV of

France, admitted it now and then in his method, but still it must be doubted if he changed the position of the hand enough to make very much difference. Bach, in his turn, seems to have faced the question thoroughly. He appears to have made up his mind to play with the hand bent, and to use the thumb as freely as the fingers, and to turn it under, or to turn the fingers over it unreservedly. But he still did not get to the system of fingering used in later times, and in playing on the organ, he used to prefer getting smooth effects by sliding some of the fingers over one another. When he was settled at Cöthen, his mind naturally turned in the direction of using what he had mastered in all these respects; for at Cöthen he was no longer in the position of a mere organist, and if he had been, there was hardly any organ worthy of his powers, and the prince, his master, was not wealthy enough to have such an establishment as a big choir or a theatre, but cultivated his musical tastes in the direction of a high class of instrumental music, and it was for this department that Bach now became responsible.

It is a curious instance both of the amount of influence a man's circumstances may have upon his work, and the advantage it may be to train energies deliberately, so as to make the best use of them. When Bach had a good organ at his disposal, and a good opportunity of testing his work and other people's, he wrote organ works; when he had a choir at his disposal, he wrote church cantatas; now, at Cöthen, he had good opportunities of trying other people's instrumental works and observing their effects and how the effects were done, and putting his own work through the same ordeal; and at Cöthen, he wrote the larger part of his most important secular instrumental works of all kinds, such as those for the clavier, as it was called; and for the violin, and for various instruments in combination. Among the best known of these in this country is the first part of the collection known as the *Forty-eight Preludes and Fugues*. But it was not forty-eight when the collection was first made, but only twenty-four, which was enough to run once through all the keys, major and minor. The second book was added considerably later. This collection is called in the German "the well or equal tempered clavier," and serves as a practical assertion of Bach's views on the important point of tuning a keyed instrument. In old days, when men did not use many keys, it was enough to have a few well in tune, and to let the keys with many sharps and flats in them be out of tune. By this means, owing to a curious scientific fact, the few keys could be better in tune and sound better in some ways than if all the keys were equally considered. But as things went on and composers wanted to use more keys, it became a question whether one should endure some keys which were out of tune for the sake of the few which were very well in tune, or whether all should be made alike. Bach saw clearly that composers could not in the end do without being able to use all keys, and by way of illustrating his opinion, he put together this set of preludes and fugues in all the keys and called it by the name which pointed to its purpose, The Well-Tempered Clavier; which means, in other words, the keyed instrument which is tuned equally well for all keys. This work was, with a few of the organ works, the first by which he became known in this country and has not only been the constant source of happiness and content and comfort to most of the musicians of any standing in the world since the beginning of this century, but it has all the elements of the most lasting value imaginable. In it, men find almost all the shades of feeling they can desire, except such as are tainted with coarseness or levity. The very depths of pathos and sadness are sounded in some numbers; in others, there is joy and lightness; in others, humor and merriment; in others, the sublimest dignity; and in others, that serenity of beauty which seems to lift man above himself and to make him free for the time from the shadows and darker places of his nature. And all pieces alike are cast in a form of most perfect art and on that scale which can be realized completely at home with no more elaborate resources than one little keyed instrument.

Another collection, which is well known to musicians under the name of the French Suites, is associated with a change in Bach's life which followed one of his most serious domestic calamities.

Bach's master, the Prince of Cöthen, used to go yearly to Carlsbad and took his musicians with him. For several years, Bach attended him. One of these years, Bach arrived home after some time of absence with his master, eager for the glad greetings of his wife, and he was met instead with the news that she was already dead and buried. Bach was a man of profound emotions, and he suffered as such men do. But he was strong and brave and had work to do, and he would not allow his loss to break him down. Before long, he was at his accustomed duties and traveled about much as before. One of his visits took him once more to Hamburg, where old Reinken was still alive and playing his organ, though ninety-seven years old, and Bach had the pleasure of meeting again the old master from whom he had begun to learn so long before, in the days when he trudged over from Luneburg on foot; and it is a comfort to find that old Reinken appreciated Bach in his turn and listened to him with interest.

Towards the end of the following year, Bach married again. The second wife's name was Anna Magdalena, and she was the daughter of a man called Wülken, the court trumpeter of Weissenfels. About her, much more is known than about the first wife. She seems to have been most wonderfully fitted for Bach. She sang, and she played; and, most serviceable of all, she had an excellent clear hand for copying music and frequently helped her husband in the laborious business of writing out the music he composed. He gave her lessons on the clavier constantly and wrote music for her to play. Altogether, their ways with one another seem to have been of the sweetest and loveliest description. There are books of the music she used to play, most of it copied out by herself, with a large proportion of her husband's work in them, and with some of his writing too. In these books, the famous French Suites soon made their appearance. Bach did not call them French in the first instance, but they were most likely called by that name later, after the suites by famous French clavier composers which consisted of similarly short and concise movements. These suites were musically far the best which had been produced up to that time, and some of them, such as the last two, are among Bach's freshest and happiest works. Besides writing in this way for the clavier, Bach turned his attention to instrumental music of other kinds. The famous suites and sonatas for violin solo, which are still the finest concert pieces of all the greatest violinists of the present day, were composed at this time, and also some suites for orchestra, which are not so often heard. The greater part of the time at Cöthen, about which but little in the way of biographical details has been left, seems to have been devoted to the study and production of such instrumental music; and this was the latest branch of art which he attacked.

Bach's stay at Cöthen lasted till well on into the year 1723. By that time, the prince had married, and the new princess, having no liking for music, her husband's attention was drawn away into other directions. Bach seemed for the time to be neglected, and he felt that his art was no longer so much honored as it had been, and the office of Cantor to the school of St. Thomas in Leipzig falling in his way, he accepted it. It was considered rather a step down for him to become a cantor after having been a kapellmeister; but this particular cantorship had always been held by distinguished men, and life in Leipzig had certain decided advantages, so, as he said in a letter to a friend, he "ventured in the name of the most Highest," and having "passed his examination, undertook to move to Leipzig."

The cantor's was a curious office. He was elected by the town council and was considered to be under its supervision. The cantor had to attend to the choir of the school and to teach them and conduct them when they sang at any festivals; and besides this, he was expected to give lessons in Latin to some of the lower classes in the school, to which duties Bach added the directorship of the music in St. Thomas's Church. He was quite ready to perform these various offices, but there were some drawbacks against him. The choir of the school had got into a most unsatisfactory state, and the town council was not the sort of body to understand either him or his difficulties. There was also a consistory which had the right to meddle in the musical arrangements, and between them all, it was no wonder that before long there was general dissension and cross purposes. The town council so utterly failed to appreciate him that they addressed a remonstrance to him and described him as "incorrigible," and resolved to take away his income. Bach was not at all subservient, but he was very much disgusted and even tried to find some new place more worthy and appreciative of his powers. But fortunately for Leipzig and the cantorship which his name has made famous, the stupidity of the town council did not have its natural results, and Bach remained in this post for the rest of his days. He was fortunate enough to find a real and appreciative friend in a new rector of the school who was elected about this time. This was a very superior man and an able scholar, named Gesner, who in a short while got the school into very much better condition and managed to make things go more smoothly with the town council, who, under his influence, had a better chance of understanding their great cantor.

At Leipzig, Bach turned his attention again chiefly to church music. In the churches there, the musical part of the service was very elaborate, and he had plenty of occasions to write for. One of the earliest works which he produced after his arrival was the music to the history of the Passion according to St. Matthew, which of late days in England has become one of the most famous of his works. The idea of appealing to people's emotions in Holy Week by performing a musical setting of this tragic crisis of the story as told in the Gospels had originated long before; and many German composers had undertaken the task before Bach, including Handel. Bach appears of all men to have been most fitted to accomplish the task with all the poetry and devotion it calls for and even with great dramatic effect at times. In thinking of this great work, it is most natural to draw comparisons with Handel's oratorios. It is not strictly an oratorio, though it has some of the external apparatus of an oratorio, such as great choruses, solos, and recitatives, and elaborate accompaniment of orchestral instruments. But the treatment of the subject and the use of these forces is extremely different in the two great masters. In Handel's work, there is grandeur, noble feeling, admirable treatment of the voices, and a great deal of the suavity and simple ease of motion which came from his frequent contact with Italians and with the great singers of the opera; but his treatment of his orchestral forces is rather crude and colorless, though vigorous and easily dealt with. Bach's work is, of all things, most thoroughly German. He broods and reflects more than Handel does; he makes superb effects with his voices, but he often treats them more as instruments or parts of an organ work. The music, on the whole, has much more character, color, and delicate variety of feeling and subtlety than Handel's; but it is not so direct and simple. In Handel's work, the influence of the opera for good and sometimes for the contrary is often apparent. Bach, on the other hand, had had next to nothing to do with opera at any time; he made use of opera forms in his airs, but the style is far removed from anything connected with the stage. Handel's work appeals readily to a great class of the public; Bach's to the more refined few and those of more delicate sensibilities.

Bach wrote other settings of the Passion besides that according to St. Matthew. That according to St. Mark appears to have been lost, but that according to St. John has often been performed in this country and has been well appreciated. It is not on the same scale as that according to St. Matthew but has the same noble and poetical qualities. He wrote a great deal of church music on a grand scale besides these works; for instance, the famous B Minor Mass, one of the most gigantic choral works in existence, and also the "Christmas Oratorio," a grand setting of the Magnificat, and an immense number of church cantatas. At Leipzig, there was a great demand for compositions of this latter class, and he seems to have been constantly producing fresh ones for performance on Sundays and great festivals at the churches where he directed the music. Before he came to Leipzig, he had probably written twenty-nine; while he was there, he appears to have produced over two hundred and ninety, some of which have been lost. This enormous mass of work seems all the more amazing when the richness and variety and the amount of labor he expended over such works are taken into account. It is not at all a wonderful thing for everyday composers to turn out cheap or popular operas and operettas by the cartload, as French composers have done, but to write nearly three hundred works of one kind, all of which have thought and elaborate artistic workmanship and individual character about them, is an amount of labor which few men in history can rival.

Bach's life continued always in the same quiet and comparatively uneventful way, which was so unlike the busy manager's life, with many journeys to and fro to foreign countries, and the association with people of all ranks and callings in the lively society of London, which was Handel's lot and his natural atmosphere. The limits of Bach's journeyings hardly exceeded a small portion of his native country, and most of the various towns where he occupied different musical posts one after another were close together and in the same district. His music made very small way with the general public in his lifetime, and the connoisseurs of other countries were rather inclined to look down upon him as a crabbed, curious old pedant who delighted in mechanical ingenuities and tiresome puzzles. This seems quite explicable and natural considering how rare is the gift of appreciating really great music. But even among the wiser people of his generation and of that immediately succeeding him, his style had but little effect. And this is the more remarkable because he was a great teacher of his art and had very great influence over his pupils, who naturally felt him to be

the greatest musician they had ever come across. His most successful pupils were his own sons, several of whom had very great musical
abilities. His favorite was his eldest son, Wilhelm Friedemann, and this
one, no doubt, had the greatest depth and character of all of them. But
he was unfortunately of a wild temperament, and though he produced
some noble works, his abilities were wasted by dissipation, and he sank
into deeper misery as he grew older and ended his life in poverty and
uselessness. The second son, Philip Emmanuel, gained great fame and
did a great quantity of invaluable work, especially as a clavier player and
writer for keyed instruments. But his line was quite different from his
father's and not by any means so lofty in sentiment or broad in style.
This was partly owing to a great change which came over the musical
world, which will have to be considered later on, and this affected the
work of another son, John Christian, even more strongly in the same
way. They all profited technically by what their father taught them, but
his style had reached too high a pitch of feeling for them to grasp, and
in the deepest things of expression he was not able to teach them to do
anything which can be said to follow naturally from his style. As time
went on and he got more advanced in years, he grew to like more and
more the quiet, orderly life of his home, with its regular round of duties
and leisure for the constant pursuit of that art which men always find
to be the more endless in its possibilities of improvement as they get
more thoroughly to understand it. His journeys consequently became
less frequent, but there was one journey which he took in the latter
part of his life which has become famous, both because it shows how
highly his powers were appreciated in Northern Germany and also
because it puts a very interesting and famous man in a peculiar light.

That extraordinary man, Frederick the Great, had all his life long
taken great delight in music, and in the intervals of fighting, orga-
nizing, diplomatising, and carrying out more great schemes than
any other man alive, he somehow managed to find time not only to
hear the select musicians whom he kept about him but to play with
them pretty regularly of an evening. Philip Emmanuel, Bach's second
son, had been appointed one of his musicians as accompanist and
so forth in 1740, and partly through him and partly through other
distinguished members of the musical circle at Potsdam, Frederick's
curiosity about John Sebastian Bach was roused to a very high pitch,

and he wished very much to see and hear him. Bach was too fond of his quiet life at home to be eager about the journey, but he was at last persuaded to undertake it in 1747. He appears to have arrived at Potsdam in the afternoon, and the news was brought to Frederick just as he had got his flute in his hand ready to begin playing at his usual afternoon concert. Frederick was generally as regular and systematic as a good clock and held discipline and etiquette to be indispensable to the right ordering of human affairs. But his eagerness overcame his usual habits. His flute was laid aside at once with the exclamation, "Old Bach has come!" and Bach was sent for and was not even allowed time to change his clothes and put on a suit of such respectful color as was considered proper at a court. When he came in, Frederick set him to work at once to extemporize and show his mastery both as a performer and an artist. He gave him a subject for a fugue, which he had to develop at once on the spot to satisfy the curiosity of the king, and he was afterwards taken to try the Silbermann pianofortes, which were then but lately invented and had been taken possession of by the royal amateur. His powers were tested in all sorts of ways, and the king seems to have shown much appreciation of the difficulties of the science of music by the experiments to which he subjected him. Bach evidently satisfied Frederick's highest anticipations and was treated with exceptional honor; and after he went home, he wrote a sort of memento of the occasion, in which he combined all sorts of wonderful musical contrivances and masterly strokes of art, which he dedicated to Frederick.

In his latter days, he continued developing instrumental music. He added the twenty-four more preludes and fugues to the collection before described to complete the work which is known in this country as the "Forty-eight." He wrote also some more suites, which are on a grander and broader scale than the French ones, which appeared soon after his second marriage at Cöthen; and he also wrote some works which make nearer approaches to the forms of later days, such as the so-called concertos, both for solo instruments and for combinations like two or three claviers with small orchestra. And all these show not only that his powers were as strong and his mastery greater as he grew older, but even that he maintained his youthful fire and geniality and freshness till the last.

Every one notices what a strong preference Bach had for fugues; and it perhaps may fairly be said that the form of fugue was as much his natural way of putting his musical thoughts as the sonata later was Beethoven's. But his fugues are utterly unlike anyone else's. Most other musicians, when they have been writing fugues, have worked as if ingenuity was the sole aim of their ambition, which makes their productions of this kind belong more to the order of sport than to the order of genuine music. But Bach looked at the form of a fugue not as an end in itself but as a means of expressing something essentially musical. He had the mastery of the art, elaborate as it is, so completely in his control that he could naturally express in this form things just as sweetly and perfectly beautiful in the highest sense as any spontaneous musical effusion of Schumann or Schubert. No other man in the world has ever written such instrumental fugues, and it may be safely prophesied that no man ever will. Very often his fugues are much less elaborately ingenious than other people's, and very often, too, they do not contain anything like the orthodox amount of technical devices which theorists say are indispensable to a good fugue. He was quite contented to show in a certain number of fugues that he could make more wonderful devices of the fugal kind than any other man, but he did not think it was always necessary to be doing so. He wanted to make music, not puzzles. At the same time, he so far divined what was possible even in instruments that he did not possess, that his works of this kind seem naturally to lend themselves to all the highest possibilities of the most perfect modern pianoforte. He himself was not much attracted by the pianofortes he had the opportunity of trying. They were, no doubt, in some ways more or less defective, and it must be remembered, too, that the ways in which the fingers have to be used to get the best effects out of them are so different from the ways he was accustomed to on his favorite little clavichord that he most likely found he could not produce the peculiar kind of delicate expression he wanted. The pianoforte did not make much way with any of the musicians in those days. His famous son, Philip Emmanuel, still went on calling the clavichord the most beautiful of instruments till long afterwards, and Haydn and Mozart in their younger days still kept to the old harpsichord. There was so much to be done in the way of changing the habits and practice of players in the positions of their hands and fingers that full appreciation of the way to manage the pianoforte does not seem to have come till a full generation and more after Bach was dead.

Towards the end of his life, his eyes began to trouble him. He had always tried them severely from the time when he copied his brother's collection of organ music by moonlight till his old age; and it is wonderful they served him well so long. It became necessary to risk an operation, and the responsibility was confided to an English oculist who was living in Leipzig. It was tried more than once, but without success, and he became totally blind. His health, which seems to have been wonderfully good throughout till this time, at last gave way, and then the fight was not long. A fever came on, and on the 28th of July, 1750, in the evening, he died and was buried with sincere and general mourning near the Church of St. John in Leipzig.

Few men of that time were capable of realizing the true greatness of the man they had lost. They admired him as a great master craftsman, a great organist, and a powerful controller of all the forces and difficulties of art. It has remained for men of full a hundred years after his time to realize the depth and almost inexhaustible fertility of his genius, and to understand fully the meaning of that saying of Schumann's, that he was a man "to whom music owes hardly as great a debt as religion owes to its founder."

IV.

HAYDN.

W HEN Bach and Handel were dead, the world of music seemed vacant and dull again, just as it did after Palestrina's death. Another mountain height had been climbed, and that a great one; and, as before, the standard of music sank to much lower levels directly, and composers had to make another fresh effort in a new direction. The art was still carried on by excellent good men, but they were perfect pigmies in comparison with the two great giants who had passed away; and their work is made to seem all the smaller and more trifling by reason of certain new influences which were coming upon the world, and old feelings and enthusiasms which were dropping away. Bach and Handel were not only the last great representatives of the older forms of art, but they were the last composers in whose works the fervor which belonged to the reformed religion in its early days showed its powerful and ennobling influence. In Bach's music, the essence of religion in the shape of deep and earnest feeling is always present, and in the best of Handel's music, it is the same. The generation which followed them lost this great source of energy and had nothing substantial to put in its place. What the national music of the reformed Church had been to Bach, the opera and people's songs and dances were to his successors; and in none of these was there as yet much of deep feeling or strong character. But since a new line had obviously become necessary, composers had to use what they could get to begin upon and make the best of their opportunities.

In point of art, too, composers were at a disadvantage. For the principles of modern instrumental music are so different from those which underlie Bach and Handel's work that the earlier composers who attempted it could not do otherwise than produce works which seem very slender and unimpressive by the side of the older masterpieces. But just as the first adventurers in new lands deserve great honor, even though they can make little progress for want of experience of the conditions they have to contend with, so do these men, though they have left little which people care to hear now, deserve great honor for what they did achieve in such unfavorable circumstances.

The foremost of these composers was Philip Emmanuel Bach, John Sebastian's second son, who was a man of considerable mental cultivation, and clear and accurate judgment, and applied his abilities successfully to the production of instrumental sonatas and symphonies. The youngest of Bach's sons, John Christian, worked also in the same line and won great popularity. There were many others too who did useful work in various ways. Some turned their attention to improving the style of execution, and some to improving the style of the music itself; and before long the taste for instrumental music became general, and little symphonies for small bands were turned out by average composers in scores, and were played by the little bands which small German potentates and noblemen kept to entertain them in their leisure, and enhance their enjoyment of their dinners.

The taste for the massive style of the previous generation died out, and people grew to like pleasant, easy music, which kept them amused and artistically pleased without much stirring of their emotions. Such music had become very general by the middle of the eighteenth century, and Joseph Haydn, who was by that time coming to man's estate, was brought under its influence.

Haydn, besides falling upon different times from Bach and Handel, sprang from a different part of Germany, where different influences were at work. He was born at Rohrau, in Austria, close to the borders of Hungary, in 1732. His father was a wheelwright, and his mother had been a cook in the household of a certain Count Harrach; so he had, at all events, the advantages of a thoroughly plebeian extraction. Both parents were musical in a quiet way and used to sing such simple songs as they could compass without the advantage of even so much science as the knowledge of their notes; and the father used to accompany himself on the harp. The stories which are told of Haydn's childhood have more appearance of truth about them than such stories usually have, as they do not set his precocity extravagantly high. He soon pleased his parents by the correct way in which he used to join their songs, and he amused them by imitating someone he had heard playing on the violin and pretending to accompany them with a couple of sticks. His mother wished him to be made a priest, but the father was persuaded that he had the making of a musician in him, and sent him to school when he was six years old in a neighboring village, where he had a chance of learning the elements of the art. The little Joseph soon developed a very good voice and picked up a little rudimentary knowledge of both violin and harpsichord; and on one occasion, he distinguished himself by the accurate way in which he played on the drum, with scarcely any previous teaching, in some music for a local procession.

A most important bit of good luck happened to him when he was eight years old. A certain Reutter, who was capellmeister at St. John's Church in Vienna, came to the village where Haydn was at school on a visit to the clergyman, and was struck by the sweetness of his voice and offered to take him as a chorister at his church. His father's consent was readily given, and the boy began life in Vienna in 1740. As a member of the choir of St. Stephen's, he was regularly taught singing and had proper instruction on the violin and clavier, and such other subjects as were taught in the school of the church, but he got little or nothing told him about harmony or any part of the art of composition. But the instinct was in him, and without knowing anything about artistic principles, he used to fill sheets of music paper with notes in the hope that something like music might come out of it. And somehow by this means, he did manage to learn a little and made a few steps towards the goal of his childish ambition.

Before long, he was thrown entirely upon his own resources. His voice began to break and lost its sweetness, and he ceased to be foremost in the choir. Reutter did not dismiss him at once, but in the end, Haydn brought about his own dismissal rather abruptly by his taste for practical joking. One day he had a new pair of scissors, and by way of trying their edge and combining amusement with practical experience, he cut off a schoolfellow's pigtail. Reutter would no doubt have forgiven him if his voice had been of any use, but as it was not, he shortly sent him about his business.

Haydn, though still but a boy, had thereupon to support himself. Some friend helped him with a small loan, and he took an attic, where he was able to keep a little keyed instrument of some sort, on which he used to practice perseveringly, and he eked out his livelihood by teaching a few pupils. Like many other great men, he was forced to develop his own education; and he seems to have done it in the same way that Bach had done before him, which was by careful study of the works of the masters of his own craft. There is no record of his having studied the masters of the old contrapuntal school to any extent, and he is not likely, with such slender resources as he had, to have been able to get many of their works. But he got some of Philip Emmanuel Bach's works, and these he delighted in and worked at them constantly; till, perhaps unconsciously, their simple and well-balanced form acted as well as a master's guidance upon him and led him to the first steps in that style of writing which was afterwards one of his greatest glories. Philip Emmanuel Bach's influence was perhaps the best he could have at that time; for as he had it in him to write in the modern instrumental style, it was vital that he should have pure models. What Haydn had to build upon, and what was most congenial to him through his origin and circumstances, was the native people's songs and dances, which belong to the same order of art in point of structure as symphonies and sonatas; and what he wanted, and what all men who aimed in the same direction wanted, was to know how to make this kind of music on a grander scale. The older music of Handel and Bach leaned too much towards the style of the choral music and organ music of the Church to serve him as a model. For the principle upon which their art was mainly built was the treatment of what are called the separate parts, which are equivalent to the separate voices when the music is sung. In the modern style, the artistic principle upon which music is mainly based is the treatment of harmonies and keys, and the way in which those harmonies and keys are arranged. In national dances, few harmonies are used, but they are arranged on the same principles as the harmonies of a sonata or a symphony, and what had to be found out in order to make grand instrumental works was how to arrange many more harmonies with the same effect of unity as is obtained on a small scale in dances and national songs. Haydn had the instinct in him for this kind of art, for from his childhood he had been accustomed to hear the people's music; and the study of Philip Emmanuel's works taught him how to direct his energies in the lines which were most congenial to him.

He can hardly have divined, however, how much stronger his gifts were for this kind of music than for any other, and his attention was given at first to other branches of art. In Vienna, even the poorest musicians had chances of hearing a fair quantity of masses and operas, and of these, Haydn availed himself. He evidently had the knack of learning when he was listening; and the results of his opportunities were shown in those directions to which young composers in modern days are most commonly drawn. One of his first attempts was a mass, and about the same time, he tried his hand at a comic opera, the words of which were put in his way by an actor with whom he had struck up acquaintance. For this work, he was lucky enough to receive some money and must have made himself a very fair advance in reputation too, for the work was successfully played in a good many of the principal towns in Germany. The next event of importance which happened to him was to fall in with Niccolo Porpora; the same who in his younger days had come into contact with Handel, and now, being well advanced in years and experience, had a considerable reputation as a composer and teacher of singing. He found Haydn serviceable as an accompanyist and took him about with him in Vienna and elsewhere and gave him the benefit of his experience in various departments of the art in return. This was of the very greatest service to Haydn, as it not only brought him into contact with the distinguished musicians of the day but enabled him to hear instrumental music more frequently and also gave him the chance of finding out how to improve his own education by the study of the works of the most famous theorists, of whose very names he might never have heard in the seclusion of his lonely attic. He turned these opportunities to the best advantage, and though he had already made some success by the little comic opera, he did not let that mislead him as to his backwardness in experience of the severer branches of art but worked at counterpoint as zealously as any beginner.

The acquaintance with some of the aristocratic patrons of art which he made through his connection with Porpora led to his first experiments in the branch of composition which, in later days, he made so specially his own. The performances of chamber music which they gave in their private houses led to his writing his first string quartets; and his chief patron, von Fürnberg, did the great service of recommending him to a certain Count Morzin, a Bohemian nobleman, who had a little orchestra of his own and was in want of a man to conduct and look after it. Haydn was appointed his *capellmeister*, and for the little band, he wrote his first symphony in 1759. Symphonies had by that time become a popular form of composition, but they were very different from the kind of works which are known by the same name in the nineteenth century. They were generally written for very small bands and consisted of four parts for stringed instruments and four for wind instruments, such as two horns and two flutes. They were only meant to be played in noblemen's houses, so they were made on a much smaller scale than they were in later times, both as concerns the actual length and the style of the music. Composers did not exert themselves much to put poetical or elevated thoughts into them or to make them deeply impressive in any way but aimed at an agreeable and easy style which was most likely to please their aristocratic patrons. As yet, great public audiences for such kinds of music were scarcely to be met with, and as long as music is written only for such little coteries and comfortable circles of wealthy aristocrats, composers are not encouraged to rise to any pitch of real greatness or depth of meaning. Haydn had to write under such influences for a long time, for after his connection with Count Morzin came to an end, he was only promoted to another post of the same kind, though it is true it was on rather a grander scale. In 1760, Count Morzin married and had to part with his band and its director, and Haydn was engaged by a rich Hungarian prince called Paul Esterhazy, who, however, did not enjoy his services for long but died in 1762. His successor, Prince Nicholas Esterhazy, kept Haydn on in his employment and became a most invaluable help to him in many ways. This prince was a man of somewhat extravagant tastes, which his wealth enabled him to gratify to the utmost. He built a magnificent palace called Esterhaz, to which he attached an opera-house and concert-room, and he collected a large company of excellent performers of all sorts and put Haydn in command of them. This became in the end one of the finest opportunities that any composer ever had, for the band was always at Haydn's disposal, and whenever he wrote a new work, it could soon be tried, and he could test its effect at his ease in every particular, and under the influence of the lesson it afforded him go on to write something better. He was always very energetic in using such opportunities, and he did not let this one slip, for he was constantly at work on new compositions of various kinds and constantly improved both in the management of his little orchestra and in the mastery of his art. The members of the band were all devoted to him and were ready to take any amount of pains to give his ideas the effect he wanted; so he could experiment as much as he pleased and keep what turned out well and reject or mend whatever turned out ill.

Under these pleasant conditions, he tried his hand at all sorts of music, such as operas and sacred music for solos, chorus, and orchestra, and symphonies; some of which were more specially fitted for the small circle in which he lived than for general publicity and consequently have not survived. But in the lines in which he was destined to excel, he made constant improvement, and without any definite object in view, he raised his standard of symphony writing far beyond any point which had been attained before. His predecessors had always written rather carelessly and hastily for the band and hardly ever tried to get refined and original effects from the use of their instruments, but he naturally applied his mind more earnestly to the matter in hand and found out new ways of contrasting and combining the tones of different members of his orchestra and getting a fuller and richer effect out of the mass of them when they were all playing. In the actual style of the music too, he made great advances, and in his hands, symphonies became by degrees more vigorous and, at the same time, more really musical.

But the limited character of the audiences he had at Esterhazy and the steady routine was still not altogether in favor of his rising to his highest mark. His master was so fond of his magnificent country palace that he rarely cared to go to Vienna or indeed anywhere else, and his band and its director had to stop there too. On one occasion when they all, except the prince, were getting tired of staying so long in one place and felt themselves in want of a change of air, Haydn came to the rescue by writing a symphony in such a manner as to express their wishes in the most delicately humorous form to their master. The earlier part of the work was just as usual, one movement following another as if there was nothing unusual going to happen. When the last movement came, all of a sudden, a few of the band stopped playing and took up their instruments and went out; then a few more followed, and then by degrees more of them dropped away, one or two at a time, and departed, till at last there were only two left, who went on and brought the symphony to a conclusion by themselves, and then departed also. The prince seems to have understood the hint, and he was too fond of Haydn to take any offense at it, so the members of the band shortly got their desires. The symphony is commonly known by the name of *The Farewell Symphony* and has been played as a sort of musical joke in later times. It is perfectly complete as a work of art, but the strong way in which the special purpose is pointed out is against its fitness for ordinary occasions.

The life at Esterház drifted on gently and uneventfully for many years, but by degrees, Haydn's music got to be known elsewhere, and about 1780, his fame was spreading far and wide over the world. On great occasions at court in Vienna, his music was played, and publishers were ready to bring out his compositions almost as fast as he could write them, which was very much the reverse of slow. Even in England, publishers were beginning to think it might pay to bring out some of his works, and a man named Forster bought a great number, including such apparently unsaleable articles as symphonies. In Paris too, his works were performed with success, and he received pressing invitations to go there. In Spain, his fame had grown great enough for him to be asked to write something solemn for performance on Good Friday at the cathedral of Cadiz; which resulted in the work known as *The Seven Last Words of the Saviour on the Cross*. Besides the invitation to Paris, many others came to him, including some from London; but Haydn always felt himself bound to his master, Prince Nicholas Esterhazy, from whom he had received so much kindness and such excellent opportunities for developing his talents, and he would not be drawn away. So his life went on still in the same steadily laborious way till 1790, when Prince Nicholas died. His successor, Prince Anton, did not care to keep on the band, so they were dispersed, and Haydn was very liberally pensioned.

Haydn was now free and went back to Vienna to settle. But the invitations to show himself in other countries were still reiterated, and at last, though he was getting on for sixty years old, he began to face the possibility of journeying abroad.

There was at this time living in London a violinist named Salomon, who, after traveling about Europe and making a considerable reputation as a player, took to giving concerts on a large scale in London. He had always had a great admiration for Haydn and gave performances of his symphonies at these concerts as early as 1786. He was also among those who had long been trying to induce Haydn to come to London, but without success as long as Prince Esterhazy was alive. In 1790, he was traveling abroad in search of singers for London concerts when he heard of the death of the prince. He saw his opportunity and went off at once to Vienna to Haydn, and this time had the good luck to secure him and carried him off in December and journeyed with him straight to London, where they arrived just at the beginning of 1791.

England seems to have been in a musical humour, and the honour paid to Haydn does great credit to the taste of the people of that day. He took up his abode with Salomon at 18 Great Pulteney Street, and there numbers of people of the highest rank and position called upon him; while poets celebrated him in verse, and all the leading musical societies of the town invited him to honour their meetings by his presence. Salomon had advertised his name in connection with his concerts, promising six new symphonies in the series. The first of these concerts came off successfully in March, 1791, when one of the famous symphonies, which are always known as the Salomon set, was performed for the first time. The English public were worthy of their guest; they came in crowds and applauded enthusiastically, even encoring the slow movement, which in those days was a most uncommon thing to do.

Haydn was in no hurry to go away again but seemed to take kindly to his novel situation, and if he was amenable to the influence of affectionate admiration, it is not to be wondered at. It shows his character in a most admirable light that such a height of success should not have spoilt him in the least. Few men have ever risen from such a lowly origin to such honour in the world's eyes. The son of a wheelwright and a cook, a poor native of an insignificant village on the borders of Austria and Hungary, almost self-educated, he had at last risen through his genius and steady perseverance to be the object of almost extravagant admiration and honour among princes and men and women of distinction in the most exclusive societies in the world. While he was in Prince Esterhazy's service, he was still more or less in the position of a servant; for the German nobles and magnates who kept musicians in their pay did not, as yet, regard them as belonging to a higher grade than their other servants. In England, Haydn was his own master, and men of high position treated him as an equal. But his genial, honest, clear-headed simplicity was not in the least affected by the change, and no hint of presumption or vanity was ever made against him. His character shines in his music, and it was no doubt its clear, straightforward, fresh geniality, free from affectation and morbidity, which endeared both him and it to the English people of that day.

The change in the character of the audience for whom he had to write had a most excellent effect upon his style; and he rose to heights of vigour and power which he had never approached before. It was the change from an audience of select aristocrats for whom he was paid to provide refined amusement to an audience of a much broader and more mixed character. The former encouraged quiet refinement, which of itself was a great good; but the latter wanted more comprehensive power and broader treatment of art. While he was chiefly concerned to satisfy a great patron and his guests, his art was inevitably rather bound to subservience to their tastes; when he addressed a popular audience, he was free to let his whole self be fully seen and to express the originality of his nature without stint. The result is that the symphonies he wrote for the English public have almost as completely eclipsed all his previous works of the kind as those had in their turn surpassed the productions of all the earlier writers of symphonies. When any of his symphonies are performed nowadays, it is almost always one of the last twelve; and many musicians of experience go through their lives without knowing more than one or two of the very numerous earlier ones. And this ignorance is not in the least a matter to be ashamed of, for Haydn is scarcely himself in this most important branch of composition till this very late period of his life. To the musical historian who traces every step on the ladder which leads from small beginnings to great achievements, there is interest in all the lesser works that throw light upon the growth of any great form of art; but to the man who wishes only to deal with things which are artistically complete, the earlier works have not much meaning. Haydn's earlier symphonies have, many of them, the marks of incomplete art. They have noble traits about them, and to a man who is intellectually cultivated to the point of appreciating them relatively to the time when they were written, they are often delightful; but for the ordinary public, who are concerned chiefly with what directly and definitely affects them without their knowing the why and wherefore, they do not have much attractiveness.

People talk of Haydn as the father of the symphony, but it seems that the title is rather misleading. Haydn took up the writing of symphonies very early, and when they were not very much advanced in style, but between his earliest attempts and his greatest triumphs, there lies the whole life and work of a genius of quite equal importance to himself; and if his position in art is to be judged by the latest symphonies which he wrote for Salomon's concerts, it must be confessed that his short-lived contemporary arrived at a very high point of perfection in this branch of art before he did his best work.

The case is no doubt involved, or historians would not have given it a misleading complexion. Haydn was the first in the field and did good work up to a certain point before Mozart did anything very notable. When Mozart began — and he began when he was a mere child — he was not under the influence of Haydn, but of other composers, such as John Christian Bach. He went on improving his own style independently for many years, and then comparatively late in his very short career, he seems to have fallen under Haydn's influence and to have modelled some of his works more or less in Haydn's style. Mozart then came to his zenith much quicker than Haydn and produced the famous G Minor symphony and that known by the name of *Jupiter*, before any of Haydn's finest works of the kind were known to the world; and then in time he more or less influenced Haydn. Such a curious case of two great men mutually leading one another hardly exists in history, and in discussing their importance in connection with the history of the symphony, it is difficult to award the palm. Mozart admired the older master sincerely, and Haydn in his turn appreciated the younger genius without a touch of jealousy or reserve. Mozart dedicated a set of his finest string quartets to Haydn, and the latter is reported to have said to the former's father after hearing one of them, that "he considered him the greatest composer he had ever heard." On another occasion, when someone had asked Haydn to write an opera for Prague, he wrote in answer that "it would be a hazardous thing to do, for it would be difficult to stand a comparison with Mozart." And he went on, "If I could transfuse into the soul of every lover of music the admiration I feel for the inimitable works of Mozart, all nations would vie with one another in trying to have such a treasure within their boundaries." At the time Haydn was leaving Vienna for London, Mozart came to see him, and they spent some of the last hours before Haydn started together. At that time, Mozart too was meditating a journey to England on similar terms to Haydn's, but it was not destined to be carried out; and before the two composers could meet again, he was dead.

Haydn wrote many other works for performance in England besides symphonies. For instance, he wrote the greater part of an opera called *Orfeo ed Euridice*, but it was neither completely finished nor performed, as the manager for whom he wrote it failed before it could be brought forward. He also wrote a march for the Royal Society of Musicians when they invited him to their annual dinner, and the original is said to be still in their possession. In July of the same year, he went to Oxford to receive the honorary degree of Doctor of Music, which the university had agreed to confer upon him at the suggestion of Burney, the historian, who was his enthusiastic admirer. He appears to have written a new symphony for the occasion, but there was not time enough to rehearse it, and a simpler work written some time before was played instead. But this did not make much difference to the gay people of Oxford, who were as much delighted with him as possible and cheered and applauded him vociferously when he made his appearance in the gorgeous gown of cherry and cream-coloured silk which is the adornment of Doctors of Music on grand occasions. In November of the same year, he was invited to Oatlands by the Prince of Wales and was treated in the most friendly way by the members of the royal family who were there. They had some of Haydn's music, and the Prince of Wales himself played the violoncello, while the young Duchess of York sat by his side at the harpsichord and sang the tunes that pleased her. It is a great wonder he managed to find time for writing, for everybody was wanting to do him honour by asking him to dinners, both public and private, and inviting him to country houses, and taking him for expeditions, and painting pictures of him, and doing everything which the most unbounded enthusiasm could suggest.

Haydn appears to have had a susceptible heart and was somewhat captivated by some of the English ladies whom he met. One of his visits was to a Mr. Shaw, whose wife he described in his diary as the most beautiful woman he had ever seen; and for many years after their meeting, he kept a ribbon she had worn upon the occasion. He also kept for a long time a short piece of manuscript music, to which there was a note appended ascribing it to "Mrs. Hodges, the loveliest woman I ever saw." Another lady friend for whom he must have had a very great affection was past the years when her beauty was likely to be a moving power, for she was over sixty. She was the widow of a musician named Schroeter and had lessons from him on the pianoforte. Their affection seems to have been mutual, and Haydn, who kept several of her letters for many years, said that if he had been a free man, he should certainly have married her. Other lady friends he had besides, such as Mrs. Hunter, the wife of a celebrated surgeon, who wrote the words for several of his English canzonets; and it seems that he himself was attractive to ladies — even in his old age — as much as they were to him. He had that simple sympathetic way about him and the sincerity and naturalness which readily draws people's liking. But, by a singular fatality, his own marriage, made in the days before fame had come to him, was an unfortunate one.

Among other interesting events of his time in England was his being present at the Handel Commemoration in Westminster Abbey. He certainly could never have heard any performance on so grand a scale before, nor anything so well calculated to give him a complete impression of Handel's greatness; and the effect it produced upon him was immense. Another occasion of a similar kind which he attended was the annual gathering of charity children in St. Paul's Cathedral. He wrote of it in his diary that he was more touched by the innocent and reverent music they sang than by anything he ever heard in his life.

Salomon's concerts came to an end with great success in June, 1792, and soon afterwards Haydn left England and went back to Germany. On his way to Vienna, he met Beethoven at Bonn, and later in the year, when he was settled in Vienna again, Beethoven came to work under him. Many stories have been told about their intercourse and the views the two great musicians had about one another. No doubt it must have been difficult for Haydn to understand Beethoven; for they were in many ways very differently constituted. Haydn was the type of the well-balanced, quiet, easy-minded artist; Beethoven the highest type of the fervent poetic genius, with a temperament burning with aspirations and deep sympathies. They belonged almost to different centuries, and the disposition which the younger artist had for splendid experiments must have seemed to the experienced old artist little better than wildness and licentious irregularity. Haydn is said to have persisted in regarding Beethoven as a pianoforte player, and not as a composer; and Beethoven in his turn was no doubt at times impatient with the apparent want of expansiveness in Haydn's mind. At the same time, they had a great deal in common. The vein of strong, healthy humour is remarkably characteristic of both of them; and so is the taste for bold and surprising effects of harmony, which Haydn had much more strongly than Mozart. Whatever may have been Beethoven's feelings about the old master in his younger days, as he grew older, he appreciated him more and more, and in the later part of his life regarded him as a truly great man.

The extraordinary success which Haydn had in England naturally increased people's interest in him elsewhere, and at Vienna, he was warmly welcomed on his return, and performances of the works he had written for London were given. His connection with the Esterhazy family appears to have revived, and Prince Anton treated him with much regard, and seemed to meditate setting him actively to work again. But whatever his purpose was, he was not quick enough in making up his mind, and in 1794, Haydn started for London again at a second invitation from Salomon, who engaged him on much the same conditions as before; the most important point for the world being that he was to provide six new symphonies, as in the first season: so making up the number written for Salomon to twelve, and putting the topstone on the great pile of his compositions of this kind. This season was even more successful than the previous one; and symphonies of his, either new or old, were given on every occasion. The one known as *The Surprise*, because of a rather comic crash which comes in unexpectedly in a very quiet and simple tune, appears to have been a great favourite; and it probably was because of the jump it gave people that they liked it. Haydn quite intended to startle them, and confessed as much to the musician Gyrowetz. Besides symphonies, new quartets and other instrumental works were brought forward, and vocal music too. He was always ready with new compositions whether written for an occasion or not; and he must have been very methodical in the management of his time, or it would have been impossible for him to produce such an enormous mass of work as he did, for he himself declared he was not really a quick writer.

The practice which is ascribed to him is that he sketched out his ideas roughly in the morning, and elaborated them into perfect works in the afternoon. He is also credited with having got his ideas into order with the help of the pianoforte or harpsichord, which most theorists have regarded as a bad habit. But if any one composer could serve as a proof to the contrary of such an opinion more than another, it is Haydn, for the neatness and compactness of his works is perfect. It is really very likely that most modern composers have used the pianoforte a good deal not so much to help them to find out their ideas as to test the details and intensify their musical sensibility by the excitant sounds; the actual sensual impression of which is, of course, an essential element in all music. The composer can always hear such things in his head, but it must be rare that the music in such an abstracted form can have quite as much effect upon him as when the sounds really strike upon his ears.

A good deal is known about Haydn's ways of composing as far as externals are concerned, though not much as far as regards his own principles of artistic development. He used to like to write in his tidiest clothes, and if he meant to make anything particularly good, he put on a ring which had been given him by the King of Prussia. Nothing could be further from the popular idea of the wild frenzy of the poet, and the life of irregular *deshabille* which is supposed to be characteristic of composers, and is the natural result of the habit of genius of watching for an inspiration and encouraging it to take possession of his whole being when it comes. This was not at all Haydn's way. It is clear from his behaviour, and such a saying of his as "genius is always prolific," that he expected such ideas as he wanted to come at call. In fact, there is the greatest difference possible between the quality of the music of his age and that of the age of Beethoven — the nineteenth century. The whole period between Bach and Beethoven was one of comparative musical tranquillity. The tone of the refined and cultivated classes was comfortable complacency. The people who enjoyed all the best things in the world in that time, before the French Revolution came and roughly awakened them, took their ease and amused themselves with perfect content, without troubling their heads much about the thousands who lived in privation and squalid misery. But just as men's lives are, such will their art and poetry be. In such times, if there is any good in them, the artistic side of music is sure to have much more attention, while those striking effects and great thoughts, which dive into the depths of man's nature, never make their appearance. A man living in such conditions may always work in his best court clothes without any danger of disarranging his frill or his periwig; and he may do very good and enduring work too. It was not Haydn's business to tear his own hair or rend other people's hearts, but to develop new forms of art to a high pitch of perfection. The conditions were favourable to him; for people did not want to be stirred deeply in those days; and it is far easier for an artist or a composer to keep his work well balanced and think of the conditions of art when he is not deeply moved by the power and passion of his thoughts. At the same time, Haydn had, behind his quiet and composed exterior, a great quantity of strong feeling, and even pathos; and he did at times sound unexpected depths.

He was capable of being moved to tears by music, as he was by the grandeur of the Hallelujah in the *Messiah* when he heard it at Westminster Abbey; and he himself said that at a performance of one of his own greatest works "he was cold as ice one moment and seemed on fire the next." It seems curious too in these days to think that there were people in his time who objected to some of his music because it made so much noise, and their criticism is not without interest as throwing a light upon similar sensitiveness among some modern critics about the music of their own time. Haydn certainly had it in him to touch upon romance and imagination, but it is not often that one man can work both the artistic side and the imaginative side; and one of his most serviceable achievements was really to prepare the way for composers who, living in more soul-stirring times, should make use of the forms of art he had done so much to perfect in his symphonies and quartets for the utterance of deeper and more passionate ideas.

The English people were more fit to appreciate the clearness and simplicity of his style than any other nation, and he himself said that he did not become famous in Germany till after he had been in England. And in England, he had the good fortune not only to be popular but to make a good deal of money. At his benefit concert alone, in May 1795, he made 400 guineas, and by the time Salomon's concerts in that year were over, he had enough money in his pocket to make him feel comfortably off for the rest of his days. His departure from London was hastened by the desire of Prince Esterhazy to revive the musical establishment as it had been in the days of his predecessor, Nicholas, and he started to go back to Vienna again in August of this same year. Soon after he arrived, a number of men of high position in the Austrian capital paid him a very touching and delicate compliment. They invited him to visit his birthplace at Rohrau with them; and when he arrived, he found they had put up a monument near his old home, with a bust of himself upon it. He visited the cottage where he was born and found the old familiar stove still in its place, where as a child he had sat and listened to the simple people's songs his parents used to sing.

The next year after this, the patriotic feelings of Austrians were raised to an unusual pitch of excitement by the proceedings of the French republic, and a hymn was written by the poet Hauschka under its influence. Haydn had been very much impressed by the English national anthem and wished to produce something which should answer the same purpose in Austria; and with this view, he set the verses to the music which is known as the Emperor's hymn; which so completely answered the purpose he intended it for that it became from that time the national anthem of the country. He himself was more fond of it than of any other of his compositions. When he was dying, he had himself carried to the pianoforte and lingered over it with evident tenderness; and it is said to have been the last thing he ever played in his life.

By the time he wrote this most successful little work, he was sixty-four years old, but his powers were as great and his thoughts

as bright and fresh as ever; and he now set about writing one of the
largest and most successful of all his compositions. In London, he had
many opportunities of hearing Handel's oratorios, as performances
were frequently given during Lent. This probably led his mind more
in the direction of large choral works than previously. Before he left
London, Salomon gave him a poem to set, which had been compiled
from Milton's *Paradise Lost*, and this he got freely translated and
reconstructed in German, and attacked the composition of the music
with enthusiasm. He was not long about the completion of the work,
as it was first performed privately in the Schwarzenberg Palace in
April 1798. It was publicly performed shortly afterwards in Vienna and
produced the greatest effect of any of his works. As soon as it could
be printed and published, it spread at once over all the musical world,
and in England, it became, as the *Creation*, the most popular work of
its kind next to the *Messiah*. In the very year that it was published, two
performances were given in London, and the next year it took firm root
in the provinces, as it was performed in 1800 at the Worcester Festival,
in 1801 at the Hereford Festival, and the year following at Gloucester.

After such a success, it was natural that his friends should press
him to undertake another work of the kind. An adaptation was made
from the poem called the *Seasons* by the English poet Thomson, and
he was persuaded to undertake the composition, though he was convinced that his strength was beginning to fail. He managed to carry the
work through and achieved another success; which at the time was
thought to be quite equal to that of the *Creation*. To all appearances,
the work is as fresh and genial as if it were the work of a young man;
but he himself felt the strain to be very great and never recovered
from it. After its completion, though he lived several years, he wrote
very little of importance. In 1806, he was engaged in writing a new
string quartett and got through two movements of it; then he felt his
musical powers failing hopelessly, and instead of finishing it, he put a
little fragment of melody with the words –

> "Hin ist alle meine Kraft,
>   Alt und schwach bin ich."[3]

3   "Gone is all my strength, Old and weak am I."

And he had the musical passage and words printed on a card and gave it to friends who called to ask after him.

He was regarded with more respect and devotion than ever in his old age; but he was forced to live in quiet seclusion and to give up all public appearances. He had many friends to see him, and when he was well enough he liked to talk over his various experiences and show the many souvenirs and tokens of affection and admiration that had been bestowed upon him in the course of his long career.

The last time he appeared in public was at a performance of the *Creation* at the University in 1808. The scene must have been very touching. He was carried in an arm-chair to a place of honour among the most distinguished people present, and was received with affectionate acclamation. But the excitement was too much for him, and after the conclusion of the first part, he was carried out; all the people pressing round him to bid him farewell. Soon after this, his strength began to fail beyond hope, and he took to his bed. At that time, Vienna was occupied by the French, after a bombardment in which some of the shells fell near Haydn's house. One of the last visits he ever received was from an officer of the French army, who sang to him his air "In native worth." As the month of May 1809 drew towards its close, he summoned his people about him and bid them farewell, and on the 31st in the morning, he died.

He was buried first in a churchyard near his house; but Prince Esterhazy had his body removed and placed with fresh funeral honours in the parish church of Eisenstadt. When his coffin was opened preparatory to being moved, it was discovered that the head had been stolen; and it appears that though a skull was sent to fill up the place, it was not the right one, which has never since been placed with the body.

The most important work of Haydn's lifetime was his development of instrumental music, in the shape of symphonies, string quartets, pianoforte sonatas, and chamber music of various kinds. When he came upon the scene, the condition of all such forms of music was very backward. Other composers had been at work in the same direction and had given the instrumental branches a good start. But neither their opportunities nor their genius had been sufficient to raise the style of the music to any great pitch of general popularity or impressiveness. In the course of his long life, Haydn managed to improve the quality of all such works and to infuse them with more definite individuality and more really musical interest; while at the same time he improved immensely the treatment of the instruments and the general standard of the art as a whole. He also wrote an enormous quantity of works of other kinds, such as masses; but these, though they have sterling and admirable qualities, have not the historical value that his instrumental music has. Being a Roman Catholic, and a devout one, he missed those noble traditions which glorified the sacred choral works of Bach and Handel; and the operatic and secular influences which had crept into the music of his Church affected his style too much to admit of its reaching those depths of earnestness or heights of sublimity which were natural to the style of the earlier masters. Under the guidance of the Italian and Southern German masters, the character of church music underwent a change, and that decidedly not a change for the better; but it was rather the fault of the fashion of the Church than through want of earnestness in Haydn that the savour of theatrical associations showed itself in his work. He was by nature of a simply pious disposition, such as is quite consistent with his origin and chances of education. This spirit was shown not only in the way he attended to the observances of his Church, but in the habits of his life. His neat and tidy manuscripts were all inscribed with the words "*In nomine Domini*" at the beginning, and "*Laus Deo*" at the end; and he sometimes added "*et Beata Virgini Maria, et omnibus Sanctis*" as well. Again, when he was writing the *Creation*, he says, "I knelt down every morning and prayed to God to strengthen me for my work"; and it was under the influence of strong religious feeling that he wrote the whole of the oratorio. Everything about him had the same natural and unaffected character, whether it was his religion or the ordinary affairs of life. Love of fun lasted on from the days of his childhood, when he cut his schoolfellow's pigtail off, till his old age; and his fund of animal spirits played an important part in the effect of his music. It is always buoyant with happy vivacity, and this quality makes up somewhat for the comparative absence of the softer and more dreamy poetry which was not congenial to his generation and did not make its appearance in music much between the period of Bach and the composers after the French Revolution.

The description which is given of his personal appearance is so characteristic that it is worth knowing. He was short and solidly built;

with legs that were too small for his body. His face was pitted by small-pox, and his nose, which had been aquiline in youth, was in his later years spoilt by a polypus which he is said to have inherited from his mother. His jaw was big, and his under lip rather large and protruding. His eyes were dark grey, and they had a very pleasant expression. His whole face lighted up very pleasantly when he was talking, as might have been expected from his genial and kind disposition; and this must have been the chief attraction in a face and figure which, though evidently characteristic, does not sound as if specially blessed with natural advantages. He wore a wig with curls at the side and a pigtail, probably like that which lawyers wear in court at the present day; and his bearing had dignity, though it is said to have suggested a touch of over-preciseness.

His prominent position in the history of music is enhanced by his being the first great representative composer of modern secular music. Till the beginning of modern instrumental music, all the highest achievements in the art were closely connected either by style or descent with church music; and the greatest composers rested their fame upon it. Haydn was the first great composer who identified himself with absolutely secular music and gave it a status equal to that of sacred music. The change from the manner of the earlier masters goes so far that while the nominally secular music of his great predecessors frequently savours of the forms of religious art, when he is nominally writing sacred music, it is often cast in secular forms and savours of the theatre. Even the traces of the grand choral style which made their appearance in his later works only came to him at second hand from Handel; as he was debarred by his circumstances from the influence of the great Protestant chorales and the traditional treatment to which the North German musicians subjected them.

But the change of front from religious to secular types and sentiments is a very important matter in history, and is met with in other arts as well as in music; for many branches of art began under religious impulses and passed afterwards into the secular or purely human condition. Haydn was the pioneer of this change in music and was the first man who achieved a glorification of the natural music which exists in the heart of the people by carrying its essence and its most healthy and vigorous qualities into the province of high art.

IV.

MOZART.

Towards the middle of the eighteenth century, most of those kinds of music which are familiar in the present day were pretty well established. The oratorio had been carried to a high pitch of perfection by Handel. The opera, in a style more modern than his, was becoming quite a common form of entertainment; and instrumental music, which is the most modern branch of the art, was progressing so well that the way to make overtures, symphonies, and sonatas was quite understood, and they were common enough to be appreciated by all men who had any pretensions to taste. The composers who had done the best work in the latter branch of art had been men of good abilities and honest purpose, but not of the highest order of genius. Among the Germans, Hasse and Bach's sons and pupils stood highest; among Italians, there were Galuppi and Paradisi, and the great school of violinists who followed the lead of Corelli, such as Tartini and Geminiani. Haydn, too, had by that time gone through the hardest and loneliest part of his career; and though he was not famous as yet, he had tried his hand in different lines, and had laid a good foundation, and was on the verge of receiving his first appointment as kapellmeister to Count Morzin, and of writing his first symphony.

In the picturesque town of Salzburg, there was living at this time a most estimable man named Leopold Mozart. He was the son of a bookbinder and had taken to music as a profession, and pursued it with considerable success. He played on the violin and wrote a good deal of music, such as oratorios, and operas, and masses, and sonatas; and was made court musician and court composer by the reigning archbishop of the principality. Besides his musical gifts, he had considerable general intelligence, which he had cultivated well, and a strong character; and he is reported to have been good-looking into the bargain. In 1747, he married Anna Maria Pertlin, the daughter of a steward of a convent, who matched him in good looks; and the two settled down with good hopes of a quiet life and an honest reputation, after the domestic fashion of Germans.

They had several children, but only two survived. The eldest of these was a girl, whom they called Maria Anna, who was born in 1751. The youngest was called Wolfgang Amadeus, and he was born on January 27, 1756.

In Leopold Mozart's household, music was held in the highest honour, and a good deal was constantly going on. There were musical friends, and there was professional work to be done, and while Wolfgang was still a baby, his sister Marianne was already learning the harpsichord; and the tiny boy did not wait long before showing that he was ready to begin too. The first symptoms of his extraordinary gifts were his wonderful ear and his cleverness at remembering tunes and puzzling out simple chords on the harpsichord. His father was quite willing to let him begin as early as he would, and set him to work when he was four years old at little pieces which he selected for him, and wrote out in a music-book of Marianne's, which is still in existence in the Mozart Museum at Salzburg. Wolfgang was eager to learn most things, but more especially music; and his aptitude was so extraordinary that the little pieces were quickly mastered one after another, and the father must have had much more difficulty in finding fit music for such tiny hands to play than he had in teaching him the technicalities of his instrument. Leopold Mozart used to make notes in this book of the dates and times the little boy learnt the pieces. Such as — "Wolfgang learnt this minuet when he was four years old;" or, again — "This minuet and trio were learnt by Wolfgang in half an hour, at half-past nine at night, on January 26, 1761, one day before his fifth year." Very soon he began to try his hand at composition too. He wrote a concerto, and when he was told it was very difficult, he said that was just why it was called a concerto. "It must be practised till it is mastered. Look, this is how it goes!" He was very much in earnest altogether, and was partly too busy and partly disinclined for the ordinary amusements of children, but he had the sweetest disposition and thoroughly natural and childish ways, which neither hard work nor early fame ever marred.

Marianne, too, got on very well, and it soon occurred to the father that as both the children were so wonderfully and unusually clever as performers it would be worth while to let them make their appearance in public; and when Wolfgang was only six years old, they started on a concert tour. Their first expedition was to Munich and took place in January 1762, when they played before the Elector of Saxony; and they were so well received that the father determined on a more extended experiment, and started off for Vienna in September of the same year. The fame of the little prodigies had gone before them, and at several places on the way they had to stop and perform to grandees and local dignitaries; and Wolfgang used his opportunities to please other people as well, for at the monastery of Ips, he entranced the Franciscan friars by playing on their organ, and when he arrived at Vienna, he saved his father the custom-house duties by playing to the officers.

When they arrived at their destination, they were summoned to make their appearance at court, where music was as highly and earnestly appreciated as it ought to be by the imperial family. Little Wolfgang was most amusingly simple in his behaviour with all the grand people; and they, of course, could not give much consideration to etiquette with such a little boy as he was. He used to run and jump into the empress's lap and kiss her, and treated the princesses like ordinary playfellows. Marie Antoinette was his favourite, and one day when he tumbled down on the slippery floor, she helped him up again whereupon he said, "You are good, and I will marry you." He was so bright and vivacious, and his gifts were so extraordinary, that it is no wonder that all the great people petted him unreservedly; and it does not seem to have done him any harm. But he was very serious about music, and when he played, he liked to have somebody near whom he considered enough of an artist to be worthy of it. On one occasion when he was just going to play to a grand audience at court, he is said to have asked, "Is Herr Wagenseil here? Let him come—he knows something about it." And the emperor good-humouredly moved out of the way to let the old musician come, who was at that time one of the most famous composers and players on the harpsichord in Vienna.

The grandees were not remiss in rewarding the subjects of their enthusiasm. The father, of course, received substantial gifts of a most serviceable kind, and Marianne received a grand court dress of white silk which had belonged to one of the archduchesses, and Wolfgang a suit of violet trimmed with gold braid which had been made for one of the archdukes; and in this dress the proud father had his picture taken.

Their successful career was brought to an end by Wolfgang's falling ill of scarlet fever. He got through it well, with plenty of sympathy from all sides; but after it was over, people were too much afraid of infection to risk having him in their houses again, so in the latter end of the year, the father and his two prodigies went back home to Salzburg. After such extraordinary successes, the father determined on trying a yet wider excursion, and in June of the following year, they started for Paris. In those days, such a journey took a long while; but people had the advantage of going by what route and in what manner they would; so old Mozart decided on visiting the country-houses of the great people that lay in his way, as they would at that season of the year be enjoying the pleasures of a luxurious country life, and were always glad to entertain people who supplied them with amusement or pleasure of any sort, whether they were strolling bands of actors or musicians. He also made his children play at the great towns they passed, such as at Heidelberg, and Mayence, and Frankfort. Goethe, then a boy of fourteen, was at the latter town, and came to one of the concerts; and many years after he wrote of Mozart to a friend — "I saw him as a boy, seven years old; and well I remember him with his powdered wig and his sword." They arrived in Paris, after the prolonged journey of several months, in November; and here, though the French were not nearly so musical as the Germans, their success was as great as it had been in Vienna. They had the good fortune to have a letter of introduction to Grimm, a German, who held a very high position in Parisian society, owing partly to his literary ability and critical judgment, and partly to his connection with distinguished men. Through him they obtained easy access to the highest society, including the royal family and the all-powerful Madame de Pompadour. They were summoned to court and treated much in the same free and friendly manner that they had been at Vienna. After playing at Versailles, all the foremost people in Paris were eager to do them honour. They played at private houses and also got leave to give two public concerts, when Marianne distinguished herself by playing the most difficult pieces which were familiar to Parisian audiences; and Wolfgang astounded everyone by his complete command of all branches of musical dexterity — such as reading at sight, transposing, and playing from memory. In Paris, too, he made his first appearance as a composer in print, as Leopold Mozart had a set of four sonatas of his for violin and pianoforte printed, with a notification on the title-page that he was only seven years old.

They stayed in Paris till April and then started for London. They found the regular packet-boat too full at Calais and had to cross in rather a small ship, and were very sea-sick. But it evidently did not take them long to recover themselves, for by April 27 they were received at George III.'s court and began a fresh career of successes as great as those at other capitals. The royal family were very musical and naturally inclined to be friendly to Germans, and the reception they gave to the Mozart family was very friendly indeed. They were summoned to a more or less private party, and King George tried Wolfgang's abilities by giving him all sorts of pieces by famous composers for the harpsichord to play, that he had never seen before. And then Wolfgang accompanied the queen in a song and did various other offices and feats to the delight of the select audience. In London, too, he first met John Christian Bach, the youngest son of John Sebastian Bach, a man who at that time enjoyed European fame and was one of the most popular composers of instrumental music and operas alive. John Christian was extremely nice and kind to him and used to take him on his knee when he played the harpsichord and is said to have shared the playing of a sonata with him in that position and to have begun extemporary fugues and made Wolfgang finish them. This genial friendliness had great effect upon Wolfgang, who ever after held him in affection. His music, too, influenced him considerably, and when he proceeded to write large instrumental works, John Christian Bach was one of the models he principally followed.

His earliest experiment in this line was very soon made. They had time to give some public concerts, which were astonishingly successful, and Wolfgang made his appearance at Ranelagh; and then for a while their career was suspended by the father's falling ill, and they went for change of air and quiet to Chelsea, which was then a separate village near London. Wolfgang would not practise for fear of disturbing his father, but he took to writing symphonies instead; so England had the honour of being the place where the first of Mozart's long series of symphonies was composed, and they were performed at the public concerts which followed the father's recovery. In London, Wolfgang first heard an Italian opera sung by first-rate singers. At that time Manzuoli's superb singing and acting were the rage of the town. The Mozart family made friends with him, and he gave Wolfgang some singing lessons, which he profited by to a considerable extent.

They left London in July 1765 and went over to Holland with a view of showing their powers there also. Unfortunately, Wolfgang fell ill at Lille; and then, after just making a good beginning by being very well received by the Prince of Orange at the Hague, Marianne fell seriously ill too and so nearly died that they gave her the last sacraments. Then she recovered, and Wolfgang fell ill again. But after these misfortunes, they still had time to give concerts — in which the music was chiefly by Wolfgang — and to astonish and enchant the Dutch as much as they had done the people of other nations.

From Holland, they went back to Paris, where the connoisseurs thought they had even improved on their former wonderful powers; but the excitement about them had toned down a little, and though they played at court and elsewhere, they did not raise quite so great a storm of wonder as before.

After leaving Paris, they visited one or two of the most important towns of France, such as Dijon and Lyons, and then they made their way back by Munich, and at last arrived home in their native Salzburg in November 1766.

The tour had been a marvellous success. In three years they had taken by storm four of the principal capitals of Europe; they had been petted and treated on terms of unusual familiarity by at least three royal families; they had made themselves known to numbers of culti- vated people in private country-houses, and in many provincial towns of importance; and Wolfgang had attained the fame of a *virtuoso* of high rank, and his reputation as a composer was already established by the time that he was only ten years old. The stories of the childish precocity of great men are rarely to be trusted; but Mozart's case was unique, and it is not probable that such a phenomenon ever made its appearance before or since. The excitement of contemporaries may have caused them to overrate his abilities as a player, but about his compositions of early years, there can be no question, for they still exist to prove his extraordinary powers. People were so surprised at his precocity that they took measures to be sure that they were not taken in. A man called Daines Barrington in England procured a copy of Wolfgang's baptismal register for this purpose, and then subjected him to a sort of friendly examination, the result of which he detailed in a paper which he read to the Royal Society; and the compositions, such as sonatas, overtures, and songs, which remain to be seen at the present day, were published in Paris, London, the Hague, and elsewhere during his first visits, so there is no possibility of misstatement with regard to them.

The period just before 1765 happened to be one in which the level of highest musical capacity throughout the civilised world was rather low, and this must have made Wolfgang's achievements seem all the more remarkable. He appeared to his contemporaries to have as much mastery of his art as most of the mature professors and compos-ers then living. But his father was too wise to let him stop without further development of his powers, and in the quiet year at Salzburg which followed the return from their tour, he set him to work at strict counterpoint and thorough-bass, and made him study the works of the ablest masters of his art, both living and of previous generations. Occasion also very soon occurred for him to turn his hand to a large composition at Salzburg. The reigning archbishop, Sigismund, does not seem to have been over-friendly to the Mozarts and was scepti-cal about Wolfgang's much-vaunted abilities. The story goes that, by way of testing him, he had him shut up for a week in a room where he could not have free communication with anyone and set him to work on an oratorio for which the archbishop himself supplied the text. Wolfgang successfully achieved the labour, and the work was performed during Lent in the next year.

In the latter part of that year, they again started for Vienna; but they were baulked of their intended concerts by the death of a member of the royal family from smallpox, which shut not only the court but the houses of the nobility. And worse disaster awaited them. In a short while both Wolfgang and Marianne fell ill of the same terrible disease at Olmütz, whither they had fled to escape it. Fortunately for them, they chanced to fall in with a rare specimen of noble and generous humanity in the person of a Count von Podstatzky, who was Dean of Olmütz and Canon of Salzburg; who disregarded the infection and took the family into his own house, where they were tended with all the care possible. Wolfgang was very ill and even blind for nine days, and was obliged to be very cautious in the use of his eyes for some weeks afterwards; but in due time, the illness ran out its course, and they were able to go back to Vienna again.

But they were not destined to find such success and welcome as they had had before. The famous Empress Maria Theresa received them as cordially as usual, but in other respects, the state of affairs was changed. The new Emperor Joseph was economically inclined, and his nobility followed his lead; so but little was done to further the cause of art in the Austrian capital at that time. One fine opportunity, however, presented itself. The emperor invited Wolfgang to write an opera and told the manager of his theatre that he wished to have it performed. This, of course, met Leopold Mozart's views, and he saw that, if it could be brought about, it would immensely enhance Wolfgang's fame. A *libretto* was procured, and the boy composer set to work vigorously, and in a very short while finished the big score of 558 pages. So far was very good; the music, or as much of it as had been seen by the performers, delighted them, and there was no reason in the natural course of things why the performance should not have come off. But there is something mysterious about opera. In other branches of music, men may make their way fairly, and a good work is often willingly accepted even when there are real difficulties in the way of its performance. But a touch of the opera seems to drive men out of their senses. The question of a performance too frequently becomes an occasion for intrigue, cabal, bribery, slander, and every mean device which can be covered by the name of diplomacy, and it was so in this case. The air became alive with trickery and plotting. The orchestra were persuaded to resent the command of a boy conductor; the singers, at first favourable, were frightened by insinuations of probable failure; it was hinted that the work was not worth performing, and when acknowledged judges declared it was, its enemies spread abroad that it was not by Wolfgang. And finally, after nine months miserably wasted in this wrestling with unseen enemies, when Leopold Mozart pressed the manager, Affligio, on the subject of the performance, that worthy answered that he would have the work done if Leopold Mozart desired, but he would take care to have it hissed off the stage by people put in the audience for the purpose. This was the end of the struggle to get Mozart's first opera, *La finta Semplice*, performed in Vienna; and one may be pardoned a little vindictive satisfaction in knowing that this same Affligio was afterwards convicted of forgery and ended his life ignobly in the galleys.

The only encouragement Mozart had was an invitation to write a mass for the dedication of the chapel of an orphan asylum, which was conducted by the Jesuit Father Parhammer, who had been confessor to the Emperor Francis I. It was a grand occasion, which gave the Mozarts a good chance of distinction; as the imperial family, and a cardinal archbishop, and numbers of grand people were present. The result was most satisfactory, as may be read in a contemporary newspaper. "The entire music was composed by Wolfgang Mozart, son of Dr. L. Mozart, *kapellmeister* at Salzburg, a boy of twelve years old, well known for his extraordinary talent. It was conducted by the composer with the utmost precision and accuracy, and was received with universal applause and admiration."

This was the end of the year's exploits at Vienna, and the family returned to Salzburg again. Here they received some compensation for the failure to get the new opera performed in Vienna; as the archbishop, proud of the achievement of his young subject, arranged a performance of it in his own palace; and when it was over Wolfgang was regularly appointed *concert-meister* to the archbishop. After this performance Wolfgang stayed quietly at Salzburg for a time, going on with work again to perfect himself yet more in his art.

Leopold Mozart now fixed his desires on making a journey to Italy. That country was still pre-eminent in music, and though the sceptre of the art was soon destined to pass away from it, the prestige of former glories, and fine traditions of style, still lingered on while the people as a whole had a greater enthusiasm for the art than those of any other country. At the end of 1769 the father and son started together in this new direction, leaving Marianne at home with the mother. As soon as they had crossed into Italy they were received with extraordinary excitement. At every great town they reached concerts were organised for them, at which Wolfgang's music was played; and when he went to play on the organ in churches he attracted such a concourse that he either had to have the way forced for him through the crowd, or else he had to be got up to the organ some back way or other. At Verona, Mantua, Milan, Bologna, the enthusiasm he excited was perfectly amazing; and rich grandees, and ordinary people, and musicians, and ecclesiastics were all equally bewitched by him. At Milan his success was so great as to induce the authorities to invite him to write an opera for their theatre, to be ready in about eight months; and this offer was of course gladly accepted. He made or renewed his acquaintance with famous singers and great musicians, such as the famous Padre Martini, who was looked upon as the most learned musician and the severest judge of art in Italy. At Florence he met the English boy violinist, Thomas Linley, who was then fourteen, and was looked upon as almost as great a marvel of promise in his line as Mozart. The boys made great friends, and played much together in the short time that Wolfgang was able to stay there, and then they parted for good. They were not destined to meet again, for Linley's promise was cut short soon after by his being drowned.

From Florence they passed on to Rome, where they arrived on Wednesday in Holy Week, and Wolfgang was taken almost directly to hear the music in the Sistine Chapel. There was a famous *miserere* by Allegri which was performed on this occasion, which was looked upon as one of the great musical treasures of Rome. It was kept especially for performance in this chapel, where its effect was always considered most extraordinary, and no one was allowed to have a copy; and the members of the choir were even forbidden to take their voice parts away with them. Wolfgang did the extraordinary feat of writing this work out from memory after the first hearing, and when it was performed again on Good Friday he took his copy with him in his hat, and corrected it. Fortunately, when it got to be known, the amazement of the ecclesiastics at the feat was greater than their wrath might naturally have been at their treasure being so skilfully stolen and the story gave an extra zest to Wolfgang's celebrity.

From Rome they went on to Naples, in some dread of falling a prey to banditti. This they fortunately escaped, and enjoyed the beauty of that famous country and the condescension of the king without further inconvenience than being upset out of their carriage on the way back again. When they were in Rome again Wolfgang was invested with the Order of the Golden Spur by the pope, which gave him the right of being called Cavaliere. This pleased the father very much, and he made him sign his compositions for a while as "Del Signor Cavaliere W. A. Mozart;" but before long he dropped the title, as well he might, for his native genius set him above all the mere 'cavalieres' in existence. Another honour which he received about this time was election as a member of the famous Accademia Filarmonica of Naples, which was regarded as a most exceptional honour all the world over; and more especially in his case, as in order to admit him they had to relax the rules that the candidate for election should be at least twenty years old, and should have passed through certain preliminary stages before being eligible for the full dignity of a *compositore.*

It was now time for them to be moving to Milan to be ready for the preparations for producing the new opera *Mitridate*, which had somehow been written during the travelling from place to place, and in the intervals between the numerous public performances. Now again they fell in with the usual troubles attendant upon operas. Intrigues began as before. Someone tried to persuade the principal female singer to refuse Mozart's songs, and sing someone else's; but fortunately she exercised her own judgment, and as she liked the music written for her, she kept to it. Then the principal tenor became difficult to manage, and lastly some of the members of the orchestra made up their minds that the work being that of a boy, and a German into the bargain, it could not be anything but a failure. But in the end the various difficulties were overcome this time, and the first performance took place on December 26. Wolfgang himself conducted, and all went well, and the enthusiasm excited was far beyond their wildest hopes. The people were never tired of shouting "Bravo, little master!" and their delight increased as the performance went on. It was given no less than twenty times, and always with equal appreciation.

After Milan they visited Turin and Venice and Padua, and then made their way back to Salzburg. The last fruits of their journey were commissions to write another opera for Milan, an oratorio for Padua, and a theatrical serenade for the marriage of the Archduke Ferdinand of Austria with a daughter of the Prince of Modena. Consequently they had to go back to Italy again the same year, to attend the festivities for the marriage. On this occasion they met old Hasse, the famous German opera composer, who appreciated his young rival with honest freedom from envy, and is said to have prophesied that he would make all the works of the older generation to be forgotten. In December they had to be in Milan yet again for the production of the new opera *Lucio Silla*, which was received with the same enthusiasm as his previous work *Mitridate*, and was performed some twenty times or so. After this they went back again to Salzburg, and remained there for the most part all through 1773 and 1774, during which years Mozart had time to compose many works of other kinds one after another besides operas, such as symphonies, *divertimenti*, serenatas, concertos, and masses. They made fresh excursions now and then to Vienna and Munich, at which latter place a new opera, *La finta Giardiniera*, was produced in 1775, and made a great impression upon musicians and public alike. Then there was a return to Salzburg again, and another period of steady and continuous work. But Mozart was now passing out of his boyhood, and the narrow limits of Salzburg life were beginning to gall him. It seemed to him as if he ought to look for some settled place with finer opportunities than were afforded him as servant of the archbishop. Besides, old Archbishop Sigismund was dead, and had been succeeded by Archbishop Hieronymus, who was almost universally disliked. Their new master always threw difficulties in their way when they wanted leave of absence, and treated them with no consideration at all. And at last they arrived at the conclusion that there was nothing left but for Wolfgang to throw up his appointment, and seek a new one at large in the world. The archbishop accepted the resignation angrily, and the poor father was constrained by the necessity of some sort of fixed income and a home to retain his own post, in face of the ill temper of his master. And as he could not get leave of absence to go with his son he had to stay at home with the daughter, and send his wife with Wolfgang. The parting was a grievous one, and the father was terribly upset by it. But he trusted his son with good reason, and knew that all the education he had given him both in music and conduct of life was such as to keep him steadfast to high ideals, and constant in self-restraint and wise resolve.

But the tide of fortune which had run so happily for Wolfgang in his boyhood seemed to turn when his manhood arrived; and though great successes came now and then, and his genius soared always into higher and nobler regions, the conditions of his life seemed changed, and he had to fight his way where formerly every step had been helped by generous sympathy and admiration. But at first he was happy in the sense of his new independence, and he wrote to his father in quite a merry vein, how he was getting clever in managing, and, like another papa, taking care of everything. "I have to pay the postilions, for I can talk to the fellows better than mother."

They went to Munich, in the hope of finding a post there. A composer was wanted, and he paid his respects to the Elector, in the hope of being appointed, but in vain. At Munich there was nothing to be won. From there they went to Augsburg, where no better fortune awaited them. They met with compliments, but with little profit and little prospect of a fixed post. Mozart had the opportunity of trying the new pianofortes, which were being made there by Stein, and that was the most interesting event of his visit; and in a fortnight they left this place also and went on to Mannheim. Here, too, his hope for a definite post was destined to be disappointed, but the period of his stay there was a very important one and influenced his career both as an artist and as a man.

Mannheim was at that time famous both for its opera and for its orchestra, which was the best in Europe for the performance of instrumental music. A violinist and composer, named Stamitz, who had lived there many years before, had turned his attention to a more delicate and refined treatment of instrumental music than had been common before. Instrumental music had previously been written plainly, without much consideration of the more delicate effects which could be obtained by attention to details of expression; and he began a great and important reform in this direction, which afterwards became a very marked feature in the progress of music written for orchestras. His traditions were kept on at the time Mozart arrived by Cannabich and the admirable band which he directed; and he had opportunities of hearing music performed in altogether a new fashion, which could not fail to influence his own style in writing the same kind of music.

With Cannabich, he soon made friends and became intimate with his family and also with many members of his band. But as his hopes of getting any definite appointment in the Elector's band came to nothing, an idea was started of his going to Paris again with some of the members of the band with whom he had made friends. It was thought there might be a good opening there for him in many ways, even without a regular appointment. His father was persuaded to give his sanction, and the preparations were made. But at the last moment, he hung back, and his friends had to go without him. His father was disappointed and puzzled; but before long, the cause was disclosed. In his letters home, there had been for some time frequent allusions to a certain Mdlle. Weber, who was the daughter of a man in a subordinate position in the theatre. He first described her to his father as only fifteen, but singing extremely well with a beautiful pure voice. And he said she only wanted action to be fit to be a prima donna on any stage. He was also drawn towards her by sympathy for her poverty and by a feeling that she was not kindly or fairly treated by the people at Mannheim. He gave her singing lessons and ended with falling in love with her. The projected expedition to Paris came therefore to a standstill for the time, as he could not face the thought of being away from the object of his devotion, though he himself scarcely realized that this was the cause of delay.

After a time, he formed an entirely new project, evidently under the influence of his affection. He wrote to his father and told him that the oppressed family had become so dear to him that it was his greatest wish to make them happy. He thought the best plan would be for Aloysia Weber to go to Italy and get an appointment as prima donna somewhere; and wanted his father to find out what sums were paid to prima donnas in such places as Verona. And he proposed if the father agreed to it all that he should go to Salzburg with the Weber family and pay his father a visit on the way. His heart was evidently set upon this project, and though he did not directly speak of marriage, it was easy for the father to guess how things were going and what sort of alliance it was likely to be for Wolfgang. He resolved to exert his parental influence at once, feeling sure that his son was only misled and blinded by his enthusiasm, and that a word from him would bring him to his senses. So he wrote to him urging him strongly to keep to his first project of going to Paris. He showed him that there was the place for a man to win fame, and there he would be beside great men who would be worthy of him. He left the attachment to Aloysia Weber unnoticed, as was indeed the wisest plan, and only put strong emphasis on an appeal to his son's ambition and good sense.

The result quite justified his hopes. Wolfgang had always been accustomed to look up to his father with special love and veneration. "Next, after God, papa," he used to say, as a little boy. And the feeling was quite strong enough still to lead him to adopt his father's views, though they were against his own inclinations; and he made up his mind to start with his mother for Paris as soon as possible. He excused his devotion to the Webers in his answer home and said he had never really hoped his father would be brought to agree with him about them; but he praised Aloysia in high terms and ended with recommending her to his father with his whole heart.

The mother and the son left Mannheim and their good friends there on March 14, 1778, and Wolfgang had to brace himself well to stand the parting. He wrote to his father directly after they arrived in Paris and described the leave-taking. "They never left off thanking me and wishing they were in a position to testify their gratitude. When at last I went away, they all wept. It is very foolish, but the tears come into my eyes whenever I think of it. The father went down the step with me and stood at the house-door till I had turned the corner, when he called out for the last time, Adieu."

The mother and son had a very tiring journey to Paris, and when they arrived, they had to take, for economy's sake, a very poor lodging, which was not big enough to hold a harpsichord. Mozart began, as soon as possible, to look up the old friends and the men in position who could help him to opportunities of distinguishing himself. But he soon saw that it was quite a different thing for a young man to make his way through the press of competition, however great his abilities, from what it had been for a rare phenomenon in the shape of a child of seven to take the town and the highest society in France by storm. Marie Antoinette, whom in his childish simplicity he had offered to marry, was now Queen of France, but he was unable to get any letters of introduction which would have admitted him to her presence. His old friend, Grimm, was immensely polite but not ready to exert himself as he had been in favor of the youthful prodigy of former times. The entry to high society's favors was not to be had. The musical public was just then so excited in the famous operatic war between Gluckists and Piccinists that they had little care for anything else, and Mozart could by no means get any prospect of the performance of a new opera or an invitation from anyone to write one.

After many and wearisome struggles with apathy and indifference, the only chance he found of distinguishing himself was the performance of a new symphony at the *Concerts Spirituels*, where some of his friends from the Mannheim orchestra were engaged to perform and could exert what influence they had in his favor. This symphony did not, of course, have the *eclat* which is produced by the performance of operas, for the public is always misled into thinking the latter the highest of musical achievements; whereas, as a fact, operas are on average far below all other forms of high-class music in actual musical value. But the symphony really marked an epoch in its composer's career and was the first in which he struck a really high point of original excellence; and this fact is to be attributed to the experience he had of really good orchestral playing at Mannheim. The Parisian public were well pleased enough in their way, and Le Gros, the director, said he thought it the best symphony on his *repertoire*, which it undoubtedly was, as no symphony had been written up to that time which could compare with it. But the success of this really important work did not make his position in Paris any better. He was able to secure a few pupils, and one or two people of high position were friendly to him; but most of the visits of ceremony which he had to pay, with those feelings of repugnance which must always arise in the minds of independent and noble natures, were utterly futile, and sometimes worse. He gave an account of one of these calls in a letter to his father, and it is so characteristic of the behavior of similar people, now as then, that it is worth remembering.

He had a letter from Grimm to the Duchess de Chabot and was invited to call. When he arrived, he was put to wait for half an hour in an icy cold room with no stove in it. He was then asked to play, and when he requested to be allowed to warm his fingers first, the duchess did not take any steps to give him the opportunity. "I had the honor of waiting an hour while she sat drawing at a table with some gentlemen. No one spoke to me, and I did not know what to do for cold, headache, and fatigue. At last, to cut it short, I played on the wretched, miserable pianoforte. The most vexatious part of all was that madame and all the gentlemen went on with their employment without a moment's pause or notice, so that I played for the walls and the chairs." When he stopped, they were all compliments, but that was not the sort of sympathy he wanted. The husband came in and behaved better, but he must evidently have been an exception amongst the selfish and self-indulgent aristocracy of Paris in those days; and it is no wonder that Mozart had not the heart to go on very actively with such dreary work.

The measure of his misfortunes was not, however, yet full. His mother, who had to be very much alone in their poor lodgings, owing to the necessity of his presence in other places, began to break down. She was ill for several weeks in the spring of 1778 and worse again in the early summer. Grimm sent a physician to look after her, but he could not arrest her downward course; and after some time spent in grievous anxiety, when Wolfgang hardly went from her bedside, she died in July.

Wolfgang was now quite alone in Paris, for his Mannheim acquaintances were gone. Grimm at this time came a little to the rescue and offered him shelter in his house, but their relations together were not happy. Grimm patronized him and at the same time told him he would never do anything in Paris, for he was not energetic and did not go about enough. And in the face of this, poor Wolfgang was driven, by the tyranny of circumstances, into borrowing money from him. It must have been a dreary world for him then, and there is no wonder that he came to detest Paris, where, though he was at that time the greatest musician living, he had for six months struggled unavailingly to make even enough money to keep him from the necessity of borrowing from an irksome patron. He turned his back upon the place in September and made his way to Germany again. He visited Mannheim once more, although most of his friends were away, and then he went on to Munich, where he found the Webers. They were of course very glad to see him, but Aloysia seemed quite changed, as if she did not care for him at all. Indeed, she confessed afterwards that she had never fully appreciated him in her younger days and only learnt to be conscious of his worth after she had tied herself to a jealous husband in the person of a court actor called Joseph Lange, with whom she did not live happily.

At last in June 1779, Mozart returned to his old home at Salzburg, after an absence of more than a year, which had been almost entirely a failure from first to last; for it had given him no advantage in enhanced position and no money in his pocket, and was marked by disaster in the shape of the death of his mother and the failure of his first love. His friends in his native town received him warmly and made much of him; but unfortunately he disliked Salzburg almost as much as he did Paris, and he did not feel it any great compensation, in the low condition of his fortunes, that his father had succeeded in obtaining for him the position of court organist to the archbishop, in the place of Adlgasser, who was dead. It was not indeed a position worthy of so great a musician as he was, but he had it at least in his own hands to use those powers which man could neither give nor take from him, and his stay at home during the following year was occupied by the production of quantities of compositions. Masses and other works for church use; songs, symphonies, serenades, sonatas, variations, concertos, and quartets, and many other kinds of music were poured out in a profusion which has never been rivaled by any other composer, and quantity did not in his case imply poorness of quality.

At last a new opening arrived which was quite in accord with his keenest desire. His friends at Munich succeeded in getting him invited to write a new opera for the Carnival of 1781. The libretto, which was called Idomeneo, was intrusted to an excellent ecclesiastic named Varesco, who lived in Salzburg and was willing to consult Mozart on every point. A good deal of the music was written at Salzburg, and then, when the time for rehearsals approached, he moved to Munich to complete it. Of course, it was impossible that a new opera should be brought forward without some sort of trouble, and there were plenty of intrigues against it. But fortunately, the forces on Mozart's side were too strong. He had many intimate friends, some among those who were destined to be performers; and some of the most influential men among the public were also keenly in his favour. The work progressed admirably, and in November 1780, the first rehearsal took place and roused public anticipations to a higher pitch than before. Old Leopold Mozart was very anxious about it all, and while the composition was progressing he gave his son about the worst piece of advice he ever had the misfortune to utter. He wrote, "I recommend you not to think only of the musical public, but also of the unmusical. You know that there are a hundred ignorant people for every ten true *connoisseurs*, so do not forget to be what is called popular and tickle the long ears." The same sort of folly is heard often enough in later days, and the answer of Wolfgang is good enough for all occasions. "As to what is called popular do not be afraid. There is music in my opera for all sorts of people, only none for long ears." This little correspondence took place between the first and second rehearsal, which followed on December 27. The further hearing increased the public interest in the coming performance, and the third rehearsal did so still more. The fame of the work spread even to Salzburg, where the father was so frequently congratulated that he told his son it would be tedious to tell him all the compliments that were paid him. But the preparation of an opera takes a long time, and it was not till the end of January that it was at last really produced. Old Leopold and Marianne came from Salzburg for the performance and enjoyed the music and the triumph of the son, who had so long waited for the opportunity to show his mature powers in a fitting sphere.

While the Carnival was still going on, he received orders from his master, the archbishop, to join him in Vienna. This he had to do at once, going by himself in a post-chaise. He was willing enough to go to the famous capital, but it was grievous to him to be at the mercy of the archbishop again; more especially as his master, though he was proud of having so great and famous a musician in his retinue, seemed determined to impress him with his dependent position and force him to realise that he was no more than the archbishop's servant. He had rooms in the same house with his master, which were sufficiently to his liking; but the position he held was pretty well defined by the company he had to keep. He described this part of the household arrangements in a characteristic letter to his father. "The two valets in attendance, the controller, the court quartermaster, the confectioners, two cooks, and my littleness, dine together. The two valets sit at the head of the table, and I have the honour to be placed above the cooks." This is quite an interesting picture for after-ages to contemplate. One of the greatest geniuses the world ever produced, after years of hard work, and after the winning of world-wide renown, having to live at the mercy of an ecclesiastical aristocrat and dine with his valets and cooks. The relations between master and servant got worse and worse. Every letter of Mozart's to his father gives accounts of fresh grievances. The archbishop's vanity was so tickled by having Mozart in his possession that he would not give him leave to play or appear elsewhere than in his own house, but for all that, his pay was small and was always withheld as long as possible. The father did all he could to prevent his son from throwing up the only definite engagement he had, but it was no use. Mozart could not help showing his independent spirit in the end, and the archbishop consequently turned upon him and called him villain and low fellow and other stronger terms of abuse and said "he would have no more to do with such a vile wretch." Mozart applied for a formal discharge and came personally to the antechamber of the archbishop next day for his final determination. Here he was met by the high steward, one Count Arco, who thereupon abused him in similar terms to those which his master had used, and it is said concluded by kicking him out of the room. This brutal treatment he could by no means get redressed, but it was some relief that it put an end to his miserable slavery under the archbishop, and he turned his mind at once to making Vienna the field of independent labours and fixed his hopes on getting an opera performed there and possibly on getting some definite appointment from the court afterwards.

The emperor had interested himself before this in trying to give a national turn to the performances at the opera house. The monopoly of Italian opera extended at that time over the greater part of Europe. England has not shaken off its paralysing dominion even to the present day, but Germany was more fortunate, chiefly owing to the genius of Mozart. The first great stroke in the direction of this reform was now undertaken, as Mozart took in hand the composition of his first German opera, under the name of *Entführung aus dem Serail*. The emperor was all in its favour, and though the usual intrigues and cabals were started to prevent its performance, it was successfully produced on July 16, 1782. The house was as full as it would hold, and notwithstanding the efforts of the opposition, the public was delighted, and one performance followed another so quickly that Mozart feared it would be run to death. But the work was much too good for any such risk and went on attracting "swarms of people," as Mozart himself wrote. This opera enhanced his fame immensely in Vienna and gave him a much better position there and throughout musical Europe than he had ever had before.

Meanwhile, another important event in his life had been approaching its culmination. When Mozart left the archbishop, he had taken up his abode with his old friends, the Webers. They looked after him very kindly and supplied him with some of the domestic comforts which, as a lonely and very busy bachelor, he could not otherwise have enjoyed. His father was alarmed at this proceeding and protested against it. But it was no use. The son tried living by himself again for a time to please his father, but he was so uncomfortable that he had to go back to his friends; and then the protestations of those who were interested in him had exactly the effect they did not want. He became so conscious of the disadvantages of a lonely existence that his mind, already set to look with favour upon Constanze Weber, a younger sister of his first love Aloysia, was now filled all the more strongly with the advantages of matrimony; and being also at that time in a hopeful humour about his prospects in Vienna, he very soon ended by getting himself betrothed. He wrote to his father a long letter about it, setting forth his inclination for a domestic life and his want of practical habits, which made a wife really indispensable to him. The father protested and threatened to withhold his consent in vain; the son held to his purpose and managed to enlist some powerful friends on his side; and in the month of August of 1782 the marriage took place very quietly, the father having just been persuaded to send his blessing in time.

In some ways, this important experiment was not a success. From the point of view of practical domestic comfort, such as he had described to his father, no good came of it at all. Constanze had no genius for ordering a household, and as Mozart was always too full of higher things to take much note of such matters as washing and darning, and similar necessities of everyday life, their existence was passed in a perpetual huggermugger and untidiness, to which the want of funds added for the rest of their lives a far from satisfactory flavour. Moreover, Constanze was far from strong, and a good deal of Mozart's precious time was spent in anxious attention to her health and comfort; and his slender resources were sometimes put to extra strain by the necessities of her condition. But apart from these matters, there was something very fitting and characteristic about their existence together. They lived in simple trust of one another, with spirits so well buoyed up by the love of art and the freshness of their mutual intercourse that the meaner troubles of life seemed to make but little effect on the enjoyment which they had in one another's society. Constanze quite entered into Mozart's ways of life and never annoyed him with importunities when he wanted to be all to himself for his work. She had, too, a thorough appreciation of his genius and could enter into all the music which he especially delighted in; and she was also able to sing well enough at sight to be useful to him, though her voice was not anything remarkable; and his devotion to her in turn was of that simple and childlike sincerity which made sunshine in their lives even at times when things looked darkest.

But in public life, matters did not improve for him. His opera had been a great success, and his appearances as performer and composer alike were always hailed with extraordinary enthusiasm. But no settled post came in his way, and even when opportunities seemed to be approaching, he was passed over in favour of less worthy men. He began to think he must leave Vienna and look for success in France or England, and wrote to Le Gros, the Director of the *Concerts Spirituels*, to find out if there might be any opening for another experiment in Paris. The news of his intended move came to his father's ears, and he hastened to put a stop to it by representing the misery it would be for a married man to lead the life of a wandering musician. The son was easily persuaded to remain quietly where he was and solaced himself by constant work at composition. He took his wife to Salzburg in 1783 to visit his family, and a couple of years afterwards, the old father returned the visit and stayed with his son in Vienna. It happened to be a fortunate time for him to come. He was made happy by finding their affairs in an unusually prosperous condition; and by a grandchild, to whom he took a great fancy; and also by the successes which the occurrence of a great number of concerts at that time gave him the opportunity of witnessing. On one occasion, Mozart invited Haydn to meet his father, and then some of Mozart's finest quartets were played. Haydn was very friendly to the father and declared to him that he considered his son the greatest composer he knew, whether personally or by reputation. Wolfgang returned the compliment by dedicating the quartets to Haydn, with a preface declaring that it was his due, for "from him I first learnt to compose a quartett."

When Leopold Mozart went away home again, he parted with his son for the last time. In April 1787, he fell ill, and though he had a temporary return of health afterwards, it did not last long, and he died suddenly in May. There is no doubt that to this singular man, the world owes much of what it enjoys in the work of his son. The extraordinary and strengthening influence which he exerted over him not only directed his studies and kept him to the work of developing his powers when he had already had enough successes to make him fancy himself a mature artist; but he also had a strong influence on his life through his affections, which made Wolfgang try so to live as to satisfy the loving anxiety of his father in all things; and kept him to high principles, which through the childlike buoyancy of his nature and his love of pleasure might have been rapidly lost sight of.

About this time, his circumstances seemed to have bettered a little. The success of *Idomeneo* and the *Entführung aus dem Serail* led to a libretto being prepared for him by a dramatist of ability called Da Ponte from Beaumarchais' play *Le Mariage de Figaro*. The opera, when finished, was brought out in the face of the most elaborate intrigues against it in 1786, and was received with the enthusiasm it deserved. A good account of the performance was written by the English tenor Kelly, who took part in it. "Never was anything more complete than the triumph of Mozart and his *Nozze di Figaro*, to which numerous and overflowing audiences bear witness. Those in the orchestra I thought would never cease applauding by beating the bows of their violins against their music desks. I never shall forget Mozart's little animated countenance when lighted up with the glowing rays of genius; it is as impossible to describe it as it would be to paint sunbeams." Soon afterwards, the opera was given at Prague, where it created unbounded enthusiasm, and as Mozart himself wrote to a friend, "the one subject of conversation is *Figaro* — nothing is played, whistled, or sung but *Figaro*, nobody goes to any opera but *Figaro*, everlastingly *Figaro*." And yet, great as were his successes as a composer, his affairs did not seem materially to improve. The opera brought him comparatively so little profit that very soon after it came out he was in pecuniary difficulties and asking for a loan from a friend. All sorts of inferior artists passed him in prosperity, while he was kept close, not only to his natural work but to other irksome drudgery. The emperor at last conferred on him the insignificant post of chamber composer, with the small stipend of about £80 a year, but this was not sufficient to make him at ease in his circumstances, though it gave rise to feelings of gratitude which prevented him afterwards from accepting a more lucrative offer. But though his circumstances were poor and depressing, his powers of composition were always vigorous, and now at their highest point. In the short space of a little over six weeks in the year 1787, he produced the finest of his large instrumental works, in the shape of three great symphonies, which were almost incredibly far ahead of anything of the kind which had been produced in the world till then, both in refinement, sentiment, form, and treatment of the orchestra. In them, he not only summed up the work which had been done by his predecessors in the same line, but all the labours and experience of his own life. Almost all the works which had appeared before on the same lines had had some traces of immaturity about them, and these may fairly be taken as the first in which the art of symphony writing attains to a perfect and complete condition.

Later on in the same year, he produced another of his most famous masterpieces. The success of *Figaro* led to his applying to the dramatist Da Ponte, who had put it together, for another libretto, and Da Ponte suggested *Don Giovanni*. Mozart began on the work with energy, but it appeared that after a time he became lazy about writing more, and put off till it became dangerously near the time arranged for its performance at Prague. He had to go there to finish it and is said to have written a good deal of it in a summer-house in a vineyard belonging to a friend, keeping up a conversation with people who were playing bowls close by all the while. It is commonly told that the very evening before the performance, the overture was still unwritten, and he had to sit up all night making the score, while his wife sat by and kept him awake by telling him amusing stories. He just managed to finish it, and the copyist, too, just managed to get the parts ready in time, and the band had to play it at the first performance at sight. This first representation at Prague was a triumph from first to last, but when it was produced later at Vienna, whether owing to cabals against him or badness of the performance, or some other mysterious reason, it was not a success; and this work, which in later times is placed almost at the head of all music of its kind, did not win its way into general public favour till considerably later.

In the year 1789, his hopes were raised a little by an invitation to go to Berlin. He took other famous places on his way and played at Dresden at court, and at Leipsic he played on John Sebastian Bach's organ in the Church of St. Thomas, much to the delight of Doles, the cantor, who had been Bach's own pupil. When he arrived at Berlin, he went at once, as Bach had done before him, to Potsdam and was received very friendly by King Frederick William II. The king was so pleased with him that he offered him the post of *kapellmeister* with a really good salary; but Mozart, thinking of his long connection with the imperial house of Austria, answered, "How could I abandon my good emperor?" Unfortunately, this journey, though artistically successful, was, like so many others, barren of pecuniary advantages of any solid kind, and he returned with very little more in his pocket than he set out. The difficulties arising from the constant illness of his wife went near to driving him to despair. At one time, his mind returned to the offer of the king of Prussia, and he tendered his resignation of the little post of chamber composer to the emperor. The emperor broke out with surprise, "What, Mozart, are you going to leave me?" and Mozart was instantly won to his fidelity again. But nothing of importance came of it except an invitation to write another opera, which was called *Cosi fan tutte*, and was performed in 1790, just before the death of the emperor. From the new Emperor Leopold, he could hope for no bettering of his condition, and he was still obliged to have recourse to the usual means of giving concerts and lessons. He made one more expedition, but it was not a long one, and again he was no better off when it was ended; if indeed he was not worse off for the loss of his plate, which he had to pawn to have enough cash in his pocket to start with.

Things were almost as bad as they could be; his wife was always ill, and even the number of his pupils had fallen to two when a queer character called Schikaneder came to Mozart with a suggestion that he might retrieve his fortunes by writing the music to a magic opera, for which he would supply the libretto and the means of performance.

Mozart was always more eager for operatic work than for any other, and he was easily persuaded to try the experiment. Both Mozart and Schikaneder were ardent Freemasons, and the subject chosen, called *Zauberflote*, was supposed to be based upon Masonic ideas and mysteries. Schikaneder had plenty of experience of theatrical matters and managed to put together a libretto which, though without real dramatic interest or an intelligible story, was capable of serving for effective situations and telling music. He knew Mozart had a repugnance to the mechanical labour of writing, and in order to keep him to his work, he prepared a little garden-house by his own theatre for him to write in. And here he kept him amused with lively company and the various distractions — not without dangers — which people who live in the exciting atmosphere of the stage commonly delight in. Mozart's wife was away for her health at Baden, where their youngest son was born, and her husband, always pressed upon by want of funds, disappointed of settled position, overtaken with perpetual labours, and gifted with a very excitable nature, was easily led by Schikaneder into more dissipation than was good for him. But the composition went on well, and the work was near enough to being finished to be put in rehearsal in the autumn of 1791.

Just at this time, when his nature was being strained to the utmost, and he was living in a way which was but too liable to rouse any morbid tendencies, his mind was much excited by a visit which had all the appearance of singular mystery about it. A tall, serious-looking man, whom he had never seen before, called on him with a note which invited him to compose a *Requiem* for someone whose name was not given, and whom he was enjoined not to endeavour to discover. It was found out afterwards that the applicant was a certain Count Walsegg, who had a whim for figuring as a composer and wanted the work to pass it off as his own composition. But Mozart never knew this, and in his excitable condition, the transaction was capable of having a much stranger significance attached to it. At first, he does not seem to have had any unreasonable fancies about it and was well pleased with the opportunity of writing another great work and making a little money. But he could not turn all his attention to it at once, as other work pressed very hard upon him at this time. A new commission was offered which he could not well refuse; which was a request from the

States of Bohemia to write another opera for the coronation of Leopold II at Prague. There were actually but a few weeks left for the work, and *Zauberflote* was not quite finished either; but Mozart did not hesitate. He wrote wherever he could and whenever he could find opportunity. Some of the music was planned and the outline dotted down in the carriage as he was travelling, and the score worked out in an inn or any other house where he happened to stop; and in good time, the work was ready and was performed on a grand scale on September 6, under the name of *La Clemenza di Tito*.

But the strain was beginning to tell, and he looked pale and was out of spirits. Moreover, people were too excited by all the whirl of festivities that were going on to take much notice of the opera so that it seemed like a failure to Mozart, and as it happened in Prague, where he had always met with more than usual sympathy, he was made seriously depressed. But *Zauberflote* had yet to be finished, so he was obliged to go back to Vienna directly. Several of the most famous numbers in it were written after his return, including the overture, which appears to have been only finished on September 28; and on September 30, they had the first performance. At the beginning, the public did not seem to take to it, and when the first act was over, Mozart came behind the scenes to Schikaneder in a great state of agitation. Schikaneder did what he could to keep up his spirits, and the rest of the work fortunately met with more favour, though it did not seem to be by any means a great success. Schikaneder, however, thoroughly believed in it and went on giving performances, and the more it was given, the more the public liked it; and before long, it became the most popular opera in existence. By November in the next year, Schikaneder had given it successfully a hundred times, and by October 1795, two hundred times, without any diminution of its popularity.

When the opera was fairly started, Mozart was able to give his whole attention to the *Requiem*; and he worked at it with unusual preoccupation and excitement. His mind had evidently lost its normal balance, and melancholy and depression seemed to be taking hold of him. According to his wife's account, he began to be possessed with the feeling that he was writing the *Requiem* for himself. Working at it evidently made him worse, and she persuaded him to give it up for a little while, and then he got better again. By way of a change, he wrote a cantata for a Masonic festival, which was performed with so much success on November 15 that his spirits revived, and he thought he could safely go on with the *Requiem* again; but almost as soon as he began, he fell back into his former state of depression. He got it into his head that he had been poisoned, and his physical health began to give way very fast. He had violent fits of sickness, and symptoms of paralysis came on, and then he took to his bed. He was a little cheered by the reports of the steadily increasing popularity of *Zauberflote*, and it looked as if at last his worldly position and domestic affairs might get into a more prosperous state if only he could hold on to life. He went on working at the *Requiem*, having the score on his bed, and writing or discussing it with his pupil Süssmayr. In the afternoon of December 4, some friends came and sang parts of it with him as he lay in bed. Suddenly, he was seized with the thought that it would not be finished and put the work away. Soon after, he became very much worse. A doctor was sent for but came too late, and the treatment he recommended brought on delirium, from which Mozart never recovered consciousness. He lingered on for some hours in this state, and early on the morning of December 5, 1791, he died.

A friend named Van Swieten undertook the matters connected with the funeral; but no idea of any public mourning for the great man seemed to have entered anyone's head. The sad ceremony took place the next day in a violent storm of snow and rain. Only a few friends attended, and after being present at the benediction in the church, they fled from the wild weather and left the bier to the tender mercies of strangers. In consequence of his poverty, no provision for a special grave had been made, and the body was lowered into a common vault, which was made to contain several coffins together. Not one human being who had been dear to Mozart stood by when his body passed below the earth. When his poor, distracted wife recovered sufficiently to go to the churchyard to see his grave, either the gravedigger was changed, or he had forgotten where it was.

It would be hard to find a stranger instance of the irony of fate in all the history of the world. After being the idol of musical Europe when a mere child, Mozart had fulfilled in maturity all the promise of his early years. But as his powers rose to nobler heights, his worldly prosperity seemed to decrease. As years went on, poverty pressed harder and harder upon him. The brave struggle with constant work, which brought him no fair and adequate reward, at last broke his health; and at the early age of thirty-five, he passed away, so little noticed or cared for that, to this day, the exact place where his body rests cannot be found.

VI

BEETHOVEN.

ONE of the most interesting things about the history of music is the way in which it invariably illustrates, in some way or another, the state of society and the condition of thought of the people among whom it is produced. Second-rate composers illustrate the tone of mind among second-rate people, and the greatest masters of their art express things which are characteristic of the best and foremost men of their time. Yet further, when some exceptionally splendid genius appears, who is fully in sympathy with the best tendencies of his day, and capable of realizing in thought the conditions and feelings which men are most prone to in their best and truest moments, he becomes, as it were, a prophet. He raises those who understand him above themselves, ennobles, and purifies at least some of those traits and sympathies which combine to make the so-called spiritual element in man; and so he comes to be a leader instead of a mere illustrator of contemporary emotion.

A little thought ought to show that this connection between music and the average mental and even moral state of society is inevitable. Appreciative audiences are as necessary to music as composers and performers. But people will never listen patiently to what is hopelessly too good for them; neither will they attend to a style of art that is altogether out of their moods. Ordinary English people might as well be expected to flock in enthusiastic crowds to the recitation of an epic in Chinese. If a man writes music that cannot find any response in the heart of the public of his time, he is predestined to failure, and his works are more likely to find a place in the limbo of useless lumber than among those monuments of art which after generations will revere. Even the best of composers can only produce genuine music in accordance with the mental state of the time in which they are born. If an age can boast of the existence of simple and sincere religion among the classes that are sufficiently cultivated and civilized to produce native art, then religious music like Palestrina's, Bird's, and Gibbons' may come out of it. If religion becomes a sham, and merely a kind of social entertainment among a large portion of the public, flimsy and theatrical religious music comes of it. So again, a generation of courtly and polite habits is illustrated by prim and polite music, and a society mentally and sympathetically enervated by frivolity, luxury, and reckless self-indulgence is musically represented by modern French opera bouffes, and those kinds of dance music and songs in which the absence of art is not less conspicuous than impudent and aggressive vulgarity. One of the things that makes the connection all the more striking is that people are entirely unconscious of the certainty with which the music they enjoy illustrates some strong qualities in themselves of feeling and disposition. They may as good as confess the basest and meanest qualities by their musical tastes; while, on the other hand, people of low circumstances and even disreputable lives may show some noble corners in their natures by the unexpected appreciation they display for great and noble things in music.

In an extremely complicated and transitional condition of society like that of the present day, a very great variety of standards of music may come to the front. The more serious and healthy-minded groups of men may be represented by really noble works, while another branch of society may be represented by the flimsiest and emptiest jingle. Like will surely go to like, and after a time, the fruit will tell its tale.

But in earlier stages of musical history, the characteristics of representative music were not so various. Music was confined to a smaller circle of human beings, and the leading musicians throughout the world were more closely connected with one another and were more at one in their views of art than they can be in later times. And so it happens that their art has a broader and more general family likeness than is the case in the nineteenth century. This is strongly felt, even by people of the most ordinary musical intelligence, about the period of Haydn and Mozart. During the greater part of their time, the prosperous aristocracies of Europe were in the highest phase of complacency and contentment. They lived easy lives, enlivened by amusements and refined by the cultivation of art and literature. Their appreciation for the various forms of art was indeed one of the redeeming features of the system in which they lived, and music met with plenty of encouragement at their hands. But their influence upon it was not altogether for good, for it was too absolutely at their mercy. Musicians, being forced into subservience to a small class, were prevented from rising to the greatest heights of independent inspiration. All art had to be devised to suit these patrons, and it had to submit to their tastes as long as they had the predominance of patronage. The result was that music had a peculiarly complacent and easy character through the early part of the eighteenth century. It was refined and graceful, but not deeply poetical or richly imaginative. It savoured of forms and conventionalities rather than strong originality and powerful emotions. But as the century grew older, a great change came over the spirit of the world. The masses of the people began to assert themselves and to claim some reasonable share in the enjoyable things in life. The conventionalism and emptiness of the ways of the courtly people began to appear in their true colours, and men of strong aspirations and natural enthusiasm turned towards the workers and the poorer inhabitants of the world to regain the sense of those realities of human life which the formal and polite manners of aristocrats seemed to have put out of sight. A kind of revulsion sprang up against the empty elegancies of the prosperous classes; and enlarged sympathies with the troubles and strivings of humanity opened out a new field for poets and composers alike, which resulted in a crisis of the utmost moment in the history of both literature and music.

The man who illustrated the change most powerfully in music was Ludwig van Beethoven; and he serves not only as the representative of the very highest type of art of the new period but also as a link between the new and the old. For he accepted all that was best and purest in the art of his predecessors and renewed and transformed it by the fervour, passion, and sympathetic imagination of his naturally democratic disposition. In music, he shares with Bach the rare distinction of attaining to those prophetic powers that do not stop short at merely illustrating the best thoughts and feelings of contemporaries but foresee and anticipate what must come hereafter, and continue to raise and ennoble their hearers for generations after their possessors themselves have passed away.

Beethoven was born in 1770 at Bonn, where both his father and grandfather had musical posts of some rather insignificant kind in the service of the Elector of Cologne. His early life must have been rough and bracing; for the family had to exist upon a wretchedly poor income, and the father was a man of dissipated habits, which grew upon him more and more as he grew older, till his drunkenness and irregularities made him utterly unfit to perform either his musical or domestic duties any longer. It was, however, from his father that Beethoven had to get the earlier part of his musical education until he was nine years old. By that time, the extent of his father's knowledge was pretty nigh exhausted, and he began to pick up stray fragments of knowledge from anyone he could find who was fit to teach him anything. Neefe, the organist of the court chapel, helped him to learn something of the organ, and he soon got on well enough to act as deputy when his master had to be away. When he was a little over twelve, he was given the post of "cembalist" in the orchestra of the theatre, and this must have been a great advantage to him, as he had to take an active part in the production of many of the most successful operas of the time and was able to gain something by the experience which would be serviceable for composition. He could scarcely have had any regular instruction beyond that, as none of the musicians he seems to have been in contact with at Bonn were likely to have much idea of teaching composition. But he nevertheless tried his hand at writing occasionally and produced works like sonatas and rondos for the pianoforte, which were of no very great importance. However, his playing and general musical gifts began to strike many people and made them think he was likely to make some mark in the world.

When he was seventeen years old, he somehow managed to get to Vienna, the greatest musical centre of that time; and there he had the good fortune to be brought into contact with Mozart, who was very much struck by his extemporizing and seems to have given him some lessons. Beyond that, his journey did not produce any remarkable result, and he had to hurry back in a few months on account of the illness of his mother, who sadly died in July 1787. This must have made the condition of affairs at home worse than ever, as the mother was of a kind and gentle disposition, and her untimely death left the young Beethoven to manage the dissipated behavior of his father and the domestic concerns of the family as best he could. Fortunately, he began to make friends among a class of people who were well fitted to help and brighten his life during this difficult time. Under the trying conditions of his early existence, his character was evidently developing and showing those qualities which all through his life exerted an extraordinary fascination upon people of all grades of society and intelligence. Among his earliest friends were a family of von Breunings, people of better social position than himself and of higher cultivation and refinement than most of those of his own rank. He gave lessons to the younger members of the family, and the mother, who was a widow and a woman of considerable intelligence, had a most excellent influence upon him. She provided him with that turn for general cultivation and an interest in literature which soon more than compensated for the scantiness of his early education in general subjects. Another important friend he made around the same time was a Count Waldstein, an enthusiastic amateur, who helped him and performed many friendly offices for him in various ways. This count was well repaid by the immortality Beethoven conferred on his name by dedicating to him one of his greatest sonatas.

In the same year that he returned from Vienna, the music at the theatre in Bonn was put on a better footing than it had been before. Several distinguished players were engaged — Neefe, Beethoven's old master, was made pianist, and Beethoven himself was appointed to play the viola in the band, besides his other duties. This new arrangement gave him opportunities of hearing better music, better performed than had been his fortune previously, and his standard of ideas probably improved under these favorable circumstances. But his position in art was still a very curious one, and very ill-defined. What struck people most was his extemporizing, which seems to have been daring and vigorous, and full of interesting ideas and surprising strokes of genius. His playing can hardly have been very perfect or finished, for he had no opportunity of learning any keyed instrument systematically or of hearing first-rate performers. But throughout his life, it seems to have been the style of expression which made his playing so impressive, rather than any gifts of facility or dexterity. His character and behavior, as well as his musical performances, must have been rather of a piece in these respects; and people were attracted by both one and the other, notwithstanding the roughness and want of polish that characterized him. This was largely due to the depth of earnestness and absolute sincerity that resided within him, along with the absence of anything like affectation.

Of composition up to this time, there was very little to show in terms of composition, and, in fact, people had not begun to regard him as a composer, even though he every now and then brought out a work of some sort. When Haydn passed through Bonn on his way to England in 1792, Beethoven took him some work that he had been writing, and Haydn praised it and advised him to continue composing. It may have been partly the result of this encouragement that the Elector, his master, began to think of sending Beethoven to Vienna again to study under Haydn for regular instruction in composition. It seemed rather late in the day to be taking such a step when Beethoven was already well past twenty; but it was evidently well worth trying, and in the latter part of 1792, the arrangements were completed. Beethoven left his native Bonn for Vienna after most affectionate partings with the von Breunings, Waldstein, and others who had learned to appreciate him at his true worth.

He began to work with Haydn as soon as possible after his arrival in Vienna, and the old master set him to do the usual, dry, technical studies in counterpoint, which are the orthodox means of gaining facility in composition. Beethoven worked with a will and produced a great deal more of this sort than Haydn had time to look at. It does not, indeed, seem that the old master can ever have given him regular and systematic teaching at any time. Before long, Beethoven began to feel restless and to think that he might do better with someone else. He felt that Haydn was too busy to attend to him properly, and he was getting old too, and was not by any means ready to appreciate the bent of Beethoven's mind. So when Haydn started for another of his journeys to England in 1794, Beethoven looked around for another master who could drill him more thoroughly. He certainly found a man as fit to do mechanical and rigid drilling as anyone known to history.

The name of Albrechtsberger is still well known to musicians as one of the most famous of theorists and one of the strictest and most mechanical of musical pedants. To this man, Beethoven attached himself, despite the obvious fact that Albrechtsberger would necessarily be more antagonistic and unsympathetic to him than even Haydn had been. For him, Beethoven ground through reams of technical exercises, from which it is probable that he could not quite contrive to keep his characteristic qualities from displaying themselves. The master, for his part, did his duty thoroughly and conducted his willing pupil through the most arid wastes of ingenuity. Beethoven bore this training as patiently as a perfect novice, even though he was by this time twenty-four, and a man of some experience and great power in certain branches of his art. Albrechtsberger had the most hearty contempt for his pupil and told some inquiring person to have nothing to do with him, "for he had never learned anything and would never do anything in a decent style." This criticism of genius is characteristic of pedants of all times and all places.

From a man like Albrechtsberger, this was to be anticipated, but it is more disappointing to find that Haydn's feelings toward Beethoven were not by any means sympathetic or appreciative. Their intercourse was naturally rendered difficult by the peculiar independence and unhesitating contempt for conventionalities of all sorts, which was one of the most striking marks of Beethoven. He detested pretension and shallow pedantry in almost equal measure and never hesitated to express himself clearly on such subjects, regardless of who happened to be in his company. An old and established musician nearly always has an extraordinary quantity of empty and dried-up formularies hanging about him, and looks upon them as articles of faith. The school of the time before Beethoven, as well as the musicians who followed it in later times, had even more of this rigidity about them than any other set of musicians in history. Beethoven, who was born to be the first and greatest exponent of a different order of things, was brought at once into antagonism with a great representative of the old order. He initially produced some works quite after the old models, and as long as he did that, Haydn was satisfied with him. But even in one of the earliest compositions which he produced after going to Vienna, there were things that were thoroughly characteristic of him. Haydn sadly shook his head and recommended Beethoven to suppress the work that contained those characteristics, advising him not to allow it to appear in print. Beethoven was quite certain that this was the best of his works so far, and posterity has thought the same, and so he must have felt that there was something radically wrong in Haydn's views of art, or else that Haydn was jealous of him. Beethoven always felt the truth and rightness of a thing he had made up his mind about so thoroughly that it was difficult for him to realize the position of people who could not follow or agree with him. Consequently, his quick and impatient temper sometimes led him to think that other people had bad motives for judgments and actions when they were really thoroughly sincere.

It is therefore not so very surprising that Haydn should have looked upon Beethoven's ways with dislike. The younger musician had, as yet, made no mark whatsoever in composition, and there was not enough of his work before the world to enable a critical man to judge how much of the new departure was the result of caprice and recklessness, and how much was the result of well-balanced judgment and genius. Haydn had, in reality, a great deal in common with Beethoven, although the things which seemed like needless violations of his rules of art were too prominent to allow him to judge of Beethoven with equanimity. The result was that their relations with one another did not run quite smoothly and equably at any time. They did not quarrel decisively, but Beethoven sometimes said rude things to Haydn, and Haydn, for his part, spoke slightingly of Beethoven. However, at the bottom of their hearts, Beethoven had a great reverence and admiration for the old master. At least one burst of enthusiastic feeling for Haydn is recorded even about this time; and in later days, when Beethoven was shown a picture of the place where Haydn was born, he said - "To think that so great a man should have been born in so humble a cottage."

Beethoven's relations with other musicians were, for the most part, worse than those he had with Haydn. There were a few liberal-minded and intelligent men whom he liked and who behaved reasonably to him, but there were also numerous self-sufficient professionals who had won success chiefly by imposing on the public with tricks of technique or by exceptional powers of self-confidence. Naturally, these individuals detested this real, true man when he came amongst them, just as similar pharisees have always done. These Viennese pharisees had a very good subject to mock at, for Beethoven's appearance was peculiar, his dialect was different from theirs, and his behavior was not of the kind affected by polite Viennese. His style of music, especially in extemporizing, no doubt seemed like perfect impudence to the taste of a genuinely well-bred pharisee of the old school. It is no wonder they threw his compositions on the floor and trampled on them, as well as otherwise showed what nature they were of at his expense. To Beethoven, this was of little consequence. It happened with him, as it happened with Wagner since; he found amongst intelligent amateurs and the public who were to be found in those days the cordial sympathy and appreciation which a large body of his fellow musicians denied him.

Among the distinguished and cultivated amateurs in Vienna at that time, he soon found enthusiastic admirers, and his music, along with his force of character, so deeply impressed them that they overcame the usual habits of the courtly classes in a capital where aristocratic rank is almost made more of than anywhere else in Europe. They placed him on equal terms with men and women of the highest position - or, at least, if not on equal terms, it was with the advantage on his side. For many of them carried their admiration for him to such a pitch that they would bear anything from him. Rudeness, bearishness, and ill temper, which they would not have endured for a moment from an equal, were taken with perfect patience and quietness when they came from him.

Almost the earliest of these aristocratic friends was Prince Charles Lichnowsky, whose name is associated, through various dedications, with some of Beethoven's best-known compositions. He was soon on intimate terms with him, and the prince induced him for a time to accept rooms in his house. However, Beethoven could not conform to the ways of such people, nor could he keep their hours, and before long, the arrangement came to an end. Nevertheless, it does not seem to have produced any sort of breach between them. Although Beethoven occasionally broke into wild tempers with his generous friend, it was long before their familiar intercourse was materially affected. Beethoven frequently played for the people who met together at Prince Lichnowsky's house, as well as at the houses of other musical aristocrats of like disposition, and the character and interest of his performances rapidly gained him more and more friends among them. However, for quite a good while after he came to Vienna, he was known more as a player than as a composer. Even as a player, he was only known to the aristocratic circles who met in private houses. The first occasion when he made his appearance in anything like a public concert was in 1795, when he had already been three years in Vienna; and on that occasion, he played his own concerto in C major, which had been finished just before. Very soon after this, he appeared in public again at a concert given for Mozart's widow, when he played one of Mozart's concertos. From that time onward, he continued to make his appearance in public more frequently, either as a performer or as a composer, and his reputation soon rose to a very high point. He also began to show himself in other towns besides Vienna, and in 1796, he traveled as far as Berlin, where he played before the king, and was treated with appreciative distinction.

In the year that followed, he continued working steadily at composition, but he still did not begin the line of grand works which would later become his special triumph. It was not until he was almost thirty that he produced his first symphony, and this was first performed in 1800. Moreover, his style did not yet approach anything like the full measure of his independent originality. Even the first symphony, which made its appearance so late in his life as compared with the great works of Mozart and many other famous composers, was still very much more like, in general character, the works of his predecessors than it was to his own more mature style. He seemed cautious and reserved in the production of the works about which he had a full sense of artistic responsibility, and he began tentatively. Only as he made sure of his ground and tested the power of his hand to express exactly what he wanted did he venture to give fuller rein to his inspiration. Every now and then, a work would emerge that encapsulated all the force of his character, and then at times he would go back again and compose another work that followed more closely the style and manner of thought of Mozart or Haydn. But to his contemporaries, even the works that seem to musicians of the present day to be the most slender and obvious among his productions appeared to be remarkably daring, and they delighted them or revolted them in proportion to their feelings for poetry and their powers of expansion.

The next large-scale work on which he was engaged after the first Symphony in C was the *Mount of Olives*, which marked his first significant choral achievement. He was at work on this project in 1801, and its first performance took place in 1803. Almost concurrently, he was busy with a second symphony, which contained much more of his own fire and independent style than the first. Several other works of considerable importance, including sonatas and chamber music, were also in progress during this time. His ideas flowed so profusely that he always had several works in development at once, and he would meditate on and contemplate these ideas for a long while before bringing them to completeness. His practice was to jot down the ideas roughly as they came into his head in little sketch-books that he carried in his pocket, and he then polished and improved these original ideas time after time, sometimes for years, before he worked them up into complete works. He had a deep fondness for the country and for open-air exercise, and the ideas would sometimes come to him as he was walking or wandering in the woods or sitting on the branch of a tree. When inspiration seized him, he was thoroughly like one inspired. His eyes are said to have dilated, and his whole being seemed to be possessed by the fervor of his thoughts. He became entirely careless of time or previous engagements as long as the excitement lasted. This must have been a characteristic trait even in the early days before he left Bonn, for his friend Madame von Breuning described him as "being in his *raptus*" at times, making him quite impossible to manage. In later times, he would stamp and stride about, singing and shouting passages that were passing through his brain, or thrum them wildly on the pianoforte.

It is altogether an extraordinary contrast to the ways of the earlier composers, with whom emotion counted for less than good workmanship. Haydn appears to have been quite quiet and self-possessed when he was producing his music. He preferred to be tidy and neat and liked to be dressed in his best clothes when he was working on anything serious. Mozart, on the other hand, wrote many of his works as quickly as most people would write an ordinary letter. He was so far from being wildly impassioned that he could quite well listen to or take part in conversation at the same time. However, Beethoven could not produce his best work except under the influence of some powerful emotion, such as that which his music represents. He considered that the emotion and the poetical or dramatic effect of the music were of the highest importance, and the title that he valued most was *"Ton-Dichter,"* or "tone poet." This characteristic of his work illustrated the direction in which art was moving, for it is the emotional power and variety that mark it as the highest expression of the expansion of the sympathies of mankind, which began in the latter part of the last century.

The third of his symphonies, at which he was working around this time, was the result of his feelings concerning the significant questions at issue between kings and aristocracies on one side and the peoples on the other. He had developed an immense admiration for Napoleon Bonaparte, who seemed to him the very ideal of a hero of the people. At that time, Napoleon's career had not yet reached the point where he appeared in his full form as an insatiable conqueror, embodying the very attributes of an imperial figure. He was still regarded as the extreme opposite of kings and monarchical traditions. To Beethoven, he seemed to be the liberator of downtrodden peoples from old despotisms and the benefactor who would give new laws to the peoples of the world, intended for the peoples' benefit and not for the advantage of despots or privileged aristocracies. In this mood, Beethoven set about writing a symphony in Napoleon's honor, producing by far the grandest, longest, and most powerful work of its kind that had ever appeared. This symphony made a profound mark in the history of the symphony, for all the greatest works that had come before it were mere shadows by its side in terms of emotion, breadth, and poetic interest. Many previous works had been perfect in terms of artistic craftsmanship and the balance of beautiful form, but composers of the previous century had never even aimed at such degrees of force or such variety of interest. His enthusiasm for his ideal hero inspired him to create the greatest music he had within him at that time. By 1804, the work was completed, and the title page bore the name "Napoleon Bonaparte." He was even preparing to send it to Paris when the news was brought to him by his pupil Ries that Napoleon had taken the title of emperor. His ideal hero was dashed from his pedestal in an instant; the man he had believed in had, after all, joined the ranks of the despots. In a fit of indignation, he tore off the page bearing the detested name, and according to the commonly accepted story, the symphony itself narrowly escaped destruction due to its connection with such a gigantic impostor. Fortunately for the world, the election of the new emperor did not produce such grievous results as that. In order to denote the ideal circumstances under which it was produced, the symphony was given the name "*Sinfonia Eroica* in Memory of a Great Man." The word "memory" carries with it a mountain of meaning.

This whole story illustrates, very happily, Beethoven's strong and independent views about great social subjects. His sympathies were all on the side of the masses and against privileges, class distinctions, and artificial dignities of all sorts. He could hardly be patient at the conventional subservience expected of ordinary people when they were brought into contact with aristocrats, for he felt that the common people were often worthier and more useful members of society than the individuals to whom they were expected to bow down. He himself ignored their claims to special respect, even ostentatiously, and many curious stories are told of his behavior towards them. On one occasion, for instance, when he was playing to a party of aristocratic people, some of the younger ones went on talking, just as people often do to the sound of good music in modern drawing rooms. Beethoven flew into a great rage and stopped the music, saying loudly that he would play no more for such hogs. Another time, as he was walking in the street, he met a group of people of rank, among whom was an especial friend of his. The revulsion against empty formalities was so strong in him at that moment that he kept his hat tight on his head and did not even give the company any sign of recognition. It is very much to the credit of the aristocratic people in Vienna that, despite his well-known views on the subject of rank and commonalty, and his brusque and unrestrained manner of speech and behavior with them, they remained his most constant friends and supporters. It is curious, too, to think that they should have embraced music that was so very different in many respects from the quiet, self-contained kind which had been prepared for their especial amusement by the composers of the previous generation. This proved, at least, that their humanity was larger and more generous than the restrictions they had to submit to by etiquette and custom allowed to appear. At the same time, it is probable they did not, in those days, realize what Beethoven was doing. They felt the greatness and impressiveness of what he expressed, but did not guess what it all meant. If they had appreciated the fact that it was an appeal from their influence on art and their exclusive patronage to a wider and more independent public, they might not have been so ready to fall in with it.

In this respect, as in the character of his music, Beethoven serves as a vital link between the old and new order of things. The rich German princes and nobles had always been remarkable for their great love of music, and they had been so long accustomed to regard it as a sort of appanage and property of their own that, even when such an independent creature as Beethoven appeared in the world, they still regarded him as their particular care, and as a person for whom it was their prescriptive duty to provide. Their generosity and helpfulness to him are so surprising that it can hardly be explained on any other grounds. The offer of Prince Lichnowsky to take him into his house has been mentioned before. Another man of rank, called Baron Pasqualati, reserved rooms for him in a house on the ramparts of Vienna, in what was called the Mölk Bastion, from which there was a beautiful view. Here, he often used to shut himself up when he was busy composing. Another patron, Count Browne, gave Beethoven a horse in return for a set of variations on a Russian air that Beethoven wrote for his wife. Beethoven characteristically forgot all about it and was very much enraged when the bill came in for its keep. Similar generosity was shown by one of the Apponyi family, who proposed to Beethoven to write his first string quartet and said he might propose whatever terms he wished for the work. However, the most striking piece of generosity came later in his life when three noblemen — Archduke Rodolph, Prince Kinsky, and Prince Lobkowitz — clubbed together to secure him a regular income, which would have amounted to 400 florins a year, but for the unfortunate condition of monetary affairs in Austria at the time, owing to long and ruinous wars, which reduced the value of the amount as paid in notes to about 210 florins. They not only did this, but when the depreciation of notes became worse and worse, and a measure had to be passed which substituted a new means of exchange for the old one at a very much lower value, they made good the difference to him as well as they could, even at their own loss.

Nevertheless, Beethoven was rarely in a prosperous condition. He could not give his mind to practical matters, and his ordinary affairs were generally in pitiable confusion. He forgot almost everything: sometimes it was his washing; another time he forgot that he had engaged rooms that he was not living in; at another time, he forgot to eat his dinner; and, as mentioned earlier, he forgot he had a horse. He was so often profoundly absorbed that things outside the range of his musical thoughts had to go by chance. It was altogether a most happy-go-lucky and uncertain existence—flying from lodging to lodging, falling out with his servants, fancying all sorts of grievances with his friends, and breaking out into wild transports of rage, pouring insults upon them, and then, if he found out he was wrong, writing the most affectionate and self-accusing letters of repentance. All his life long, it was the same and showed a childlike and transparent simplicity combined with a force of character and nobility of soul, such as is always one of the most attractive compounds in human nature. People's interest in him was also enhanced by his troubles and misfortunes. Chief among these was his deafness, which began to show premonitions of its approach as early as 1798 with singing and buzzing in his ears. By 1800, it had become serious enough to require the attention of doctors, and its progress from bad to worse was so steady and unmistakable in its march that he foresaw that it must end in total deafness. To a man whose whole organism was centered in the beauties of sound, it must have appeared a most fearful prospect; the anticipation tortured him. He endeavored to face it with determined courage. He looked forward to moments when he would be the most wretched of God's creatures, but he made up his mind to grapple with fate and not allow it to drag him down.

There is something very tragic in the whole story of his life. He had a most sensitive and excitable disposition and was in a constant state of suffering, either from his own headlong mistakes or from the troubles that fate brought upon him. As he grew older, the net seemed to get closer around him, and the worries and misfortunes became more desperate and were less often relieved by brighter moments. Finally, he was shut out from all communication with the outer world by means of sound, and from all sensation of his beloved art. But though he was also pressed upon incessantly by poverty and bad health, and harassed by the baseness of the nephew in whom he had centered his affections, yet he always went on rising to nobler heights of art and achieving greater and more powerful accomplishments, with a Titanic power and endurance, and a spirit which misfortune seemed rather to purify and exalt than to subdue.

The indications of approaching deafness, which were becoming more and more conspicuous about the beginning of this century, appeared only to increase his ardor for work, as if in anxiety to get as much completed as possible before the time when he would no longer be able to hear what he had made for all the world to hear. Among the most important things that he set to work upon soon after the *Eroica Symphony* was the opera *Fidelio*. He had long been wishing to try his powers in opera writing and had even accepted engagements from managers to write works for them, as, for instance, for Mozart's old friend, Schikaneder. However, these had all fallen through. One of his difficulties was very characteristic of him. The opera writers of previous generations had been content to set the most inconceivable and idiotic rubbish to music. So long as there were some points that were effective for the stage, or which gave opportunities for the display of qualities of voice or acting for prima donnas and famous tenors, the public did not mind the dramas being unintelligible nonsense. The patrons of the earlier operas went to the theater to be amused, and if such a thing as a variety entertainment had been invented in those days, it would have sufficed to give the performance an imposing name and the pretense of a story to satisfy its highly cultivated audiences that they were listening to a work of art. Even Mozart, whose dramatic sense and power of character-drawing in music were of the highest kind, did not inquire too minutely into the nature of the stories upon which his librettos were founded, but accepted the silliest and most empty things to set to music. Beethoven's point of view was altogether different. He felt that, in an artistic sense, the dramatic side of the matter was as important as the music, and that to be worthy of the name of a work of art, an opera must be complete and intelligible in all respects, and not like the creatures of old Norse fable - a face and front with neither back nor substance underneath. And this was not all. He felt the need of the thing being sound throughout and he felt also that the subject must be of the noblest and broadest kind to be worth setting to music. He knew that silly and empty commonplaces could be only set consistently to silly and empty music. The connection between the music and the words and dramatic situation was so close in his mind that he could not bring himself to write music to anything ignoble; or to deal with anything as opera which was not a great type of some sort.

In the end he fixed upon a story of brave and unconquerable womanly devotion for his subject, and this was embodied in the libretto of *Leonora*, or *Fidelio* as it was afterwards called and by the end of 1805 the work was ready for performance. He took enormous pains over it, and tried and tested the various parts of it with even more than usual patience. It is said that he made as many as eighteen different versions of one famous passage, and ten of another, and similar changes and experimental improvements through-out. The result was a work thoroughly worthy of him and of the labour he had given to it. To modern musicians it has a unique place in the whole province of opera; and in nobility and truth of sentiment, and depth of musical feeling, and insight into the possibilities of operatic art, it is beyond rivalry among the works produced before the present generation. But unfortunately, when it was brought out in its first form, it had all sorts of unfavourable circumstances against it. The first performance actually took place when the French army were in possession of Vienna, and had just driven out the high society of the place, and among them many of Beethoven's most faithful friends and admirers. Besides this it was evidently too long, in its earliest form, for the endurance of any average audience, and he was so determined not to alter anything when he had once thoroughly made up his mind, that it was almost hopeless to try to get him to cut it down. The singers complained that some passages were unsingable, but he simply refused to make any changes for their benefit. He had come to a decision as to how the music ought to go, and so it was to remain. It was the same with the difficulties that troubled the band, and when his friends protested that it was too long it threatened to be the same with them. But after long wrangling, which made Beethoven violently angry, he finally gave in and agreed to reduce the length of the work materially. The impression it produced seemed to improve after this, though its success was evidently not striking or enthusiastic; and after no very great number of performances, disagreement between Beethoven and the intendant brought them to an end early in 1806, and no more were given anywhere for many years.

Beethoven thenceforward gave up opera writing and went back to the lines of art for which he found more sympathetic audiences. He was by this time arriving at the full maturity of his powers; and the traces of the formal style of the composers of the previous generation, which had again and again presented themselves, even in *Fidelio*, were by degrees being pushed altogether out of sight by the growth and increase of his own individuality. He was one of those rare men whose energy and vitality continue so constantly unabated through life that they grow and improve even up to the days of their old age. Neither weariness nor excess of labor could make him write conventionally or formally. Formality is often the fruit of indolence and want of earnestness, which makes men put empty phrases, which cost them nothing, in the place of the real ideas which exhaust their nature. Beethoven was always possessed with such thorough enthusiasm for art that every work he wrote served as a stepping-stone in some way to further advance. He would rather not write at all than write things without any artistic or emotional point in them; and now that he had arrived at complete mastery of the resources of art after the manner of his predecessors, he turned all his energies to the improvement of the emotional qualities of his work.

The chief works which he was engaged upon immediately after *Fidelio* were symphonies, the famous *Violin Concerto*, a *Mass in C*, and some overtures. The most important of these is the *Symphony in C minor*, which has in later times had the greatest popularity of all his larger works for orchestra. It was almost the first in which the full force of his originality came out untrammeled by conventions or traces of the old formal traditions. It had no external name or association, like the *Third Symphony*, to define to the public the kernel of poetical meaning upon which it turned; but it seemed to tell its own tale without that. Every movement in it expressed something as a whole which the public could grasp and feel, apart from the mere technical development of the work of art, and each successive movement set off and illustrated what had gone before it. The last of all was at such a pitch of grandeur, weight, and force as the world had never heard in a last movement before. The people who clung to the old traditions, the conservatives by inclination from their birth, often found its originality intolerable; but it sometimes happened that even those who began with mocking ended with enthusiasm.

A similar wealth and power of imagination now began to make its appearance in all his instrumental works and gave them the peculiar character now recognized as belonging to his most vigorous and warmly poetical middle age, before sorrow, trouble, and the isolation from deafness gave his music the peculiar cast which it bore throughout the later years of his life. In these works, the character of a new line of music is completely fulfilled; the prominence of art from the craftsman's point of view gave place to a high poetical conception, and from this starting-point, the whole course of modern music has since flowed. He seemed now to have thoroughly matured his plan of operations, and new works followed one another rapidly. Some of them merely appeared with the usual formal names, Symphony No. 4 or No. 5, or Sonata, Opus 55; and some had descriptive names given them, such as the *Pastoral Symphony* and the sonata called "*Les Adieux, Absence et le Retour*," inspired by a parting with his friend, the Archduke Rodolph.

But Beethoven was not altogether in favor of giving definite names to musical works to fix their meaning. He probably knew that the public was attracted by such a procedure, but he felt it was not without its risks. It happens very often that music can express things which words lack the subtlety to describe; and the practice of tying a composer down by a definite program sometimes leads him to try to express things unfit to be said by music, potentially preventing him from rising to heights where music surpasses even the most refined language in expressive power. The impulse which led him away from the old formal methods of composing often made him conscious of the connection between his music and some poetical idea external to music, and at certain points, it was possible to state the connection in words; but his feeling and judgment set him against trying to paint scenes or events in musical sounds. The vulgar conception of program music, which consists of actually reproducing scenes or events in music, was naturally repugnant to him. If he had to make music to any idea or scene, he would try to express not what was seen by the eye but what was felt inwardly. Music, to be true to itself, must refer to the inner emotional workings, not outer sensations. If that were kept in view, program music might always be admirable except for the fact that words would often be behindhand in the race.

The power of music to express subtle gradations of feeling is so much greater than language that, in most cases, attempts to describe the meaning of music through words are almost hopeless. Words can often give no more than the baldest suggestion of the outline, leaving the characteristic elements and internal workings of the music untouched. Nevertheless, Beethoven seems to have had an inclination toward defining the feelings he expressed in his music, and he allowed it to sway him occasionally, as appears from the names he gave to a few of his works and the manner in which he developed some of them in connection with words. But many of the familiar names by which his works are known, such as the *Pastoral Sonata*, the *Moonlight Sonata*, and the *Sonata Appassionata*, were neither given nor authorized by him but were either invented by publishers, who knew the value a name has with the ordinary public, or by admiring amateurs; and a general impression of their usefulness has kept them in use despite the protests of good judges and the fact that one at least is perfectly inappropriate. In the case of the *Pastoral Symphony*, the name was given by Beethoven himself, and the plan was deliberately worked out by him. It contained some things which certainly came very near being attempts at musical scene-painting, as, for instance, in the movement representing the storm. But Beethoven was careful to point out that he intended it all to be more about feeling than painting; "*mehr Ausdruck der Empfindung als Malerei,*" as he himself wrote. Actual imitation of birds' notes and of the whispering of the brook does come into it, true, but such things only enter as accessories, and the removal of what is implied would make very little difference to the effect of the work as a whole. The music is perfectly intelligible and complete by itself and does not depend on the coloring or influence of the external idea on the minds of the audience.

This may serve to illustrate Beethoven's position as the greatest composer of pure instrumental music. The object of successive generations of composers who worked on this branch of composition before him was evidently to produce works perfectly interesting and intelligible in themselves without the help of words or explanatory names or text. They had to content themselves at first with very simple and slender works, as the whole scheme and system upon which music could be made intelligible of itself had to be discovered. They put dance tunes together and found that their contrasts were effective, spinning out the time by making variations and so forth. Each generation improved upon the work of the generation before, learning to do more with the instruments and how to make movements longer and more interesting. This continued until the time of Haydn and Mozart, who produced very perfect works of art in the form of symphonies and sonatas, relying on the principles upon which they were constructed as the means of making them intelligible. Then Beethoven came and added a greater element of interest and a stronger bond of connection in all parts of the work by bringing ideas and moods and various means of arousing impressions more strongly forward. He filled his music as full of emotion as it would hold without upsetting the balance of those qualities upon which the existence of pure, unadulterated *instrumental* music depends. The fact that he did adopt a name in the case of the *Pastoral Symphony* provides a clue to his principles in creating works without names; but his art was perfectly pure in that it was completely interesting and intelligible in itself.

The story of the middle period of his life is altogether centered in his art. It would have been impossible for him to produce works so full of deep and earnest feeling without giving all his vitality to them. And even though he concentrated all his energies upon them, he produced much less than his predecessors had done. The conditions under which he worked were altogether different from theirs, and much more exhausting. They had been able to produce little elegant works to please their refined public without much exertion, but he wanted to appeal to his hearers and move them in a deeper way. To him, art was not an amusement or a means of passing hours that might otherwise hang heavy on men's hands, but a means of elevating them and giving them interests and feelings that would take them away from the sordid and material cares of everyday life, supplying a counterbalance to their hardening influences. He worked essentially for the same ideals as a poet and put his whole soul into his work in a way that no composer before, except perhaps Bach, had thought of, and the result naturally was that the vital force was concentrated into fewer works, instead of being diffused in a thinner stream in many.

Besides this, there was much more actual exertion in making his works than there had been in those of his predecessors, both in the matter of thought and mere manual labor. Composers had gone on increasing the number of instruments they used for their symphonies, and they had tried to increase the force and fullness of sound of their works, even when they wrote for only one instrument. The symphonies that numerous forgotten composers used to write for the delectation of aristocratic patrons in the early part of the eighteenth century, just before or about the beginning of Haydn's career, had usually been written for small bands of eight instruments—such as two violins, a viola, a cello, two flutes, or two oboes, and two horns, with a harpsichord allowed to supply a sort of accompaniment and filling-in at the conductor's discretion. At first, composers used this small band very roughly, doing little in the way of refined or delicate expression. But as time went on, musicians were impelled to attempt more finish and artistic effect, and to experiment with more instruments. Stamitz earned a good title to be honorably remembered for the way in which he taught the band at Mannheim to play in a more finished and intelligent way, using more subtle shades of *piano* and *forte* than had been thought of before. Mozart profited by this when he went to stay at Mannheim and afterward devised his symphonies with much more attention to such matters. Both he and Haydn did an immense deal to make the treatment of the band more refined and artistic, and they also increased its usual size by adding instruments like trumpets, drums, bassoons, and sometimes clarinets. Beethoven, in his time, immediately began to make the band larger and more powerful and treated the instruments with more artistic independence. In some cases, he introduced trombones; sometimes, he used four horns instead of two, and he constructed the works altogether on a more elaborate and grander scale. So, of course, there was much more work in even the actual writing of such works than in the early symphonies, which had neither half the instruments he employed nor the labor of writing out their parts, greatly reduced by the simple device of directing several to play the same passages together for entire pages in succession.

A similar change came about in works written for solo instruments. Beethoven's career corresponds with the regular adoption of the pianoforte by the musical world in general in place of the old harpsichord. Both Mozart and Haydn had been brought up to the harpsichord and wrote many of their sonatas for it. And even when Mozart took to playing and writing for the pianoforte, he continued to treat it in a subdued, quiet, harpsichord style, disliking the energetic and muscular kind of playing necessary to get the proper and characteristic effect from the pianoforte. The first great representative of genuine pianoforte playing was Clementi, who did the world some service by leading the way in the development of a proper treatment of the new instrument. By Beethoven's time, the requirements of the instrument were becoming much better understood. The prejudices and conventions of the old harpsichord school were giving way before the rising school of regular pianoforte players, and music was devised in a way better suited to the character of the new instrument. The result was a much grander scale of writing in sonatas, just as there was in orchestral symphonies, and Beethoven was the composer whose share it was to bring this branch of art to perfection also. Mozart's and Haydn's sonatas were even slighter and more unimportant in proportion than their symphonies. The larger portion of them were the merest trifles, neatly put together but containing very little of striking character. They both wrote a few tolerably large works of the kind, but harpsichord traditions and their craftsman-like point of view prevented them from producing anything very impressive or striking in this genre. Beethoven began from the first to put his full energies into writing pianoforte sonatas. In his early days, he was so drawn in this direction that a good deal more than half of his first fifty works were in this form. He soon developed an extraordinary insight into the nature of the instrument and produced new, deep, and noble effects with it. He found out how to express his own individuality in this branch of composition earlier than in any other, and he gave such color and character to what he wrote that the whole standard of pianoforte music has been raised to a higher level. He continued writing pianoforte sonatas for nearly twenty-five years, always endeavoring to add to their interest and improve the form of art. In no branch of music can the course of his musical life be more clearly traced, from the beginnings under the influence of Mozart and Haydn to the mature richness and warmth of his middle age, and on to the great and unsurpassable utterances of his deepest latter days.

As years went on, his fame spread abroad. In England, his works were brought to a hearing and met with enthusiastic appreciation to a certain point. The appearance of his new works was eagerly antici-pated, and he was occasionally invited to write works specifically for publishers or audiences in this country. Among these invitations was one from a publisher called Thompson in Edinburgh, for settings of Scottish national tunes, for which he was ready to offer Beethoven very liberal remuneration. Beethoven accepted the task and arranged over 150 of them in his own style - a labor that took him many years to complete. The result illustrates his views of art and idiosyncrasies more than anything Scottish.

In 1814, the opera *Fidelio* was revived. Though Beethoven had been difficult to persuade to make alterations at first, time had made him regard such changes from his settled intentions with more patience. He allowed the *libretto* to be revised and set to work himself to make considerable changes throughout the music. In its new form, it was performed in May and seems to have been received with much more appreciation than at first. In the same year, he brought out one of his most interesting and romantic symphonies, which was received with enthusiasm. His position in public estimation was further demonstrated in the same year by the way he was received by the many dignitaries who came to Vienna for the Congress. A great hall was lent to him by the authorities, where he gave two grand concerts, inviting crowned heads as well as aristocrats. The first concert was attended by fully 6,000 people, and Beethoven met with all the sympathy and apprecia-tion he could have desired, and gained some substantial profit as well. For a time, things seemed to be prosperous for him.

But the tide soon turned, and from 1815 onward, troubles constantly thickened around him until the end. In that year, his brother Caspar died. This was unfortunate for him, as Caspar had been very helpful in managing his worldly affairs, with which Beethoven was utterly unfit to deal. But there were other and heavier misfortunes that followed from this occurrence. Caspar left behind him a son, who was confided to the care of his brother, and Ludwig took the charge upon him with more than paternal assiduity. His first difficulties were with the widow, whom he could not endure; and he was entangled in several successive lawsuits in the endeavor to get sole custody of the son. They went on from year to year, sometimes in his favor and sometimes in hers, and his sensitive nature was harassed and tormented with anxiety, and his time wasted in letter writing and conferences with his advisers and friends on the subject; and when finally the case was decided in his favor, the object of all his solicitude turned out to be desperately unworthy, and showed a thoroughly bad and unlovely nature. But Beethoven's affection had become centered in him, and nothing could destroy it. It was a sort of infatuation, which made him seem to beg tenderly for forgiveness whenever he was obliged to take the object of his devotion to task for incessant wrongdoing. In one part of a letter, he found fault with him, and then, as if afraid that it would make a bar between them, went on - "Only come to my arms: not one harsh word shall you hear. You shall be received as lovingly as ever - only come." Letter after letter is in the same style, but the only effect it had upon the unworthy object was to make him thoroughly callous.

The fruit of all this worry and distress of mind was naturally to increase Beethoven's irritability and to aggravate the ill health which troubled him more and more as he grew older. He was frequently obliged to resort to doctors for matters of general health, while his deafness became so serious that in 1816 he began to use an ear trumpet. He gave up playing in public in 1814, and everything which depended to any extent upon hearing, such as conducting or superintending rehearsals, had in like manner to be brought to an end. After a time, it became difficult even to take part in ordinary conversations; and he had to carry a notebook and a pencil about with him, and people who wanted to talk to him had to write their part of the conversation. Another misfortune which came upon him at the end of 1816 was the death of Prince Lobkowitz, who was one of the three aristocratic friends who had guaranteed him a fixed income. No arrangements seem to have been made for the continuance of the payments after the prince's death, so Beethoven's income was from that time seriously diminished.

But no amount of pinching or distress for funds would make him sacrifice his art, or try to make musical sham and pretty twaddle to catch the pence of the public. At the very time when want of money was beginning to tell most hardly upon him, he devoted all his best energies to the production of works which were even more than usually unsaleable. The worry and waste of time arising from the guardianship of his nephew seem to have prevented his working at any large orchestral works for a while, but he set to work instead to produce the finest and grandest of his pianoforte sonatas, which were so terribly difficult that there was no chance of any but very able and experienced players attempting them; while they were constructed at such a high pitch of art, and the things they expressed were so noble and exalted, that there was no chance of any but the few who were exceptionally gifted with musical sense being able to understand them. It shows how entirely the impulse to compose was an artistic and poetical one with him. His gift was too sacred to be desecrated for ignoble uses. He was often driven to try very hard to get money's worth for what was done, but such a thing as altering or lowering the standard of his art with the object of making it more saleable seems never to have been allowed to enter into his head. In this, he is the greatest type of high and unyielding honor; for the idea of degrading and cheapening his precious art seems to have been so entirely impossible to him that he probably never allowed himself even to consider it for a moment. In this respect, German musicians have always been patterns to all the world. In all other countries, composers have been too easily led by cheap sophistries to escape from the taint of dishonoring their art, and publishing what they knew to be bad, vulgar, and commonplace, because it is easiest to get the ignorant public to pay for what pleases them most easily. The public are, in fact, helpless in matters of taste if they are not led and directed by true artists and sincere judges, and it is so difficult for ordinary people to understand in what real art consists that it is no wonder they often seem not to appreciate the devotion of those whose true love and feeling for the honor of their art is stronger than their desire for popularity and well-fed ease. But nevertheless, in Beethoven's case, the sense of his perfectly heroic determination to work for art and art alone, and to make his music as perfect as possible without one thought for profit or fame, must have given the people of his time a very exalted notion of his true-heartedness; and was no doubt one of the sources of the great admiration in which he was held in the latter part of his life by musicians throughout the world. For, as far as appreciation of his works went, it is quite obvious he was leaving musicians more and more behind. It took many people some time even to understand his early works, and while they were coming on to that point, he was going on to more and more perfectly original and grand conceptions, so that the people who really understood him grew fewer, instead of more plentiful, as time went on. Most people found his latest sonatas and quartets hopelessly unintelligible, and it has only been in later times, through the power and devotion of such men as Liszt and Büllow and Joachim, and a few less widely known but hardly less able and earnest performers, that these greatest of musical works have been put within the reach of the public. In Beethoven's own time, even works which now seem perfectly natural to ordinary musical amateurs were regarded as chaotic extravagances; and people only pardoned things, which seem like master-strokes now, as the "eccentricities of genius." It went even so far that some well-intentioned amateur wrote to him and offered him a good round sum if he would write something in the style of his early days, thinking thereby to benefit humanity as well as himself.

But Beethoven was not to be turned aside, and devoted himself to carrying out works according to his own highest ideals of art in all forms; and two of the greatest of all his works were yet to come. The first of these is the great Mass in D, which he wrote for the installation of his friend—the Archduke Rodolph—as Archbishop of Olmütz. The sacred music of the Roman Church had long been suffering under various degrading influences, and had passed through a meretricious and theatrical phase, which was altogether unworthy of the depth and seriousness of the words of the Mass, and other ecclesiastical literature. Beethoven had given one earlier example of his notion of how such things ought to be treated, and he now attacked the matter again from a still more exalted point of view. He idealized religious emotions of the broadest and most comprehensive kind, as things belonging to all men, and all creeds and forms of religion; and he endeavored to express them in music of the most vivid, powerful, and earnest kind. He became extraordinarily absorbed in it, and more wildly possessed by inspiration than ever. A characteristic account of his ways of working at this time has been given by his friend Schindler, who saw a great deal of him, and wrote a book which is not considered entirely trustworthy but has plenty of characteristic matter in it. In 1818, Beethoven had gone for the summer, according to custom, to a country place near Vienna, for fresh air and the country scenes which he loved. Here he used to be shut up in his room, sometimes all day, shouting, stamping, and tearing about the room under the influence of the excitement of the emotions which he was trying to express in his music. He used to forget all about time and rest and food for whole days at a stretch, and to come out disheveled and haggard and exhausted at the end. But notwithstanding the vehement way he worked at it, the Mass took a long while to finish, and was actually not complete till two years after the installation for which it was intended.

When that was finished, all his attention was directed to the completion of the greatest of all his works. He had long been attracted by Schiller's *Ode to Joy*; and ever since his youthful days, he had been meditating a setting of it in some form or another, and many years before this time, ideas for it had been roughly indicated in his sketch-book. At last, when he was over fifty, he set his hand definitely to the task of embodying it all in a grand symphony. Again the composition took possession of him, and he seemed to forget all the comforts and conveniences of life, and even ordinary necessaries, in the wild fervor of inspiration. The symphony which resulted is entirely unique. It all turns upon Schiller's poem, though the first portion - consisting of three movements like the ordinary first three movements of symphonies - is purely instrumental. In this part, he seems to express various conditions in man's existence while searching for the truest and highest form of joy and being denied step by step. At last, after several attempts, the true conception wanted seems to be found, and with the entry of the voices come varying forms of utterance - sometimes wild and exuberant, sometimes gay, sometimes earnest and serene - of the ideal of joy as conveyed by the great and noble melody he at last developed to express it.

The reception which the great work had from the public in general was disappointing. It was fearfully difficult to perform, and even in Vienna it was not understood; while in London it was looked upon as a distressing failure. A critic of the day went so far as to discuss the causes for the falling off and failure of the powers of so great a master, as shown in this work, to parts of which he applied such epithets and expressions as "odd" and "almost ludicrous rambling," "chaos come again," "obstreperous roaring of modern frenzy"; and endeavoured to account for it as the result of the deafness which cut Beethoven off from the rest of the world of music. One of the most painful inferences he draws is that Beethoven found "that noisy extravagance of execution and outrageous clamour in musical performances more frequently insured applause than chastened elegance and refined judgment, and that he wrote accordingly." Anything so diametrically opposite to fact could hardly have been proposed. If Beethoven ever thought of a public at all it was of an ideal public gifted with like insight and like feelings with himself. He knew that the public had to be considered, but he felt also that the public could be led; and his belief has proved right. In the course of the time that has elapsed since, the public has so far advanced under his guidance that this great symphony has become a special feature of all series of concerts of the highest class, and the work to which conductors and performers address themselves with most ardour and eagerness; and the one which most intelligent amateurs and professed musicians alike look upon as the highest and most noble and enduring enjoyment which can be presented to them.

This was Beethoven's last work on a grand scale. After it he only wrote string quartets and other works of less dimensions. His aspirations were as great as ever. He hoped yet to write another opera and to set Goethe's *Faust* to music, and to write more symphonies and other works still greater than what he had already done. He went on sketching ideas into his notebook, and even got on some way with fresh works; but nothing more on so grand a scale was destined to be finished. In 1826 he went with his nephew to stay with a brother who had a little property at a place called Gneixendorf, not far from Vienna. An account of his daily ways there was given by a Michael Krenn, which is so characteristic of him that it is worth quoting[4]: "At half-past five he was up and at his table, beating time with his hands and feet, singing, humming, and writing. At half-past seven was the family breakfast, and directly after it he hurried out of doors, and would saunter about the fields, calling out, waving his hands, going

---

4   Taken from the article "Beethoven," by Sir G. Grove, in his Dictionary of Music and Musicians.

now very slowly and now very fast, and then suddenly standing still and writing in a kind of pocket-book. At half-past twelve he came in to dinner, and after dinner he went to his own room till three or so, then in the fields again till about sunset, for later than that he might not go out. At half-past seven was supper, and then he went to his room and wrote till ten, and so to bed." But his brother did not make him comfortable or treat him well, and the whole conditions of life were such as he could not endure for long, so he started with his nephew to go back to Vienna on December 2, 1826.

Unfortunately, they could not get a closed vehicle to travel in, and the journey had to be done in an open carriage. The condition of his health rendered him quite unfit for such exposure, and when he arrived home he became very ill with cold, which developed into inflammation of the lungs, and was followed by dropsy. The illness lasted long; but it did not at first alarm him or his friends enough for them to think there was any serious danger. His most faithful attendants were two members of that same von Breuning family who had been almost his first friends in the old Bonn days and Schindler, who left the account of him before referred to. He was not allowed to compose, so he took to reading, both literature and music. He tried Sir Walter Scott, but could not get on with him, as he thought "that he wrote for money." He also read some of Schubert's songs, and thought they were real music, and he had a great quantity of Handel's works by him, apparently for the first time in his life. About the middle of March, 1827, he got seriously worse, and was unable to go on even with writing letters, and now foresaw that the end was coming. He said to his friends in a grimly humorous way, characteristic of him, "*Plaudite, amici, comedia finita est*"—Applaud, friends! the comedy is ended. The struggle with death was long and terrible. His strength was so great that he seemed to wrestle with it. On the evening of March 26, there came on a sudden storm of thunder and lightning, and in the midst of the rattle of hail and wild commotion of the elements, he died.

The funeral, which took place on the 29th, was attended by an enormous crowd of people, mourning in real earnest; and masses were performed, and addresses on his memory were read, and every token was given of the immense admiration in which he was held. All over the civilised world it was felt that a man of the most powerful character and unique genius was gone; and yet to the public of that day his music was not a tithe of what it is to musicians of the present. His far-reaching mind went beyond their understanding; and even now, though half a century has passed away, there is still a vast store of beauty of the most exalted and noble kind which the public has not attained to. He is one of the few great creators of art whom a man, though he be ever so blessed with musical intelligence, may study for a lifetime and never exhaust.

VII.

CARL MARIA VON WEBER

UNTIL near the end of the eighteenth century, all the greatest composers had sprung from the masses of the people. Carl Maria von Weber was the first who came of an aristocratic stock. His ancestors were Austrian barons, the bulk of whose property had been lost in great European wars, and some of whom had latterly led the demoralising kind of life which was too often the lot of their class, in the second-rate courts of Germany. They went by degrees down the hill, and funds and circumstances got lower and lower as time went on, till in the lifetime of Carl Maria's father, Franz Anton, they had become as low as they well could be. In his case, even the struggle for the ordinary means of subsistence had become a hard one, and the tone and style of his life followed the downward course of his fortunes and became thoroughly unsatisfactory.

The family had long had the reputation of being musical and of having a taste for the stage, and in Franz Anton's case these qualities appear to have come to a climax. He began life as a gay officer in the guard of the Elector of the Palatinate. After seeing some service and a good deal of dissipation, he made one step towards settling down in life by marrying a lady of some means, and getting the appointment of judge and municipal councillor in the domains of the Elector of Cologne. But his tastes and his erratic character stood in the way of his fitness for a steady career, and after wasting his wife's fortune, and possibly accelerating her death by his unsatisfactory ways, he lost his good position, and became first a director of a travelling theatrical company, then a Kapellmeister; and he was finally reduced to the not over-dignified or remunerative position of a town musician in a second-rate place called Eutin. Before he settled down there he was married again to a lady of good family in Vienna, by name Genovefa von Brenner; and he took her with him to Eutin, where the famous composer Carl Maria was born in 1786.

The mother appears to have been delicate, and her health was not improved by her husband's ways, and the son was weak and sickly from his birth. The father's treatment of him was not calculated to strengthen him; for he had been smitten with a fancy for playing the part which Leopold Mozart had played with his famous son, and figuring as the guide and proprietor of a youthful prodigy. To attain this end, Carl Maria was vigorously educated in music from his earliest years, though in a very different manner from Mozart. The father was at best no more than a flashy amateur, and was not so anxious that his prodigy should be substantially grounded as that he should astonish the public by his performances. He could not educate his son himself, or even wisely superintend or regulate the system of his education, so he put him under several masters in succession; the best of whom were Heuschkel, Haydn's brother Michael, and Kalcher, the court organist at Munich. The youthful prodigy was pressed onwards to produce large musical works before his education was complete, and when he was barely fourteen, an opera, called *Das Waldmädchen*, or *The Dumb Girl of the Forest*, was produced first at Freiberg in Saxony, and then at Chemnitz. Its success was not great, but the father persevered and pressed him on to fresh exertions, and two years later another opera, called *Peter Schmoll and his Neighbours*, was written and performed at Augsburg, in 1803, without making any great mark.

Carl Maria was already showing signs of genius, but the whole method of his life and education, except so far as it gave him intimate acquaintance with the stage, was thoroughly prejudicial to his character and the standard of his art. His father shifted him from place to place and from master to master. After Michael Haydn, he chose a fashionable musician, called the Abbé Vogler, as master for his son, and Vogler did him the good service of advising him to study *Volkslieder*, and also helped him to gain the appointment of conductor at Breslau. Some good at least came of this, for the son was removed from the immediate influence of his father, and had a good opportunity to apply his mind to the practical concerns of theatrical management and the conducting of an orchestra; for both of which occupations he showed considerable aptitude. But the advantages of this position only lasted for a short time. He was too young to bear so much responsibility, and jealousy or other causes made him enemies. So, after two years, in which time foolish connections and dissipated living had loaded him with debts, and the singular accident of drinking some chemical acid by mistake, instead of wine, had additionally weakened his constitution, - the appointment had to be abandoned.

Soon afterwards, he had the good fortune to be made conductor of the band of a prince of the house of Württemberg for a little while, and when the establishment had to be broken up, owing to the pressure of the wars, his master recommended him to head-quarters at the court of Württemberg. Here, he figured in a new position as private secretary to Duke Louis, a younger brother of the king; and with a mind already unsettled by the frivolous tone of his father's life, along with the complete absence of any healthy principles of conduct, he was subjected to the seductions of one of the most dissipated and extravagant courts of Europe. The excitability of his artistic nature helped to lead him astray, and the least that can be said of his life was that it burdened him yet more heavily with debts. Before long, matters were made worse by the appearance of his father upon the scene. His influence must always have been bad, but on this occasion, he brought about more substantial evil in the shape of very serious disgrace upon himself and his son.

The account of this important point in Weber's life has been told differently by various biographers. But whatever the true explanation may be, there can be no doubt that the source of trouble was the money difficulties which the folly and extravagance of both father and son brought upon themselves. The necessity of getting supplies, of course, devolved upon the son, as the father did nothing but spend; and in order to procure a loan, he had to condescend to some expedient which laid him open to disgrace upon discovery. The king regarded him with animosity, both as an accessory to Duke Louis's extravagance and also for the charming practical joke of sending someone who asked him where the royal washerwoman lived into the king's own apartment. The king was, therefore, only too glad of the opportunity, and chance aided him to make it more effective. Just at this time, a new opera of Weber's, called *Silvana*, was being rehearsed; and the situation was enhanced by the appearance of the police in the theatre, who carried off the unfortunate composer there and then, and threw him into prison. At the trial that followed, Weber's innocence was said to be established. But the king would not relent, and both father and son were conducted to the frontier and expelled from the kingdom.

This event marked a significant crisis in the earlier part of the career of the composer. He did not, by any means, succeed in throwing off at once the inclination for frivolity and dissipation, which must have had a strong hold upon him after the long traditions of his family and the vicious influences to which his father had subjected him in his youth. However, the disaster acted as a sort of check upon him, and from that time he began to set his face toward a more steadfast cultivation of his art; and his character, which had always had some good and even beautiful elements mixed up with the bad, began to gain in solidity and steadiness from this time forward.

He took up his abode first in Mannheim, where he had some excellent friends, the most notable of whom were Gottfried Weber, a famous musical theorist; a young friend called Gänsbacher, with whom in after years he carried on a very large correspondence; and a clever young Jew called Beer, who at that time had a great name as a pianoforte player, but in later days was famous all over the world as a composer of operas, under the name of Meyerbeer. With the latter, Weber became intimate, and his great gifts as a pianist stirred him to exert himself in the same line; for Weber also had great advantages in a large and supple hand and a decided instinct for effect in pianoforte playing, and the rivalry he now found himself drawn into made him put his gifts to good uses.

He set to work again vigorously at composition, and in Gottfried Weber's house, he began a new opera called *Abu Hassan*, which was finished in the course of the year. His fame as a player and composer began to spread abroad, and he was not only encouraged to give concerts in various towns but found opportunities to get his operas performed as well. The opera *Silvana*, which had been so grimly interrupted at Stuttgart, was performed at Frankfort; but, according to his own account, it was deprived of the success it ought to have had by a lady balloonist, called Blanchard, fixing the same evening for an ascent, which caused "restlessness and distraction in the public in the theatre," who had only half their minds to attend to the opera with, the other being occupied with the prospect of the excitement which was to follow. Nevertheless, it seems to have been well enough received, and in the next year, *Abu Hassan* was performed with more substantial signs of approval at Munich, from whence it spread over Germany and even reached to England.

To himself, he seemed in those days to have been dogged by perpetual ill luck, and his letters and writings are full of complaints of the perversity of fortune and cruel want of success. This probably arose from his delicacy and ill health, along with the excitable life he had gone through, which produced morbid sensitiveness and made him lay extra stress on everything that seemed to thwart him or check the flow of his wishes. A curious paper written by him about this time throws light on his character, with its interesting mixture of gaiety and melancholy. It is evidently a sudden outbreak of feeling, which must have been very acute to make him put it on paper. It begins by describing himself as "weighed down by the struggle against adverse circumstances," but having attained "such apparent calmness that few under the cheerful exterior would be likely to discover the grief which distressed and consumed him, oppressing and irritating both body and soul." He goes on, - "How could any poor mortal boast of circumstances more adverse and oppressive, or more unpropitious to all talent, than myself? From the hour of my birth, the path of my life assumed a very different aspect from that of other men. I cannot revel in the remembrance of a gay, frolicsome childhood; no uncontrolled youth gladdened me; still young in years, I am old in experience; all comes through myself and from myself, and nothing from others. I have never loved, for reason always too quickly showed me that all those by whom I foolishly fancied myself beloved were only trifling with me for the most pitiful motives. My faith in womanhood, of whom I cherish a high ideal within my heart, is gone forever, and with it a large share of my pretensions to human happiness." And so he runs on in one piteous wail, ending - "In short, misery is the lot of man; never attaining to perfection, always discontented, at war with himself; unstable, yet ever moving on, devoid of strength, volition, and repose; the fleeting impressions on his mind vanishing as soon as made, of which these utterances from the depths of my heart are proofs."

It is probably not uncommon for young people of poetical or artistic temperament to have fits of this sort, especially if they have ever been demoralized by dissipation and happen to have aspirations. But in Weber, it points to a condition of morbid weakness which was part of his constitution and was only kept from expressing itself in his music by the show of excitement and gaiety, along with the brilliant effects which make it sometimes appear rather shallow and superficial; and it was only kept in the background of his life by constant activity, which in his later years scarcely gave him time for the lonely luxury of melancholy.

Not long after writing this paper, he began a more active life and started on a prolonged concert tour through Germany and Switzerland, during the greater portion of which he was accompanied by a friend called Baermann, who was a remarkably able clarinet player. He visited Prague and Leipsic and Dresden and Berlin and Gotha and Weimar, and many other places, making friends everywhere and rousing enthusiasm by his playing. While he was at Berlin, the news came from Gottfried Weber that his father was dead. He was, of course, prepared for such an event, but he seems to have been a good deal affected by it; and if the accounts that exist of the father's history are true, he hardly seems to have deserved such dutiful words as the son wrote in his diary: "It is beyond measure painful to me that I could do no more to promote his happiness. May God bless him for all the great love he bore me, which I did not deserve, and for the education which he bestowed upon me."

When his long tour came to an end in 1813, he went to Prague, where he had the good fortune to be appointed musical director to the theatre. The opera there had gotten into a very bad condition, and the public had become quite apathetic about it. Weber set himself vigorously to work to regenerate it. He went to Vienna to gather a proper company together and then instituted a series of frequent rehearsals with a view to making the performances as good as possible. In the course of these events, he was brought into contact with a woman called Thérèse Brunetti, who had been a dancer and had risen to take small parts as an actress. He was completely fascinated by her and fell an easy victim to her designs. For some time, he led the most pitiable and unedifying life at her mercy. He did indeed manage to keep level with the actual work he had to do for the theatre, but in other respects, his art was neglected, and he seemed to exist only to strive for some return for his misplaced adoration. This was fortunately his last folly on a grand scale, as his hitherto erratic affections soon became concentrated on an object more worthy of him.

In his search for singers to strengthen his company, he bethought himself of a certain Caroline Brandt, who had very much pleased him in the principal part of his opera *Silvana* when it was performed at Frankfort. He procured her engagement, and on her arrival, she soon justified his hopes and delighted the public as well. She was the very opposite of Thérèse Brunetti, and Weber had quite enough appreciation of good qualities to feel the superiority of her refinement and quiet self-restraint over the vulgar wildness of the object of his late adoration. Through a fortunate accident, he was much thrown together with Caroline Brandt, and very shortly thereafter, he transferred his affections to her; and after no long time, they were engaged.

Other circumstances combined with this happy arrangement to call out all the better side of his nature and to direct him into a more healthy and noble style of thought and living, which he followed from that time forward. The German people were, at this time, roused to an unusual pitch of patriotic enthusiasm by feeling themselves free from their long troubles with the French. Napoleon appeared to have been successfully tamed and exiled, and the Germans felt themselves strong and triumphant. Art has often profited greatly from a powerful stimulus of this kind, and the national enthusiasm of this time raised Weber to a height which he had never attained before. The first fruits were some of the finest national songs ever produced, the most popular of which are the settings of Lieder from Körner's *Leyer und Schwert* as choruses for men's voices. The success of these songs immensely improved his position before the world and probably helped to steady him. However, it did not at once help to make his life any smoother. One trouble arose directly from it, for Caroline Brandt was a great admirer of Napoleon, and Weber's superb national songs only served to intensify the difference of opinion between them on a most important subject. Various other difficulties sprang up, and while he was away for a time on leave, she wrote to him that their engagement must be broken off. Fortunately, this trouble did not last for long, as on his return, he showed himself to be in such a very miserable condition that she was brought to a better mind.

A more serious disaster shortly followed. For unexplained reasons, he appears to have made enemies among people in power at Prague, and a very harsh and unfair report was made upon the condition of the opera under his direction. He could not do otherwise under the circumstances than send in his resignation, and he was once more thrown upon the world without any definite fixed position. His first thought was to try to get the Kapellmeistership at Berlin, where, in order to prepare the way, a performance of a new patriotic cantata of his called *Kampf und Sieg* was performed. This project was, however, interrupted by a proposal for him to undertake the organization of a German opera at Dresden, where for nearly a century the German inhabitants had been obliged to content themselves with operas in a language they could not understand, in deference to the Italian tastes of their rulers and the courtly aristocrats who attended upon them. The King of Saxony was strongly opposed to this arrangement, as he preferred his Italian singers and the aristocratic traditions of Italian opera in Germany. But through the activity and enthusiasm of a certain Count Vitzthum, it was nevertheless carried out, and Weber was successfully installed as Kapellmeister.

The task he was set to do was not by any means an easy one, and he had an uphill battle to fight. The King of Saxony himself had every reason to dislike Weber, as his interests were all with Napoleon and strongly against the patriotic enthusiasm of which Weber's national songs were the finest musical expression. Besides this, all the people who clung to the Italian opera looked upon Weber as the center of antagonism, and the Italians themselves, headed by their own director Morlacchi, had more reason than they usually required to incite them to work underground. They were paralyzed and kept quiet for a time by Weber's vigor and ability, but their native talent for intrigue asserted itself in the end, and they succeeded in worrying him into a state in which his feeble constitution was singularly open to the attacks of disease.

But they could not prevent him from achieving those works which have given him the right to be counted among the few great composers. The first step which led to an actual beginning of his greatest masterpiece was his meeting with the poet Friedrich Kind, who had some experience in writing and some knowledge of the stage. Weber had come across the story of Der Freischütz some years before in a book of Apel's called *Gespenster Geschichten*, and had taken a fancy to it. He now proposed to Kind to turn this into a libretto for him, and in a very short time, Kind finished the work. Weber's first idea was to call it *Jägersbraut*, or The Hunter's Bride, and under that name, it is referred to in a letter to his friend Gänsbacher, written in March 1817, where he says, "I mean soon to set to work at a new opera which the well-known poet, Friedrich Kind, has written for me, the *Jägersbraut*, a very romantic, mysterious, beautiful work." It is again mentioned under the same name in his diary as having been begun in July of the same year. However, it was not permitted to be worked out at once, and he suffered from many and long interruptions in the course of it. Not only was his work as director of the new opera house very severe, but he had to attend to preparations for his marriage with Caroline Brandt and for housing her afterwards. They were married at last in November 1817, after several years of waiting, and there can be no doubt that Weber's life was immensely improved both in happiness and in character from that time forward, though his health began to show signs of serious collapse. The worries which the intriguing partisans of the Italian opera brought upon him culminated in a severe illness which lasted some time and evidently stopped his work. But he still must have had a great fund of spirits and a power of elasticity, for almost before he was well, he produced the famous *Invitation à la Valse*, the happiness and delicacy of which seem perfectly serene and unclouded. In the next year, 1819, he was able to return more steadily to work at his opera, and early in 1820, it was finished. His spirits rose, and his health improved in congenial work, along with the sense that what he was doing was thoroughly worthy of him; and this year was probably the happiest of his life, as it was also the climax of his career.

Owing to the hostility of many people in power at Dresden, it was not possible to have the new work first brought out there; but arrangements were made for its performance in Berlin, where at that time Weber was really better appreciated. The performance took place under Weber's direction in the Schauspielhaus on June 13th, 1820, and the success it won did great credit to the audience.

The occasion marks an epoch in the history of operatic art. It was the first great opera that was German through and through. In the early days of the history of opera, the German race seemed to have but little aptitude for composition in that line. All through the seventeenth and the first half of the eighteenth centuries, the Italians had been complete masters of the field. Even Handel, though by birth a German, had become a disciple of the Italian school in opera writing; and Gluck, after beginning in the same line and following the usual models, tried to carry on his most necessary reforms at first in Italian at Vienna, and later not in Germany at all, but in Paris. Mozart, in his turn, had experimented with a German opera comparatively early in his career at the instigation of the Emperor of Austria, but it was with an eastern and not a national subject, and after writing it, he was driven by force of circumstances to resume the Italian line again and only made one more attempt at German opera at the end of his life in the shape of the Zauberflöte. How ripe the public were for native products is shown by the success which this work ultimately achieved; and in many respects, it was characteristically German, though the fairy elements and many of the characters and much of the music were certainly anything but Teutonic. Then came Beethoven with *Fidelio*, in which the music was most essentially German, and the story so also as far as earnestness and thoroughness were concerned; but still, it was not so in respect of the actual circumstances, scenes, and personages of the play. At last, Weber comes into the field and puts the final touch to the efforts and aspirations of generations of composers by producing a work that is German in music and in story, both as concerns the spirit and the actual scene chosen, in which the characters are essentially German, and the poetry is infused with such thoughts as are dearest to the German mind. Besides all these advantages, it had qualities that would have given it the highest rank based on its own merits. As a play, it was, for the most part, extremely attractive, and the best parts had been set to music by Weber with unsurpassable insight into the situations, whether it was Agatha in anxiety over the fate of her lover, or in the weird scene in the Wolf's Glen, or in the situations of lesser prominence. All the characters, from the wild and headstrong meddler in magic to the light and simple-minded Aennchen, were perfectly expressed in the music allotted to them. The most superb orchestration, melody, dramatic climax, and even musical form all worked together to make the work of art as high and perfect in its way as it could be. The success with the public was great, and its position as one of the great masterpieces of operatic art was not long in becoming established. However, as usually happens in such cases, the wiseacres decided against it. What the music expresses to people in these days seems so simple, so natural, true, and spontaneous that it appears utterly incomprehensible how anyone could have failed to recognize its merits. Nevertheless, Spohr, the famous violinist and composer, wrote of it in terms that imply irritated contempt; and Zelter, the renowned master who drilled Mendelssohn in his younger days, also spoke of it in terms of elaborate derision. Others joined in swelling the adverse chorus. Weber was singularly sensitive to such matters, as successful men sometimes are, and he suffered from them and resented them. Nevertheless, setting aside such drawbacks, the visit to Berlin on this occasion was the brightest moment in his career, and his success placed him in a position among living composers in which his only superior was Beethoven.

When he got back to Dresden, he found that his well-earned success made little difference to his position there. He had to take up his work just as he had left it, with no diminishment of its drudgery or the slights that he suffered. *Freischütz* was ultimately performed there also in 1822, but the opportunity seemed to have been wrung from the authorities with difficulty, and its success was not followed by any sort of recognition from them.

But its general success in the country was too great for him to rest upon his laurels, and it was time to be looking out for another subject. Unfortunately, Kind, the able writer of *Der Freischütz*, had quarreled with him, either on the grounds that his work had been meddled with or that he had not received a fair share of the profits arising from its success. In his search for someone to replace him, Weber fell into the clutches of a conceited aspirant to the fame of a poetess called Helmina von Chezy. She proposed a romantic and rambling story of knights and fine ladies, which went by the name of *The History of Gerard de Nevers and the Beautiful and Virtuous Euryanthe*, and Weber was unwisely persuaded to accept it without testing the lady's literary abilities or her powers of putting it into a dramatic form. The work, almost before it was begun, was assigned to Vienna for its first performance. In order to see what sort of artists would be available for the performance and to adapt his music to their requirements, he went there at once. On his way, he stopped at Prague to conduct a performance of *Freischütz*. At Vienna itself, where a mangled version had been given until his arrival, he was able to superintend its performance in its original state and to be rewarded by the enthusiasm of the public.

After his return home, he took his wife to a farmhouse at Hosterwitz, a place overlooking the Elbe, near Pillnitz. In the midst of beautiful countryside and forest scenery, for which he always had a very great liking, he continued with the composition of the new opera, *Euryanthe*. It was a common practice for Weber to do a great part of his composing in his head while he was walking or journeying, before he put it down on paper. Several of the famous patriotic songs set to Theodor Körner's words had been produced in such a manner, and a good deal of *Euryanthe* was developed during lonely walks in the woods near Pillnitz. However, as he progressed with his work, he began to realize what hopeless stuff he was committed to by his connection with the ridiculous Helmina von Chezy, and great was the trouble that was spent in endeavoring to make the story in any way effective. Fortunately, he was spared such frequent interruptions as had come during the composition of *Freischütz*, and he finished the whole work at his farmhouse in the country in August 1823. A short spell of hard drudgery at Dresden followed, and then he set out for Vienna for the performance of the new opera. While he was there on this occasion, he paid a visit to Beethoven, a most graphic account of which has been given by Sir Julius Benedict, who was Weber's pupil and was with him at the time.

Weber's opinions of Beethoven had undergone a significant change since he had learned to take a higher view of art. In his early years, he had written contemptuous criticisms of Beethoven's mature work. In a letter to Nägeli, the publisher, written when he was about twenty-five, he said, with complacency worthy of an ignorant amateur, that "his view differed far too much from Beethoven's for them ever to come into contact. The fiery inventive faculty that inspires him is attended by so many complications in the arrangement of the ideas that it is only his earlier compositions that interest me; the later ones, on the contrary, appeared to me only a confused chaos, an unintelligible struggle after novelty, from which occasional heavenly flashes of genius dart forth, showing how great he might be if he chose to control his luxuriant fancy." He tried to atone for this folly and presumption in the years when he had grown wiser, by making an energetic attempt to get a thoroughly fine performance of *Fidelio* while he was directing the opera at Prague in 1822. At the time he was in Vienna, his feeling for the great master had risen to as high a pitch of reverent appreciation as anyone could desire. Beethoven, in his turn, highly appreciated the composer of *Der Freischütz* and sent an invitation to him to come and see him at Baden, the place near Vienna where he used to go to enjoy country air and freedom. Benedict accompanied his master, and they found Beethoven in his dressing gown in a room that was a perfect chaos of papers and clothes, cups, and other things he had been using, all covered with dust. He gave Weber a vigorous welcome and took them out as soon as he was dressed to the place where he usually dined. They talked congenially with the help of Beethoven's pencil and notebook, and Beethoven took an interest in hearing about the prospects of Euryanthe. Weber, for his part, wrote of the interview in his diary: "We dined together in the happiest mood; the stern, rough man paid me as much attention as if I were a lady he were courting and served me with the most delicate care. How proud I felt to receive all this attention and regard from the great master spirit!"

The performance of the opera took place after numerous rehearsals at the Kärnthnerthor Theatre in October. Expectation was wrought up to the highest pitch, and the house was so full that the portly Helmina von Chezy, who arrived rather late, loudly demanding "room for the poetess," had to be passed to her place over the heads of the audience. The earlier part of the opera was received with vociferous enthusiasm. Several numbers were encored, and the performance seemed likely to be dragged out in consequence to an unseasonable length. As the libretto passed drearily into an unintelligible stage, the interest of the audience flagged, but towards the end, it revived again; and when the curtain fell, the applause and shouts for Weber seemed to betoken another great success. In fact, there are things in *Euryanthe* as superb and beautiful as anything in *Freischütz*, but the drama is so desperately foolish and unintelligible that the music cannot save it. The public and capable judges took great delight for the time in the beautiful passages, but in the end, the libretto dragged it down, and in the course of the performances that followed, the public and the performers alike grew apathetic, and adverse criticisms began to make their appearance. Weber, before that time, had gone back to his wife at Dresden in the full belief that the opera was, after all, a success. As usual, the unfavorable criticisms took a heavy toll on his overstrained constitution, and he began to show signs of breaking down. Composition came to an end for a long time, and everything seemed to presage the approach of a fatal malady. He himself felt that he had not much more time before him, and after first trying to do his usual work with assistance, he was obliged to take complete rest from the routine of his office as Kapellmeister and go into the country.

About this time, he received an invitation from England to write an opera in English for performance at Covent Garden. This opportunity opened to his mind a prospect of making enough money to leave his family fairly well off if his life should not last much longer. For as far as he had gone, he had been able to lay but little by, chiefly owing to the debts he had contracted in his early years and the legacy of similar obligations left to him by his father. However, he felt at the same time that a journey to England was a considerable risk, especially in his enfeebled state. He called in his doctor to advise him, and the doctor's stern verdict was that the only hope for his life was a visit to some warm climate. Nevertheless, Weber was so buoyed up with the hope of making some money for his family that, in defiance of his doctor's decision, he made up his mind to accept the invitation. The subject chosen for the opera was *Oberon*, which was adapted into an opera-book by J. R. Planché, who had considerable reputation in England as a writer of theatrical pieces.

To add to his labors, Weber had to begin learning English, as it was a language he was almost totally ignorant of. Notwithstanding the wretched state of his health, the opera progressed rapidly, as did his knowledge of the new language. He also resumed his duties as Kapellmeister and superintended performances of other men's works with the same care as usual. Before starting for England, he paid one more visit to Berlin to direct another performance of *Euryanthe*, and he was received with affectionate enthusiasm by both the public and his old friends. Then he returned once more to his family at Dresden, where he put the final touches to the new opera. It would have been a great thing for him if his wife could have accompanied him; however, her health and that of one of their younger children was too poor for such a thing to be thought of, so he had to make up his mind to go by himself. Fortunately, a friendly flute-player, by the name of Fürstenau, offered to go with him to take care of him. On February 16th, 1826, with dreary forebodings, he bid farewell to his wife and family and started on his journey.

He went by way of Paris, and though he intended to keep quite quiet, he could not resist the temptation to pay visits to many of the famous musicians there, such as Cherubini, Auber, and Rossini, who welcomed him with the utmost kindness. When he arrived in England, the weather happened to be good, and he was delighted with the scenery, the fast traveling by coach, and the friendliness of the people who called upon him. He anticipated a brilliant success and substantial profit from the journey. He was comfortably lodged in the house of Sir George Smart, in Great Portland Street, where every attention was paid to his needs and the greatest care was taken of his health. He wrote to his wife that "no king could receive more proofs of love and interest, for he was spoiled in every possible way." He had to make his appearance and conduct at public concerts; and in the hopes of making a better sum total out of the expedition, he even condescended to attend private concerts at the houses of rich and fashionable aristocrats. This was, of course, not conducive to his health, nor was it conducive to his happiness, for he very soon found out what hollow affairs such private concerts for fashionable crowds almost invariably are. The only occasion which afforded him a pleasant experience in his relations with people of high position was a visit he was invited to pay to members of the royal family at the Duchess of Kent's, where, like Handel and Haydn in similar circumstances, he met with both kind sympathy and appreciation.

As the rehearsals of his opera proceeded, his hopes began to fall. The performers who had been chosen for the work could not bear any comparison with those he had been accustomed to abroad. Many of them were quite inefficient, and the more able ones gave themselves airs and demanded all sorts of alterations to suit their convenience. He submitted patiently to their whims and accommodated them as well as was possible; and by one means or another, in the course of sixteen laborious rehearsals, he made sure of a good performance.

This took place on April 12th, 1826. The house was crowded as full as it could hold, and the audience was completely wrapped in delighted attention throughout, and at the end burst into reiterated shouts for the composer. He wrote to his wife the same night that he had perhaps never before experienced such a perfect success. "When I entered the orchestra, the whole house rose as of one accord, and an incredible applause, cheers, and the waving of hats and handkerchiefs received me, and was hardly to be quieted." However, the excitement and strain were too much for his broken state of health, and the next morning, Fürstenau found him in a state bordering on collapse. He was longing to see his wife and boys again and began to look forward to the day when he would be starting homewards once more. But he had promised to conduct twelve performances of *Oberon* first, and this engagement, notwithstanding the critical condition he was in, he made up his mind to fulfill. He arranged to give a concert on his own account, hoping that after the success of his opera, people would come in crowds, and that the receipts would make a weighty addition to his treasury. Upon this concert, he set great expectations. Almost all the conspicuous musicians in London were to take part in it, and the program was prepared with great care to make the whole affair as attractive as possible. Weber wrote a new song for Miss Stephens, a favorite singer of the day, and promised to play her accompaniment himself. The day of the concert arrived, but not the audience. Some people were drawn in another direction by horse races; all the most fashionable people went where they were sure of meeting one another and of being able to talk, which was to a concert given by a fashionable singing-master in the house of a noble duke; and to complete the adverse fortune, the rain came down in torrents. When Weber came into the concert-room, it was only half full. The performers did their best, and as far as music was concerned, Weber thought it was one of the most brilliant concerts he had ever given, but a good performance could not alter the receipts. Instead of a good lump sum, which was worth trying for, even at a risk to his health, all he had to show for his efforts was the paltry sum of £96.

The disappointment evidently affected him very much, and his health took a decidedly worse turn. The doctors concluded that the only chance for him was to avoid all excitement and to rest. He had to be persuaded to give up any hopes of more concerts or benefit performances and to be satisfied with the rather disappointing financial results he had attained thus far. His thoughts now all centered on getting back to his wife and children, and he wrote to the former not to address any more letters to him in London but to expect him very soon, as he intended to avoid Paris and take the shortest route back to her.

In a letter dated June 2nd, he mentioned that he was still very excited and suffering but longing to be on the way. He ended: - "As this letter requires no answer, it must necessarily be very short. Isn't it nice not to be obliged to answer? Fürstenau has given up his concert. This may enable me to come perhaps even a few days sooner. Hurrah! May God bless you all and keep you well. Would I were amidst you! I send you the tenderest kisses, my beloved wife. Preserve your love for me and think joyfully of him who cherishes you above all." These must have been the last words he wrote to his wife. He had made up his mind to start homewards on the 6th. His condition was so bad, and he suffered so much from pain and exhaustion that his friends tried to persuade him to postpone the journey for a little while. But this only seemed to annoy and upset him. On the evening of the 4th, he had a few friends with him at Sir George Smart's house, who looked after him anxiously and persuaded him to go to bed early. He thanked them affectionately for all their kindness and bolted himself into his room. They, being in great anxiety about him, sat up long consulting how they might persuade him to postpone his journey. However, their decision on that point was not required; the journey was postponed for a long while without their interference. Early the next morning, they went to his door but could get no answer. It had to be broken open, and then they found him lying as if in sleep, having passed tranquilly away.

His body was embalmed, and after a few days, it was buried in Moorfields, where an imposing ceremony was organized in the Roman Catholic chapel. The orchestras and choruses of the principal theatres, where *Der Freischütz* and *Oberon* had been performed, offered their services, and a performance of Mozart's *Requiem* was prepared. The feeling of sympathy and regret was universal; crowds even lined the streets where the procession passed between Sir George Smart's house and Moorfields. The chapel was full to overflowing with people who were anxious to pay their last respects to the composer. In Moorfields, his body remained for many years; but Germans, who felt how strong a national representative he was, could not be content that he should rest in a foreign land. Finally, in 1844, partly through Richard Wagner's exertions, the body was conveyed back to his native country. The second funeral was even more imposing than the first, for by that time, his works had thoroughly established their right to the highest place as great national works of art, and they had taken possession of the hearts of the most musical nation in the world. The body was brought by sea to Hamburg, and thence it was slowly transported up the Elbe, being delayed by hard frosts. At last, in December, it arrived at Dresden, which now paid him the full honors it had grudged in his lifetime. The streets were filled with people, and between long lines of mourners carrying torches, he was borne to the chapel of the Catholic cemetery in Friedrichstadt. The next day, in the presence of a crowd of people, the body was lowered into the grave while music of his own was performed, and Richard Wagner made a speech of farewell. "There never was a more German composer than thou. Into whatever distant, fathomless realms of fancy thy genius bore thee, it remained bound by a thousand tender links to the heart of thy German people, with whom it wept or smiled like a believing child listening to the legends and tales of its country."

It is this thoroughly German and romantic spirit which gained Weber his great position in the history of music. It is not through depth of thought, or greatness and nobility of poetical conception, or power of technical ingenuity, or counterpoint, or perfection of form that he stands so high, but rather through the natural, spontaneous outburst of genial and bright thoughts which express almost more than any other man's work the character of the nation to which he belonged.

His greatest works are his three latest operas and the music to the play *Preciosa*, and they are, in themselves, enough to establish his fame. Next in importance comes his pianoforte music. In this branch of art, he was also one of the few greatest masters. His brilliant style was quite his own, and even the way in which he uses his hands is original. He himself had a very large hand and could grasp chords which, to most people, are impossible and often need to be arranged slightly to make them playable by ordinary hands on modern pianofortes. The style of his writing is brilliant in the extreme and most effective from the point of view of an experienced performer, such as Weber himself was. In depth of feeling and richness of tone, he never approaches Beethoven, and the balance and form of movements on a grand scale, as in sonatas, are often rather unsatisfactory. However, his romantic feeling, along with his brightness and neatness, are all his own and go far to atone for these deficiencies.

A curious account is given of one of his most famous works for the pianoforte, in which he appears to have tried to tell a sort of story. It was on the very morning of the first performance of *Der Freischütz*, while all his friends were in the greatest anxiety about the critical moment that was approaching, that Weber brought to his wife and his pupil, Benedict, a new work that he had just finished, which he sat down to play for them. He first gave them an account of what it was all about: how a lady is supposed to sit in her tower thinking of her knight who has gone to the Crusades, and imagining that he may be lying wounded on the field of battle, perhaps dying, and longing for one more sight of her. In her excited imagination, the picture is so real that she faints away, when suddenly from the woods without, comes the sound of men approaching. She looks out anxiously, and there is her lover, and with a wild outburst of joy, she rushes into his arms. And thereupon, Weber played for them, for the first time, the famous *Concertstück*, which all great pianists since have regarded as among the most effective of such pieces, and which is one of his most successful works on a large scale for the pianoforte. This story sheds some light on his ways of thought and illustrates the curious liking for legends and romantic stories of knights and ladies, which was probably at the bottom of his being led to the unfortunate mistake of setting Helmina von Chezy's inspirations to music. It also illustrates his connection with the very important tendency of modern composers of instrumental music to adopt programmes.

Composers had long been smitten with the idea of illustrating things through music, but they had never found out how to do it successfully, or what the true subjects to illustrate were. In the seventeenth century, old masters like Kuhnau and Froberger had tried their hands at illustrating biblical stories, such as David killing Goliath, or battle scenes, such as a German army crossing the Rhine in difficulties, or even such abstruse things as the motions of planets. Bach had made one interesting little programme piece on a much more suitable subject in the *Capriccio on the Departure of a Beloved Brother*. In Mozart and Haydn's time, the principal composers paid attention chiefly to design and devised regular principles on which one tune should be made to balance another. They modulated with such effect as to achieve a good impression of the whole from the point of view of form, without much thought for the meaning or spirit of the work. Beethoven began to give his attention to meaning as well, and he realized, first of all, clearly what sort of subjects and what sort of treatment was possible in music which was based on a programme. He saw that what was wanted was not musical pictures, but rather the expression of the emotions that belonged to the story, articulated in musical terms. He gave great illustrations of the most perfect ways of carrying it out in the *Eroica* and *Pastoral Symphonies*, and in other great works. Weber was moved by a similar impulse, for it was always more natural to him to feel the poetical side than the formal side of his art. In the latter respect, it is probable that his early training under the supervision of his scatterbrained parent was defective. However, when he was aided by lyrics such as Körner's, or by dramatic situations like those in *Der Freischütz*, or by a romantic conception such as he took as the basis of the famous *Concertstück*, he immediately found the natural outlet and form for his musical ideas.

He had the advantage in working out his operas of being a man of some culture and superior perception in other matters besides music. He possessed no inconsiderable literary gifts, and besides leaving a considerable collection of letters, he produced, chiefly in his early days, numerous critiques, which often had the generous objective of helping forward a fellow composer.

Some prominent traits of his character came out strongly in his music. That gaiety of disposition, which led him into unsatisfactory ways in his youth, shines with a purer light in his music until the last.

Even when weighed down by suffering and worry, and when he almost saw death in the way before him, the brightness and freshness of his musical thoughts came out untarnished.

Oberon, written when fatal disease had set its hand irretrievably upon him, is as full of happy, genial ideas as any work he ever wrote. No doubt, in his interactions with other people, he maintained this appearance of a good heart until the end. Another feature of his character was his excessive sensitiveness, which was demonstrated in all sorts of ways. An apparent slight was enough to make him ill, especially if it came from anyone in a high position. The way in which he allowed himself to be affected by criticisms of his work is truly surprising. Instances of composers thinking so much of printed criticisms are not indeed rare, but they are more common among second-rate men and the impostors who think more of social success, or of seeing their names in print, than of their art. Masters and men of mature judgment know how to estimate them at their proper worth. It is true that most men are naturally inclined to resent the stupidity, perverseness, or careless haste of their critics, but strength or experience generally enables them to throw off the impression without excessive annoyance. Weber's weak constitution was probably the cause of his inability to do the same, and it is likely that among the various worries that played an important part in bringing about his too early death, the critics of his time must take their place. The public were always his friends, as was indeed natural, for his music possesses all the best qualities of the people's music - broad, healthy, vigorous melody, and a clear, though not commonplace, rhythm. It also has a genuine wealth of sentiment, which is sufficiently heartfelt and sincere to escape that most common pitfall of the injudicious public: sentimentality, which is the cold-blooded aping of real feeling by shallow beings who are incapable of it.

Weber was eminently capable of real feeling, and on the whole, no trait distinguishes him more satisfactorily than his amiability and affectionate appreciation of his friends. An early expression of these qualities comes in a letter to Gänsbacher written in 1810, where he says: "These are among the happy moments of life that outweigh years of chagrin, through the feeling of having acquired the love and esteem of worthy men." A similar sentiment is put even more nobly in a letter to a friend named Susann, written fourteen years later, *apropos* of *Freischütz*: "Believe me, a great success weighs like a heavy debt upon the soul of the honest artist, and he can never pay it as he earnestly desires. What experience adds to our faculties is taken away by the decaying force of youth, and nothing remains but the consolation that everything is imperfect, and that at least we did as much as we could do."

The man who could write such words showed that the noblest qualities in his disposition had survived the dangers of his early years, when the lack of judgment and the absence of solid example in his father had almost wrecked his whole life. When he had finally left his youthful levity behind him and learned to aspire to a nobler life and a more elevated function in art, his whole nature seemed to become different. He was tried in the fire and found not wanting. The devotion he showed to his art, along with the steadfast and conscientious labor of his latter days, wiped out the mistakes of his youth and deservedly earned for him the love and admiration of the nation whose musical feelings he so fitly expressed, as well as that of all those who appreciate what is most worthy of appreciation in musical art.

VIII

FRANZ SCHUBERT.

EVERY one notices that the greatest composers have almost always had some special province of their own and have established their right to the highest rank by producing something thoroughly ripe and perfect of a kind that had not been matured before. The reasons for this phenomenon are commonly overlooked, but they are not hard to find. The processes by which great forms of musical art, such as masses, motets, oratorios, operas, symphonies, and sonatas, were made, were gradually perfected over time and have always culminated in some happily constituted individual, to whom it has been allotted to produce the first completely mature examples and to sum up in his work the labors of the musical generations that had gone before. It was conspicuously so in the cases of Palestrina, Handel, Bach, and Beethoven, and at the beginning of the present century, it came to the turn of Schubert to become the representative composer who first brought the artistic form of musical song to its mature perfection.

It may seem strange to people who have not considered the matter with any attention that song should come to perfection so late. It seems to be the simplest and most natural kind of music, as well as one of the easiest to produce and to understand. And yet, it had to wait for the development of almost all the greater forms of art before it began to appear in its perfect lineaments; it was only by means of the enormous quantity of musical work done in all the other branches, both in terms of form and expression, that song, as it has been produced by the German composers of this century, became possible.

The conditions under which perfectly artistic songs can be produced are most complicated and difficult, and all sorts of favorable circumstances have to combine for their consummation. In the first place, a genuine song requires a well-developed national style and a treatment of melody that is perfectly adapted to the language. For languages not only differ in such important matters as accent and inflection or the changing pitch of the voice, but even in the quality of the actual sound produced when they are sung. Italian naturally produces beautiful sounds when sung, and a singer requires comparatively little teaching to make his notes sound well with it; but the languages of northern nations, such as German and English, have to be managed with considerable art to make them sound agreeably. Thus, in the ordinary course of things, it is more natural for an Italian to sing and to care for beautiful vocal sounds than it is for a German. The German has to go through much more to achieve a refined and satisfactory result, and however much he manages his language, he can never make it sound as purely beautiful as an Italian does; the result has been that Germans have ultimately come to give much more attention to the effect of musical declamation, as well as to the spirit and meaning of the words, than the Italians. The latter have often been content to ignore the meaning altogether and to set the most trivial and empty sentiments to music because they only wanted words at all as something to excuse their use of their voices.

Besides this, the Germans have been driven, partly by the same causes, to give much more attention to purely instrumental music and to develop all that has distinct meaning and definite individuality in it, while southern nations have been more readily content with soft and sensuous sounds that have little real purport in their figures and subjects. This same condition of things seems to play a considerable part in deciding the curious fact that the music of the Italians has always had a decidedly vocal character and depends upon the paramount consideration given by them to vocal effects, while Germans have looked at music from an instrumental point of view, sometimes treating voices themselves too much like instruments.

These circumstances have had a great effect upon the history of songwriting, and the difficulties Germans labored under made them all the more careful and consistent in their art; this also made them much slower in coming to their maturity. For a long time, they were, as the English have been, almost entirely dominated by Italian influences in secular vocal matters. Up until Mozart's time, German composers failed altogether to produce a national opera of any solid kind, and the people had to be content with works that were Italian in spirit, Italian in style, and Italian in form, sung to them in a language they did not understand. This necessary submission to foreign rule also prevented them from producing anything thoroughly genuine in the nature of artistic song; instead of taking lyrics and dealing with them according to the poet's indications of rhythm and accent, they always tried to force their poems into the Italian forms of musical art, which had next to nothing to do with their spiritual plan. In fact, the music - as has generally been the case in England from the same cause - was really independent of the words, except in a very moderate sense; it was devised in accordance with certain supposed limitations of musical art that were believed to be necessary for its healthy maintenance, much like it was once thought necessary for the orthodox maintenance of Christianity to limit the world to the old continents, bounded on the west by the Atlantic, because the way to America had not been discovered yet.

In reality, musical art was not sufficiently advanced until Mozart's time to allow for the free development of German opera or song music; for it is much more difficult to combine sentiment and emotion with form and to make them agree together than it is to consider form first and make sentiment submit as the less important factor. In Italian works, the form was, as it were, preordained, and every item was made in the same shape, which worked very well in the Italian style of art, as it was based chiefly on the pleasantness of sound in singing. However, from the German point of view, which took ideas so much more into consideration, anything so limited would not work; thus, they had to figure out how to make the form turn and vary much more freely, without ceasing to maintain balance and proportion, and this was destined to be accomplished in their great instrumental music. They also had to figure out how to adapt the melody to their language; for as long as they wrote to nothing but Italian words, they were making no progress in that direction. These circumstances explain sufficiently why none of the great German masters, such as Haydn, Mozart, or Beethoven, made any notable contributions as genuine songwriters.

Beethoven came closest to it, as he lived more in the conditions that made it possible to deal with poems independently; he was also less inclined to submit emotional expression to the dictates of supposed laws of form, and did more than anyone else to show that the narrow confines in which theorists used to stand were only limited by their misconceptions of the conditions of art. But even he wrote very few songs and was too busy developing larger-scale works to dedicate his whole mind to the subtleties and refinements of the smaller lyrical kinds of art. However, the condition of things had progressed far enough before he passed from this world, and by the beginning of this century, there was a profusion of lyrical poems readily available to the composer, and everything combined to bring the fruit of this labor to maturity.

Franz Schubert, the illustrious composer to whose lot fell the grand opportunity of creating timeless music, was born on January 31st, 1797. The stock from which he came was a thoroughly plebeian one, for his grandfather had been a Moravian peasant. His father had migrated from the countryside to Vienna, where he became a parish schoolmaster. He married a woman by the name of Elizabeth Vitz, who was a cook, and together they had fourteen children, several of whom sadly died young. Franz was the youngest son of the first family, separated from his eldest brother Ignaz by a space of twelve years, and from his brother Ferdinand, to whom he was most deeply attached, by three years. Schoolmastering was a characteristic occupation of the family. Franz's uncle was also a schoolmaster, and these two brothers became schoolmasters as soon as they were old enough, and Franz himself, in his turn, had for some time to adopt the same calling. The family also exhibited notable musical tastes. Both Ignaz and Ferdinand played the violin, while their father played the 'cello, and they were fond of making music together. The brothers became Franz's first masters, and as soon as he surpassed their capacities, which did not take long, he was passed on to the parish choir-master Michael Holzer, who taught him the violin, pianoforte, organ, and some harmony. Holzer was immensely impressed with the boy's musical powers and said afterwards, "If ever I wished to teach him anything new, I found he already knew it. I cannot be said really to have given him lessons at all; I merely amused myself and looked on." The truth of the matter appears to have been that Franz's friends and neighbours were scarcely thorough musicians enough to know what to do with him, and many people consider that it was a great misfortune that he was not more thoroughly drilled in his youth in the mechanical part of the art. But at least it can be said that mechanical drilling and discipline could not have improved the sensitive impressionability, which was the source of his masterpieces in song writing, and it might have taken away some of his spontaneity and originality for the sake of what a theorist would consider correct and well-balanced treatment.

He developed a beautiful voice as a boy and was taken first into the choir of Lichtenthal, the parish where the family lived; from there, he was advanced at the tender age of eleven years to the school that was called the Convict, where boys were educated for the choir of the Imperial Court chapel in Vienna. In this school, his musical opportunities were significantly improved. Besides singing, the boys had a regular little band in the school, which was good enough to play the simpler kinds of symphonies that were popular in those days. Franz took his place in the band at once, as his violin practice at home and his natural ability gave him some advantages; it is also recorded that this engagement won him at once a good friend. At the time he arrived in the school, a boy called Spaun was the best violin player and led the band. One day, upon hearing someone playing unusually well behind him, he turned round to see who it was and discovered it was "a small boy in spectacles called Franz Schubert." Spaun was nine years older than Schubert, but the latter's remarkable ability bridged over the gulf which often separates boys of such different ages, and Spaun became one of his truest and most helpful friends. Franz was very poor, and Spaun appeared to be rather better off, and he did not neglect any opportunities to help his small friend. The impulse to try his hand at composition seems to have taken possession of Franz by this time, but it was hindered by the difficulties of getting anything to write upon. Among other kindnesses, Spaun helped him in this respect, and when he realized what Franz's talents were, he took good care that they should not be wasted for want of paper.

As time went on, Franz rose to be quite an important individual in the school. He became first violin in the boys' band, and his school-fellows regarded his compositions as marvellous. However, he had no one to direct him or advise him, and his early works were, for the most part, wild and irregular attempts to express himself with no better guidance than his own instincts and the knowledge he had of such models as the works they performed at the school. He wrote hugely long pianoforte pieces, as well as songs, overtures, quartets, variations, and church music; in 1813, he produced his first orchestral symphony, which marked his last composition as a boy at the Convict, for his time there came to an end in that same year, and he returned home to live once again.

The life at this school seems to have been a hard one, especially for a boy as poor as Franz was. A letter of his to one of his brothers, written late in the year before he left, gives a strong impression of the absence of any sort of enervating luxury: "I have been thinking a good long time about my position, and find that it's well enough on the whole, but might be improved in some respects; you know that one can enjoy eating a roll and an apple or two, and all the more when one must wait eight hours and a half after a poor dinner for a meagre supper. The wish has haunted me so often and so perseveringly that I must make a change. The few groschen my father gave me are all gone to the devil; what am I to do for the rest of the time?[5]

So thought I. Suppose you advance me a few kreuzers monthly. You would never miss it, whilst I should shut myself up in my cell and be quite happy. As I said, I rely on the words of the Apostle Matthew, who says, 'Let him that hath two coats give one to the poor.' Meanwhile, I trust you will listen to the voice, which appeals to you to remember your loving, hoping, poverty-stricken — and once again I repeat, poverty-stricken — brother, Franz." Besides poverty, the boys suffered bitterly in the winter from living and working in unwarmed rooms, so altogether, the picture is a very harsh one to contemplate. Nevertheless, the school afforded some advantages to Schubert, for there he gained a good deal of experience with solid music and plenty of sympathy from the other boys, and there also he made some excellent friends who remained faithful to him throughout his life.

When he got home, he found one significant change; his mother had died the year before, in 1812. However, there is very little recorded

5   'They that hope in thee shall not be ashamed.'

of the effect it had upon him or upon the ways of living at home, and before long, his father married again. The new wife did not come up to the conventional and traditional reputation of a stepmother, but treated Franz well, and she appears to have been regarded by him with affection.

It was now necessary for him to do something definite for his living, and being somewhat in dread of being taken off as a soldier, he shortly became a schoolmaster at his father's school, where he taught the lowest class. This, of course, entailed a considerable amount of drudgery, but he somehow managed to find time to pour out a constant flood of new works, and even to have lessons in composition from old Salieri, who was then *capell-meister* of the Viennese Court and had a great reputation among his contemporaries. Salieri was a man of the old school and sought to try and get Schubert into the traditional ruts, wherein respectability prefers to go leisurely along. He naturally thought most of Schubert's productions to be wild vagaries, and cautioned him against the great lyrical poets of Germany, Goethe and Schiller, whose thoughts and words seemed to him too wild and irregular for music. He even tried to make Schubert write vocal music in the old conventional forms after the Italian manner and to Italian words. This, fortunately, had very little effect upon Schubert, and if Salieri had any influence upon him at all, it probably was in lines which were less vital to his position as a representative composer. On the other hand, it must be confessed that Salieri was not a stubborn pedant altogether and had enough vital expansion in him to win a good word even from Beethoven; moreover, he was not really incapable of seeing how great Schubert's genius was, though he naturally tried to direct it into channels more congenial to his own tastes.

The extraordinary impulse to compose, which seems to have possessed Schubert more powerfully than any other composer known to history, drove him to try his hand in various directions. The year after he left the Convict school, he produced a mass for the Lichtenthal church, where his old master Holzer still reigned over the choir. The work was well performed under the boy's own direction, with some very good musicians among the performers, and it was received with enthusiasm by his friends and relatives, including Salieri, who appears to have been very complimentary and to have publicly recognized Franz as his own pupil. Another large work soon followed, which was no less than an opera called *Des Teufels Lustschloss*, and this was succeeded by another mass, as well as various other works of large calibre.

However, among these works, and in some ways more important than any of them, are the first great songs, which made their appearance around this time. A most extraordinary thing about them is that in this line, he seemed to require no preparation or education; for some of his very finest songs were produced within the year of leaving the Convict while he was still endeavouring to imbue infantile minds at his father's school with the elements of knowledge. In some branches of art, such as symphonies, he began at rather a low and uninteresting level and went on growing and gaining in mastery all throughout his life. However, the tamer style of his instrumental works was probably due to the same causes which made his songwriting so remarkably exceptional. In instrumental music, he was rather at sea at first, and from a lack of education and advice, he did not know what to aim at or how to carry on the music in an interesting way. However, in relation to songs, the want of discipline had its advantages, for it left him all the more open to the impression that the poet produced upon him, and the music seemed to flow out as a natural reaction from it. The poems themselves appeared to supply him with the principles of form upon which to construct his music, along with the best musical ideas to intensify the situations and even with a characteristic style. Thus, he needed no guidance other than the receptiveness of his nature, which led him at once to his goal.

It was as early as 1815 that he produced one of his most famous and most powerful songs. The subject is a weird ballad by Goethe called "*The Erl King*," in which a father is represented as carrying his child on horseback through a wild winter night. The terrified child fancies that it sees the Erl King and believes he is calling it to come to him. The father tries desperately to pacify the child and assures it that there is nothing but wafts of cloud and the howling of wind. The fancied voice of the Erl King mockingly calls the child to come to him, and the excitement waxes wilder as the child's terrors increase, while the despairing father urges on his horse and folds the child closer to his breast, but in vain. For when he arrives at his own door, the child is dead.

It was a splendid opportunity, and splendidly did Schubert master it, giving it an impressiveness and a power which no reading of the poem by itself could approach. He conveys the impression of the wild elements and of the headlong career through the night; the terror of the child, the anxiety of the father, and the mocking summons of the Erl King are all combined in sounds that rush with excitement, ever increasing from moment to moment, until, with their arrival at the door of their home, the music - like their headlong career - stops suddenly. In the stillness of despair, the father's horror at finding his child dead in his arms is simply conveyed in six quiet words, which supply exactly the dramatic effect that is wanted. This was one of Schubert's earliest songs, and it contains all the marks of the artistic song in complete maturity. Such an effect, of course, cannot be obtained by the voice alone, using the old methods; the most elaborate resources of instrumental music must be employed to express the terrors of the situation, while the voice, at times, does little more than declaim the words. However, Schubert never meant to degrade the voice to a secondary position, nor did he allow the song to become merely a pianoforte piece with a voice that only explained what it was about. His instincts led him to utilize all the opportunities at his disposal to convey the poet's meaning in musical terms. In some other songs, the voice is far more musically prominent, and the pianoforte provides little more than a subordinate accompaniment in the usual sense of the term. However, this is the case only where it seemed right and possible to him to treat the poem in such a way. In most cases where he dealt with an impressive poem, the balance between the voice and the instrument is such that each has a full share in conveying the poet's meaning as best it can.

The story of the first appearance of "The Erl King" has been told by Schubert's friend Spaun, who called upon him at his home one afternoon in 1815 and found him in a state of excitement over Goethe's ballad, which he had only just discovered. The song was finished and written out before the evening, and they took it to the Convict, where some of the old friends were gathered, and they tried it together. As was very natural, they were rather bewildered than pleased with it. Everything thoroughly genuine and original tends to puzzle people at first, and in this instance, the work was not only very much out of the beaten track but extremely wild and dramatic into the bargain; so it is not to be wondered at that his audience did not take it all in at once. However, they admired and loved Schubert too well to discourage him, and before long, all his friends had learned to understand and delight in it.

The rapidity with which he wrote this famous song is characteristic of him. He devoured everything that came in his way in the line of lyrics and scarcely ever paused to consider whether the poetry was good; but if it conveyed any impression to his mind, he set it to music at once. At one time, he lived with a poet by the name of Mayrhofer, whose acquaintance he made in 1815. They used to sit in their room together, one writing poetry and the other composing music. As Mayrhofer finished a poem, he would toss it across to Schubert, who would read it through and immediately begin to make the music for it directly. As a rule, this speed was almost a necessary condition of Schubert's work across all branches of art. He had no taste for the patient balancing, considering, and re-writing again and again, which were characteristic of Beethoven. The thought possessed him and must go down on paper, and luckily, in the matter of recording what was in his head, he was tolerably certain of the effect he wanted. What he wrote expressed what he meant, and that was enough for him. At the same time, though he did not often alter works once written with a view to improving them, he improved immensely in his successive works, especially in the more arduous kinds of composition such as symphonies and quartets. This was because there was in his nature an appreciation of the possibilities that lay beyond his first efforts in such lines. In songwriting, it was difficult to find how he could do better than he did even before he was twenty years old.

He was still slaving away at the school and pouring out ceaseless floods of music during the intervals of work when a new friend sought him out and, at least for a time, helped to put him in a position more suitable for his genius. This was a certain Franz von Schober, a young man of some means, who had come across Schubert's songs and had been very much struck by them. He called upon Schubert and was very much impressed by the apparent unfitness of circumstances that saw a composer of such extraordinary powers devoting his strength and many hours daily to the education of small infants. He proposed that

Schubert should go and live with him, pursuing his art more freely and with less interruption. This generous proposal was accepted, and as Schubert's temperament was for the most part easy and accommodating, the arrangement worked out very well as long as it lasted. Schubert devoted himself to composition and congenial company, while his moderate wants were chiefly provided for at von Schober's expense. He never troubled himself to think much about providing for the future.

Meanwhile, his compositions were not making any great headway. His friends appreciated him fully, but the public knew next to nothing about him, and publishers would not even look at his works, let alone accept them as a gift. The friends he had made hitherto had scarcely been in a position to help him before the public, but soon after making von Schober's acquaintance, he had the good fortune to make friends with a famous singer and actor called Vogl, whose position in the world as a highly cultivated, enthusiastic, and intelligent man offered him the very best opportunities for serving anyone in whose abilities he believed. Spaun has given an account of their first meeting in Schober's rooms. Vogl had been persuaded by Schubert's friends to see him, and arrived one evening. Schubert, with a shuffling gait and incoherent stammering speech, received his visitor. Vogl, the man of the world, was quite at ease. Taking up a sheet of music paper that lay close by, he began humming the song Schubert had written on it. Then he tried one or two more and concluded by saying, "There is stuff in you, but you squander your fine thoughts instead of developing them." He was not carried away by enthusiasm all at once and made no promise that he would come back again. However, he became acquainted with more of the songs and was increasingly impressed with the style of the music; thus, he began to visit Schubert more often, and Schubert, in turn, began to pay Vogl frequent visits. Vogl gave him excellent advice and helped him in the choice of poems, discussing and critiquing them. More practically useful than all this, he began singing Schubert's songs in the many houses in Vienna where he was welcomed and sometimes took Schubert with him to accompany him. In this way began the friendship that had the most important effect upon Schubert's career.

To this same period, or near it, belong some of the few remains of written expressions of Schubert's own, which throw some light on his character. Fragments of a diary from 1816 contain the most curious passages, such as aphorisms, exclamations, criticisms, and but few biographical details. One passage that gives a clue to his musical mood at the time is particularly interesting. It is dated June 13th.

"This day will haunt me for the rest of my life as a bright, clear, and lovely one. Gently, and as from a distance, the magic tones of Mozart's music sound in my ears. With what alternate force and tenderness, with what masterly power did Schlesinger's playing of that music impress it deep, deep in my heart. Thus do sweet impressions, passing into our souls, work beneficently on our inmost being, and no time, no change of circumstances can obliterate them. In the darkness of life, they show a light, a clear, beautiful distance from which we gather confidence and hope. Oh, Mozart, immortal Mozart, how many and what countless images of a brighter, better world hast thou stamped on our souls!"

Three days afterwards come the words, "To-day I composed for the first time for money — namely, a cantata for the name-day festival of Herr Professor Watteroth von Dräxler. The honorarium was 100 florins, Viennese currency." Then follow a whole string of general remarks that have nothing to do with one another and tell nothing of his life, except in so far as they illustrate the state of his mind. Such remarks include, "Natural disposition and education determine the bent of man's heart and understanding. The heart is ruler; the mind should be. Take men as they are, not as they ought to be. Town politeness is a powerful hindrance to men's integrity in dealing with one another," and so on, with whole pages produced in a single day. The marvel of it is that he could find time to write so much when he was incessantly producing one composition after another, and at such a pace that it is wonderful how he could even manage to put it all down.

He made an attempt every now and then to secure some fixed musical appointment that might bring him in a little money regularly. In 1818, he was invited to go with the family of Count Johann Esterhazy to their country house at Zelesz in Hungary, where he was to make himself generally helpful in various musical ways and to give the daughters music lessons. All the members of the family were musical in their pursuits. The Count and Countess, along with their two daughters, all sang, and the two latter also played on the pianoforte. Additionally, they had with them a friend, the Baron von Schönstein, who possessed a fine voice and sang well, soon entering into Schubert's songs with great enthusiasm. The opportunity presented itself with some decidedly advantageous aspects for Schubert; the countryside was beautiful and healthy, the company was good, and moreover, he had abundant opportunities to hear Hungarian music in its own cultural home. He was naturally attracted by the distinctive style of this music, as many other great musicians have been throughout history, and he wrote down many of the captivating tunes he heard sung or played by gipsies or servants. Among other creative results was a very fine *Divertissement à la Hongroise*, which is said to have been founded on some tunes he heard a kitchen maid singing as he and the Baron von Schönstein were returning from a pleasant walk.

But Schubert was not altogether in love with his circumstances. He was too much of a Viennese at heart and could not get on without his friends and the characteristic ways they used to live together in their familiar camaraderie. He gives his view of things in a letter to his friend Schober: "No one here cares for true art, unless it be now and then the Countess." After a few reflections on his art and work, he sums up his company as follows: "The cook is a pleasant fellow; the ladies' maid is thirty; the housemaid is very pretty and often pays me a visit; the nurse is somewhat ancient; the butler is my rival; the two grooms get on better with the horses than with us. The Count is a little rough; the Countess is proud but not without heart; the young ladies are good children. I need not tell you, who know me so well, that with my natural frankness I am good friends with everyone."

He probably returned to Vienna and to his loved companions there about the end of 1818, and it must have been near that time that he went to live with the poet Mayrhofer. The friends were extremely intimate, calling one another by peculiar nicknames and being very fond of rough joking and lighthearted banter, which showed that their animal spirits were very much alive and vibrant in those days. Schubert was constantly busy producing music and had his mind so entirely centered upon that occupation that he is said to have slept in his spectacles to be ready to begin writing directly as soon as he woke. He commonly worked until dinner time, after which he liked to go for a walk in the beautiful countryside. The evening was often divided between visiting a friend's house, attending the theatre, and finally stopping by a *gasthaus*, where friends would sit smoking and drinking beer or wine, making merry after the customary manner of Viennese society until the small hours of the morning. From this, it would appear that Schubert's only regular working time was in the morning, during which he could squeeze in about five or six hours of concentrated effort. However, this did not preclude him from working at other times when the mood came upon him. He wrote his songs anywhere and at any time when the thoughts came to him, or when a particular poem moved him; even works on a considerable scale were sometimes written at the spur of the moment in out-of-the-way places. It sounds rather like an easy, happy-go-lucky kind of life, but when he did work, he must have worked thoroughly and rapidly, getting the very best out of himself.

Owing to Vogl's passionate advocacy, Schubert's name was brought more and more before the public eye; and in 1820, a comic operetta called the *Zwillingsbrüder* was performed in one of the Vienna theatres. Additionally, a work called the *Zauberharfe* was also performed later in the same year, so things must have seemed to be growing a little brighter for him. In the next year, a more important event occurred, which was the first publication of some of his songs. This significant consummation was at last brought about owing to some concerts given in the house of a family called Sonnleithner, one of whom had been at school with Schubert and had cherished his friendship, as all men seem to have done when they had once won it. At these concerts, many of Schubert's works were performed, and among them were some of his finest songs. The audience was so pleased that everyone began to think a decided effort ought to be made to enable people to possess such treasures. Schubert's friend Leopold Sonnleithner, along with Gymnich, an amateur who sang the songs admirably, made up their minds to try and find a publisher. They searched in vain. The publishers thought the works were too difficult and too uncommon and that the composer's name was not known enough. Finally, in despair of succeeding any other way, Schubert's friends determined to publish sets of songs on their own account and get the copies subscribed for among the people who attended the Sonnleithner concerts and other friends. A selection was made, and the publications began in April 1821, continuing for the rest of the year at various intervals. The friends did all they could to bring the songs before the public and to keep the interest alive, and the result was that sufficient copies were sold to encourage the cautious publishers to go on bringing out more of them at their own expense. This, to a certain extent, improved Schubert's position as a composer, and the sale of copies even temporarily put him in funds. This was perhaps the most successful financial result his compositions ever brought him, for in the whole course of his life, the publishers could never be induced to give him more than the most absurdly trifling sums, even for his most attractive songs. About the highest price he ever received is said to have been 3 florins, and for some of his best songs, quite late in his life, he got just 1 florin apiece.

Not long after the successful launch of his first compositions into print, he went on an expedition around the country with his friend Schober, visiting certain relatives and friends of Schober's. The principal result of this journey seems to have been the composition of a large opera called *Alfonso* and *Estrella*, to words written by Schober during their journeyings together. It was finished early in 1822, and then came the usual disagreeable operations necessary to get it performed. He seems to have brought it to the notice of all sorts of people at various periods in the succeeding years but met with nothing but excuses or rebuffs. One well-known passage of arms between him and Weber is reported to have arisen from it. Schubert certainly criticized Weber's opera *Euryanthe* rather unfavorably, and it appears to have reached Weber's ears, who was annoyed by it. Schubert, meaning no evil, afterwards took his score of *Alfonso* and *Estrella* to show to Weber; whereupon Weber expressed his opinion of that work by saying that it was "usual to drown the first puppies and the first operas," under the supposition that it was Schubert's first attempt in that line. Later, he repented of his sharp speech and is even said to have considered performing the work himself in Dresden. Schubert made another attempt by sending his work to Berlin to a friend called Anna Milder, who was a great singer. She returned him a very friendly answer but held out no hope of getting a performance, as she said, "It pains me to remark, but I must do so, that the libretto does not suit the taste of the people here, who are accustomed to the grand high tragic opera or the comic opera of the French." At the Vienna theatres, he had no chance of getting a performance, as two of them were in the hands of a thoroughly mercenary man who would not dream of undertaking anything that was not sure to bring him in good profits. Schubert's friends would have organized a performance but for the fact that the difficulties of the work were beyond their powers of execution. In the end, all hopes had to be given up, and the work was never performed until long after his death, when Liszt brought it out at Weimar among several other apparently forlorn hopes which he gallantly led in 1854. However, even then, its success was doubtful, less from the characteristics of the music than from the poor arrangement of the story and ineffectiveness on the stage. A few years ago, it was again revived in Vienna, and having been elaborately revised by the conductor, it met with more success than before.

Of course, the failure to get a performance must have been trying for him, but he was always too busy and too merry with his genial friends to allow such rebuffs to weigh heavily upon his spirits; he still had his heart set on doing something significant in the same line. In 1823, he wrote a little one-act opera called The *Conspirators*, and this too, after being in the hands of the licensers of plays for a year, was returned to him and was never performed during his lifetime. He followed up this work by yet another in the same line, but on a larger scale - a regular full-sized romantic opera in three acts, called *Fierabras*. The words were put together by a man named Josef Kupelwieser and were all about contests of Franks and Moors, as well as kings and knights, and noble ladies. Of this work, Schubert really had some hopes of getting a performance, as the libretto, foolish as it seems, was already accepted by the manager of one of the theatres before he began to write the music. As soon as the words came to him, he set to work and wrote at a most astounding speed. According to the dates given, he wrote the entirety of the first act - which consists of 300 pages of manuscript - in just seven days, and the whole opera, which filled up more than three times as many pages, was composed and finished in every detail between May and September; though he appears to have been so ill at some time between those two dates that he had to go to a hospital for treatment. As soon as it was finished, and before the fate of its performance was decided, he was engaged upon yet another

work for the stage called *Rosamunde*, the words of which were supplied by that absurd old poetical aspirant, Wilhelmina von Chezy, who
previously wrote the words for Weber's *Euryanthe*. The story was titled
Rosamunde, the Princess of Cyprus, and was of the same preposterous
romantic texture as Weber's opera, and it had the same pernicious
effect upon the fortunes of the music associated with it. It was not so
much an opera as it was a play with incidental music accompanying it,
and it did not take Schubert long to write his share; but his contribu-
tion was beautiful and far too good to be dragged down into oblivion
by the foolishness of the words. The opera was performed in 1823,
and the music was well appreciated, but so much depended upon the
play that the combination was inevitably a failure, and both the music
as well as the literary part were laid aside and forgotten. Long after,
in 1867, the work was discovered in the cupboard where it had been
left, by Sir George Grove when he was hunting for relics and forgotten
beauties of Schubert in Vienna. Much of the music has subsequently
been revived in concert halls and is always received with delight by
all lovers of Schubert's works. In the same year, he wrote many more
beautiful songs, among which the most celebrated are a set of twenty,
called the *Schöne Müllerin*, upon which he was engaged at different
times in intervals of work on the opera *Fierabras* - some of the songs
being said to have been written while he was ill in the hospital. Early
in the next year, the fate of *Fierabras* was also decided. It was returned
to him unperformed, and without any prospect being held out of his
ever hearing a note of it. These repeated disappointments seem at last
to have seriously depressed him. Several written expressions from
him around this time show how deeply he felt them. In a letter to the
brother of the friend who had put the poem of *Fierabras* together, he
poured out his grief, stating, "I feel myself to be the most unhappy,
the most miserable man on earth. Picture to yourself a man whose
health can never be re-established; who, from sheer despair, makes
matters worse rather than better; a man whose most brilliant hopes
have come to nothing, whose enthusiasm for the beautiful (an inspired
feeling at least) threatens to vanish altogether; and then ask yourself
if such a condition does not represent a miserable and unhappy man.
Your brother's opera was declared impracticable, and no demand of

any sort was made for my music. Thus, I have composed two operas to no purpose whatsoever."

Belonging to the early months of the same year, there remain several entries in his diary that tell nothing of his outward life but express pointedly the deep sorrow and depression of his inner man. Grief and bitterness are present in every line, and all the consolation which he derives is that grief is better for a man's soul than happiness, and that his best productions spring from his sorrow; "those works which are the product of pain seem to please the great world most."

In words, he was often sad after this manner, but his music always supplied the contrast; for when the wells of musical thought were open, joy seems to have possessed him again, and outward disappointments never clouded its serene beauty and freshness.

In the same year in which *Fierabras* was rejected, he took another expedition to Zelesz in Hungary to stay with the Esterhazys and make music with them as before; and no doubt, it did him a great deal of good. A letter to his favorite brother, Ferdinand, contains allusions to tears that he had shed and former sadness, but his general frame of mind seems to be very much improved. He expresses, "Certainly that happy, joyous time is gone when every object seemed encircled with a halo of youthful glory, and what has followed is the experience of a miserable reality, which I endeavor to embellish as far as possible by the gifts of my fancy (for which I thank God). People are wont to think that happiness depends on the place which witnessed our former joys, whilst in reality, it only depends on ourselves; and thus, I learned a sad delusion, and saw a removal of those very experiences which I had already made at Steyr, and yet I am now much more than I was formerly in the way of finding peace and happiness within myself." The last sentence seems to express a much better-balanced mood than the style of his letter to Kupelwieser. But indeed, there was enough to make him depressed. The very fact that his friends believed in him so thoroughly and had regarded him for so many years as a favored genius served to throw the perpetual want of success and the reiterated rebuffs he received into a darker relief. Few men could have borne such trials so patiently, or with such constant returns of good spirits after occasional fits of gloom; and it was probably the constant outpouring of composition that prevented him from dwelling too much upon his position. However, this does not take away one iota from the honor that it is to him to be among those few who produce their music for itself from the genuine love of it, especially when so many ordinary composers produce theirs for the sake of what they can gain by it, whether in monetary rewards or praise. Perhaps his disappointments may have been good for his character in this respect, for, having never tasted the sweets of public success, he was less likely to be tempted to sell his soul for more draughts of that dangerous intoxicant. At all events, the perpetual outpouring of fresh music was never relaxed, and in some lines of art, he mastered greater and greater results as he continued on his creative journey.

The next year seems to have been a brighter one for him. Its chief incident was a country excursion which he took with his friend Vogl; during which, for five months, he enjoyed the delights of traveling through beautiful scenery, mixing with pleasant company at the various places where they stayed, and finding thorough sympathy and appreciation for his music on all sides. Vogl would sing Schubert's songs to the people whenever they met congenial friends, with Schubert accompanying him on the piano; and, as Schubert wrote to his brother, "the way Vogl sings these things and I accompany him - so that whilst the performance lasts we seem to be one - is quite an unheard-of novelty amongst these people." They indeed took a great fancy to him and made much of him, and everything combined to make him happy and hopeful. When the summer came to an end, Vogl went off to Italy, and Schubert returned to Vienna, resuming his usual ways of life there.

Nothing occurred to mark the course of his life for some time after this beyond the appearance of fresh compositions. The chief events that happened in the following years were two more attempts to gain a definite musical post, such as might supply him with a small but regular income and a definite position among his fellow artists, but both attempts came to nothing. Another interesting event was his visit to Beethoven's bedside just before that great master passed away. Schindler, Beethoven's admirer and biographer, was a great believer in Schubert and tried to bring them together, but he had failed until the end was manifestly approaching. When Beethoven was laid up with his last illness, Schindler brought some of Schubert's best songs to show him. Beethoven became very much interested in them and was greatly surprised when he heard what an enormous quantity of such works Schubert had produced. He is reported by Schindler to have said, "Truly Schubert has the divine fire within him." It is probable that it was owing to these favorable expressions that Schubert was persuaded to visit the bedside of the great man. Very few words were exchanged, but they must have been sufficient to show Schubert that Beethoven had discovered his gifts and appreciated them. He went again later, but at that time, Beethoven was not able to speak and could only make signs with his hand. Within three weeks after this visit, Beethoven was dead. At the funeral, Schubert was one of the torchbearers. When he and two of his friends were returning, they stopped at a *gasthaus*, and Schubert and his friends each drank one glass of wine to the memory of the great man departed, and a second glass to the one of the three who should first follow him into the afterlife. Schubert little thought then how short his own time was destined to be.

Around this time, he began to receive communications from publishers with a view to bringing out more of his music, as well as some encouraging proposals to write works specially for various societies. In the same year, he was elected a member of the representative body of the Musical Society of Vienna, which he regarded as a pleasant honor. He continued his composition with even greater ardor than ever, and by the spring of 1828, he had finished his greatest symphony, the only one that was destined to be thoroughly characteristic of him and also complete, alongside other instrumental works, such as sonatas, a very fine quintet for strings, a cantata called Miriam's War Song, and numerous songs, which succeeded one another rapidly. He seemed to think it was time to give less attention to songs and more to works on a larger scale, as he expressed to a friend that he hoped to hear no more about songs, but rather to devote himself to opera and symphony.

In March, for the very first time in his life, he gave a public concert in the hall of the Musik-Verein of Vienna. The program included part of a string quartet of his, a trio for piano and strings, music for men's chorus, and several fine songs. Many excellent performers came forward to help him, among them his old friend Vogl; and it serves to show how his genius was beginning to become known and appreciated, that the hall is said to have been fuller than had ever been remembered before, and the audience was delighted. The good attendance also brought about 32% into his pocket, which must have made him feel quite rich. As was usual with him, his friends got the benefit of his prosperity, and he spent his wealth royally as long as it lasted; and by summer time, he was as badly off as ever. The idea of going for another excursion into the lovely country of Styria was again entertained but had to be given up because of the low state of his funds, and he had to remain in Vienna all the year round.

Early in September, he went to live with his brother Ferdinand in a house in the suburb called the Neue Wieden. He had been bothered with an old trouble of inclination of blood to the head and giddiness, and it was thought it would do him good to be nearer to the country and to have readier opportunities of getting away for exercise and fresh air. The house they occupied was a new one, and it is supposed this aggravated his unhealthy and over-strained condition. He became decidedly ill, and doctors had to be called in. Then he picked up a little and went for a five days' excursion with some friends into the neighborhood of Vienna, visiting, among other places, the grave of Haydn at Eisenstadt. He seems to have regained some of his usual gaiety for the time, but when he got back to Vienna, the illness returned.

One evening, when having supper with some friends at a hotel, he suddenly threw down his knife and fork, saying the food tasted like poison. He still walked about a good deal after this, but he took scarcely anything to eat and got steadily worse. But he did not seem to have any anxiety about himself and spoke to the composer Lachner, who came to see him, of his intended work on a new opera he had in hand called *Graf von Gleichen*. He went to hear music and was very much excited over a performance of one of Beethoven's latest quartets. Among other ideas, he had one of developing his mastery of counterpoint more thoroughly; a purpose which arose from his becoming acquainted with Handel's works so late in life; and he applied to a man called Sechter, who was considered an authority in that branch of art, to give him lessons; and the matter even went so far that he went to see Sechter and discussed what would be the best books to work upon and arranged dates for the lessons. The last music he heard publicly performed was a mass by his brother Ferdinand, which was done in the church at a village called Hernals on the 3rd of November.

When he got home again, he was very tired and ill and grew worse day by day. He wrote to his old friend Schober, "I am ill. I have eaten and drunk nothing for eleven days, and am so tired and shaky that I can only get from the bed to the chair and back." And he asked for some books to amuse him, suggesting some of Cooper's novels. Some of his friends came to see him, but there seems to have been a dread of infection, and he had not so much company to cheer him as was desirable. He occupied some of his time correcting proofs of the latest set of his songs, called the *Winterreise*, and still had hopes of doing more work. But after a few days, he became delirious, and the doctors announced that he had typhus fever. The faithful brother Ferdinand attended him constantly. Franz was possessed with strange fears and asked, "Brother, what are they going to do with me? I implore you to put me in my own room and not to leave me in this corner under the earth. Don't I deserve a place above ground?" Ferdinand did all he could to quiet him and assured him he was in his own room; but Franz only shook his head, saying, "It is not true, Beethoven is not here." He never became himself again but died on Wednesday, November 19, 1828, only thirty-one years old. Two days afterwards, the funeral took place, and his body was borne, accompanied by many friends and admirers, to the cemetery at the village of Währing, where Beethoven had also been buried; and it was deposited as near as possible to the last resting place of that great master, towards whom in his latter years he had been so strongly drawn by sympathy and admiration. Many performances were given and articles written in honor of his memory, and the proceeds of concerts and subscriptions were enough to pay for a monument over his grave, upon which were appropriately inscribed the words:

> "Music has here entombed a rich treasure,
> But still fairer hopes."

Several great musicians have been cut off even before what might be fairly considered the prime of their life and vigor, but of all the greatest ones, Schubert's time was shortest; yet in those few thirty-one years of life, he produced such an enormous quantity of music that the amount would have been noticeable even if his life had been rather longer than most men's. He wrote over 500 songs, at least seven entire symphonies, and two incomplete ones, of which latter, one is among his most beautiful and popular works; over twenty sonatas; numbers of string quartets; six masses; and other large and fine examples of church music; several operas, part songs, cantatas, overtures, and so forth. His rapidity of thought and of writing must have been marvelous. As fast as he finished one thing, he generally began another and often wrote several songs in a single day; and those not songs of the cheap, ephemeral description familiar in modern times, but works of art, with real thought and point and good workmanship in them.

Of all these various works, comparatively few came before the public before he died, which may be partly accounted for by the shortness of his life. But when he was dead, the interest in his music began steadily to grow, and the publication of songs went on unceasingly for such a long time that one critic, in facetious terms, suggested that someone was trading on the popularity of Schubert's name and passing off as posthumous works of his, things that were written by somebody else. But in fact, even in the present day, great as is the number of his songs which are known to the world, there are still many which remain in manuscript; but a very considerable portion of his works of all kinds are now in print, and many works on a large scale, such as his latest symphonies, are great favorites with really musical people. The revival of his last great symphony was due to Schumann, who did more than any other man of his time to bring before the public works by all sorts of composers, living and dead, who, without his advocacy, might have been ignored, or at least have had a very long fight to win recognition. Schumann went to Vienna in 1838, ten years after Schubert's death, and found an enormous quantity of manuscripts which were still in the possession of the faithful brother Ferdinand, and among them was the last symphony in C, which he had written in the year that he died. Schumann soon recognized what a splendid work it was and sent it to Mendelssohn, who was then conductor of the famous Gewandhaus concerts at Leipzig, and it was performed there early in 1839 for the first time. Mendelssohn had but little sympathy with Schubert's large instrumental works, but he was, nevertheless, willing to champion a work on such a grand scale and brought it to England with him to have it performed under his direction at the Philharmonic in 1844; but the band failed to understand it at the rehearsal and behaved so badly that Mendelssohn withdrew it; and the prominent English critics of the day not only pronounced their verdict against this and other instrumental works of his but even against his songs. For instance, the song known as the *Junge Nonne*, which is one of his most impressive works, was sung at a Philharmonic concert in the same year, 1844, and was described by the critic who was considered to have the greatest ability and judgment in the country "as a very good exemplification of much ado about nothing—as unmeaningly mysterious as could be desired by the most devoted lover of bombast." For many years, the same tone was kept up; but in defiance of critics, Schubert's music grew more and more into favor: the public felt that what it said to them was true, and it moved them as genuine music should; and in the end, it was accepted as a regular feature, even in places where little but well-tried classics are admitted, and nowhere has it been better received than in this country, where at first it met with such contemptuous opposition.

The position which Schubert's larger instrumental works have won in the end is rather a significant one; for, judged by comparison with the great works of such masters as Haydn, Mozart, and Beethoven, they certainly have artistic defects. The nicety of adjustment of details of form, after the manner of such masters, is defective, and self-restraint, concentration, conciseness, and judgment are too often absent; and yet the works have taken their place among things which are most delighted in, through the beauty of their ideas, and their color, character, and spontaneity. It is this state of things which makes his instrumental works specially interesting, as pointing to the position occupied by the intrinsic qualities of music in this century compared with the prominence of formal qualities in the last century. The success of Haydn's and Mozart's work depended to a great extent upon beauty of form, and not very much upon strong individuality. Beethoven alone balanced form and idea upon equal terms, and made strong character one of the essentials, and after him instrumental music began to move into more erratic forms, and to depend much more upon ideas and character; and Schubert was one of the first composers of mark who gave point to this tendency. There only exists one symphony and a half of his which represent him thoroughly, and yet that is enough to outweigh a whole dozen of symphonies by composers whose works were looked upon with complacency by his contemporaries at a time when his were ignored. But though the symphonies and the masses, and the operas and the sonatas and pianoforte pieces, have a place in history, they all must yield in importance to his songs, and it is as the first great representative song-writer that he must be chiefly remembered. With him begins that wonderful flow of songs which are as characteristic of Germany as the symphony and the sonata; for no other nations have been able to produce a natural kind of art-song like theirs, any more than they have been able to produce symphonies. Symphony and song fill up the extreme limits of the picture, and the thoroughness of the German people in musical matters has won for them the first place all through.

Schubert is another example, like Beethoven, of that supreme devotion to art which makes all convenience and comfort of daily life of secondary importance. His, too, was that singular and untarnished honour of persistently writing what he felt to be best and most beautiful, without ever thinking of what he might get by accommodating his music to his hearers. Popular sophisms could have no hold upon him, because there was no weak place in the armour of his belief. He believed in what was good and not in what was convenient, and it was quite impossible for him to act against his feeling. If other nations could show a few such men among their composers they might rise in time to equal musical honour with the great Germans.

IX

MENDELSSOHN.

THE story of Mendelssohn's life is in strong contrast to those of the great composers who preceded him. They all but one had sprung from the ranks of the people, and most of them had been obliged to fight their way to success, and to pass through stern ordeals in learning the mastery of their art. He was the first who came of a rich family, and enjoyed the apparent advantages of able instructors to guide his youthful steps, and careful and wise friends and relations to superintend the system of his education; and what is still more exceptional, a constant flow of success from his childhood till his death. To the general world the ease and well-being of his early life, the personal comforts, and the refined society that was always at his command, seem to have placed him in a most favourable position for the development of his genius. But worldly advantages are not without their drawbacks when art is concerned; for the trials the earlier masters had to go through strengthened their independence and force of character, whereas all he gained by his immunity from sordid cares was an accurate knowledge of what kind of art was appreciated by eminently respectable people, an equable, refined, and placid style of expression, and a ready facility in managing the resources of his art.

The original name of the family was Mendel; the name of Mendelssohn, "son of Mendel," was taken by Moses, the grandfather of the composer, a famous philosopher in his time. His son Abraham became a very prosperous banker, and was settled in Hamburg at the time Felix was born in 1809. The ancestors had been Jews in religion as well as descent, but Abraham came to the conclusion that it was advisable

199

to adopt Christianity, so he made his children German Protestants. It was Abraham also who added his wife's family name, "Bartholdy," to his own, to distinguish his branch from other branches of the family.

Soon after the composer was born, Abraham moved his household and his bank to Berlin, in consequence of the inconvenience they suffered from having the French in Hamburg in the time of the great wars caused by that nation; and from that time the family took root there, and became thorough Berliners. The house they lived in was a large one, and became a favourite meeting-place of people of intelligence and artists of distinction. The mother was an eminently clever woman, and thoroughly fitted to act as hostess to such gatherings, as well as to see that the children were well brought up and properly disciplined. Felix received a very thorough education in every respect, and was taught Greek and Latin and drawing as well as music. But music naturally became the most important item, and his extraordinary gifts in that line caused his parents much anxious consideration as to whether he should be allowed to devote himself to it as a profession. They showed their wisdom in deciding that it should at all events have the best opportunities available, and immediately set about to find the best masters for him. A man called Berger, who had some reputation at that time, was chosen to teach him the pianoforte, and Zelter, a great friend of Goethe's, undertook to teach him composition. Zelter's views of art were extremely strict, and even old-fashioned; but that is not altogether a bad thing for a master of composition if the pupil has any real stuff in him; and Zelter certainly appreciated the responsibility he had undertaken with such an extraordinarily gifted pupil, and endeavoured to ground him thoroughly.

The young musician's powers developed at a wonderful speed; in fact, it is probable that no other human being except Mozart ever had such natural gifts. His memory and facility in playing an instrument were as remarkable as his powers in composition, and even from his boyhood he developed such a talent for extemporising as has rarely been heard of. By the time he was twelve years old he had written a couple of operas, and a psalm with extremely elaborate vocal writing in it, and many other works of less magnitude, and his fame began to be noised abroad. Old Zelter was very anxious that he should not be spoilt, and was chary in his praises to the boy; but his amazement at his pupil's precocious powers was so great that he made up his mind to show him to Goethe at Weimar. The meeting was brought about in 1821, when the boy was thirteen years old, and the old poet was so delighted with him that the visit, which was intended only to last a fortnight, extended to a month, the latter sixteen days of which were spent in Goethe's own house. Goethe made him play to him frequently, and tested his powers in extemporising, in playing all sorts and styles of music, and also in reading, and even in deciphering a rough manuscript of Beethoven's. The opinion he formed of him was the very highest imaginable. Some one asked him how he stood comparison with Mozart, whom Goethe had seen and heard at Frankfort when he himself was twelve years old and Mozart little over seven. Goethe thought Mendelssohn's performances bore the same relation to Mozart's that the cultivated talk of a grown-up person does to the prattle of a child, and that his ideas were more independent than Mozart's had been at the same age. The relations between the old man and the precocious child became charmingly intimate, and lasted till Goethe's death.

In the following year Mendelssohn first made acquaintance with Ferdinand Hiller, with whom he formed an intimate friendship which lasted for a great part of his life. This well-known musician, who still lives and adorns the copious ranks of German composers and pianists[6], has given a charming account of their early intercourse, which conveys a lively picture of the boy's character and intelligence. Hiller had received almost incredible accounts of Mendelssohn's abilities from his master Aloys Schmitt, and when Schmitt offered to bring them together at Frankfort, Hiller was in a great state of wonderment to see what the boy would be like. He describes himself as watching out of the window of his house and seeing Mendelssohn running behind Schmitt and jumping up on to his back as he walked along, and holding on for a little and then slipping off, and going through the same operation again and again in the merriest way and he thought he "must be jolly enough." But when they came together Mendelssohn was grave and dignified at first, and Hiller was even more impressed by his personality than he had been by the account of his performances,

6   During the interval between the printing and first publication of this article, Ferdinand Hiller died at Cologne, at the ripe age of seventy-three.

and when they came to make music together the impression was still further intensified. But Hiller noticed certain peculiar traits in him, too, when they used to meet together more intimately later. His opinions about art and artists in his youthful days were rather over-ripe and assertive, and he had a way of expressing himself "with a certain precocious positiveness which was evidently characteristic." This quality he may have got from the society of Berlin, of whom Goethe said, "they were such a forward set that delicacy was thrown away upon them. One must have one's eyes wide open and even be a little rude to keep above-water." But Mendelssohn's enthusiasm for what was good, and his wild and happy spirits and genuine quickness of thought and speech set off most favourably on the other side.

At home at Berlin, the boy had exceptional opportunities for developing his gifts. There used to be regular gatherings of friends and acquaintances at the house on the Neue Promenade, where the Mendelssohns lived, on alternate Sunday mornings, when music was performed in a large dining room. For these occasions, a small orchestra was engaged, and the boy-composer's early symphonies and other instrumental works were regularly performed. Felix himself always conducted, even in the days when he was so small as to have to stand on a stool to be visible. This was, of course, of most excellent service to him, and an advantage never enjoyed so early by any other composer. He was able to test the effect of what he wrote, to get familiar with the requirements of a conductor, and to be accustomed to facing an audience. When he arrived at the age of fifteen, his fourth opera, called *Die beiden Neffen*, was performed, apparently at home, and afterwards, at supper, old Zelter jokingly advanced him from the grade of "apprentice" to that of "assistant, in the names of Mozart, Haydn, and Bach." In the same year, he made the acquaintance of Moscheles, who at that time enjoyed a great reputation as a pianist, and the opinion of the new friend was that he was already a mature artist and in no need of lessons. But the parents were still just a little doubtful as to whether a musical career was, after all, the right one for him; and report says that a journey undertaken by the father with his son to Paris, in the year 1825, was partly to see what Cherubini would say about it.

Cherubini was at that time a sort of critical autocrat on musical matters in Paris, and rode roughshod over all the younger musicians of his time with free impartiality. To one who played to him, he would say, "Perhaps you paint well;" sometimes he would say nothing, but only make faces; if he said nothing and made no faces, it was quite a favourable symptom; and the estimation he was held in was so immense that no one, except, perhaps, Berlioz, ever dared to do anything but bow and accept his decision as incontrovertible.

To such an autocrat, it was proposed to subject the youthful Mendelssohn. The result surprised the French musicians as well as his own friends; for when Cherubini had heard one of Mendelssohn's works, he even smiled and nodded, and said, "The boy is rich; he will do well. I myself will talk to him, and then he will do well." Mendelssohn himself viewed the old master critically and with some appreciation; but he thought he was an extinct volcano, still throwing out occasional flashes and sparks, but quite covered up with ashes and cinders. Of the state of musical art and taste in Paris, he had a poor opinion, and of the musicians, with a few exceptions, the same. He found, as has generally been the case, that they cared mostly for glitter and show and had no taste for anything solid and genuine. A passage in one of his letters to his sister Fanny is a good specimen of his quick intelligence and ready way of expressing himself. He says: "The people here don't know a note of *Fidelio*, and look upon Bach as a mere full-bottomed wig powdered with nothing but learning. The other day, at Kalkbrenner's request, I played Bach's organ *Preludes in E and A minor*. The people thought them both sweetly pretty, and somebody remarked that the beginning of the *A minor prelude* bore a striking resemblance to a favourite duet of Monsigny's - a French writer of operas!"

They went homewards in the spring and paid another visit to Goethe on the way. Meanwhile, the stream of composition was constantly pouring out. He had already passed his thirteenth symphony, and the year 1825 saw the completion of another opera called The *Wedding of Camacho*, and striking advances in point of style, such as were shown by his now well-known octet for strings. The very next year, 1826, found him at his best, for the overture to The *Midsummer Night's Dream*, which he then wrote at the age of seventeen, was never surpassed by him in neatness of expression, freshness of ideas, good management of form, and delicacy and finish of orchestration. According to Hiller's account, it took him the best part of a year to write; and it was a year well spent. Mendelssohn told him how he had been working and spending all the spare time he could find between the lectures on philosophy and history and so forth, which he was attending at the university at Berlin, extemporising at it on the pianoforte of a beautiful lady who lived hard by. It was first played privately in a garden house of the Mendelssohns', and publicly at Stettin early in the next year, 1827; and its extraordinary success marked the conclusion of his actual studies with Zelter; though the old master continued to watch the progress of his pupil with anxious interest and to report it to Goethe as long as they lived.

This same year saw the public performance of the opera *The Wedding of Camacho* at the theatre in Berlin. He had to experience some of the worries and annoyances composers are generally subjected to when their operas are first performed, and criticisms which were distasteful to him; and though his friends received the work with acclamations, he did not care to exert himself to get it performed again, and from that time his connection with the history of the opera ceased. His life went on somewhat uneventfully for some time after this, but the ways of his home at Berlin were not such as to allow him to grow dull. The house was constantly alive with vivacious guests, and as he came on to maturer years, he became more and more a centre of attraction. It seems as if the rattle of gaiety and perpetual succession of distractions and amusements must have prevented his cultivating his deeper feelings, but it certainly kept his wits up to the mark and made him the more ready in practical matters. Even Zelter, who took part in some of the joking and merriment that went on, was not altogether content with his remaining constantly in such an atmosphere. He wrote to Goethe that he was fearing to see him "dissolve like a jelly in the midst of the idle family tittle-tattle of the place." His circumstances made Mendelssohn what he was, as is the case with every man, and among them were the years of such social vivacity as he spent at home up to his twentieth year. The head was cultivated, but not the poetical side of his disposition or his deeper and finer emotions; but at the same time, he had an instinct for what was noble and lofty in art and showed it during this very period by one of the most honourable achievements of his lifetime.

It appears to have been in 1827 that he began trying the effect of Bach's Passion Music according to Matthew with a select choir of sixteen voices. The matter grew on his hands, and people became more and more interested in the work, till it became the general desire of his friends that a public performance should be given by the society called the Singakademie, with over 300 voices under Mendelssohn's direction. Zelter was against it, and the general public were not very eager for it, but in the end, the enthusiasm of a few friends carried the point, and in 1829, the first performance of this great work since the death of Bach took place. Contrary to expectation, the success was great, and the work was repeated, and from this point no doubt began that revival of J. S. Bach's great choral works, which has been one of the happiest and healthiest features in the progress of musical taste in the last fifty years.

In this same year, it was that Mendelssohn made his first independent step out into the world, to try his fortunes as a musical artist. His parents agreed with the many wise friends who were interested in him that it would be good for him to travel in many countries and see people of various tastes and of eminence in different styles of art; and his first journey was to England. The separation from the home circle seems to have been a serious wrench, but his cheerful spirits were not at that time capable of being clouded long, and he found plenty of distraction in new scenes and the friends which his genial disposition made for him wherever he went. He came to England by steamer from Hamburg, and had a very rough passage, and was very ill. He arrived in April and took up his abode in London, where he found plenty of congenial musicians. The place was very much to his liking, and he expressed himself delighted with everything. The public were not less delighted with him. He made his first appearance at a Philharmonic concert in May, when his youthful symphony in C minor was performed with great success. He also made his appearance as a pianist and played several great works, becoming more and more a favourite of the public at every step. A curious incident of his stay in London was that after a most successful performance of his *Midsummer Night's Dream* overture, the score of the work was left by someone in a cab and entirely disappeared; but the story goes that

Mendelssohn wrote it all out again by heart, and it was found to be almost perfectly exact when compared with the band parts.

After a most successful stay in London till the end of the season, he travelled about England and paid visits to people who appreciated him. From England, he went on to Scotland, where he began to gather those impressions which ultimately found their expression in the popular *Scotch Symphony* and in the *Hebrides Overture*; the principal musical subject of which seems to have come into his head when he was enjoying the wild and rugged scenery of Staffa and the neighbouring islands. From Scotland, he went to Wales, where a visit to a country house has since served as the occasion of a very characteristic account of him by one of its inmates. His merry, genial disposition always seems to be the principal trait in such accounts, as he was always ready to throw himself into the enjoyments of expeditions, picnics, sketching parties, and such social distractions. Dancing was with him quite a special passion. His talk was witty and pointed, and sometimes fanciful. He did not seem to be otherwise than perfectly natural and modest, but was always ready to use his gifts, whether musical or otherwise, to the best advantage. "He was so far from any sort of pretension or from making a favour of giving his music to us, that one evening when the family from a neighbouring house came to dinner, and we had dancing afterwards, he took his turn in playing quadrilles and waltzes with the others. He was the first person who taught us gallopades, and he first played us Weber's *Last Waltz*." Of his characteristic appearance and manner the same writer says: - "I suppose some of the charm of his speech might be in the unusual choice of words which he, as a German, made in speaking English. He lisped a little. He used an action of nodding his head quickly till the long locks of hair would fall over his high forehead with the vehemence of his assent to anything he liked." In the latter part of this same year, 1829, he came back to London, and it is surprising and interesting to find him writing of that town as "indescribably beautiful." He was extremely happy, and made the people he was with happy too, and no doubt gave rise to plenty of regret when he left at last for Berlin in November.

He stayed at home in the winter, and then started on a new journey in the direction of Italy. On his way he paid another visit to Goethe at Weimar, and a most interesting visit it was. Goethe was getting to care less and less for much company, but Mendelssohn's arrival evidently brightened him, and he was as sociable as of old with his lively young friend. The pianoforte, after long silence, was opened again, and every morning the old poet had what he called his music lesson, which consisted in listening to Mendelssohn for an hour or so while he played to him a quantity of music of all styles, and as Goethe would have it, in chronological order. Mendelssohn described him as sitting in a dark corner like a Jupiter Tonans with his old eyes flashing fire, occasionally criticising and making favourable or questioning remarks. After dinner they used to talk, and Goethe poured out wise and pointed words which Mendelssohn, in his able way, commemorated; and it is easy to see what admirable company the young musician made for great men like Goethe, as well as for ordinary gay and thoughtless people. When he went away, Goethe wrote to the old master Zelter that his coming had done him a great deal of good. "From the Bach period downwards he has brought Haydn, Mozart, Gluck to life for me, has given me clear ideas of the great modern masters of technique, and lastly has made me understand his own productions and left me plenty to think about in himself." It was the last time they met, for before Mendelssohn had another opportunity of visiting Weimar again, Goethe was dead.

After parting with the old poet, he went on to Nuremberg, and Munich, and Vienna; at which latter town he was not over-pleased with the condition of musical taste, but he found society very amusing, played the pianoforte at numberless parties, and made many gay and amusing friends. By October he reached Italy and began to enjoy his life more than ever in a new phase. He entered fully into the enjoyment of the numberless masterpieces of the sister art, as well as the scenery and the glories of the climate. He appreciated less the monuments of ancient times and appears to have had little sympathy with things depending for their interest on historical associations. He described a scene in which the sea lay between the islands, and the rocks covered with vegetation bent over it as in the days when Brutus and Cicero were there. "These are the antiquities that interest me, and are much more suggestive than crumbling masonry." It is a gratifying trait in his character that he loved the sea and thought it the finest object in nature. He always felt happy when he saw the wide expanse of waters.

But his nature was capable of finding enjoyment in almost everything enjoyable. In Rome, he enjoyed not only the scenes and the paintings and the music, and the picturesque effects of religious ceremonies and religious music, but also all kinds of society. His looking-glass was stuck full of visiting cards, and he spent every evening with a new acquaintance. His capacity for tasting fresh sensations was insatiable. Among his new friends were famous artists, such as Thorwaldsen the sculptor and Horace Vernet, and English people, as well as musicians and fellow-countrymen. At the same time, he arranged his time so as to get through a regular methodical amount of composition every day, and he allowed nothing to interfere with it. The works which he was engaged upon at the time are among his most successful productions. He had been spurred to set Goethe's *Walpurgisnacht* to music during his late stay with the poet, and the first version was completed during this time in Italy. The *Hebrides overture* too was finished during the same period, and one of his most mature symphonies, afterwards known as the *Italian*, was rapidly progressing, besides many lesser works. He also imitated Mozart's famous feat of writing down by heart some of the music he heard performed in the Sistine Chapel in Holy Week.

When he left Italy, he went back to Munich, where he played his famous *G minor Concerto* for the first time and received a commission to compose an opera for the Munich theatre, the preparations for which went even as far as choosing the subject and a man to make it up into a libretto, but apparently never got any further. In order to visit his librettist, he had to go to Dusseldorf, where he was very much pleased with the people and their friendliness to him, and then he moved on to Paris.

In Paris, he found his friend Hiller, and a great number of other musicians of fame and genius, such as Chopin, Meyerbeer, and Liszt. He "cast himself into the vortex," according to his own phrase, and went in for a great deal of society and merriment; and enjoyed everything that came in his way, from theatres and the company of able and distinguished men to frolics in the streets. He was introduced to the Parisian public by Habeneck, at one of whose concerts he appeared as a pianist with Beethoven's great *G major Concerto*, and as a composer with his *Midsummer Night's Dream* overture. Hiller gives an amusing account of the circumstances of the first performance of this latter work. Just as they were going to begin, they found out there was no drummer. Whereupon Mendelssohn jumped on to the orchestra and seized the drumsticks, and "beat as good a roll as any drummer in the Old Guard," probably to show his proficiency. Parisian audiences are rather conventional and technical in their appreciation of classical music, and they were more inclined to be amazed at his brilliant gifts than to appreciate first-rate points in his composition; and after some pleasant experiences with the orchestra, he received an unpleasant impression through the rejection of his *Reformation Symphony*, which had been written a year or two before. A French critic, upon whose judgment much depended, considered the work too learned, too much fugato, and containing too little melody. This verdict and refusal to perform the work certainly pained him a good deal, more especially as he had been accustomed up to that time to carry all before him. It was in Paris also that he received the news of Goethe's death, and that of another friend called Edward Rietz, to whom he was attached. But otherwise he spent his life very gaily. A good deal of his time was spent in playing chess, in which he excelled. One of his frequent antagonists was a brother of Meyerbeer, and of another - Dr. Herman Franck - an amusing story is told. How Franck would not admit that Mendelssohn was the best chess-player, and how Mendelssohn every time he beat Franck used to say, "We play equally well - quite equally well - only I play a very little better."

Mendelssohn used to be annoyed at being bantered for a certain likeness of appearance to Meyerbeer, which arose partly from the fact that both composers wore their hair rather long. One day, when he had been teased a good deal about it, he went and had his hair cut quite short, much to the amusement of his friends, and of Meyerbeer himself when he heard of it.

During this same stay in Paris, he renewed his acquaintance with Cherubini, and the old autocrat criticised some of Mendelssohn's compositions, in a way that was not much to his taste. He broke out to Hiller one day, "What an extraordinary creature he is! You would fancy that a man could not be a great composer without sentiment, heart, feeling, or whatever else you call it; but I declare I believe that Cherubini makes everything out of his head alone." Still, he had a thorough appreciation of the old master, and found his remarks worth taking note of when he got over his annoyance. Not much new music was produced during the month he was in Paris, but he spent his working time chiefly in polishing up old compositions. The impression he made upon the public of Paris seems not to have been very great. The French said of him, "*Ce bon Mendelssohn, quel talent, quelle tête, quelle organisation!*" But when he was no longer amongst them, they did not care to play his music, and his name dropped out of notice for many years.

In the spring of 1832, he went on to London again and seemed to be as delighted as ever to be there. He described it in a letter from Naples as "the smoky nest which is fated now and ever to be my favourite residence." Here he always was thoroughly appreciated both personally and artistically; and that made him busy in the ways he liked best. His *Hebrides Overture* was played at the Philharmonic, and he presented a manuscript score of the work to the society. He played at concerts and on the organ at St. Paul's, and otherwise enjoyed life till July, when he went back to Berlin. Music at home was revived, and he gave some public concerts, chiefly of his own works, such as the *Walpurgisnacht*, which he had finished in Italy, the *Reformation Symphony* which had been refused in Paris, the *Hebrides Overture* which had been thoroughly revised after the performance in London, and the *G minor Concerto* which had made its first appearance at Munich, on his return from the Italian journey. He was still working at the *Italian Symphony*, and his anxious meditations upon it are recorded by himself to have cost him "the bitterest moments he ever endured." The "bitter moments" do not appear in the result, which owes much of its great popularity to its brightness and cheerfulness, and clearness of expression and orchestration. The Philharmonic Society wrote to him asking for a Symphony and some other pieces for their special benefit, offering handsome remuneration, and the new symphony was accordingly copied for them as soon as it was finished. The first performance took place in May, and for this he went over to London for a flying visit, going back to Germany in time to be present at the Düsseldorf Festival, which began on the 26th of that month. The result of the success of this festival, which seems to have been mainly through his exertions, was that he was invited to undertake the whole management of the musical arrangements at Düsseldorf, and he accepted the responsibility.

But before he began operations, he had to make yet another visit to London, and on this occasion, he took his father with him. The father did not find London quite so fascinating as his son did, and had the bad luck to have a spell of ill health, which did not improve matters. But the son spent his time very gaily and made as much music as usual. His duties at Düsseldorf began in the latter part of the same year, and he threw himself into them with his usual energy. He routed up the church choirs and set them to work at thoroughly good music, and he performed Handel's oratorios at concerts, and *Don Juan, Figaro, and Cherubini's Deux Journées* at the opera. But this course was not destined to last. He found the work at the theatre uncongenial and more trouble than it was worth and resigned that part of his engagement; but he kept on some of his duties and the position of general supervisor for some time longer.

In the spring, he went to Aix-la-Chapelle for a musical festival and met his friends Hiller and Chopin there. They were very welcome to him, but being direct from Paris brought a flavour of showiness in their art which was not altogether to Mendelssohn's taste. He wrote to his mother that they had both improved in playing, and Chopin especially was "quite a second Paganini, but they both labour a little under the Parisian love for effect and strong contrasts, and often sadly lose sight of time and calmness, and real musical feeling; perhaps I go too far the other way, so we mutually supply our deficiencies, and all three learn from each other I think; meanwhile, I felt rather like a schoolmaster, and they seemed rather like *mirliflores* and *incroyables*."

When the festival was over, Hiller paid Mendelssohn a visit at Düsseldorf and found him altogether in a flourishing condition. He was already at work at *St. Paul* but doing it without effort, and riding and spending much time with young painters and other lively and congenial company. He had begun the work in 1834, at the invitation of the Cacilien-Verein of Frankfort, but it was not finished till early in 1836.

Things did not go on very satisfactorily at Düsseldorf; he found it difficult to distribute his duties with his fellow workers and to judge who was to have precedence among them, and ultimately he became irritated and threw up his connection with the principal theatre. But his position in Germany was by this time so good that there was no lack of opportunities for making himself useful. Early in 1835, he was invited to conduct the famous Gewandhaus concerts at Leipzig. Besides this, he was asked to conduct the Lower Rhine Festival at Cologne in the same year, which went off with great success, and all his family came for the occasion. When that was over, he had to begin his work at Leipzig. It began in the most promising way, and he felt the contrast to the uncongenial troubles he had at Düsseldorf very strongly. He himself wrote that when he first went to Leipzig, he felt as if he were in Paradise. In the interval between the concerts at Leipzig, he paid a merry visit to his family at Berlin. It only lasted two days, but was marked by even more than usual gaiety, his home being crowded with guests who were animated by the merriment and jokes and playing of the pianoforte which always went on wherever he was. It was the last time the circle was to be complete, for his father Abraham died during the next month. Mendelssohn hurried back from Leipzig to Berlin to comfort his mother for a short while, but his duties necessitated his presence in Leipzig, where many important works were due for performance at the concerts, and he had to return to his lonely house there. He was prevented from thinking too much about his loss, however, by the necessity of getting on with *St. Paul*, and he was no doubt helped by the society of the place, where he was adored. His band were devoted to him, and his friends were ready to help him in every way, whether it was in practical matters or in sympathy.

St. Paul was finished in due time, but owing to the illness of Schelble, who conducted the Cacilien Society at Frankfort, the intention to perform it there for the first time had to be given up. But no harm was done by this, as an alternative was found in the Lower Rhine Festival at Dusseldorf. It was performed there on May 22, and notwithstanding the drawbacks of too small a room and great heat, was enthusiastically received by the public. Hiller gives a picture of the Festival, which shows Mendelssohn in the usual light, as the central point round which everything turned. "Not only as composer, director, and pianist, but also as a lively and agreeable host, introducing his visitors to each other, and bringing the right people together with a right word for everybody. But even Mendelssohn was not safe from the critics, and Hiller makes mention of one who spoke of *St. Paul* "in that lofty, patronising, damaging tone, too often adopted by critics towards artists who stand high above them." It was some time before

Mendelssohn could get over the fact that the first criticism of his beloved work should be so offensive."

From Düsseldorf, Mendelssohn went on to Frankfort to fill Schelble's place at the Cacilien-Verein, and here again he was with Hiller, who was consequently witness to one of the most important series of events in Mendelssohn's life. At Frankfort, he made acquaintance with a family of Jeanrenauds, consisting of the widow of a pastor of the French Reformed Church and her family. He found them extremely attractive and paid very frequent visits at their house. The truth was, he was especially attracted by one of the daughters, whose name was Cécile; but in such a case, he put a guard upon himself and behaved with so much cautious reserve that people thought the mother, who was still comparatively young and handsome, was the principal attraction. But Hiller was soon let into the secret by his pouring out his enthusiastic praises of the young lady when they were alone together; and things evidently tended towards a climax when Mendelssohn suddenly left Frankfort and went to Scheveningen, in Holland, for a month, and one of his friends says he did this deliberately to see how much he was in love. The result of this singularly cautious experiment was satisfactory, and soon after going back to Frankfort, they were formally engaged, and early in the following year, 1837, they were married.

Of course, they went for a honeymoon, during which Mendelssohn occupied himself with a good deal of composition, as the well-known *Forty-second Psalm* and the *Concerto for pianoforte in D minor* are said to have been the fruits of this happy time. He was also thinking already of writing a new oratorio, *St. Peter*, and corresponded with an intimate and cultivated friend called Schubring about it, but in the end, it came to nothing.

In the first year of his married life, he had to leave his wife to fulfil his engagements in England, and for the first time, he found himself positively cross and out of temper when he arrived in London alone. He wrote from there to Hiller: "Here I sit in the fog, very cross, without my wife, writing to you because your letter of the day before yesterday requires it; otherwise, I should hardly do so, for I am much too cross and melancholy today. I must be a little fond of my wife because I find that England and the fog and beef and porter have such a horribly bitter taste this time, and I used to like them so much." But he threw himself into the musical life of the town as much as ever, played the organ in St. Paul's and other places, and attended a performance of the oratorio *St. Paul* at Exeter Hall in the capacity of a listener and thought it "very interesting." He also began to think about a new oratorio, which was to be called *Elijah*, and had various consultations with a friend called Klingemann about it. Very soon he was obliged to hurry off to Birmingham, where he had to help in various ways, as conductor, and pianist, and organist, to the wonder and delight of everyone. From Birmingham again he had to hurry back to Germany, to be in time for the commencement of the Gewandhaus concerts at Leipzig. On his way there he arrived in London by coach at midnight, and was met by a committee from the Sacred Harmonic Society, who presented him with a silver snuff-box, which had an appropriate inscription on it. The whole stay in England, which contained so many experiences and so much active work, only lasted just over a month, and he was in his place again at the Gewandhaus concerts on October 1.

In the spring of the next year his eldest son was born, and in the summer he took his wife for the first time to his home at Berlin. He was very busy with composition, and had entered into correspondence with Planché about an opera. He wrote to Hiller, "I am thinking of composing an opera of Planché's next year. I have already got two acts of the *libretto*, and like them well enough to begin to set to work. The subject is taken from English history in the middle ages, rather serious, with a siege and a famine. I am eager to see the end of the *libretto*, which I expect next week." But, as happened in other cases, the projected opera came to nothing.

Other works, which depended on less troublesome conditions, went on more prosperously. The famous violin concerto was begun about the summer of this year, and before the year was out the composition of *Elijah* was also progressing. But it had cost a good deal of consideration before he settled on it, for some other subject besides the *St. Peter* before mentioned had also been thought of. Mendelssohn himself planned a good deal of the book of both his first oratorios, and had a clear idea of the need for thoroughly dramatic treatment of such a form of art. According to Hiller, one of the first incitements he received towards the composition of *Elijah* was the passage beginning, "And behold the Lord passed by," etc., which struck him as such a splendid opportunity for an important feature in an oratorio, and ultimately formed one of the most striking features in the completed work.

His life continued for the most part in the same tenor for some time. He had to conduct again at Düsseldorf in May, 1839, and in the summer he went to Frankfort; he was always a good deal in society, as usual, and always steadily composing. In the autumn he had another child, a daughter, and near the same time Hiller, who had lately lost his mother, came to stay with him at Leipzig. Hiller's account of the arrangements of Mendelssohn's house and their domestic habits are very characteristic. The house Mendelssohn lived in looked out upon St. Thomas's church and school, where Bach had spent so much of his life. The main features of the inside were a sort of hall, with a large sitting room and some bedrooms to the right going in, and to the left Mendelssohn's own study with his pianoforte in it, and opening out of this a fine large drawing room, which was doubtless very serviceable to a man who saw so much company. They used to breakfast at eight on coffee and bread-and-butter, but Mendelssohn never ate butter himself, "but broke his bread into his coffee like any schoolboy." They dined at one, and though Mendelssohn despised butter he always liked a good glass of wine, and they often had to try some special sort, which he would produce with great delight and swallow with immense satisfaction. They made quick work with their dinner, but in the evenings, after supper, they used to sit round the table for hours, chatting, but not smoking, and sometimes they used the pianoforte. Mendelssohn took an idea into his head that he and Hiller must compose at the same table together, and they tried it. It answered well enough when they wanted to make nothing more serious than part songs, but Hiller did not find it to his liking when more important work was in hand. In fact, he found it impossible to work in the same house with Mendelssohn at the oratorio he was then writing. He said it was impossible to feel at ease at the pianoforte with the consciousness that every idea had a listener, and such a one! Besides, I afterwards discovered by chance that Mendelssohn equally disliked his communings with his genius to be overheard. How could it be otherwise? At last, Hiller had to move to a lodging hard by, and then both of them pursued their work with less constraint.

Mendelssohn was always very careful in getting the best form of expression for what he wanted to say musically, and many of his works were frequently revised with the utmost care. Hiller came across a curious instance of his anxiety in this respect, about this same time. One evening he found him looking flushed and in an unusual state of excitement; and when he asked him what was the matter, Mendelssohn answered, "Here have I been sitting for the last four hours trying to alter a few bars in a part song, and can't do it." He had tried twenty times without being able to satisfy himself; and it appears that in the end he had to leave it till another time. Such patience and expenditure of time as this over a small detail makes all the more marvellous the amount of work and society which he managed to get through. He superintended the performance of numbers of important works at the Gewandhaus concerts, carried on a voluminous correspondence, translated several difficult sonnets of Dante, Boccaccio, and other Italian poets for an uncle called Joseph, and drew up an important memorial to the Home Minister of the King of Saxony about the application of a legacy, which had been left by one Herr Blumner, to the foundation of a regular musical academy at Leipzig; which had important results, as it led to the foundation of the famous Conservatorium there in 1843. Besides all this, he found time and energy enough to produce his famous *Lobgesang*, or *Hymn of Praise*, at the request of the Town Council of Leipzig, for the Gutenberg festival which was in commemoration of the invention of printing, and took place there in June, 1840. As soon as this festival was over, he had to go to Schwerin to conduct a performance of *St. Paul* and when he came back he began to exert himself to get a worthy monument erected in Leipzig to the memory of John Sebastian Bach, and at the same time gave an organ performance in the church of St. Thomas - sacred as much to the memory of the great cantor as to the nominal patron saint - by which he realised a good sum to improve the pay of the men in the Gewandhaus band.

It sounds like a perpetual storm of work, but it never seemed to impair his clearheadedness, or hamper his musical powers in any way. But the strain seems in reality to have had some effect upon his health at this time, and his medical adviser was anxious for him to relax a little. He was generally as brilliant in society as ever, but he had days of exhaustion and depression, which were ominous. But rest was impossible, for he received a new invitation from England to go and superintend the performance of the *Lobgesang* at Birmingham in September, and he had accordingly to squeeze in a hasty visit to this country in that month which passed, much as usual, with playing on the organ in Birmingham, and at St. Peter's, Cornhill, and visiting his numerous friends, and superintending rehearsals, and winning more successes everywhere; and then by the beginning of October he had to be back again for the Gewandhaus concerts. The new *Lobgesang* was, of course, to be performed at Leipzig, and it affords another instance of Mendelssohn's care about finishing his works. Theorists and critics often talk about music as if it sprung straight from a man's brain in its perfect shape, and could not be satisfactory or spontaneous if it did not flow out under the immediate influence of a single inspiration. Beethoven is well known to be an exception, in so far as he always hammered and plied his works time after time before he could get them to answer to his intentions; but he is generally set aside as too peculiar to be counted. Mendelssohn is, however, in fact a more difficult instance against the favourite theory than Beethoven to explain away; for the plan upon which he dealt with his art was so much simpler, and the style of his musical thoughts so much easier to express; and his education too had been all on the side of making sure of details. And yet even he had many fierce struggles to get things to go as he wanted them and in the case of the *Lobgesang* he altered and re-wrote so much after the experience he had gained at the first performance at the Gutenberg Festival and the performance at Birmingham, that the plates which had been engraved for the publication of the work in England had to be destroyed, and the entire work re-done; and a performance of the work in its new shape, as the world knows it now, was first given in December, nearly six months after the first performance. Hiller tells a similar story about the popular *D minor trio* for pianoforte, violin, and cello, which was published in this year. Mendelssohn went on correcting and altering it up to the last minute, and many of the plates had to be engraved over again.

The next year, 1841, did not make things better for his health and freshness; for he was invited by the King of Prussia to undertake the musical part of a great scheme he had for founding an Academy of Arts on a grand scale at Berlin. Correspondence and interchange of views on the subject absorbed nearly all his time in the most unprofitable and vexatious manner. Of course, Government officials, as well as Royal personages, had their own views of the way in which the scheme was to be carried out, and the result was that Mendelssohn was thoroughly worried and bothered. He did not believe that Berlin could take a high place among the German musical capitals. But he could not refuse the commands of the king, and so the arduous labours had to be faced, and he took up his abode in his old home to be on the spot for the conferences which were necessary. One satisfactory result came out of it, which was his setting of the *Antigone* of Sophocles. The king took a fancy for reviving the ancient tragedies with music, and Mendelssohn, finding the matter congenial, threw himself into the task with his usual energy, and the work was first performed at Potsdam in October, and soon became a favourite with the public both at Leipzig and Berlin. But the audiences at the latter town were very different from what he was accustomed to at Leipzig. They were cold and apathetic, and he was not happy with them. The usual musical parties at his house must, however, have been some solace to him, and there he could always meet clever and congenial people. He found time also to get on with his *Scotch Symphony*, and finished it early in the winter of 1842. It was first performed at Leipzig in March, and early in the summer he had to go over to London to superintend its performance by the Philharmonic Society there.

This visit passed much in the usual way, but it was made memorable to the public by a private visit he was invited to pay to the Queen and Prince Consort at Buckingham Palace, the account of which in a letter to his mother is familiar to many musical people. He also saw a great deal of society as usual, and seems to have specially delighted people with his extemporising on the organ. He used very frequently to play voluntaries after service in churches where there were good organs, and his favourite plan was to take one of the hymn tunes they had just had in service, or a piece of an anthem or chorus which had just been heard, and make a sort of extemporary fantasia or fugue upon it, in a manner which evidently impressed his hearers greatly. He had a great reputation for such performances, and for playing Bach's fugues; and when people got wind of his being in church they always stopped for a long while after service to listen to him; - sometimes to the annoyance of the vergers, who are recorded to have withdrawn the organ-blower on one occasion at St. Paul's in the middle of a fugue, in order to clear out the congregation.

Before the end of the year he had to be back at his uncongenial work at Berlin. The scheme for the formation of the musical department in the great Academy of Arts seems to have come to a standstill, and finally it became evident that nothing more could be done in that direction, so all the worry and vexation he had undergone about it so far had been in vain. All that resulted was the formation of a very select cathedral choir, and the title of General Music Director, with a good salary for Mendelssohn, and a commission from the king for him to compose music to *Edipus Coloneus*, after the manner of the Antigone, as well as music to the *Athalie* of Racine and Shakespeare's *Tempest*, and to complete the music for the *Midsummer Night's Dream*.

The consultations about the Berlin school being ended, he could give more time to his schemes at Leipzig, and there he was at last successful in getting the Conservatorium started, about which he had been drawing up the memorial three years before. The concerts went on again as usual, and early in 1843 a grand performance of the *Walpurgisnacht* was given in a completely revised form. For he dealt with that work as he had dealt with the *Hymn of Praise*, and rewrote most of it, and added two airs to the original scheme so that the form in which it is now so well known is considerably different from its first version.

Berlioz came to Leipzig early in this year, and Mendelssohn received him very affably. Mendelssohn's opinion of Berlioz was expressed in a letter in which he wrote of his music: "I cannot conceive anything more insipid, wearisome, and Philistine - for, with all his endeavours to go stark mad, he never once succeeds." Berlioz's opinion of Mendelssohn was naturally of a similar cast, but from an opposite point of view; but this did not hinder them from appearing in public as friends. Berlioz gave an account of his visit to Leipzig in a letter to Stephen Heller, and of the first meeting with Mendelssohn just after a performance of the *Walpurgisnacht*. According to his own account, Berlioz asked for the baton Mendelssohn had been conducting with, and Mendelssohn answered that he would give it if Berlioz would send his in exchange.

Berlioz courteously answered, "I shall be giving copper for gold; but never mind, let it be so." And next day he sent his stick with a characteristic note, calling Mendelssohn great chief, and their exchange an exchange of tomahawks, and ending, "Be my brother! and when the great spirit sends us to hunt in the land of shades, may our warriors hang our tomahawks together at the door of the council chamber." Mendelssohn in his turn gave Berlioz what help he could, and offered him the concert-room of the Gewandhaus, and asked to be allowed to play one of Berlioz's works at one of the concerts; and Berlioz says further in his letter to Heller that in helping him to organise his concert Mendelssohn did behave like a brother towards him.

The events of the early part of 1843 were the regular opening of the Leipzig Conservatorium in the buildings of the Gewandhaus, and the unveiling of the monument to John Sebastian Bach. Another event was the appearance of Joseph Joachim, the violinist, at Leipzig, then twelve years old; and the friendship which thereupon commenced between him and Mendelssohn. The compositions which he had been commissioned to produce for the king took much of his time in the middle part of the year, and in September the *Midsummer Night's Dream* with his music completed was performed at the New Palace at Potsdam with great applause. An amusing feature of the occasion was the condition of mind of the Berliners towards the play, which was considered by them as rather a low piece. Some distinguished individual confided to Mendelssohn that he thought the music was very good, but that it was a pity it should have been wasted on such a poor play!

Mendelssohn was now drawn by the force of circumstances to remain more constantly in Berlin, and the connection with the Gewandhaus concerts had definitely to be given up. In November he moved his family and his goods and chattels to Berlin, where he took up his abode in his old house, which since the death of both parents had become his property.

Early in the next year he received a fresh invitation from the directors of the London Philharmonic Society to conduct some of the concerts of the approaching season, and in May he accordingly began operations with them. He had one rather disagreeable collision with the band, which redounded immensely to his credit and very little to theirs. He had brought with him Schubert's greatest symphony, which had been unearthed by Schumann at Vienna, thinking to make it a welcome feature at the concerts. But the band did not understand it, and behaved so badly that Mendelssohn withdrew it in real anger, and along with it his own new *Ruy Blas* overture. But after that his relations with them became excellent. They felt that they had a conductor who knew thoroughly what he wanted and took infinite pains to get the best effect out of the works performed. He made himself clearly understood, and was patient and good-tempered over difficulties as long as the players did their best; but he could be very sharp and severe where such methods of management were wanted. The concerts which he conducted were a great success, and his playing and extemporising caused as much excitement and delight as usual. The whole visit was full of pleasure for him. He wrote home to his sister describing it as "a mad, most extraordinarily mad time, a glorious visit. I was never received anywhere with such universal kindness, and have made more music in these two months than I do elsewhere in two years."

In July he came back to his family again, and spent a time of rest at last with his wife and children near Frankfort. Of course, composition was not considered to interfere with his holiday, and during his two months of comparative quiet he finished at last his famous *Violin Concerto*, which had been begun long before. He played with his children and gave his little daughter Marie lessons on the pianoforte, which occasioned the amusing remark that he had forgotten how to finger the scale of C.

This pleasant time was brought to an end by his presence being required at Berlin again for the regular succession of concerts. Here he met as before with coldness and discouragement, and not being able to endure the uncongenial musical atmosphere of the place any longer, he begged the king to release him finally from his engagements, and left the place with relief. He naturally returned to Leipzig again, where he was so thoroughly appreciated, and threw himself not only into the work of the concerts but into the work of the new school. He gave a certain number of lessons in pianoforte playing and composition, of which the members of the classes ever afterwards treasured the remembrance. He gave the pupils minute attention, and made them work hard, and no doubt they felt it to be a great privilege to be taught by him, though sometimes he was rather quick-tempered and spoke sharply to them. But it would have been difficult not to profit from such a man's teaching, even if it was true, as stated by men of the same standing with himself, that teaching was not a strong point with him.

Besides all these various occupations, he was now busy with the composition of the *Elijah*. The arrangement of the book of words had spread over a very long time, and he had evidently taken extraordinary pains over it; but now at last he was able to go on with the making of the music; and he was very pleased with what he did. He writes to a friend, "If it only turns out half as good as I fancy it is, how pleased I shall be!" Interruptions frequently came in the shape of performances which he had to conduct at various towns, but the work progressed pretty steadily. The whole seems to have been completed before the summer was over; and in August he took his journey to England once again to superintend the preparations for the first performance at Birmingham. This took place in the Town Hall there on August 26th, amid such enthusiasm and excitement as has rarely been witnessed over a new musical work. He himself was delighted and said he never in his life heard a better performance; and eagerly shook hands with as many of the performers as he could get to afterwards, thanking them for what they had done. But the work was very severe and began to tell upon him, and on his way back to Germany he was forced to break his journey and rest. In *Elijah* again he made many alterations in consequence of his impressions at the performance, which cost him some labour and time, and then once more he seems to have taken to the idea of writing an opera, and had some correspondence with a theatrical manager as well as with Scribe, the famous French librettist, on the subject. But yet again the project came to nothing after causing him some annoyance.

He was himself becoming conscious that the strain of work and excitement was too great and constant, and he suffered from pains in his head. But he could not take much rest. There was a great quantity of work to be done at Leipzig in the latter part of the year, and early in the next he had to go to England once again for more performances of *Elijah*. He still played as brilliantly as ever and was as merry and bright in society as long as excitement kept him up; but the kind of life he led was taking more and more serious effect upon him. When he returned to Frankfort in rather an overstrained condition he received too suddenly the news of the death of his sister Fanny. The shock was too great for him, and he fell to the ground insensible. He became so ill that it was necessary to give him complete change of scene and rest. For this purpose he moved with his family to Switzerland, where he amused himself chiefly with sketching. He seemed to get a little better by slow degrees and regained his spirits, but his nerves were completely out of order, and he could not bear the least noise. He never played on the pianoforte and was shy of trying an organ. Applications came for a new symphony for the Philharmonic in London and other works, and propositions for more performances of *Elijah* under his direction, but he refused to entertain most of them for the present, hoping for a more suitable time. In the latter part of the summer he began composing again and worked at a new oratorio which was to be called *Christus*, and at the *Loreley*, a last experiment in opera, and a string quartet. But he was very much changed, and his brilliant spirits had given place to frequent fits of apathy and depression.

In September they moved back to Leipzig, but he could take no part in the Gewandhaus concerts and avoided public performances. He still looked forward to going to Vienna and directing the performance of *Elijah* there, and he was occasionally in something like his old spirits; but there was no sign of solid improvement, and he looked old and worn. On October 9th a fit of shivering and coldness came on which necessitated the immediate attention of doctors and the application of leeches. Again he got a little better in a week or so and was able to go out walking with his wife towards the end of the month. But the attack returned, and after lingering without consciousness for almost a day he died on November 4, 1847, only thirty-eight years of age.

His funeral was attended by the principal representatives of the Conservatorium and civic officials and members of the university and crowds of sympathisers; and after due honours at Leipzig the body was removed to Berlin and buried there close to the grave of his sister Fanny. His death produced a great sensation both in England and Germany; the time seemed so short since he had been delighting everyone he met with his brightness and vivacity. People felt that they had lost a dear friend as much as the world a great composer. Performances in honour of his memory were given in London and

Manchester and Birmingham, and at Berlin and Leipzig and Vienna, and other German towns; and even in Paris the first concert of the Conservatoire, in 1848, was consecrated to his memory.

It has not been the lot of many men to win so much affection or to give so much pleasure. His various gifts were in constant employment for the benefit of all people who were capable of enjoying music and good company; and he squeezed as much work into his short life as most men get into a life of twice the length. The spirit in the end wore out the body; indeed, it seems wonderful that it stood the strain so long. But his nature would not allow him to live otherwise, and the enjoyment of all the things that came in his way was a necessary condition to enable him to produce the happy, genial style of music which is characteristic of him. The least that can be said of him is that, though he was most eminently capable of enjoying life and society, he never sacrificed his ideals of art to gain an extra moment for gay frivolity. He was too full of occupation to brood over the troubles of the world or to think much of tragedies and stern workings of fate; but all moods must have their expression in art, and those which were natural to him to express he dealt with in the most delicate and artistic way, and the results have afforded healthy and refined pleasure to an immense number of people.

X

ROBERT SCHUMANN.

IN the early part of the history of modern music, the aims of the greatest composers seem easily intelligible to those who come after. The roads to great achievements were open in all directions, and after preliminary difficulties had been overcome by men whose names have for the most part passed out of remembrance, the great heroes of the art came upon the scene, and with strenuous vigour made sure of one new province of art after another, till by the second quarter of the present century there hardly seemed any new lands left to conquer. The great provinces of oratorio, opera, symphony, and song were taken complete possession of, and the artistic principles upon which they needed to be worked out seemed theoretically to be so thoroughly well settled and decided that it is not easy to see what was left for great composers to do. The matter of merely improving upon an established form of art is not nearly so enticing as the perfecting of one which is not mature and does not seem to offer such opportunities for individual distinction. In art, just as in the circumstances of outward life, it is always more inspiriting to adventure into new lands and open them up for the first time than it is to cultivate and improve them when someone else has discovered and conquered them. When great material resources are at the command of many people, there are plentiful opportunities for average men to make themselves useful, but less for individual men to tower into rare eminence above their fellows. The sum of work done may on the whole be greater than what was done in earlier stages of history, but it is more diffused, and more hands have a share in it. Individual greatness may show itself still, but its signs and tokens seem less clearly marked out, and to depend on subtler conditions and to have less of monumental and isolated conspicuousness about them. Men have to use what has been used before and do what has been done before, and their individual prominence depends chiefly upon the way in which they can adapt themselves to phases of mind and action in their time or the manner in which they use established forms so as to illustrate the taste and characteristic modes of feeling of their generation. They may rise to eminence as illustrators, as many painters do, or they may revive and combine different branches of art, or they may become great critics, and by appreciating thoroughly what has been done in the past, find out also where there is something which has not been done, or at least not done in the sense which appeals most powerfully and naturally to the people of their own time. The mere copying of other people's ways of expressing themselves can never be of much use to the world. People who only write blameless symphonies and sonatas after the accepted models, with nothing of their own to mark them by, might just as well let composing alone. They are only taking up time which would be better employed in attending to the original masterpieces. The only chance for the composer who has no new point to make is for him to have a genuine spur in himself arising from some phase of contemporary life which appeals strongly to him, or a deep and unusual feeling for poetry and romance and colour, which makes him produce spontaneous effects as the result of his exceptional organisation and can be achieved by him alone.

The immense accumulation of material which had been organised sufficiently for musicians to work upon by the end of the first quarter of the nineteenth century produced a very great number of fair composers, who ministered to the average wants of the day. The works of the great masters supplied them with the outlines of ideas and the principle of arranging them in an orderly manner, and they sometimes attained to a point of real usefulness without breaking new ground. Some obtained a place of mark in history by doing exceptional work of a special kind, such as enlarging the resources of the pianoforte, improving the management of orchestras, or by introducing national elements of a striking character into the domain of art. But the power of thought and character which is wanted to make a really memorable composer becomes no commoner with the increase of fields to work in. Reputations are more plentiful than master minds; for nearness of time always makes it difficult to escape from misleading influences in judging who are really first-rate and who are only made-up successes. Men who fifty years ago were universally regarded as among the great composers of all time, and were hailed at every appearance with wild enthusiasm, are beginning to drop so entirely into neglect that the younger scions of the living generation know of them as little more than empty names. But as these lesser lights die out and sink into obscurity, some few names stand out all the clearer and with more steady brightness for being free of the crowd of ephemeral stars; and at least one among them, after being looked at rather suspiciously by professors of classical views in art, and fiercely opposed by critics, even till some time after his death, has been of late years becoming gradually more and more established in the affections of all people of large musical sympathies and not only wins appreciation for what is lovable in his work among those who only care for what pleases them, but also a place in musical history as a foremost and most characteristic champion of the progressive tendencies of musical art.

Robert Schumann was the first composer who illustrated several thoroughly modern traits of character in his life and work. He was the first composer of dignified instrumental music in whom certain romantic and mystic influences came to a head; the first who combined singular gifts of appreciative criticism and a capacity for analysing the inner meaning and purport of music with a power of original musical production; and the first of great mark in whom the modern tendency to luxuriate in warm and rich colouring in every department of art became decidedly pronounced. The circumstances of his parentage and education were peculiar for a musician, and though favourable in some ways, evidently unfavourable in others. His father, August Schumann, was a publisher and bookseller in Zwickau, in Saxony, who had decided literary tastes and gained some distinction by translating Byron's *Childe Harold* and *Beppo*, as well as some things of Scott's into German, and by writing some original treatises. His wife was the daughter of a surgeon of some repute in another town of Saxony, and she is recorded to have been extremely practical and at the same time inclined to sentimentality, but to have shown no traits which could account for the direction taken by her son's genius; for she certainly had no kind of sympathy with it. Four children preceded Robert into the world, where he made his first appearance on the 8th of June, 1810.

The bent of his nature towards music seems to have asserted itself early, and it must have done so without encouragement. He was sent to school when he was six and received some musical teaching, probably of no very high order, from an excellent man called Kuntsch; who, though not capable of grounding him very securely in music, nevertheless inspired him with affection and esteem. At school, he is recorded to have shown a peculiar ability for taking off the characters of his schoolfellows in extemporary pieces which he played on the pianoforte before he was ten years old. From school, he advanced to the Zwickau Academy, where again he showed his musical inclinations by making special friends with any boys who had any liking for the art; and he even succeeded in organising a few of them into a little band consisting of two violins, two flutes, a clarionet, and two horns, and with his accompaniment on the pianoforte they managed to perform works of solid artistic merit and also some things which Schumann himself wrote for them. To these performances, the father was not at all averse and indeed seemed ready to fall in with his son's tastes; for he even went so far as to make overtures to Carl Maria von Weber to take him as a pupil. But unfortunately, in 1825, when the boy was yet only fifteen years old, the good father died and the mother, always averse to the son's musical inclinations, insisted on his preparing himself to become a lawyer. His education was carried on with this view for some years, and when he was eighteen, he was sent to Leipzig University, where he was entered as a student of law. But wherever he went his inclination for music asserted itself; he always sought out friends who could sympathise with him and spent his time in the enjoyment of making music with them and practising, and occasionally trying his hand at composition. The only taste which vied with music was that for poetry and literature of a sentimental and imaginative kind. He was chiefly taken possession of by the writer Jean Paul Richter, familiarly known to the world as Jean Paul, whose peculiar fancy and style of thought coloured his ways of looking at things for the greater part of his life. He took to writing poetry of his own and setting it to music, and otherwise showed the state of his mind by breaking into effusions which were inspired by the influence of his favourite writer, and were by him called Jean-Pauliads.

The most important friendship he made at Leipzig was that of a very able teacher of music and the pianoforte, called Friedrich Wieck, under whom he studied. This master had a daughter called Clara, who was an astonishing musical prodigy, and though at that time only nine years old had made her appearance in public as a pianist with great success. He became more and more determined to adopt music as his profession but was obliged by force of circumstances to keep up the appearance of studying law, and with that view, after a year at Leipzig, he passed on to Heidelberg to complete his education, where he was placed under the direction of a famous professor of law by name Thibaut, who happened also to be musical. The professor, seeing in course of time the decided disinclination of his pupil for legal studies and his equally decided musical gifts, was inclined to encourage him in the latter. At Heidelberg, he went on practising with more ardour than ever and began to gain a reputation as a pianist; while at the same time, he also made experiments in composition, some of which had sufficiently solid qualities in them to be kept among the works which he recognised as worthy of his ideals in later years. At last, he made an appeal to his mother and his guardian to release him from the drudgery of the legal studies to which he had never really succeeded in accommodating himself; and when his master Wieck backed his appeal by expressing his belief in the boy's powers, they yielded to the inevitable, and he was allowed to prepare for the career of a musician unchecked.

But it was as a pianist that he intended to come before the world; and with the view of making himself fit for the career of a performer, he returned to Leipzig and took up his abode with his master Wieck, with whom he remained for two years. But the rather amateurish way in which he had been forced to work at the piano till this time caused him to be somewhat behindhand for his age in matters of technical mastery, which are very necessary for a pianist in modern times; and though he worked very hard, he did not get on fast enough to satisfy himself. His impatience at last drove him to try and discover some means of making his fingers more pliant without such prolonged drudgery, and he invented a machine which he supposed would enable him to arrive at complete facility at once. He applied it to his right hand first, and instead of curing its deficiencies, maimed it completely from that time forward. At first, he hoped it would come right and went on practising with his left hand for some time; but though everything was tried which could be thought of, it was without avail, and the chances of his becoming a public pianist were entirely put an end to.

This naturally made him turn his attention more fully to composition, and the work he had gone through in practising was not by any means wasted, as it served him in very good stead in writing for the pianoforte and in songs. But he had a good deal of lost time to make up, and though he felt he had something in him which was worth putting down, he found it hard to express it at first. He was of course obliged to give up working at the pianoforte with Wieck; but he still lived in his house and worked at composition and the departments of musical art which go with it, under a man called Dorn, who held the position of conductor in the opera at Leipzig. With him, he began almost at the very elements and worked his way through the drudgery which most aspirants to the fame of a composer complete almost in boyhood. But his spirits were high, and he never seems to have been particularly cast down by the necessity of having to give up all hopes of being a great pianist. Composition supplied him with a thoroughly congenial alternative, and he did not know how hard and trying the fight would have to be to win a hearing for his works.

He tried various lines of composition at this time, and works both of large and small calibre. A symphony was completed, and the first movement of it was played at his native town, Zwickau, at a concert where Clara Wieck, then a girl of thirteen, also made her appearance as a pianist and fired the quiet people of the place with musical enthusiasm for the first time in their lives. He also wrote a concerto, which, with the symphony, was ultimately consigned to oblivion. The larger works of this time were all afterwards laid aside by him, and only the lesser works for pianoforte have survived; and in reality, he expressed himself most naturally in the latter line at first, partly owing to the lack of education in the principles of composition and partly to his sympathy with the instrument to which he had lately given so much attention. This sympathy was still all-powerful and made him think most of his music from the point of view of a pianist

- a condition which he never altogether freed himself from, though it grew less prominent as years went on. But in this line, his poetical and susceptible disposition served him in good stead, and in the early years of his work as a composer, he produced many of his happiest and most successful compositions in the form of highly imaginative pianoforte music. The line he chose was one in which few composers of the highest rank had hitherto done much, but it was thoroughly in consonance with the spirit of the age. His bent was towards short, vivid pieces, in which he expressed some definite idea. They belonged to the same order as Mendelssohn's "Songs without Words," but were far more characteristic and original, and more poetical and romantic. Even when he went to work to make large works and long movements, he constructed them by knitting a series of such little pieces together in a style more like mosaic than the continuous development of the sonatas by earlier great masters. But the standard of his ideas was so high, and his treatment of the instrument so rich in colour, that he raised this branch of art to a point which it had never attained before and left a mass of genuine lyrics that are the most enduring and enjoyable of all the thousands of such works which have come into existence in the present century.

The circumstances of his life, and even the apparent defects of his education, seemed in this way to make him a high representative of the tendencies of his time, and enabled him to treat forms of art which have too often been of very slight value and of very flimsy construction, so as to give them a standing among works of real artistic importance. He also tried his hand in the line of sonatas, but he could not bring himself to the proper standpoint of a sonata writer of the conventional type; and rather experimented than wrote with deliberate and conscious judgment as to what was possible and worth doing in that form of art. For either his poetical impulses dominated him, or else he had to sacrifice something in the constraint of confining himself to accepted regulations. It is natural to suppose that this was partly caused by a want of discipline in his earlier years; but it is certain that if his nature had been regulated by much of the work necessary to make a composer of the old-fashioned classical pattern, he would never have produced the kind of pianoforte music which is so characteristic of himself and also of the time when he lived.

In the early years of his musical career, after the necessary abandonment of the project of becoming a great pianist, he was drawn into another line besides that of composition, which is equally characteristic of his position in relation to his art. Many of the young and enthusiastic musical friends he had made in the course of his time at universities used to meet together in a restaurant, and their talk turned chiefly upon music. They discussed the lowness of the taste of the public and the badness of musical criticism and came to the conclusion that they might do something themselves to remedy it. Schumann himself had tried his hand at criticism and made his first appearance in that capacity with a warmly appreciative article on an early work of Chopin in one of the principal newspapers of the time. They now determined on a definite and decisive plan of action and founded a regular musical newspaper, in which the friends were to write criticisms and discuss important subjects connected with music. Among the helpers Schumann had in the work was a friend called Schunke, his pianoforte master Friedrich Wieck, and an able writer called Knorr. The first number of this paper, which was called *Die Neue Zeitschrift für Musik*, came out in April 1834. Schumann himself, in after years, wrote a preface to the series of his own articles which appeared in it, and gave an account of the conditions under which the newspaper was started and the objects of its enthusiastic promoters. In it, he said, "The musical situation was not then very encouraging in Germany. On the stage, Rossini reigned; at the pianoforte, nothing was heard but Herz and Hünten; and yet but a few years had passed since Beethoven, Weber, and Schubert had lived amongst us. One day, the thought awakened in a wild heart, 'Let us not look on idly, let us also lend our aid to progress, let us bring again the poetry of art to honour among men.' From such ideas, our most unique newspaper began. But the original band could not long hold together. Schunke died; others were drawn away from Leipzig by the necessities of their lives, and it nearly came to an end."

Schumann then goes on to describe himself, and his words clearly define his position in relation to art at that time. "One of the party - the musical visionary of the society - who had dreamed away his life until then rather over the pianoforte than among books, decided to take the editorship of the paper into his own hands and carried out his decision for ten years until 1844." Hence began a series of articles and sketches on music and musical subjects, which are without parallel in the literature connected with the art. The style is fanciful but singularly telling and attractive, and deals with all subjects in the genuinely appreciative spirit which is so extremely rare among writers upon music. His is not the spirit which speaks well and in words of well-regulated enthusiasm of an established great work, or pats a dull composer on the back because he has written respectably and according to rule, but the spirit which searches out what is really and substantially good in the byways as well as the high-ways of art; and endeavours to show the public where the point lies and how and wherein the power and value of a new work may be felt. It really was a splendid mission to undertake, and no man in the world was more fit for the office. His position as a genuine composer himself gave him insight into many ways and virtues of his brother composers, which it takes a long time for the public or even a good critic to grasp, while his generous sympathies and his poetical disposition, and even the way in which the work of Jean Paul had influenced him in earlier years, gave him a tone and style which were peculiarly happy in dealing with a subject which really is a difficult one to manage, so as to avoid coldness on the one hand and frothy exuberance on the other.

In this way, he was able to play a most honourable part, for nearly all the rising musicians of the day were at one time or another liberally helped by the generous words he wrote about their works. Of Chopin, he had written already before the paper was regularly started, and further criticisms upon his works followed later on. In its pages, he also wrote of Mendelssohn, Gade, Sterndale Bennett, Franz, Henselt, Stephen Heller, Berlioz, Liszt, Thalberg, Hiller, Ernst, Vieuxtemps, Moscheles, and Johannes Brahms, and always in a way which showed marvellous perception of their good points and touched their faults lightly and generously. It was the mission he had undertaken to further good and sound art, and he did it rather by extolling freely what was worthy of such treatment in the works of his contemporaries than in the more easy but less lovely way of pulling rubbish and impotence to pieces. His position was a really singular one, for most of the men he praised were immeasurably inferior to him in the very department of art about which he was writing, and yet he never put himself forward or showed any bitterness at the absence of encouragement and sympathy for his own work, which he so liberally gave to others; and it is not less remarkable that several of the men he praised and helped so generously were utterly incapable to the end of their days of showing any appreciation of the work of the man who had been their public champion.

His position in these respects is altogether a most noble one, and the familiar truth that it is harder to see real beauties than blemishes enhances it, for he always aimed at hearty praise, even of things which were absolutely new to the world, and when dealing with works which an ordinary critic would either have written an involved account of so as to prevent anyone knowing whether he meant to praise or to blame, or else have endeavoured to amuse the public by extravagantly abusing.

Schumann's insight in such respects was a quarter of a century ahead of his contemporaries. The most signal instance of this fact was the enthusiastic article he wrote about Johannes Brahms, who, as a young man, was sent to him by Joachim, the famous violinist. Schumann saw into him directly and recognised in possibility what he has come to be in the world's estimation in ultimate reality, and he no sooner saw it than he proclaimed it in no measured terms. It so happened that the musical public did not accept his judgment at the time, and Brahms had a very long fight to win his way to the front; but this only enhances the acuteness of Schumann's insight, especially when it is remembered that Schumann himself was by that time getting on towards the end of his musical career, when most people are less open to fresh impressions than they are in young and expansible times.

The newspaper was not, of course, solely devoted to praising and expressing sympathy for brother composers, but also contained articles and discussions about great masters of the past and their works. And not a little of this was carried on in a most peculiar way, which serves to connect Schumann's music with his literary work. He invented a fanciful name for the group of friends who joined with him in carrying on the newspaper. They were the Davidsbundler or Davidites, whose mission was to wage war against musical Philistinism and obstruction - that is, against narrowness, pedantry, commonplace, and vulgarity, and all the many other forces and perversities which mislead or bewilder the well-intentioned public. This Davidsbund comprised many names, which partly represented types of thought and feeling, and partly real persons, so far as the persons could be identified with the types. Schumann himself was represented by several names, which personified the various qualities which he felt to exist within himself. "Florestan" represented his impulsive and ardently imaginative side; "Eusebius," the more thoughtful and critical side; "Meister Raro" stood between the two and interposed in their discussions. Other names were now and then used to express the different moods in which different articles were written. Mendelssohn was Felix Meritis, Clara Wieck was sometimes "Chiarina," sometimes "Cecilia," and numbers of other less-known persons had characteristic titles. By using the names representing different types of mind, dialogues were carried on upon matters of musical interest from different points of view; or a string of aphorisms with the names of the personified types appended gave similarly effective impressions. An instance will give the best explanation of this curious device. Florestan, the impulsive Schumann, says, "Where is the use of dressing a hair-brained youth in his grandfather's furred dressing-gown and putting a pipe in his mouth to make him regular and orderly? Let him keep his flowing locks and easy attire. I love not the men whose lives are not in unison with their works." Meister Raro - the moderating Schumann - follows with another aphorism: "Warn the youth who composes. Fruit that ripens too early falls before its time. The young mind must often unlearn theory before it can be put in practice." Eusebius, the reflecting, meditative Schumann, follows with yet another: "It is not enough that I know something unless I can make use of what I have learned in the conduct of my life." There is obviously no dialogue here, but each character, taking the same thought in mind, supplies something from his point of view towards a complete judgment in the matter. Another ingenious plan is for two or more articles upon the same subject to be given side by side. In this way, one of Chopin's concertos is discussed by both Florestan and Eusebius, and on such a question as a proposed monument to Beethoven, no less than four personified abstractions write independent articles. Sometimes Florestan and Eusebius discuss things adversely, as happens over Hummel's Studies, on which occasion "Meister Raro" steps in at the end and disagrees with both of them. The idea is clearly a new one in musical criticism, and it is singularly happy and entertaining, but it could only be possible with young and fresh minds and can hardly be imitated successfully by anyone.

This literary device was also carried on in connection with Schumann's own music, which was in some cases attributed to different personalities. The largest of his sonatas, that in F sharp minor, was attributed at first to both Florestan and Eusebius. Another work with many different pieces in it is called *Davidsbündlertänze*: in the "Carnival," he returned to the practice which was attributed to him as a boy at school and gave fancy musical portraits of several members of the ideal confraternity, including Chopin, himself in different moods, Clara Wieck, and Ernestine von Fricken, a person by whom he was at one time considerably attracted; and the whole ends up with "a march of the Davidites against the Philistines." In such ways, the curious fancy of the "Davidsbund" coloured all the first period of Schumann's musical life and represents his ardour for advancing the art by both teaching and example, and infusing it with poetical fancy. As he advanced in years, the names were dropped, and he lived more in practical realities. They ceased to appear in connection with his musical works early, and the last is said to have appeared in his literary works in 1842.

Editing a newspaper is hard work at any time, but when a man has a cause at heart and throws himself into it with all his soul, it is most exacting. Schumann had to supply something for his readers constantly and would never do it without getting something genuine out of himself. He had facility in writing, but it is not to be wondered at that in the earlier years of his editorial work, he did very little in the way of composition; but what he did do was of a very high order; and at least one of his most successful large compositions for the pianoforte, the *Etudes Symphoniques*, was written in the first year that he was busy as the representative Davidite. But this absorption in literary work can hardly be regarded as a misfortune. The world is a gainer by what he wrote, and the cause of first-rate music was a gainer. Besides, it is probable that he also profited greatly by his drudgery. He himself said that in earlier years he was inclined to dream his time away at the pianoforte; and the necessities of the editorial work were bracing to his mind and forced him to get something definite done. As he got more into the habit of doing his literary work systematically, his impulse to compose returned, and after a year or two, a flood of works for the pianoforte came forth, many of them among his finest works; such as the great *Fantasia in C*, the *Fantasiestücke*, *Humoreske*, *Novelletten*, and many others. In these years, and as long as he only seemed to represent the branch of pianoforte writing, the reception of his works by critics was decidedly encouraging, and he had good reason to hope well of his prospects; but the representatives of classical respectability soon showed signs of being suspicious of him, and their feeling became more pronounced as he began to attack branches of composition which were considered to have more importance and to entail greater responsibilities.

Among the circumstances which are said to have exercised influence upon Schumann's career must be mentioned the arrival of Mendelssohn in Leipzig as conductor to the Gewandhaus Concerts. Mendelssohn acted without actual intention or invitation as a very able coadjutor in the cause of the Davidites; for his presence seemed to have an electric power to stir people up and make them energetic about performing and hearing good music. Schumann was roused to a pitch of very high enthusiasm about him. He admired the mastery of art which he showed and the balance and clearness of his works; and may have been impelled to admit a little more consideration for classical form, together with the poetical impulse, after contact with the better-regulated master. Mendelssohn, on the other hand, seems scarcely to have thought of Schumann as a composer at all, but only as a literary man and art critic, and consequently there must always have been a sense of antagonism lurking in his mind, such as is natural between the producer and the appraiser. But they were a good deal together, chiefly owing to Schumann's admiration, and they discussed musical matters as freely as Schumann's singular taciturnity admitted of.

Another most important influence which began to exert itself about this time was the love which developed in him for Clara Wieck. He had been a great deal with her in the days when he was living in her father's house, but she was too young then to inspire him with any great passion. He admired her powers enthusiastically, but personally she had not sufficient influence upon him to prevent his susceptible disposition from being captivated by Ernestine von Fricken and other sympathetic ladies. But as Clara Wieck developed into womanhood, a far more powerful feeling took possession of him than any he had before experienced, and her feelings responded to his. When they both found out the state of their affections, Schumann applied to the father to allow them to marry. But the father, on considering his prospects, saw little that was promising in them and refused. From a worldly and practical point of view, he seemed right, and Schumann for the time acquiesced. He set about at once to find a sphere of action which might give him a better chance of winning the father's consent, and struck upon Vienna as a likely place for getting something to do, and, with Clara Wieck's consent, went there to see if anything could be achieved.

His idea was to bring out a newspaper like the one he had worked upon in Leipzig and get enough support in a place which had such a reputation for being musical as Vienna had, to bring him both position and funds. But he was cruelly disappointed. The Viennese people no longer cared for really great and good things, but were altogether under the dominion of Rossini, and light dance writers, and virtuosi of the pianoforte who delighted their frivolous minds by spinning endless tinkling variations and fantasies on familiar tunes.

He stayed there for half a year, and the greatest fruit that came of the visit was the routing up of Schubert's manuscript compositions. He had always been an enthusiastic admirer of Schubert, and being now in Schubert's own native town, he naturally sought out traces of him. He went to see Beethoven's and Schubert's graves, which were close together in the Währing cemetery; and it is illustrative of his character that he took possession of a steel pen which he found lying on Beethoven's tomb and kept it, as if it had some mystical sanctity, to use on special occasions, one of which was the writing of his own *B-flat Symphony*. But a more tangible result came from his visiting Schubert's brother Ferdinand, who still kept many of Schubert's manuscript compositions. While he was turning these over, he came across the score of the great *Symphony in C*, Schubert's last, written but a short while before his death. He was so struck with it that he asked to have it sent to Mendelssohn for performance at the Gewandhaus concerts. Mendelssohn duly brought it out in March 1839, and it interested people so much that it had soon to be played again, and from that time began by slow and sure degrees to win a prominent place among the most successful great works for orchestra in existence, and the impression it made at the time also began to draw people's attention more to other works of the same master besides his songs.

When Schumann returned to Leipzig, he could no longer refrain from pressing his suit for Clara Wieck. He had a little money of his own, and his newspaper also brought him in a tolerable profit, and he felt confident that his compositions would help further to augment the sum total. But the father did not take the same view, and in the end, Schumann took his case into the law courts - for in Germany a man who refuses to let his daughter marry can be forced to explain the reason for his refusal in a court of justice. It must have been an unpleasant operation to go through and cannot have conduced to a happy frame of mind as long as the contest lasted; but fortunately, the courts decided in Schumann's favour, and after about a year of anxiety, the marriage took place in 1840.

His marriage was the beginning of a new life for Schumann in more ways than one. One of the happiest results was that he burst into song for the first time. The winning of the object of his love seemed suddenly to open the floodgates of a stream which till then had been pent up and unknown in him; and in the one year that succeeded his marriage, he poured out in rapid succession all his finest songs, to the number of over 130. In them, he showed powers with which no one till then would have credited him. There was no laborious process of developing his style in the particular branch of art; he no sooner faced it than his mastery seemed complete. In this respect, he resembled Schubert, who had written many of his finest songs in the earliest years of his mature productive period. Schumann adopted much the same method of dealing with his poems that Schubert did. He did not aim at making tunes with accompaniment and fitting the words to them, but he looked to the poet's conception to guide his own inspiration. Everything available was made to minister to the purpose of intensifying the design, thought, and metre of the poet by the music. The pianoforte part and voice part had well-balanced functions. The voice did all that was possible in the way of melodious declamation, and the accompaniment supplied colour, character, rhythm, and all that must necessarily fall to its share, in the most perfect manner possible. Moreover, Schumann, by nature a poet himself, seized the purpose and spirit of the poems he set with an astonishingly powerful grip and conveyed infinite shades and varieties of meaning in forms which are almost always perfect works of art in detail and in entirety. He expressed with equal success pathos, passion, bitterness, humour, joy, exultation, and even gaiety and sarcasm. It was probably the happiest period in his life when he did this work, and the work itself represents him in his best and clearest phase.

When the year was ended, he himself thought he had done all he could of the best kind in songwriting, and to someone who expressed hopes of further achievements in that line, he answered, "I cannot venture to promise that I shall produce anything further in the way of songs, and I am satisfied with what I have done." The way in which he grappled at once with this branch of art and worked it out to the full limits of his powers to the exclusion of other work became characteristic of him in his best time. He had written all his best pianoforte music before his marriage; in the year following it, he wrote all his best songs; and in the years that succeeded, he worked in a similar manner at one province at a time, taking up new ones in succession and achieving a great quantity of work in each before passing on to another province. Immediately after the long bout of songwriting, he went to work at symphonies, and in one year produced three of his most important works in that line. The first one was in B-flat, which was performed in the spring of the year 1841 at Leipzig under Mendelssohn's direction; and this, being regular and clear in form and expression, was received with favour. Two more were performed at the end of the year, and these, possibly owing to their containing some rather experimental features, were not so well received.

In the following year, Schumann took up yet another province in the shape of chamber music, and in this again, he was surprisingly successful. His earliest essays were string quartets, one of the most difficult branches of art for a composer of high aims to succeed in. His work interested people very much and even surprised men who had not up to that time recognised his abilities; but he himself seems to have felt that they were not the best that he ought to do. He followed these with the famous quintet for pianoforte and strings and the quartet for a similar combination, which have gained him most popularity in Europe by their thoroughly modern qualities of rich colour, volume of sound, romantic style, extraordinary attractiveness of melody and rhythmic figures, and genuine go. They stand by all the qualities which appeal to sympathetic imagination and feeling and not by the old ordinances of classical form, and in this sense, they mark Schumann again as a thorough representative of his time.

In the next year, he took up yet another new line and attacked choral composition for the first time. The work with which he presented himself before the public was a setting of a cantata adapted from Moore's Lalla Rookh, called *Paradise and the Peri*; and this was received with such evident delight that he forthwith proceeded to another attempt in the same line but on a grander scale; and in the course of 1844, he began to set scenes from Goethe's *Faust*. But after writing four numbers, his work was interrupted by a serious breakdown in health.

Since his marriage, he had lived very quietly, devoting himself chiefly to composition. But he had found other work to do which taxed his strength. He had managed to reduce his work upon the musical paper by degrees, but in its place, he had taken up the labours of a professor in the new Conservatoire founded at Leipzig through Mendelssohn's exertions, which was probably less congenial to him than literary work. It is recorded that he had no great aptitude for teaching, and this of itself must have been trying to him. But he found it also trying to be obliged to hear so much music, and he became oppressed with exhaustion and weariness. He began to be troubled with loss of musical memory, sleeplessness, and strange and uncanny fancies; showing a decided disorganisation of some kind, either of nerves or brain. For the sake of rest and quiet, he determined on leaving Leipzig and going to Dresden, where he soon found some relief. He wrote to Ferdinand David, "Here one can get back the old lost longing for music; there is so little to hear! It just suits my condition, for I suffer still very much from my nerves, and everything affects and exhausts me." This state of things was better for him than the turmoil of Leipzig, but it was long before he had a return of really satisfactory health, and little work could be done. He lived very much alone, and the habits of silence and abstraction which had always been characteristic of him began to grow more and more marked. It was not till 1846 that he showed signs of being more himself again, and then he began at once to turn his attention to composition with his former ardour.

It is curious that he became at this period more eager about clearness of part-writing in his music. He had always been a most ardent worshipper of J. S. Bach, but had loved his works rather for what they express and the general power of intellect and emotion which they display than for their technical merits. But now, late in the day, he began working more decidedly at counterpoint, Bach's own special field of technical triumphs; and the results of this study were a number of works such as canons for pedal pianoforte, pianoforte fugues, and a set of very fine fugues for the organ on the notes representing the letters of Bach's name. Other great works were also brought forward soon after his reappearance in the world, such as his most important symphony in C and the famous concerto for pianoforte. These works must have been partly written during the period when he was more or less withdrawn from society, but it must be confessed they show little sign of obscurity of mind or failing of nerve. The symphony is full of vigorous thoughts, and is clearly expressed and well worked out; and the concerto has won its popularity by a profusion of most attractive ideas and beautiful melodies, which often have a certain pensive sadness in them, but no traces of morbid melancholy. Early in the year 1847, he and his wife paid a visit to Zwickau, where they were most cordially welcomed, and these two new works were both performed with success.

Schumann now had his mind set on trying an opera. He had long had desires in that direction and thought German composers had not done enough in that field. In 1842 he had written in his newspaper, "It is high time German composers should give the lie to the reproach that has long lain on them of having been so craven as to leave the field in possession of the Italians and the French. But under this head there is a word to be said to the German poets also." It might be reasonably answered that one of the reasons why German composers had done so little in real German opera in comparison with other nations was that they took a more serious and thorough view of art, and unless very considerable compromises are admitted, and a very light view taken of the requirements of reason and criticism, an opera is a most difficult thing to arrive at.

Schumann himself was brought face to face with these difficulties just as Beethoven had been. He first of all found it very difficult to settle on a story which satisfied his high ideas, on the score of being suitable and worthy of setting to music. Many were the subjects which came sufficiently near to satisfying him to be mentioned - such as *Faust, The Veiled Prophet, The Wartburg Tournament of Song* - but for one cause or another, they were all dropped. At last, he fixed on the story of St. Genevieve, which had been already put into a poetic and dramatic form by two German poets. But when he had settled upon his subject, he met a new difficulty. The literary form in which the story stood in the works of Hebbel and Tieck was not fit for musical setting; and it was no easy matter to find anyone to recast it. Hebbel himself refused to reconstruct his work; another poet called Reinick tried but failed to satisfy Schumann; and in the end, the composer was driven to try his own poetical powers and make up the opera book for himself. That and the work of composition necessarily took time, and it was not till 1848 that the opera, under the name of *Genoveva,* was ready for performance. Then it was the sensitive Schumann's turn to realize the usual miserable and repulsive preliminaries of such theatrical performances. He tried to get it done at Leipzig, where he knew he had many friends; and his hopes were raised by a promise to bring it out in the spring of 1849. But when the time came, first his own circumstances stood in the way and then other people's, so that with evasions and postponements, the whole year passed without a sign of performance. Schumann naturally grew irritated, and when a promise by the director on his honour that the work should be performed in February 1850 was likewise broken, it was as much as his friends could do to prevent Schumann making the director's apparent dishonour public, and taking his case into a law court. In the end, the opera was performed in June of that year, and Schumann himself superintended. The result was not altogether satisfactory, and Schumann attributed it to the unsuitable season of the year for bringing out a new work. "Who goes to a theatre in May or June, and not rather into the woods?" But nevertheless, he had many friends and admirers to support him with their presence, and they were delighted with much of the music, which is indeed in parts superbly beautiful and appropriate; but they were not convinced that opera was one of Schumann's special provinces, nor were they roused to any great enthusiasm. Schumann was disappointed and distressed by the want of sympathy which he felt, and by the tone of the criticisms which appeared in print. The cold impression left by the work is probably owing partly to the way in which the plot is worked out. For the characters do not all explain themselves spontaneously to an audience as they should do, and there is a want of clearness and balance in the form of the drama. This Schumann was inclined to lose sight of through feeling that the music satisfied his sense of the requirements of the situations, and the coldness of the public and the strictures of critics only struck him as galling stupidity.

Another work which employs similar resources to opera was the setting of scenes from the second part of Goethe's *Faust*, which he carried to a condition fit to be performed by the time the opera was brought out. This work was received with much more favour than the opera in Leipzig and was soon repeated at other musical centres, and its fame spread widely. The choruses at the end of the work have generally been considered to be among his finest conceptions, while the music of some earlier scenes expressed so well the poet's intention that people said things were brought home to them in the poem which they had never understood before. In later years Schumann added considerably to the work and wrote an overture and scenes from the First Part, but these bear traces of his failing powers more than any others of his great works, and hamper its fitness for general performance.

Schumann's stay at Dresden came to an end when political disturbances broke out there in 1849. He was unfitted by his reserved and retiring disposition to take any part in such public manifestations, and he retired first to a village called Kreischa, where he went on working quietly at his compositions even within a few miles of the exciting scenes of the insurrection. This first move was soon followed by a more decided one. While in Dresden, he had first had a little experience of systematic conducting. A men's choral society had been prospering there under the direction of Schumann's friend Hiller, and when he left to take another post in Düsseldorf, Schumann went on with the work. But Schumann was not really fitted for the ways of a German singing club, and the chief advantage of the experiment was that it led to his getting the command of a larger choral society with mixed voices, where he had better opportunities and a more congenial atmosphere. This roused him a good deal in many ways and afforded him opportunities of trying the effect of choruses in the setting of Faust, and doing practical work which took him a little out of himself. The experience so gained led to a hope that he might get some definite post as a conductor, and when Ferdinand Hiller moved on from Düsseldorf to Cologne, Schumann obtained the appointment of Kapellmeister there. At first, this new line of work seemed a success. The people of Düsseldorf welcomed gladly such an acquisition to their musical forces as he and Madame Schumann represented; and his enthusiasm for his art and his reputation gave a decided impulse to music in the place. But Schumann appears to have been no more really fitted for conducting than for teaching. The natural impulse in him to look inwards rather than outwards, and his reserve and habits of silence were all against it. He had a singular disinclination for asserting himself, and this prevented his beat from being as decisive as it ought to be; and when the band made mistakes, it also prevented him from calling their attention to the fact, and all he did in such cases was to make them play the passage over again, and if the mistake happened again he only got angry and yet could not bring himself to explain. His want of fitness for such work increased as time went on, and the signs of a return of mental troubles such as he had had before when he left Leipzig first for Dresden began to make ominous appearance. But the work of composition still went on steadily, and as yet the material produced was of admirable quality; one of the greatest works of his time at Düsseldorf being the important one known as the *Rhenish Symphony*, which is full of vigour, colour, and character.

The failing of his mind showed itself much in the concerns of outward life but most seriously in his conducting. Among the stories that are told of its effects are that he fancied music was taken too fast and slackened the pace of things that were performed under his direction in an unintelligible manner. He is reported to have gone on beating time after the band had stopped; and when such infallible signs were added to the fact that he was unfitted by nature and disposition for the business of conducting, it became obvious to the directors that someone must be found to take his place. They tried all they could to spare Schumann's feelings, but it was impossible to get through such a difficult operation with a man whose mind was in an unhealthy condition without disaster. Schumann could not be persuaded to meet the directors halfway and ease the rupture, and in the end, the parting was effected in a manner which left a painful impression upon the composer's mind.

When he left Düsseldorf, he went with his wife for a concert tour in Holland, which seemed to enliven him, and the sympathy they met with in that country soon raised his spirits; but his health was gone too far in a serious direction for return to the happiness and clearness of spirit and work of earlier days. Hallucinations of a strange kind began to present themselves, and nervous disorder and depression became more frequent and irresistible. The working of the disease was intermittent, and in the intervals he still continued to work and to carry on his relations with people as usual. He himself felt so unsafe from the effect of these visitations that he even wished to be taken to an asylum - though for many years past he had had a morbid horror of such places. At last, the crisis came, and in the afternoon of the 27th of February, 1854, in one of his fits of acute depression, he tried to put an end to his life by throwing himself from a bridge into the Rhine. His life was saved by some boatmen, and he was taken to a private asylum near Bonn, where he remained for the rest of his life. He was still able in his happier and clearer moments to carry on correspondence and see friends and relations, but no more composition of importance was undertaken, and after two mournful years, he died on July 29th, 1856, in the arms of his noble and loving wife.

The nature of the disease which brought his life so sadly and prematurely to an end is said to have been the formation of bony masses in the brain. Schumann appears to have inherited this disorder from his mother, who also was subject to violent headaches and depression, and the earlier stages of the development of the evil began to exert influence upon his character and habits long before a serious crisis came about. It seems that even before his marriage he was subject to fits of excessive depression and gloomy forebodings, and he had a singular dread and horror of lunatic asylums. His extreme irritability may also have had some connection with the disease, and that presented itself to a noticeable degree even as early as his twenty-fourth year. The most curious feature of his character was his silence in company. In his most familiar circle and at home with his family, he was bright and talkative, but outside, with acquaintances and strangers, it was difficult to get him to utter a word. The natural bent of his disposition seemed to be to look inwards and not to act or initiate. He listened to others and took in what they said, responding sometimes to anything that he sympathised with, especially by a peculiarly bright and expressive look. But words became constantly rarer as he grew older. When he was in Dresden, he used to go often of an evening to a particular restaurant, where he drank beer; but he did not join friends or enter into conversation, but used to sit at a particular table alone, with his back to the rest of the people and his face to the wall, either working out musical ideas - which he sometimes whistled softly to himself - or meditating about things which interested him. Even with friends that he was very fond of, he liked to maintain silence if he could, without intending to show any want of appreciation of their company. A story was told by a great friend of his in comparatively early years, called Henriette Voigt, how after she and Schumann had been enjoying music together one lovely evening in summer, they went out in a boat together. And there they sat side by side for over an hour without either speaking a word. When they parted, Schumann said, with a pressure of the hand that expressed his feelings, "To-day we have perfectly understood one another."

These silent habits certainly stood in the way of his exchanging and discussing views with other musicians or doing much in any practical line, such as organising or conducting; but on the other hand, they served to intensify his originality and allowed his views of art to develop undisturbed by doubts and hesitations. Fortunately, he was always inclined to be extremely liberal, and isolation never made his judgment narrow or pedantic. He had too powerful a sense of the meaning of music to be led into the common trap of taking details for essentials and expending his force upon technical matters. This is illustrated by the style of his writings on music, in which he showed that most rare gift of going to the heart of his subject and carrying the reader along with him, and convincing him without any of the affectation of learning which is commonly used as a cloak for total barrenness. His principle rested upon the broad foundation of apprehension of the historical progress of music and the feeling that art cannot stand still, but must either advance or deteriorate. He felt as much as most men similarly placed, that it is always hard to tell what direction the new paths are to take; but he was ready to welcome any endeavour that seemed to be made in an earnest spirit. This was one of the spurs which drove him to write about art, and he expressed his hopes and views in many places, both in the newspapers and in letters to his friends. "Consciously or unconsciously, a new and a yet undeveloped school is being founded upon the basis of the Beethoven-Schubert romanticism, a school which we may venture to expect will make a special epoch in the history of art. Its destiny seems to be to enter into a period which will nevertheless have many links to connect it with the past century." The last sentence clearly implies that he felt that the work of the past must be the basis of the progress of the future, and this conviction may be seen also in his own work. He knew that art could not make a totally new start or ignore the principles which had been discovered in the course of centuries of musical development. He knew the difference between clap-trap or tall talk and genuine performance, and did not seek to find new principles, but to understand better the principles of the past and apply them to liberal uses in that spirit of poetry and romance which was the increasing tendency and feature of the music of modern times and his own most notable characteristic. He also knew and understood the doctrines of most revolutionary men, such as Berlioz, and as far as he found them earnest and clear-sighted, and gifted with qualities which would really further good art instead of misleading the public, he cordially expressed his sympathy with them; but he never had any patience with people who showed great gifts and put them to sordid and ignoble uses, or truckled to low public tastes for the sake of success.

He was yet another example among Germans of that type of the musician so entirely possessed by the love of his art that any other view than that of improving it and spending all his energies to master higher and higher ground seemed inconceivable. His aims were always of the noblest, and the style of his musical expression corresponded with them. His habits of introspection made him critical of himself even more than he was of others; and as long as his health lasted, he was always trying to improve and enlarge his powers. But the growth of the disease against which it was impossible to contend made it inevitable that all the most attractive part of his work should be done in his earlier years, when youthful power and enthusiasm were yet vigorous in him, and he was able to shake off the obscuring influence of the fits of melancholy. It is true he kept his art wonderfully free from traces of morbidity long after the disease had laid its remorseless hand on him, and long after his relations with people in everyday life had become strange and uncertain. But the average of really successful works became smaller as the years rolled by, after the first brilliantly productive time directly after his marriage; and most of the works of the latter part of his life contain but an uncertain reflex of the vigorous breadth, imaginative power, and freshness of his earlier years.

It was natural that the works of a man having such liberal and advanced views about art should be slow to make their way. His position as editor of a successful musical newspaper certainly helped him in early years. He himself knew it and expressed it in the words, "If the publisher were not afraid of the editor, the world would hear nothing of me." To the average critic, his works were a sealed book. They could find little that they understood, and much that altogether revolted their conventional notions of propriety; and the result was that even till long after his death, when the public were becoming universally captivated by his works, they were condemned by the journalists in the most reckless and unrestrained terms. But he left his message to the world in the very best possible hands. His wife, having won a position as a pianist almost unrivalled in Europe, and having perfect knowledge of the meaning of his works and the way he wished them to be expressed, could carry on the most grateful task of making his music known to all the world by her playing; and so triumphantly has she maintained the cause that he became one of the best-loved composers of the generation after his death, and to many people, whose hearts and sympathies are warm, the composer who most truly represents the tendency of modern art since the days of Schubert and Beethoven. The success which was won first by his pianoforte works and songs and chamber music was ultimately won also by such large works as overtures and symphonies; and though other men have attained greater popularity in the last branch of art, his works stand at the highest level of nobility and vigour of style and variety of interest between Beethoven's time and our own. His influence has naturally been very great upon later composers, and some have gained even remarkable popularity by doing little more than reproducing his style and methods. His influence upon the musical world in general has also been great and of the very best quality. His style of criticism first awakened people to more generous and self-respecting views of art, and his music in its turn roused them to feel what is really beautiful and nobly emotional, rather than to rest content with a cold and mechanical emptiness which too often succeeds in passing itself off as classical art because it does not violate conventional proprieties.

The spirit which lived in Bach and Beethoven lived also in him, and in spite of the deficiencies of his education and the troubles of his later life, it finally gave him a secure place among the immortals.

XI

RICHARD WAGNER.

People commonly speak and write as if they thought that works of art and imagination, and all products of what they call genius, sprang by inspiration from nowhere and were the independent creations of their originators. They can understand how natural laws work elsewhere; that a plant will not grow unless the seed is put where it can germinate, and that it requires light, heat, moisture, and nourishment to bring it to mature perfection. But they seem to think it is quite different with art and things which grow in the human mind, as if it were a pure matter of chance whether a genius made his appearance; and that everything depends upon such chance, and nothing upon previous experience and development. But in truth, it is quite the other way, and the matter is obvious enough when it is considered with a little attention. Primeval savages did not find out how to draw horses, elks, men, and such familiar objects all of a sudden, just as the thought struck them; but they began thousands upon thousands of years ago to find out that certain lines and curves scratched upon bone, or clay, or stone looked rather like men or beasts. In the course of succeeding ages, they improved step by step upon their first crude efforts, and by helping and criticizing one another in a rough way, they got their pictures more and more like the objects they were meant to represent.

It is just the same in modern times with music; and no art affords better opportunities for tracing the gradual growth of the powers of the human mind and the certainty of its submission to circumstances and conditions. Its development lies in a singularly small compass, and the greater part of the materials which a philosopher requires to analyze and make his conclusions upon are ready to hand. If only the study was a little more advanced, it would be interesting enough even to engross people who care very little for music itself, because of the certainty with which each step can be followed, and the curious manner in which traits of character in nations and individuals come out, and the ways in which misconceptions and false theories lead into inevitable absurdities, of which the immediate actors in the story have not the very least suspicion. So that music, from this point of view, affords a singularly entertaining study of humanity itself.

There is no kind of music which shows the nature of development and the way in which art is hedged about with diverse conditions than opera. The whole of its history can be traced from its crudest beginnings up to the present day, and the earliest conception formed of the way to combine a drama or a theatrical poem with music is the same in principle with that of its latest great master, Wagner. The process of perfecting the form of art took over two centuries; and in the course of that time, men tried all sorts of roads and were often led astray by false ideals. But even their mistakes are interesting, because they illustrate so clearly the way in which music has been developed; and serve better than anything else to point out which must be the right road, by showing how men have been led by obvious but natural mistakes and misconceptions into taking the wrong one.

Men began the history of opera just at the end of the sixteenth century, by setting plays and pastorals to a very simple kind of music, which consisted of little more than musical recitation supported by occasional chords. What they supposed was wanted was something as like speech as possible, made singable by defining the notes. They did not try to introduce tunes and airs, or dramatic and emotional effects, for they thought the right way to manage the matter was to take the play exactly as it stood, and merely sing it straight through, repeating nothing. The result was excessively vague as far as the music was concerned, but it pleased the people who heard it because their minds were fixed on the poem and regarded the music merely as a help to the general effect of the performance. But composers could not rest satisfied with such limited opportunities, and they soon began to introduce passages of more definite form and of more decisive character. To help themselves in designing their tunes, they began to repeat the words, so that the straightforward declamation of the play was interrupted, and the whole began to be broken up into more and more definite sections. While this was going on, solo singers began to develop new powers, for when the history of opera began, there was little or no solo singing. But the new kind of art soon called new means of effect into play; and as these became more and more conspicuous and more and more appreciated by the public, the composers had to give them correspondingly more attention. It naturally followed that the drama fell by degrees into the background. The original purpose of the first experimenters to develop a musical drama was lost sight of, and the opera became merely a form of entertainment, consisting of a string of solo pieces to show off the abilities of singers. Dressing up in character and appearing on a decorated stage were continued and served, of course, to please the eye; but the real drama had so little place in the scheme that it counted for next to nothing in the prosperity or failure of the performances. The public liked to hear great singers sing such things as showed off their abilities, even if they consisted of nothing but runs and flourishes; and people did not trouble their heads about the stiff and utterly undramatic effect of the succession of airs of exactly the same form interspersed by formless recitatives, so long as their ears were tickled with good tunes and good voices, or at least a sufficient display of clever vocalization.

When people take up with sophisms and cheap and false ideals, they generally go a long way into the depths before they find out it is time to turn back and take another road. The absurdities of the conventional plan upon which Handel's operas were made are striking enough, but his successors reached a far profounder depth of empty twaddle. Handel at least had genius and feeling; but after his time, opera writing became a mere knack. Composers learned a few tricks and were then able to turn out so-called arias by the thousand. But in due time, the crisis came, for people always get sick of their own stupidities in the end, and a strenuous effort was made in the latter half of the eighteenth century to re-establish the position of the drama and to make the play at least of equal importance with the music. Composers again made up their minds to be guided by the poet and to intensify the situations of the play, and to express the dramatic points by their music, instead of torturing and twisting the story and making a mockery of the dignity of human speech in order to catch the public by trumpery jingle. Great things were done, and a form of opera more dignified, and more varied, and more worthy of the name of art was arrived at; but complete reform was impossible as yet, partly because at that time there was not sufficient expressive material developed to supply composers with figures and subjects to carry on the music simultaneously with the play, and partly because Italians still had chief power in the operatic branches of art; and they had so entirely sacrificed everything else for the sake of vocalization that their influence acted as a dead weight against all possible progress, and it was not until genuine German art began to establish itself that the incubus was displaced.

Meanwhile, in other branches of art, the musical language was being rapidly enlarged, and composers were soon able to enrich their operas with greater variety and freedom of form, and to follow their dramas more directly and more naturally. Poetry and emotion came by degrees to play a more and more prominent part in musical effect in all branches of art. It became more and more necessary for a composer to be a poet, at least in disposition, in order to give his work enough character and originality of design to satisfy the craving of the public for something better than mere neatness and balance. Beethoven, Schubert, and Schumann all had poetical sympathies; and two of them at least had great poetical feeling, though they did not get as far as producing poetry in words. Their musical works are poems, and it is upon the poetical qualities they possess, rather than their classical formality, that their effect depends. Such a condition of musical art obviously tends towards giving the best opportunities for realizing the ideal of opera, considered as a drama set to music, without sacrificing one element of the form of art to another, but allowing both the drama and music to have an equal share in the result. Musicians had long been misled by thinking that their part of the business was of supreme importance, and that everything must give way to the supposed necessities of musical form. It was very natural that they should think so, for they could scarcely fail to have a very low impression of the effect of poetry when their acquaintance with that branch of literature was probably limited to the wretched formal twaddle which second-rate poetasters turned out for them to make into operas. Musicians failed to recognize that in a form of art in which several elements are combined, there must be more or less of a compromise between them. When the singers insisted that everything should be sacrificed to them, the opera became intolerable through the preposterous degradation of language and musical sense. It was only a shade better when composers insisted that all dramas must be cut up into sections and devised upon an invariable scheme to enable them to make their special effects. The drama was still in a very inferior position, and indeed betrayed the fact by intrinsic frivolity as well as its extrinsic qualities. But it required a man who could look upon the matter without glorifying either department at the expense of another to work out the reform. A mere musician could not see both sides of the question clearly enough to shake himself free from the conventions which had grown up over the years. The only chance seemed to lie in the advent of a man who had strong sympathies with both poetry and drama, and insight into theatrical as well as musical effect, along with a mastery of all the resources of modern musical expression of the dramatic kind. Furthermore, as it turned out, it required a man of the utmost force of character and determination to win his way against the furious opposition which the greater number of musical critics invariably raise against a man who ignores the barren conventions that are their only criteria of excellence. Richard Wagner had such gifts and opportunities in a very singular degree. His father, who occupied some rather insignificant official position in Leipzig in connection with the police, was a man of good education who took much interest in poetry and theatrical matters. Richard was the ninth child and was born in 1813 in an old house called the "Red and White Lion" in Leipzig. Tragically, his father only survived his birth by a few months. His mother was left very badly off, with a large family of young children on her hands; and in two years, she was married again to one Ludwig Geyer, an old friend of the family who was an actor and a writer of plays. As he was engaged in the royal theatre at Dresden at the time he became Richard's stepfather, the family had to leave their native town and relocate there. Geyer appears to have made a very good stepfather and was always remembered with affection by his son. He did not, however, live long enough to exert much personal influence on Richard's career, as he died in 1823 when the boy was only ten years old. Nevertheless, it is probable that his profession added strength to the already strong theatrical influences present in the family, thereby helping towards the favorable conditions necessary for the achievement of the special work the boy was destined to do in the world of music.

Richard showed an aptitude for literature from the very first. He was sent to a school where he was taught Greek and Latin and made very rapid progress in Greek. He also began to read Shakespeare very early on and was impelled by the profound impression our great poet made upon him to attempt a grand tragedy on his own account when he was just fourteen. Music also began to occupy him, and he took especial delight in Weber's *Freischütz*, regarding the composer, who was at that time in Dresden, with profound veneration. The theatrical influences were yet further intensified before long, as three of the elder members of the family went on stage, and the boy soon began to think of writing music for his own tragedy. His first master was not successful in controlling and directing his energies. Young Wagner tried his hand at various large works that did not fit in with the master's views. Since the pupil did not find the adverse criticisms to his taste, they had to part company. The boy could not rest satisfied with moderate experiments, but must needs try his hand at once at works on a grand scale and wrote an overture that was played at the theatre in 1830, much to the apparent bewilderment of the audience.

Soon after this, he had the good luck to find a master more capable of managing his difficult and aspiring disposition. This was an excellent musician called Weinlich, who was cantor of the Thomasschule. He put before him the most admirable models and did him good service by helping him to understand them, showing him what was to be done in the way of art by following them. His connection with this intelligent master lasted for the short space of six months, and from that time forward, he had to develop his powers for himself. A great impulse was given to his taste by hearing Beethoven's works, and he studied them constantly with the greatest enthusiasm. According to a writer who afterwards turned against him, he knew most of that master's greatest works intimately before he was even twenty. The first fruit of their influence was a symphony in C, which was performed at a Gewandhaus concert in Leipzig.

But these attempts at abstract instrumental music soon came to an end. The influence of Beethoven, and the sense of power with which his works impressed him, remained in his mind but was ultimately destined to bear fruit in other lines of art.

Wagner was one of those men who develop very slowly. His aims were exceptionally high, and he had to go through an immense amount of experimentation and experience before he discovered how to express himself fully. His earliest attempt at writing a book for an opera was called *Die Hochzeit*, which was produced in 1832. This work was not considered satisfactory and was consequently given up. When he was twenty, he went to join his elder brother, Albert, who was an actor and stage manager at a theatre in Würzburg, and he himself became the chorus master there. The experience he gained in this role led to the production of a three-act opera called *Die Feen*, parts of which were tried out at Würzburg, but it was never performed in its entirety. Another opera, called *Das Liebesverbot*, modeled on Shakespeare's *Measure for Measure*, soon followed, and this was ultimately performed under very unfavorable circumstances. He was appointed "musik-director" of the theatre at Magdeburg in 1834, where there was a small theatre and a slender company. In 1836, the new opera was scheduled for performance, but somehow the rehearsals were postponed until it was too late. Even though all the singers worked very hard to master it, they could not get ready in time. Wagner's vigorous conducting appears to have carried it through at the rehearsal, but when the performance finally came, he was not so successful, and desperate confusion ensued. The public, whose expectations had been raised to a great pitch, were utterly bewildered and disappointed, and when the work was brought forward a second time, the theatre appears to have been so empty that the performance was not continued.

Soon after this, Wagner left Magdeburg and secured an engagement as conductor at Königsberg, where, in 1836, he married Minna Planer, an actress who had been with him at Magdeburg and had taken an engagement at Königsberg at the same time he moved there.

His life was necessarily very unsettled during this period, as he was driven by high aspirations yet held back from achievement by the inability to find any large field for his work. His stay at Königsberg was short and unprofitable, and from there, he moved on to Riga in

1838. His aspirations began to turn toward Paris, where, in his imagination, the Grand Opera presented a worthy object of ambition for a composer. Consequently, he set about writing the kind of opera that he supposed would win success there. The Parisians favored pompous displays, immense masses of noise, glitter, and everything which excited the senses. There is a feeling of power and mastery in works that are successfully contrived to satisfy such cravings, and Wagner, in his younger days, could to a certain extent sympathize with them. The work produced to address these purposes was called *Rienzi*, and it was the first that brought him fame. He finished the poem while he was in Riga and planned the music on a grand scale.

In the latter part of 1839, he started with his wife and a big Newfoundland dog on a sailing vessel for London, intending to make his way from there to Paris and to have his new grand opera performed. The voyage was a most tempestuous one, taking over three weeks. The storm was so violent that the captain had to take refuge in a Norwegian port. The impression produced on Wagner's mind by the wild weather, the rushing seas, and the manners and customs of sailors was profound, and bore remarkable fruit later on in his works. They rested in London for a few days to recover themselves and then embarked on their important journey to Paris. They stopped along the way at Boulogne, where Meyerbeer, who was all-powerful at the Grand Opera, was staying, with the purpose of gaining whatever assistance might be obtained from him for the coming campaign. It is clear that Wagner's powers must have appeared remarkable at this time, for Meyerbeer was sufficiently impressed to provide him with letters of introduction to various important persons connected with the opera in the capital, which ought to have served him in good stead.

He arrived at his destination late in 1839, and Meyerbeer's letters ensured his being received at least with outward courtesy. The various officials were profuse in compliments but very chary of making definite promises. All efforts to get *Rienzi* performed at the Grand Opera completely failed. He very nearly succeeded in getting the earlier opera *Das Liebesverbot* performed, but all his hopes were dashed one by one, and the struggle for bare existence became very grievous. At one point, he was reduced to the extent of trying to secure a position as a member of a chorus at an inferior theatre; but even that failed. In order to support himself and his wife, he took to making easy arrangements of popular airs, even for cornet-a-pistons, writing articles for musical papers, making pianoforte scores of popular operas, and correcting proof-sheets for publishers.

But grievous as the struggle was to keep himself and his poor wife from starvation, he would not quit the place where he hoped to gain so much without a good fight. *Rienzi* was finished and laid aside with a view to getting it performed later elsewhere, and then a new work was begun on a very different plan. This time, Wagner determined to depend less upon theatrical effect and more upon the profound interest of a romantic story. The subject he chose was the famous legend of the sea captain who, for an untimely oath, was condemned to sail the seas for ages until he could find a woman whose love was powerful enough to face even death for him. He was only allowed to come ashore for a limited time at long intervals apart to find his liberator. Wagner planned out his story, and on the recommendation of Meyerbeer, showed it to M. Pillet, the director of the opera. That gentleman studied it thoroughly and then informed Wagner that he was so pleased with it that he wished to have it translated into French in order to have it set to music by a French composer. Of course, Wagner protested, but it was all in vain, and his plot was actually taken and worked up into a play, which was duly set by a Frenchman and performed in 1842, with Wagner receiving a moderate sum by way of compensation. Meanwhile, Wagner had moved from Paris to a village nearby called Meudon, and set to work vigorously at his own version and musical setting of *Der Fliegende Holländer*, and in a very short space of time completed the entire work. But there was no chance of getting it performed in Paris any more than *Rienzi*, and he began to face the necessity of beating a retreat, trying to find if his own countrymen would not treat him a little better.

But he had to meet with yet more rebuffs before any gleam of sunshine came. Both at Munich and Leipzig, the new opera was refused "as unfit for Germany," and though a promise was obtained to perform *Rienzi* in Berlin, the prospect was a distant one. Finally, a great opportunity was opened to him by *Rienzi's* being accepted at Dresden, where he had friends to support him, and in April 1842, Wagner relinquished the hopeless fight in Paris and returned to his own country. The performance duly came off and was successful. The leading tenor was delighted with the opportunities his part afforded him, and the band, chorus, and conductor all threw themselves into the work vigorously. The public was delighted with the display, and possibly also interested in the story. Wagner obtained at once a considerable reputation, and the way was prepared not only for the performance of The *Flying Dutchman* but also for his appointment as "Hof Capellmeister," or principal conductor of the opera, at Dresden, in which office he was installed in February 1843.

Rienzi, however, by no means, represents him fairly. It serves only as the one remarkable illustration of the time before he had found his true path. The public found this out very soon when The *Flying Dutchman* was presented to them, for they naturally expected something that would affect them in the same way as the previous work, and they were considerably bewildered by the difference. Wagner, like most men of great mark, had to find out his principles of art by degrees. No man who makes a great step of any sort contrives an abstract theory and works to it, for reason always moves slower than artistic instinct in the heat of production. Thus, the theory is made after artistic invention has led the way. In Wagner's early time, he was working with his face set towards the public and his soul bent on fame. When he wrote The *Flying Dutchman*, his position was already changed; he was then thinking less about fame than of doing something thoroughly good that should satisfy his own criterion of what was wanted in opera. This was therefore the first important step in asserting his own individuality, which did not consist solely in a style but in a way of seeing things as they are, leaving conventions behind in favor of realities. He meant for the drama to assert itself as much as the music, with both elements helping one another. His experience of the sea on the voyage to England was quite enough for his susceptible temperament, and he was able to give a decided tinge of nautical life to the whole piece. His musical expression of storm and tempest was excessively powerful. The drama itself would be impressive even without the music, as it is not only full of points of vivid interest but also goes on from step to step, taking the sympathies of the audience along with it. The principal characters, especially the heroine Senta, are drawn with a vivid distinctness which shows, even as early as this, what a master Wagner was in literary as well as musical matters. Nevertheless, when it was first performed at Dresden, its reception was doubtful. The famous actress, Mme. Schroeder-Devrient, made a great impression as Senta; Schumann thought it the most original presentation of a character she had ever given. However, the public was not worthy of the work, and this was the first real indication Wagner must have had of the fact that genuineness and real interest are often a decided hindrance to success when the public is not prepared for them. Furthermore, a man who sets about taking people out of a worn-out road into a much better one generally receives more abuse and ill-usage than thanks for his pains.

He had a great deal of hard work to do as conductor. As many as three or four operas were given every week, along with theatrical performances as well; and besides that, he had to give a certain amount of attention to the music of the Catholic Court chapel, which was very distasteful to him, as he had to put up with conditions that made any kind of artistic excellence impossible. Another heavy responsibility was the direction of the concerts given in connection with the opera establishment, where he gained special fame for the superb performances he delivered of Beethoven's finest symphonies.

Every day must have been full to overflowing without considering other work, for a conductor of an opera has to keep on at high pressure for many hours at a stretch when rehearsing. There is always plenty of other work to do in preparing and settling plans and arrangements, and the whole evenings, sometimes for upwards of six hours, were taken up by the performances. But between whiles, in the first two years of his life at Dresden, he managed to bring to completion another of his most important works.

The subject of *Tannhäuser*, or the contest of the Minnesingers, struck him soon after the completion of The *Flying Dutchman*. This choice marked the beginning of his labors upon the line of the Teutonic popular stories, which represent great types of men and men's circumstances. The difficulty of finding a fit subject for musical treatment had struck him as much as it has struck most other people possessed of any sense of criticism. Everyone whose judgment has not been vitiated by careless acceptance of conventions feels the necessity of removing the characters who have to sing their dialogue away from the familiar associations of modern life. In order to be fit for music, the words need to be thoroughly poetical, and the characters should be types rather than ordinary individuals. If they are only commonplace men and women, it seems absurd for them to be singing what is more fit to be spoken. Wagner struck on the mine of the great old German stories early. *Tannhäuser* was the first he came to, and in gathering the materials for it, he was led to read other old German poems which contained the stories of *Lohengrin* and *Parsifal*.

The whole work of *Tannhäuser* was completed and carefully revised before the end of 1844, and it was first performed in the next year. Here again, the composer asserted his individuality even more strongly than in The *Flying Dutchman*, and the result was an increase in the growth of opposition among musicians. A great deal of the work was not appreciated at all; the public was bewildered, the critics proclaimed that there was no melody in it, and musicians thought the licenses Wagner took were outrageous. The composer himself, having taken infinite pains with his work and having carefully tested and considered it until he was sure it was as it ought to be, was very much astonished at its reception. At all events, it opened his eyes thoroughly to what was in store for him if he continued to do what he believed was artistically right and just and refused to make any compromise with the dulness of the public. Yet he determined to stand by his colors and carry the public with him. He wrote of his state of mind at the time: - "A feeling of complete isolation overcame me. It was not my vanity. I had deceived myself and felt numbed. I saw a single possibility before me, namely, to induce the public to understand and participate in my aims as an artist." He realized how easily the public may be misled by the sophisms and platitudes of journalists, and that they always have a chance of understanding even unfamiliar things if they have a few facts pointed out to them. In the end, he was driven to take up his pen to lay before the world the views he had formed in the experience of combined poetical and musical composition.

The disappointment he felt at the reception of *Tannhäuser* did not put any stop to his work, for by 1846, he had finished the poem of *Lohengrin*, and in the following year, he was at work upon the musical composition. He lived rather a retired life in order to give the best of his powers to it. However, he began to feel that the result of his labors was uncertain, for each step in advance took him further away from the familiar path to which the public was accustomed, and he himself was not without doubts as to whether the uncompromising line he had chosen could be worked out. He was clearly not in a happy position. He had gained a certain notoriety, but the force of character he showed in whatever he undertook raised enemies against him on all sides. Moreover, the reputation his works gained for being extremely difficult to perform, and at the same time doubtful of popularity, made conductors and managers shy of him. So, instead of it becoming easier to get his works done as his name became widely known, it was rather the reverse. *Lohengrin*, however, was completed in 1848, and without waiting to consider what its future might be, he was soon engaged in the search for another fitting subject. He tried many lines and, at last, fixed upon the grand mythical stories which are connected with the race of the Nibelungs and the hero Siegfried. Thus, he began at once to put some of the most interesting points into poetry. But the subject was an immense one, and the whole development of it was destined to occupy the greater part of the remainder of his life.

His connection with Dresden was, unfortunately, suddenly severed. Political troubles sprang up rapidly. The poorer classes suffered very much from want, while people connected with the Court were always enjoying their ease and luxury. Patriotic and revolutionary clubs were founded, and a great deal of fierce speech-making went on, which had to be taken in hand by the police. Wagner, of course, sympathized deeply with the suffering classes, and he made a few speeches, which were not by any means unreasonably violent, at one of the revolutionary clubs. His behavior and views brought him under suspicion, and he was subsequently warned by the police authorities. Finally, the people rose against their rulers in 1849, and the Court fled in fear. Prussian soldiers were sent to stamp out the uprising, and various individuals, who were supposed to sympathize with the rioters, were proscribed. Wagner was prepared to find himself among those to be seized upon, and he had retired in good time to Weimar, where Liszt was established; and when the news came that the warrant for his arrest was out, Liszt, through his popularity with the Court people at Weimar, was enabled to procure a passport, and Wagner was safely conveyed out of Germany.

At first, Wagner felt happy in being free; but he was more isolated than ever, and the feeling that he could not enter Germany again for a long time, or take any share in the music that was going on there, soon told heavily upon his spirits. A few years later, he wrote of his condition at the beginning of his exile: "I was thoroughly disheartened from undertaking any new artistic scheme. But recently I had had proofs of the impossibility of making my art intelligible to the public, and all this deterred me from beginning new dramatic works. Indeed, I thought everything was at an end with my artistic creativeness." But fortunately, he left a friend behind in Germany who was quite competent to fight his battles for him, and he soon received sufficient encouragement to make him take to his work again. On his way through Weimar, and on the very morning when he had to fly into exile, he had heard Liszt superintending the rehearsal of *Tannhäuser*. Up to that time, Wagner had not divined Liszt's powers, but he was suddenly made aware of them in the most pleasant possible way. He said himself later, "What I had felt in inventing the music, he felt in performing it; what I wanted to express in writing it down, he proclaimed in making it sound." When he was in the lowest point of depression and disappointment in Paris—whither he had fled from Weimar—the news came to him that Liszt was preparing the performance of *Lohengrin*, which had, by that time, slumbered untouched for two years since its completion. Wagner himself had no chance of hearing the result, but he knew that the work was in the best possible hands, and that nothing would be left undone to gain its success, and he was roused out of his depression and inactivity to vigorous labor again. *Lohengrin* was, in fact, first performed at Weimar in 1850, under Liszt's superintendence. It met with much the same kind of reception which fell to *Tannhäuser*. There were many who were open-hearted to it, and some who were persuaded in spite of themselves; but by that time, a considerable body of musicians had declared war to the uttermost against Wagner, and nothing he could do had the least chance of favor from them. Their violent and indiscriminate hostility lasted for the rest of his life, and even beyond it, and *Lohengrin* had to suffer like the rest of his works. But the public, in defiance of their professional advisers, soon found enjoyment in the work, and it became, in no long time, one of the most popular of modern musical dramas, and helped to open the doors of theatres where his works were as yet not admitted.

What made him go to Paris when he was driven from Dresden owing to his complicity with the revolutionists cannot be decisively explained. The deeply-rooted feeling of his younger days, that it was the greatest operatic center, may still have had some power over him, and he was probably right in supposing that if he could get a performance of any of his works at one of the principal theatres, it would rapidly spread his fame abroad and make managers more anxious to perform them. But Paris was no fit field for him and his uncompromising ideas. The French people, with all their taste for what people call "Bohemianism," and readiness to take up and act upon daring social theories, have no aptitude for thoroughness in art. They have always had a surprising affection for little obvious tunes and commonplace rhythms, and prefer their large works to be cut up into short and easy conventional forms, which relieve them of any intellectual effort or vigour of attention. The only chance of getting them out of such habits was to appeal to their senses in some violent and exciting manner. Wagner does appeal to the senses with enormous power, but his way of expressing himself is so original as to be almost a protest against concession or conventionality, and that is a thing which can only appeal to French musicians after a long period of probation.

The short stay in Paris was, consequently, altogether unfruitful; and from there, he moved to Switzerland, where he took up his abode in Zurich. Here, too, he was still more or less isolated from his fellow musicians and from practical work. However, he found occasion to conduct performances now and then, and his mind soon began to ferment with many new projects.

One of the most important results of his exile was his writing a great quantity of theoretical and critical works on the philosophy of his art. He had become conscious of the difficulties which composers had to face who addressed the public in unfamiliar ways, and he had also more or less realized the reasons behind this. He saw what the stumbling-blocks were that hindered ordinary musical people in distinguishing between things which were merely incoherent and rhapsodical extravagances, and things which were well-considered and artistically devised but out of the common path. In both cases, the public only feels that they do not understand what they hear, and judge equally unfavorably from similar impressions; while they will accept and go on listening over and over again to things which are absurdly imperfect and incongruous if they are like what they are accustomed to and contain something which takes their fancy. However, of such things, they eventually get tired in the end while if they can be persuaded to be patient and take their pleasure with a little less levity, they find things that afford them much more lasting enjoyment, and that of a higher kind.

Wagner was forced by his circumstances to explain his own position, and he expounded at length the views which had grown to distinctness in his mind in the course of his artistic labors. The effect was manifold. One immediate result was to intensify the detestation of a certain definite section of musicians against him. This was partly due to the thoroughness of his views on art, which was offensive to the conservative portion of musicians, who believed all their habits to be truths; and partly to his criticisms of Judaism in music, and the characteristic part which Jewish musicians have played in modern art. Another effect was no doubt to make him consider and realize his own position and views about music and drama more thoroughly. For most people, even men of great eminence, are singularly hazy and illogical in their artistic theories until they are brought to the point of putting them in order in writing. Under that ordeal, what is unsound commonly betrays itself; and if the writer has any power of self-criticism and does not lose himself in cloudy rhetoric, he may find out where his pathway is in a wrong direction; while, on the other hand, things that are radically true lay hold of the mind more and more strongly and are carried out more steadily to their legitimate conclusions. This is what appears to have happened in Wagner's case; for the works which followed his period of theoretical and philosophical writing were far ahead of his earlier works in the decisive and uncompromising way in which he carried out his theories. In the first place, the theories came out through his instincts, but they only presented themselves in a modified form in the works before his exile; in those which followed, they seem to have been realized intellectually as well as instinctively, and appeared in their most complete maturity.

About the same period when he did such an enormous amount of prose literary work, he was becoming engrossed in the great circle of heroic stories before alluded to, which served as the basis of the largest work of his lifetime. The legends of the Nibelung dwarfs who live in the bowels of the earth, of the Rhine maidens, and of Wotan, Thor, Freia, and the other gods and goddesses who inhabited Valhalla, and of their dealings with heroic mortals such as Siegmund and Siegfried, seemed to afford the finest opportunities for carrying out his convictions on the subject of musical drama. The stories have been dear to northern nations for fully a thousand years, and their fascination seems rather to mellow than decay with age. Even the cold spirit of nineteenth-century analysis and criticism grows warm under their influence; for the mysticism, which formed so much of their charm, is no vague cloudland of dreams and sensational episodes, but an expression of the feelings and reflections of a noble and warm-hearted race of human beings on the circumstances of life and the mysteries of the world; and the stories as wholes are an attempt to explain, either in an allegorical or direct narrative way, their idea of the origin of things and the forces of nature, and the inevitable and inscrutable fate that seems to hang over all. They are just the kind of things that a composer of Wagner's calibre wants; for the characters, the situations, and the general outlines of the stories are of the grandest and most typical kind, and they express deep truths of human nature without either complication or commonplace. Wagner had begun some time before by putting some of the most impressive parts of the story into poetry first, such as, for instance, the magnificent scene of the death of Siegfried, which ultimately formed one of the most sublime passages of the fourth division of the great work when it was completed, and that work was called "Dusk of the Gods." Now he went to work steadily from the very beginning. He wrote both the drama and the music of the first work of the series, called *Rheingold* - corresponded in size and scope to a complete opera, before the year 1854. There were, therefore, nearly six long years between the completion of *Lohengrin* and that of the first opera of his thoroughly mature style. He went on quicker with the next work of the series, and he finished the drama and music of the *Walküre* in the year 1856. Then, he continued again at once with the next installment, and in the following year, he completed the earlier part of *Siegfried*; and there he broke off for some time.

An important incident, which it is necessary to notice during the years that he was working on the earlier part of the Nibelung series, was his visit to London. This visit was brought about by the directors of the famous old Philharmonic Society in the year 1855. They had tried a good many conductors in the course of the preceding years, but had settled satisfactorily on none. There was no great choice available, for some foreigners who were fit for the position were better employed elsewhere. Wagner's reputation was still of rather an ambiguous kind, but the experiment seemed worth trying, and so he was invited to come over and conduct for a season. He was naturally severe about execution; and he found that while the tone of the band was fine, the opportunities for getting thoroughly good performances of first-rate works were simply not sufficient. Audiences wanted too much music with too few rehearsals. The trouble was just the same as it is at the present day. "The Philharmonic people, both orchestra and audience, consumed more music than they could possibly digest," said Wagner. Enormous programmes were planned, with barely sufficient time for rehearsing to secure an apparently correct performance, which was a task for even an astute conductor. With such a man as Wagner, correct performance was merely a beginning; infinitely more time was needed to achieve the expression and interpretation he knew to be required by a great master's work. Playing the notes is, of course, necessary to start with, but all the expression, which is undoubtedly the hardest part of a competent executant's work, lies far beyond that. But the chances of getting further than the mere notes were, and are still, too often very faint, considering the immense expense of rehearsals for orchestral performances and the immense number of works the public require for their money. Wagner found, too, that the band were sometimes listless and negligent, and on such occasions, his quick temper is recorded to have flashed out; but they seem to have taken it well, and the impression he made upon both the public and the performers by his visit is said to have been favourable, though he did not try the experiment again.

While he was in England, he did part of the work of the *Walküre*, at a house located in Portland Terrace, Regent's Park, where he was staying. But even at that time, his attention was beginning to be drawn aside by some of the other noble stories which he afterwards developed into great works. He was again thinking about that of *Parsifal*, and *Tristan* and *Isolde* received so much attention that he worked the story up into a dramatic scheme. His impulse to go to work upon it was quickened by a surprising invitation he received from the Emperor of Brazil to write an opera for the theatre of Rio de Janeiro on whatever terms he pleased. *Tristan* was thereupon vigorously attacked, and his labours at the huge group of Nibelung dramas were suspended for a time. By the end of 1857, the whole poem and the music to the first act were completed. The second act was finished in Venice early in 1859, and the last act was completed before the end of the same year.

Wagner appears to have had hopes that it might not be difficult to get *Tristan* performed; but it ultimately proved to be the most arduous of all his single works. To begin with, it was the very first of the single dramas in which he completely carried out his principles and with thorough mastery. The whole is also executed at a greater heat and intensity than any of his earlier works, and consequently, greater demands are made upon the voices of the singers and upon their dramatic capacities; while the several acts are so perfectly con-tinuous that a greater demand is also made upon the earnestness and attention of the audience. It seems probable that in the excitement of composition, he did not clearly realize how great the abilities of his performers would have to be to cope with it. He naturally wrote what he knew to be within human powers; but the highest and noblest works require the greatest gifts in the performers, and composers who are capable of producing such works think less of degrees of difficulty than they do of the perfection of their art and the possibilities of human execution. Wagner was made to realize in the course of time the result of aiming at the highest ideals, and for many years, *Tristan* remained unperformed.

Once again, he centered his hopes on Paris and went there with the view of getting *Tannhäuser*, and if possible, *Tristan* also performed. By this time, his name was better known to the directors and managers of theatres, and he set to work to influence them by a series of concerts, in which extracts were given from *The Flying Dutchman, Tannhäuser, Lohengrin,* and *Tristan.* The result was a heavy expenditure, and there was no spontaneous advance on the part of managers. However, Madame de Metternich, the wife of the Austrian Ambassador, who was a person in very high favour at Court, was so bewitched by the music that she persuaded the emperor to order a performance at the Grand Opera. Wagner exerted himself to get as grand an effect out of it as possible, and no money was spared. A picked group of singers was secured, and the chorus and band were strenuously drilled in an unusual number of rehearsals. But as the time drew near, Wagner's relations with the French officials grew worse and worse. The conductor was quite unfit to grapple with such an undertaking, and Wagner's differences with him made affairs most critical. A cabal was organized against the work, in a manner such as Parisian opera-goers have been celebrated for, and the performances were disturbed by the wildest noises and signs of opposition. Some people disliked the work simply because it was not what they were accustomed to, while yet more deliberately refused it a hearing; so that disappointed frivolity and determined enmity between them wrecked Wagner's hopes. He ultimately had to give up the campaign and retire.

But it was not without its results. A few men of high soul and generous disposition recognized a great kindred spirit and rallied to his side. Moreover, his compatriots saw the ill-usage he had received at the hands of the Parisians, and they took up his cause with enthusiasm. Just at the right moment, the edict which had banished him from his native country was revoked, and he was free to return to any part of Germany he pleased. Everything seemed most promising. But though his countrymen received him with open arms, he was in sad straits. The campaign in Paris had loaded him with debt and had absorbed even the sums paid for works that had yet to be written. Attempts to perform *Tristan* had to be abandoned, and he was reduced to giving concerts to keep himself going, and for years he struggled with almost hopeless adversity.

But even when things were at their sorest with him, he produced his brightest and most genial work. Just as it had been with Beethoven and Schubert, the heaviest pressure of poverty and the gloomiest outlook failed to affect the vigorous qualities of his art, and the very years which verged on driving him to despair saw the production of his most genial, warm-hearted masterpiece, the *Meistersinger*. This again was a story of medieval life, in which the love of the Germans for an early poetic hero had mixed up quasi-legendary elements with historic facts. Its circumstances were such as gave Wagner an opportunity to intertwine with a delightful love story a merry satire on the common human weakness known as pedantry. The real hero of the piece is the famous and much-loved shoemaker-poet, Hans Sachs, who is presented in the picturesque surroundings of the medieval city of Nuremberg, as a member of the famous guild of master-singers. The members of the guild are bound by all sorts of fantastic rules, which are supposed to be necessary to the purity of art. The lover in the story is the true poet, who, in his youthful fervour, pours out his inspirations under the guidance of no rules but the true instincts of genius, and hopes to win admission to the guild and the hand of the daughter of one of the burghers thereby. The satire turns upon the horror with which the members receive his lays, in which they find nothing but an outrageous violation of their technical regulations as to melody, rhythm, and plan, and they are quite incapable of seeing the real beauties of the poet's songs, because their whole souls are wrapped up in trivial details. The most humorous character in the piece is the thorough-going old pedant, Beckmesser, who sets himself to oppose the poet with all the weapons of his order; and contests with him, by songs concocted according to its regulations, for a prize - which is no other than the hand of the same lovely daughter of one of the worthy burghers of the city and a fellow master-singer, whom Walther the poet is in love with. Hans Sachs alone is worthy of the occasion. He is puzzled by the violations of the rules of his craft, but he has clear enough perception and sympathy to see the true poetry that lies beyond his horizon and cannot be measured by his usual canons of taste. He gives the young poet his help and wisely advises him that though genius is pre-eminent, it cannot disregard true principles, and shows him that there are points and rules of art which are not merely pedantic. In the end, the decision is left to the general public. A great meeting of the inhabitants of the city is called in the open fields without the city walls, and before all assembled master-singers and burghers, the true poet and the pedant contest for the prize. The pedant, whose position is made more effective by his having tried to steal the poem of his rival under the supposition that it was the production of Hans Sachs himself, makes a most ludicrous and fantastic exhibition of himself; and the true poet rouses the enthusiastic joy and sympathy of the people and wins the hand of his lady-love. The story is perfectly unique. It is full of humour of the most refined and, at the same time, telling kind. The qualities of pedants of all time are taken off inimitably and made merry sport of in a manner which is no more than perfectly just and moderate; at the same time, the love story is one of the prettiest and sweetest imaginable, and the character of Hans Sachs is one of the most lovable and humanly genuine in all dramatic literature. The music is so thoroughly in character with the play that it has forced expressions of delight and appreciation even from some of Wagner's bitterest opponents, while to the public and those who have real human and poetic sympathies, there is no work to surpass it for fresh and kindly-hearted enjoyment.

But even when he was just on the verge of completing this work, Wagner was in despair. Things had gone so badly with him, and the prospect of getting his works performed or gaining any livelihood by them seemed so desperate that he finally gave up hope and made up his mind to retire to Switzerland and abandon his further career as a composer. Then, in the very nick of time, the young King of Bavaria came to the rescue. Wagner was actually on his way to retirement when he received from him an offer of a moderate annual income and an invitation to go and live in Bavaria and continue his great work in peace. One part of the burden was lifted from his shoulders, and he could, at all events, meet his creditors and live without fear of penury. But he was not suffered to live in peace, for his enemies still worked hard to destroy him; and though most musicians of genius have had grievous things to bear at the hands of critics and fellow musicians, probably no one has been so ferociously and bitterly vilified and ridiculed as Wagner.

Fortunately, the belief of the young king in the worth of his work was not to be shaken, and he supported him steadily and helped, as no one but a man in such power could do, to bring about the recognition of Wagner's work. The first fruit of his sympathy was the performance of *Tristan and Isolde* at Munich for the first time in 1865. The performance of the *Meistersinger*, which was finished in 1867, followed in 1868. A very important event in Wagner's life about this time was his second marriage with Cosima Liszt, the daughter of the famous pianist and composer, and his great friend and helper. It took place in

1870. After his return to Germany, Wagner lived partly in Munich and partly at Lucerne, and at last, in 1872, he moved to Bayreuth, which was destined to be the home of his latter years, the scene of his greatest triumphs, and his last resting place. Here, through the enthusiasm of his admirers all over the world, he was supplied with means to begin the building of a great theatre, on purpose for the performance of the gigantic work called the *Ring of the Nibelungs*, which had been begun with the *Rheingold* and the *Walküre* long before, and interrupted by the composition of the *Tristan* and *Die Meistersinger*, was continued in *Siegfried*, which was finished in 1869, and was ultimately concluded with the immense work called *Götterdämmerung*, or *Dusk of the Gods*, in 1874.

The foundation stone was laid in 1872 and inaugurated by a performance of the greatest of musical masterpieces - Beethoven's *Ninth Symphony*. The building was carried out in accordance with Wagner's plans to form what he conceived would be an ideal theatre for the performance of musical dramas. The immense stage was devised with every appliance of machinery and every opportunity for scenic effect; the orchestra, which often makes such blatant and head-splitting uproar in the usual open space in front of the footlights and distracts the attention of the audience by the grotesque movements of players and conductor, was sunk below the level of the stage, where it was invisible to the audience but proportionately even more than usually audible to the actors and singers, and the places for the audience, in a long, shelving incline, gave everyone a perfect view and enabled every sound to be perfectly heard. The first performance of the great series of dramas, *Rheingold*, *Walküre*, *Siegfried*, and *Götterdämmerung*, took place in this ideal theatre under his superintendence in 1876. It was an occasion unlike anything else in modern times. The little quiet town of Bayreuth gave a tone of remoteness from the usual everyday hackneyed associations of busy life. It was as if one stepped out of the hurry and frivolity and commonplace of modern existence into a quiet corner and set aside a complete little piece of life to the joy of art and the enthralling interest of a great old heroic story.

Each performance spread over a week, as the four divisions were given on alternate days, and the intervals between seemed as just nothing more than sufficient to absorb the enthralling music and drama which had passed and to become fresh for the next. There was no hurry and bustle about it, and for those who were worthy of the works, nothing was needed to fill up the interspaces but quiet life and reflection or contented discussion of the works. The performances were superb and were of course enthusiastically received, but the expenses were too great, as things were done too liberally, and the result was that at the conclusion a heavy debt was remaining over, notwithstanding that most of the performers gave their labour for nothing.

It was then suggested that public curiosity was so far aroused that a festival given in the Albert Hall in London might bring in enough profit to wipe off the deficit. For this, everything was planned on a gigantic scale, but without sufficient practical wisdom and foresight. It was thought that if high prices were charged, the wealthy classes would come in sufficient numbers to make a financial success. The result proved, if indeed it wanted proving, that the wealthy classes are not those who support music. The first performances were fairly attended, indeed, but were so far from drawing the numbers required that it seemed as if Wagner would be burdened with yet more debt. Then, at the last moment, the tactics were changed, and two extra performances were given at prices which admitted a less wealthy public, with such good results that Wagner was able to set aside a few clear hundreds to pay off the debt on the first Bayreuth performances. At this festival, a copious selection from all Wagner's works, from *Rienzi* to *Götterdämmerung*, was given with very great effect; and an enormous number of people who had as yet had no opportunity of judging his work were roused to enthusiasm thereby, and by this means a good step was made towards introducing his greater and maturer works on the English stage. Till that time, the cause of Wagner's works had seemed almost a forlorn hope in this country; nowhere had the influence of old established musicians, who professed to be classicists, been so powerful to keep his name in bad odour. A few performances had occasionally been given, but regular English opera-goers were hopelessly behindhand and cared only for works that showed off celebrated singers and gave them time to gossip and stare at their neighbours' dresses between the songs; and the leading professional musicians, and the critics who were their familiars, played into their hands. But after the so-called Wagner Festival, the really musical public began to assert itself, and in no long time all Wagner's greatest works were heard on the English stage.

By the time Wagner was in England, he was already meditating his last work. Every great man is serious at bottom, and in Wagner, there was a deep vein of religious sentiment, which took shape in his last years in the music-drama of *Parsifal*. The poem was at that time finished, and he read it out to a group of friends who gathered together one evening at Mr. Dannreuther's house in Orme Square, where he was staying. It was at the end of 1877 or the beginning of the following year that he began to make the music to it; and he kept on steadily and quietly, as seemed fitting to the subject, till it was completely finished in 1882.

A series of performances followed at the theatre at Bayreuth in July and August of that year and produced the deepest impression on everyone who attended them. They were lifted out of themselves and made to experience in their inmost nature those mysterious religious feelings which have formed a part of man's emotional being in one form or another for thousands upon thousands of years. As a work of art, balancing all the elements of poetry, music, and scenic effect in fair proportions into one harmonious whole, *Parsifal* was a worthy conclusion to the labours of a lifetime; and as a work illustrating his position in the history of the art, it is most significant. Taken by itself, the music is not so powerful nor so rich as in others of his works; and the drama, read by itself, is not so striking, nor are the characters so distinct, as in *Tristan* or the *Nibelung* series. But all the elements of art help one another. The music throws light upon the drama and intensifies it, and the situations and action on the stage react upon the music and give it a meaning which is otherwise overlooked, except by people of a highly imaginative temperament. Again, no subject could be more fit for treatment as a musical drama. The religious element, the fact that the interest of the play turns so much upon mental processes rather than upon action, and even the nature of the situations express a musical mood. Repetition of words or conventional forms seems almost inconceivable in relation to such a work, for the musical ideas attend so closely upon the action and poetry that the two elements only express the same forms in their respective ways; and, as it were, present two sides of the matter at once.

At the time *Parsifal* was performed, Wagner seemed in the best possible spirits. His vigour and decisiveness were as remarkable as ever, and at home, in congenial company, he was as merry as a boy. His triumph seemed complete at last, and it was as though the signs and tokens of the storm of opposition had passed away into the distance; and the friends who had helped in the long labour of getting his works acknowledged were gathered in numbers, with less of exultation in their mood than a sense of serenity and content. It was a fitting close to his long career of strife and wrangling; but no one thought that the end was near, and Wagner even talked of attacking a new subject. In the latter part of the year, he took up his abode in Venice. His health was not very good, but there was nothing to make anyone anxious. The end came suddenly. On February 13th, 1883, in the afternoon, without a struggle, he ceased to live. His body was conveyed back to Bayreuth and placed in the vault which he had prepared some time before, in the garden of his house.

Wagner, like many other great men, was short of stature, but neither stumpy nor dwarfed. His face was extraordinary. The eyes capable of being either piercingly brilliant or tender. His forehead was immense, and the whole expression vivid, decisive, and commanding. His speech in private life was always full of point and character; and he had a way of driving his meaning home by some striking expression, which vividly conveyed his thought and made it live in the memory. In public speaking, his voice was sonorous and his words slow; he then almost declaimed, and the sound was musical and rolled from point to point in varied tones. He always acted upon the thought of which he was convinced and had little talent or patience for compromise. This may have been a hindrance to his popularity in earlier times, for he spared no one's susceptibilities. A notable and characteristic instance of this occurred at the first performance of *Parsifal*. The public called for him at the conclusion rather too vociferously, and when he came on to the stage to acknowledge their plaudits, he almost instantly turned his back on them and addressed a long speech to the performers, who stood in a semicircle at the back of the stage, and then added some more words to the orchestra, acknowledging their devotion and ability; but of the audience, he took scarcely any notice at all. He had before that interrupted the applause by pointing out that the work was not meant to rouse their excited enthusiasm, but to give birth to a sense of devotion and quiet rapture. His view was perfectly well understood by the audience, and his desire acquiesced in. And so it was with all reasonable and sound-minded people through his life. His severity was generally found to be just and his purpose wise, and sensible men liked him all the better for his vigorous assertion of what he believed to be necessary and right.

His character and abilities were extremely comprehensive in many ways, and it was this diversity of artistic gifts which gave him pre-eminence in his particular branch of art. He had at once great literary talents and power of verbal expression, an astounding sense of colour and rhythm, an insight into the meaning of the highest music, and the right way to deal with it; a strong sense of human character and a feeling for its greatest beauties; dramatic fire, passion, tenderness, and even a very acute sense of scenic effect, and of what was thoroughly adapted to theatrical treatment. Such a combination was just what was needed to achieve the highest artistic possibility in a musical drama; for all the elements necessary were in one man's hands. As long as the different branches have to be worked out by different individuals, there is always danger of one being sacrificed to the other, or one leaning too much on the other. The marvel in the case of Wagner was that prior to his time so little had been done in the direction which he took, and the great pitch to which he carried the new treatment of his art. He seemed to do all the work himself. But in this case, appearances are misleading. He did, it is true, develop, step by step, from comparatively unpromising beginnings. His earliest productions gave but little indication of the great possibilities that existed in him; and even after he found his true sphere of activity, every step showed an enlargement of his power and a greater and surer grasp of the most difficult problems of art. Scarcely any man known in the history of art grew so immensely in the course of his life. But, nevertheless, his work is no exception to the rule of regular progress. There is no real gap between his music and that of the time which was before him, because he did not build it solely upon operatic lines. He absorbed all that was available in his predecessors' works, and by drawing the stream of far nobler art into the operatic river he achieved his end. As he himself said, even before he wrote *Tristan and*

Isolde, "It seemed feasible to realise my idea by leading the whole rich stream into which German music had swollen under Beethoven into the channel of the musical drama." It was the general development of the language of music and its instrumental resources, in symphonies, overtures, sonatas, and quartets and so forth, that made his attempt possible. The infinite variety of melody and the gradual expansion of forms enabled him to wed music to words without sacrificing sense or dramatic propriety; and the development of the dramatic story enabled him to dispense with the regular systematic outlines, which are necessary in pure instrumental music, and in their place admitted a freer emotional form, depending on a balance of emotional crises - moments of passion alternating with moments of comparative quiet in infinite gradations.

In this way, the ideals of the early Italian experimenters, Peri and Caccini, were at last achieved, by using the results of 200 years of musical development in all directions. Operatic art having passed through all sorts of phases, some healthy and many vicious, and being helped by the development of other kinds of music, was finally brought to a consistent and well-balanced artistic condition by the vigour and determination of one man. If Wagner had not had an extraordinary power of persistence in the face of adverse circumstances, besides all his other gifts, the cause of the really artistic musical drama might have had to wait a long while yet. His force of character won the day; and hereafter, whatever composers may think of the style of his expression, they will have to consider the principles of his achievement, if they would attain to a point which is worth any musician's taking note of. His work is indeed accomplished; not fate itself, nor all the malevolence of unsympathetic critics, can now annul it.

XII

CONCLUSION.

P EOPLE'S opinions differ as much about composers as about all other subjects under the sun, more especially when they are discussing contemporaries and neighbours. The enthusiastic amateurs of a provincial town think the local professor who publishes an occasional anthem or part-song, or a piece for the organ or pianoforte, to be quite among the marvels of the age; and similarly, on a larger scale, nations who do not know much of solid music set a man who can make the sort of jingle that pleases them far above the greatest masters of the art, if the latter happen to belong to other countries. In both cases, there may be something to excuse the misplaced admiration; for the provincial organist or professor may be an excellent master of counterpoint, and the popular composer may produce some really good tunes, or write so well for the voice as to give the singer very exceptional opportunities. But the extravagant opinion of their admirers is always received with caution by persons of experience; for they know that it is likely to be the result of want of experience and understanding of what is really first-rate.

Music does not stand alone among arts in this respect. Poetry and painting suffer almost as much from the want of taste and discernment of the public; and considering how difficult all art is, and what an amount of patience and intelligence is necessary to master even a few of the principles which help to a correct judgment, and what stumbling-blocks there are in the constitution of the human mind itself, it is not to be wondered at. People cannot see either through fogs or brick walls, neither can they understand things which they have not the mental machinery for grasping. They must climb the walls to see what is on the other side, or wait till the fogs clear away. Most men are mentally walled up somewhere, but they manage to find a way over or through the obstruction if it is of vital importance for them to do so. But it does not seem of vital importance to anyone to clear away the hindrances to the understanding of music, so, on the whole, that art suffers more than any other from the want of free vision and clear judgment among its nominal votaries.

To a musician, it naturally seems rather a pity that people should take such trivial views of art and be so easily led by the silly sophisms and misleading platitudes which happen to flatter their weaknesses or excuse their indolence. For not only is it really worthwhile to make a little effort to appreciate what is first-rate, but in point of fact it is only the object of getting nearer to understanding and feeling what is thoroughly good and noble that makes art worth taking any trouble about at all. The silly sipping of one sweet after another, and passing day after day and week after week from one ephemeral piece of elegance to another, just to make acquaintance with a new sensation, or get through an hour which might otherwise hang heavy on the hands, is utterly unworthy of the dignity of a human being; and the people who misuse art in such a way justify the views of the active and practical people who look upon music as a foolish waste of precious time, and an occupation only fit for gushing and empty-headed triflers.

There must be music for all orders of intelligence, but even in the most different standards there are positive degrees of goodness and badness. Music such as a ploughboy or a boot-black can appreciate may be thoroughly good, and the music which people who have every chance of being refined and cultivated do enjoy is often thoroughly bad. But when a being of low intelligence and undeveloped feeling has something sound and wholesome to feed upon, it is a step towards something better; and when a well-developed, thinking, and feeling being feeds upon something rotten and meretricious, it is a step towards something, if possible, worse, or at least towards a state of incapacity to enjoy any longer what is wholesome and good. Really good music is worthy of all men - even the highest and noblest - bad is worthy of none, and second-rate or one-sided music can only be upheld on the grounds of its leading to something higher and helping people to understand what is better; or of doing something really worth achieving in the way of technique or expression, or presenting in an interesting form some new phase of art or national style. A successful second-rate composer is sometimes useful in helping people to get accustomed to the style of a greater master, whose manner and methods he, perhaps unconsciously, imitates. Men without any remarkable genius have also done good work by finding out some new and serviceable ways of using the fingers or violin-bow, or by producing new effects upon instruments. There is indeed plenty of work for many men short of the greatest to do, but in all stages, there is the work which serves good purpose and ill. The sum total of the efforts of small men who do well in proportion to their gifts may be an immense gain to art, but every man who writes cheap, vapid, and meaningless commonplace, or panders to a taste for vulgarity and show, adds his share to its degradation.

Great composers are the men who sum up the labours of their good predecessors both great and small. They are the men whose instincts are good enough to distinguish what is noble and worthy from what is base, and have the mastery of resource to present their thoughts in the greatest and most perfect forms, and with the deepest impressiveness. Of the very greatest, who stand at an immeasurable height above all others both in power and imagination, like Bach and Beethoven, there are very few; and even of those that are worth calling great at all there are scarcely more than a dozen in three hundred years.

In the early days of music, the greatest heroes stood rather far apart, but as time went on, they seem to have come closer upon one another. This is partly because at first there were but few roads opened up; and as the art developed up to a certain point there were more and more opportunities found in instrumental music, vocal music, and dramatic music, and, consequently, a greater diversity of things for men of great gifts to do. It has even happened that two great composers have lived side by side pursuing totally different lines of art, and never approaching one another in style or method. But as time goes on, the fields get exhausted, and in order to get to a high point without deliberately imitating the works of earlier composers, it becomes necessary to get more and more complicated, till at last the endurance of man will go no further; and then most probably the greatest type of musicians will become rarer and rarer, and the people who require new music to gratify their insatiable taste for change will have to put up with more and more of the cheap trifles which are only fit for a moment's tasting and then to be thrown aside for good; and those who have a taste for greater and nobler music will have to feed more scrupulously on the great masterpieces of the past.

The world has fortunately not arrived at that point as yet, but can still enjoy works by a living master worthy of being numbered with the greatest. The pre-eminence which the Germans have gained by their thoroughness and clearness of judgment, and true nobility of thought in music, is still maintained by Johannes Brahms, a descendant in the direct line of Bach and Beethoven. He represents a totally different kind of art from Wagner, who is nearest to him in point of time, for all his fame is centred in instrumental music and songs and choral works, and none in dramatic music for the stage, while Wagner's position is entirely due to his great achievements in the latter department.

Brahms was born in 1833 at Hamburg, and began to show his powers early, but fame was very slow in coming to him. When he was twenty, he was sent with an introduction to Schumann, and his playing and extemporising as well as his compositions produced such an impression upon that sympathetic composer that he wrote an enthusiastic article in his newspaper about him, describing him as the man the world had been waiting for, and the great master of the future. Schumann's generous insight was never more happily shown, and it was so far ahead of the standard of musical intelligence of his contemporaries that his praise produced almost as much scepticism as sympathy. It made people curious about Brahms, but did not convince them. The strong character of his style, which depends not a little on a certain roughness and sternness, was to many people quite repellant; they had to get over his apparent want of consideration for their weaknesses before they had equanimity to listen to what he had to say. There is no second-rate suavity about his work nor compromise with fashionable taste, but an obvious determination to say only such things as are true and earnest, and to hold no parley with musical luxury and sensuality. And this earnestness is not only shown in nobility of thought, but the power to do without formularies and padding; which also is a great trouble to people of feeble musical organisation.

In music which falls short of the highest, a great deal of what is called accompaniment, and some of the less prominent parts even of the melodies, are a sort of common property. Thousands of composers write the same figures and the same successions of chords over and over again, and think they have done enough when they have mixed up other people's tunes in a way which the public will not recognise - at least in the short period that their works are likely to last. By such a process the public are saved a good deal of trouble, for they know a great part of what they hear already, and have only to give their attention to a tune or two. The greater respect a composer has for himself and his art, the more he tries to get rid of this element of empty fudge; but very few are strong enough to succeed, for it is only possible for those who have a strong grasp both of the theory and practice of art, and a positive feeling, as well as a mere dry rule, for the total effect of any great form of composition, and the relation of details to the whole.

Brahms has achieved this to an exceptional degree, for in every part of his work the powerful character of the man is felt. The way he treats the inner parts of the harmony is as much his own as the melody at the top; and even the way in which he treats an instrument like the pianoforte is quite different from the usages of other composers, and players have to accustom themselves to new ways of using their hands, and their heads as well, before they can master his works. Then again he scarcely makes any pretence of writing tunes or trusting the effect of his works to neat phrases. The principle of his art is to develop his works as complete organisms, and their artistic value depends upon the way in which they are carried out and the total impression they make rather than the attractiveness of the details. There must, of course, be passages of stronger and passages of lesser interest, and the features that are meant to stand out often have high beauty in themselves; but it is the relation in which they stand to the rest of the work of art which gives them their full effect. Even the passages of lesser interest have their share in the total impression, and not the negative kind of function of similar portions in the early sonatas and symphonies. The balance between subject and episode, or subject and continuation, is much more even than in the typical sonata of the Haydn and Mozart period. Instrumental works of that time seemed to be made upon simple tunes strung together by links which were often completely devoid of any kind of interest. The tendency of art has since been to make the passages between the subjects interesting also, and to lessen the sharpness of the outline which marked off the subjects from the rest of the work - in other words, to make the whole more homogeneous.

Brahms has carried this to the highest point, chiefly by reviving in his work more strongly than ever the principles of the great old contrapuntal school, and working into his instrumental forms the most musical qualities of the polyphonic method of Bach, of which the modern composer is a most powerful master. But this welding of old methods with new is accomplished without a trace of pedantry, as it is not the details but only the principles which are used.

The manner and spirit are genuinely modern, but the matter is managed with the full powers which the earlier masters of the great choral age developed, as well as the powers of the later sonata writers. That is to say, the design is capable of being tested in all directions. It is neither only in blocks nor only in lines and curves, but combines both in a way that is thoroughly characteristic of the man and of the time in which he lives. And thereby his work gains in continuity and consistency, for the gaps which used to appear between the subjects in old times disappear, and one subject is made to lead on to another, and each is made to minister without break of interest to the effect of the other.

The works in which he first made his mark in these respects were chiefly in the form which is known as chamber music; that is, works on the same lines as sonatas or symphonies, but written for combinations of a few solo instruments. In the old days, when musicians depended very much upon the patronage of rich people and aristocrats, when public audiences and public concerts were extremely rare, a great deal of first-rate music was written to be played in comparatively small rooms, before small groups of intelligent people. It did not, therefore, require much power of sound, but was contrived especially with a view to refinement and elegance. But as great players addressed themselves more and more to large audiences in big concert rooms, composers began to use greater volumes of sound. Moreover, as long as the harpsichord was the chief resource of composers as a keyed instrument, duos and trios which were written for stringed instruments in combination with it could not have much sonority; but when pianofortes came in and gained steadily in the capacity for making a volume of sound, the style of chamber music changed, and rapidly gained in power, breadth, and comprehensiveness. The change began in Beethoven's time, and he succeeded in producing much more massive works without losing the refinements of the old style. After his time, the style of the best and most popular works of the kind became much louder and more symphonic, and the details were more richly treated; much more color was introduced, and more vehemence of expression. From the point of view of the worshipper of the old delicate and refined style of chamber music, this was naturally a great falling off, but this branch of art was undergoing an inevitable change, and though it still kept the name, chamber music ceased to be designed only for small audiences or private rooms. Under these conditions, Brahms found a comparatively fresh field, and he developed his pianoforte quartets, trios, and quintets on an immense scale, aiming at the most powerful effects the instruments were capable of, and replacing the refinements of the older school by the interest and complexity of his details.

This branch of art was most favorable to his peculiar gifts, as, writing for first-rate solo players, he had no need to stint himself in difficulties and could revel in elaborate combinations and ingenious rhythms. But he has always been faithful in principle to the traditions of the classical school in matters of design, and he shows no signs of sympathy with the ultra-romantic modern school which seeks a new field for instrumental music by the help of program and speculative devices of form. Brahms is, therefore, a representative of the classical school, but he combines with his asceticism a strong vein of poetry of a rather mystical and severe type. He has some of the qualities of the heroes of Scandinavian sagas, for, like them, he seems to be conscious of the inevitable fate and destiny which overhang all men and things, but has the force and dignity of mind to face them resolutely and to act with the vigor becoming a man. Seriousness and earnestness are the keynotes of his system, and all his music has the most bracing and invigorating character. The example of a noble man tends to make others noble, and the picture of a noble mind, such as is presented in his work, helps to raise others towards his level; and the influence which his music already exerts upon younger musicians is of the very highest value to art. Brahms has worked in many lines, but always in the same range of style. In somewhat advanced years, he has brought out four extremely fine symphonies, which are as characteristic of him as all his other works; and he has shown his mastery in such lines as variation writing - a branch of art in which only the very greatest masters have excelled - and in overtures, pure choral music, and works for solo, chorus, and orchestra, such as the grand German *Requiem*, which in its line is one of the finest works of modern times.

But he has shown the freshness and poetry of his genius most remarkably in his songs. It is not usual for the giants of art, who excel in the sternest and grandest forms of music, to give much attention to songs, but Brahms has made songwriting quite a special province, and has not only produced an enormous quantity of such works but by far the finest individual songs that have made their appearance in the present generation. In fact, Schubert, Schumann, and Brahms make a triad of great songwriters such as no other nation can approach, and Brahms can well stand comparison with the other two. His principles of songwriting differ chiefly from theirs in the greater elaboration with which he deals with the poet's ideas. Even his simpler songs are so original as to present considerable difficulties both to singer and player; but the difficulties are always well worth overcoming, for they arise from his determination to get the most thorough musical expression and not to surrender anything for the sake of putting his work within the reach of feeble executants. It is never really worth-while for a man who has anything genuine to say in the way of music to try and accommodate himself to inefficient performers. Reducing the difficulties generally reduces also the artistic completeness, and nothing is gained, for second-rate performers have not the sense to perform the works of men like Brahms or Wagner even when they are simplified, and so it is better to keep them out of their reach. Brahms' songs represent the most advanced stage of artistic song in the mat-ter of perfect balance of the elements of art, and they present also endless phases of feeling and emotion, from light-hearted merriment and childlike innocent gaiety to a high pitch of passion. They are often dramatic in the same sense that Beethoven's music is dramatic and portray the characters of various kinds of human beings with an amazing subtlety and power. Finally, it is in his songs that Brahms shows the most easily recognizable examples of what people call beauty, and it often is genial beauty of the highest order. Tunes are, of course, not too common, but melody is in profusion, and melody in genuine intelligible form, such as only differs from tunes in the fact that the design is not familiar.

Brahms is not yet past the prime of his vigor, and he is of that type of artist, like Beethoven, who goes on growing all through his lifetime and may yet produce works beyond even the great height he has already attained. But what he has done has gained for him a place among the few greatest in the history of music, and by slow degrees all the musical world is learning to know him and value him as he deserves. The treasures of art he has made are for coming generations as well as the present, and his influence and character may, in the end, be rated even higher than they are now.

The list of the greatest composers closes with him, and though his work may be little more than half done, his position in history is quite clearly defined, and the greatness of his music is stamped upon the very face of it, both in the mastery of art and the dignity, force, and nobility which it expresses.

There is, of course, no clearly defined line that marks off great composers from their fellows. Even those who have done great things for art are not necessarily those who have the highest powers; and not a few of those whom public favor has canonized, or critical presumption unduly exalted, may yet sink to an average level; and composers' names who are almost unknown to the public at large are sometimes worthy of the highest honor. In the time when great composers seemed rarer than they do in the present century, many men of comparatively moderate gifts did most useful work. The early development of modern vocal music was carried on by quite a large number of excellent Italians who were gifted with a great enthusiasm for beauty and a real feeling for art. The names of the foremost of them in the early days, between Palestrina and Handel, were Carissimi, Monteverde, Cavalli, and Cesti, of whom the first two were men of really great genius. After they had done their work and advanced a good way from the crudest elementary stage of opera and cantata, Lulli came into the field and made a very considerable mark in the history of music. He left his native country in such early years that he missed the influence of pure Italian traditions, and his employment in the household of the French king made him accustomed to the passion for ballet and spectacular display, which has been a prominent characteristic of French taste from the earliest days of theatrical representation till the present time. Lulli won favor with the king and ingratiated himself with men in power at Court, and partly by favor and dexterity in pushing his own cause, and partly by genuine ability, he managed to suppress all rivalry and gain the highest position in operatic matters in France. He made his mark in the history of music by contriving his works so as to meet French tastes. He filled his operas full of ballet pieces and choruses and supplied plenty of opportunities for pageantry, and by that means established the characteristic type of French grand opera on a firm basis before he died. His sense for theatrical effect was stronger than for dramatic effect, but he managed in a few cases to write some scenes that have real dramatic merit, and he did good service by the ability with which he designed his overtures, making them at once more interesting and effective and more definite in form than his predecessors had done.

In Italy, the principal figure in the latter part of the same century was Alessandro Scarlatti, whose genius and views of art were infinitely higher and nobler than Lulli's. Scarlatti was a master of many lines of art; a great writer of sacred music, no inconsiderable master of instrumental music; but most successful in operas, of which he wrote over a hundred between 1680 and 1725. By his time, opera had progressed very far from the crude state it was in at the beginning of the century; composers had found out how to make definite and well-designed portions which they called arias, and had also learned something in the way of dramatic expression; and Scarlatti's operas are not only well planned, but contain a good deal of really fine music, most of which is unknown to the public because nearly all these works remain in manuscript.

At the same time with Scarlatti lived the first of the instrumental composers whose works have kept any popularity up to the present day. The violin was just coming into use at that time, and players rapidly developed the art of playing on it. Corelli was the first representative of a great Italian school of violinists whose influence soon extended over the musical world, and has lasted on till the present day.

Most of the greatest living players belong to the Corellian school, and the direct ascent through successive generations of master and pupil can be traced with ease from such great modern violinists as Joachim, Ernst, Hellmesberger, Rappoldi, Sarasate, Leonard, and others, through Rode, Viotti, Pugnani, and Somis right up to old Corelli himself.

England was not behindhand in those days, but in Purcell had a representative worthy to take his place with the foremost of all the living musicians of his time. Purcell's talents lay chiefly in the direction of dramatic music, and he produced a form of opera which had real national traits about it, as it had close kinship with the kind of entertainment known as a masque, which had been popular in England for hundreds of years. The kinship is shown in the number of choruses and dances with which his principal works are full, and the rather excessive predominance of literary and allegorical matter over direct dramatic effect in the plays. Purcell had a most remarkable feeling for musical expression, considering the time when he lived, and attained a point in advance of any other composer of his century in that respect. Unfortunately, when he died, there was no one capable of carrying on the good work he had begun, and English opera got no further than a most excellent start.

After these numerous composers had done their share in the improvement of opera came the great days of Handel and Bach; and from their time there were fewer and shorter gaps between composers of the highest mark. Between them and Haydn, the principal figure in musical Europe was Bach's son, Philip Emmanuel, who took up quite a different line from his father, and was the first composer of note to give his attention principally to instrumental music of the modern sonata type. His works do not seem profoundly interesting to modern lovers of music, and their elegance and simplicity of form is a very poor substitute for the richness, vigor, and nobility of his father's style. But by comparison with the other composers who were producing symphonies and sonatas in enormous quantities in his time, he thoroughly deserves the high reputation he gained, and his works are not by any means entirely dead even in the present day.

Another very interesting figure also made his appearance in the world a little before Haydn. Gluck was born in 1714, and began writing operas of the usual Italian kind in 1741. He had powers sufficient to succeed fairly well in that line, but the fact that he possessed intelligence and critical faculty as well as musical gifts raised him to a very high place in musical history. By his time, opera had got into a very bad state. The object of the original experiments in musical drama had been lost sight of in the effort to supply great singers with opportunities for showing off their voices and abilities; and the public were satisfied not only with absurdly undramatic pieces, but with the most trivial and empty music, so long as their taste for clever tricks of singing was gratified. Gluck saw the falseness of this kind of art and made up his mind to bring back truer and more artistic relations between the drama and music. According to his own words, he "endeavoured to reduce music to its proper function, that of seconding the poetry by enforcing the expression of the sentiment and the interest of the situations, without interrupting the action or weakening it by superfluous ornamentation." He began a practical illustration of his theories in the operas *Orfeo ed Euridice*, *Alceste*, and *Paride ed Elena*, which were performed in Vienna in 1762, 1767, and 1769. But in Vienna, he made no great impression and had to give up the prospect of carrying his point there. He then took the bold resolve of going to Paris, and convincing the people of the principal operatic centre in Europe of the truth of his views. *Iphigénie in Aulide* was written on purpose and performed at the principal opera theatre in Paris in 1772. The work was very successful; but the believers in the old-fashioned kind of opera were strong in numbers, and not altogether weak in a rival composer called Piccini, who was prepared to face Gluck as representative of the regular conventional opera. Their rivalry is one of the most famous things in musical history. All Paris was divided into Gluckists and Piccinists, and their differences of opinion were discussed with extreme heat. In the end, Gluck thoroughly eclipsed his rival in his *Iphigénie in Tauride*, and won one of the earliest victories of good over bad art. Nevertheless, opera did not get established upon a sound basis at once. The vicious traditions of the Italian school were too deeply rooted to be got rid of, and music was hardly advanced enough anywhere to be dealt with according to Gluck's ideal theories. But his success had the best possible influence, and opera continued to improve from that day forward.

After Gluck's time came the great achievements of Haydn, Mozart, and Beethoven; and there seemed always less and less for composers whose powers were short of the greatest to do, when the giants of art produced works of every kind, and were not to be excelled in any. Yet plenty of men worked contentedly and well at lower levels.

Contemporary with Beethoven was Cherubini, a most singular figure. He was a representative of all that was old-fashioned and conventional in art, and yet so great was his mastery within the limits he allowed himself that he almost attained to the highest rank among composers. As Mendelssohn said, he seemed to have no feeling, only science, and made all his music out of his head. But he nevertheless managed to leave behind him things of real beauty and to write church music and operas which have really splendid and genial qualities. In some respects, he was a perfectly colossal pedant, for he seemed to consider grammar and old-fashioned rules far more important than feeling; but he won the respect of all men of judgment and discretion, and held such a position in light-hearted Paris that his decision on questions of art was considered as final as the word of an irresponsible despot.

A figure equally characteristic in the opposite pole of art was Berlioz, a southern Frenchman through and through whose contempt for arbitrary rule and precedent was as unbounded as his revolutionary ardor in relation to art. Berlioz had a great feeling for what was really noble and expressive in art, and was one of the first Frenchmen to appreciate Beethoven. His own views of art were rather theatrical; but he had a sense of rhythm and color and general effect of the most gigantic kind. If he had been brought up under more favorable conditions he might have been among the greatest composers. As it is, his productions are in their way unique. He loved especially to deal with enormous masses of sound and to produce effects which were most extravagantly exciting, but his instinct for orchestration was so abnormally acute that whatever experiments he tried, from the most delicate and slender combinations to those of utmost volume, were sure to sound as he intended. He won better success in other parts of the world than in his native country, where he had a severe struggle to keep his head above water; and had to depend chiefly upon his literary gifts, which were considerable, for making even a poor livelihood. He only left a few works behind him, but the rare occasions on which they are performed in the present day are always regarded as quite important events, and the impression they produce does not show any sign of diminishing.

Almost contemporary with him was a man who exercised a far greater influence upon art, and whose works are as familiar in musical home life as Berlioz's are rare. Chopin was born in 1809 in Poland; but he was not of pure Polish descent, as his father was a Frenchman. His claim to a high place among composers rests on his connection with the pianoforte; and the work that he did for that instrument alone is so superlatively artistic in the development and use of its resources, and so refined in texture and so poetical in thought, that it ranks in importance with works of far more imposing dimensions. His was not a strong nature, nor is his music bracing or elevating, but it has typical modern qualities to a remarkable degree. His coloring is both rich and pellucid, his rhythms wonderfully varied, and his fancy free and exuberant. It is rather the music for highly cultivated and wealthy society, loving luxury and delicate excitements of sensibility, than for strong, energetic, and intellectual natures; but it has fascination also for all beings who have sympathy with imagination and rhythm, whether their characters are strong or languid.

The list of composers who came near to the greatest would not be complete without mention of Spohr. At one time the musical public certainly thought him worthy of highest rank, and his facility in all branches of art was without doubt very remarkable. He also, like Chopin, has a well-defined place in history, as in his connection with modern music for the violin he is without rival. It was as a violin player that he first began cultivating music, and in comparatively early years he won recognition as the finest player in Germany. He also showed his talents in composition very early, but it was chiefly with a view of suiting himself with effective pieces to play that he began writing. The violin concertos, which served him as show pieces at his concerts, had such real solid merits, and showed such a gift for artistic management of a difficult form of composition, that he was led on by degrees to try his power in oratorios, symphonies, songs, and operas. The circumstances in which he found himself were generally the main sources of these experiments; but the confidence of ability with which he inspired people with whom he came into contact gained him plenty of opportunities, and before the end of his life his fame rested even more upon his compositions than upon his superb playing. In person, he was large and powerful, and he was gifted with happy self-reliance and healthy geniality. But his music does not seem to represent him faithfully in these respects, for it is the lack of genuine energy and breadth which has caused it to lose much of the estimation it was held in during his lifetime. Spohr's merits are a wonderful mastery in writing for the orchestra, a considerable sense of colour, and an agreeable and well-rounded style. But the music is rendered distasteful in the end through excess of sweetness, and a want of directness and decision, which arises from the affection he had for rather languid harmonies, and an excessive use of chromatic notes. There is individuality about his music, but it is not altogether of a desirable kind; and though he had influence upon a few of his younger contemporaries, he has not given rise to a school, or left such a mark as his fame in his own time led people to expect. His long life extended from the days of Beethoven's boyhood till some years after Mendelssohn's death, and the greater part of its story has been most amusingly told by himself in his autobiography.

The series of distinguished composers of second rank thus attends upon the great line of composers of first rank, sometimes filling gaps between them, and sometimes illustrating them and acting as intermediaries between them and the public; and some few had special provinces of their own, and left work which was of real service to art, and gave them a definite place in history. This last is a position of very high honour, and is near being the most decisive basis for a claim to foremost rank among composers. But there is after all something higher even than having a province all to one's self.

During the lives of great artistic workers of all sorts, public judgment is constantly misled by personal considerations. One man has the gift for contriving or even organising success; another has an equally remarkable gift for preventing his own attainment of it. One man catches a fashionable taste and is adored; another wages war upon it and is vilified. But when they have passed away, men begin to ask in more judicial mood what their works represent artistically. Do they open up any new vista? Do they show mastery of any new resource? Do they put things in a light never thought of before? Do they lead anywhither? But mixed up with such questions are still more important ones. Men ask what is the quality of the things they utter, whether they express great and noble traits of character and thought, whether they appeal to noble sympathies and arouse healthy and exalted emotions.

In literature, fine language, clearness of expression, mastery of design and power of laying out an argument, craftsmanship, and even correctness, all count for a good deal; but in the long run the man who has the noblest thoughts takes the highest place. And so it is in music. Finished art, mastery of resource, clearness of expression, all go for something; they are in fact indispensable, but however remarkable in their way they cannot atone for levity and shallowness. The greatest composers are not those who merely entertain us and make us for a while forget boredom and worry in trivial distraction; but such as sound the deepest chords in our nature and lift us above ourselves; who purify and brace us in times of gladness, and strike no jarring note in the time of our deepest sorrow.

THE END.